NITS'O'KAN/ HIS DREAM
Johan Pursnipen

Text copyright © 2016 John M. Olson aka Johan Pursnipen

All rights reserved

Key words: Legends of the Blackfeet Indians of Montana /Journey of self-discovery/ Ghost stories/ love at first sight/ Dreams

Description:

After the death of the man that raised him as his own, Daniel begins to have reoccurring dreams about people and places unfamiliar to him. The dreams make him begin to wonder what his life would have been like, if his birth parents had not been killed when he was four years old. The dreams seem to be a key to finding the answers to these questions and his search takes him to Browning, Montana, where he discovers many details of the life he had been separated from and falls in love with the very woman he may have been intended to be with all along.

At the same time, someone from his past is reaching out to a higher power to reconnect the past and present, so the next generation will know the ways of their people.

In addition to finding family and love in Montana, Daniel gains a deeper understanding of the world around him, as he begins to see it through the eyes of the Siksikawa(Blackfeet) and comes to realize after seeing the ghosts of Mary and Ray, as they try to warn him of danger, that he is comforted by the visits of their spirits, as they appear in the form of animals and birds. They help him see, he is a link in a chain that connects the past to the future and also makes him see his role in helping forge the next link.

Throughout the story, the language of the Siksikawa(Blackfeet) is used to help perpetuate its existence and for the purpose of reminding people that before the west was won there were people already here, with their own beliefs, living their lives. In doing the research on the Siksikawa language, I found contradicting information, some might say, it is because I do not understand and the words of the 'Old Ones' should be left alone. To them, I say as a child who saw his Mother, who spoke German and wanted to teach it to her son, fight with his father over it, because his own Ojibwa heritage had been banished by the government and lost; I do understand and I will continue to try and get it right.

Naapi (Old Man) who can be kind or a trickster to the Siksikawa is embedded in the story and as Daniel learns his own story, he learns he is part of something that began long ago, when Naapi got in the middle of a dispute between the Chief of the Wolves and the Chief of the Grizzlies; as he shaped the world of the Siksikawa(Blackfeet.)

I would like to thank everyone that contributed to the process of making this book possible. Especially my wife, Jeanette, who's Tech. skills, numerous proof reads and thoughts, helped make the characters and stories, in my head come to life. Their journey which started out written in long hand, made the leap to Windows 7 and then Windows 10 and Amazon KDP, because of her encouragement to keep learning new things.

Any similarities between the Characters and any person living or passed is coincidental. Some of the locations are real and if you get to Montana, I would recommend checking them out.

Chapter One: The Old Ones trail

Chapter two: Mountains and trees

Chapter three: The Indian in the mirror

Chapter four: Small world

Chapter five: Dreams in the night

Chapter six: The reunion

Chapter seven: Stepping stones

Chapter eight: Party of three

Chapter nine: New boots

Chapter ten: Field trip

Chapter eleven: Lessons

Chapter twelve: A hand to hold

Chapter thirteen: Memories

Chapter fourteen: Eyes on the road

Chapter fifteen: Questioning the answers

Chapter sixteen: Trouble

Chapter seventeen: Shaking the bush

Chapter eighteen: Grilling and Chilling

Chapter nineteen: Birds eye view

Chapter twenty: Meeting Mother

Chapter twenty-one: Nice threads

Chapter twenty-two: Return / Review / Regroup

Chapter twenty-three: New York state of mind

Chapter twenty-four: City life

Chapter twenty-five: Planting seeds

Chapter twenty-six: New Office / New Policies

Chapter twenty-seven: Nothing stays the same

Chapter twenty-eight: Family retreat

Chapter twenty-nine: Old stories / new faces

Chapter thirty: Just the facts

Chapter thirty-one: Sifting through the ashes

Chapter thirty-two: Taking another bite

On a mountain in Northwest Montana.

CHAPTER 1

"'Aka'ista'ao'" (place of many ghosts), he said, glancing back at the old house, as he settles back down on a metal chair in front of the fire pit, after putting more wood on the fire.

"I will be the last one," he says, to no one but the night.
Thoughts of days gone by, run through his head, like gently rolling waves lapping rhythmically on a lake shore. The sun is disappearing behind the mountains to the west. He clears his throat and begins a chant, one he had made his own, many years ago.

"Hey, Yo… Hey, Yo, Hey… Hey, Yo …Hey, Yo, Hey… Hey, Yo… Hey, Yo, Hey…" he sings over and over, as he makes the journey in his mind toward the border land, between this world and the next.

"Aa'ini'hkwa'! Aa'ini'hkwa'! (sing! sing!)," Naapi' (Old Man) calls out to him.

"Hey, Yo! Hey, Yo, Hey! Hey Yo! Hey, Yo, Hey!" the man sings even louder as he follows the trail left by the Old Ones, in his mind.

He stops at the edge of the river separating the two worlds. On the other side, in the half light of the Sand Hills, he can see six shadowy figures. It is his family!

"In time my son," his father's voice calls from across the water, "In time… there is still more you must do. 'Naapi (Old Man) will guide you."

Then the dim light starts to fade, the silhouettes of his family are gone. He is alone in darkness so black; he cannot see his hands in front of his face. Then he hears a voice.

"Joe Standing Bear, there are still those that will follow…. If they are not shown the path, they will follow another and only the wind will speak of the ways of the Niitsitapi (Real People.) You must reach out to them. Be the fire that guides the lost travelers' home. Be the one who cries out from the wilderness," a voice tells him. It is the voice of Naapi (Old Man.)

****

Joe Standing Bear opened his eyes. The blazing fire was now only orange and black coals. The journey into the boarder land had taken several hours. He stared into the coals and for just a second, he saw the sun cresting an ocean, as it begins to rise and light up a new day. He felt the Spirt World release its' grip.

"There is one other," Joe says.

He put more logs on the fire, and as the flames grew, he thought of a time his father had taken him and his brother hunting. They had split up to ambush a group of elk. When the elk turned and went up and over the mountain, the boys followed. They were trying so hard to out maneuver the elk, they hadn't paid much attention to anything else and when the sun set, they panicked, instead of starting a fire and staying put until morning, they started back to where they thought they had come from. They climbed up and down two mountains, before they came out of the timber and admitted to themselves they were lost. Then they saw a fire way off in the distance. They started out for it and as they got closer they could hear a familiar song, one they had sung with their father hundreds of times at home.

The song told the story of Sip'is'too'(owl) and the night he spent on the ground, after falling from his nest. The boys started singing the part of the young owl as they made their way toward the fire and their father, as he began to sing just the part of the mother owl as she watched for danger from the branches above. In no time at all, they were standing by him. What where the words again? He smiled as he sang a couple lines. He caught himself listening for a reply….

It made him think about other old songs his father would sing, when they would sit around the fire together. Many of them were about the adventures of Katoyis (Blood Clot Boy.) His favorite had always been how Katoyis had helped the elk get back its bugle after it had been tricked by an old woman, a witch, who lived alone in a deep ravine. He remembered when he was very young, how scared he'd gotten when his father would start to tell the part when she turned into a mountain lion and nearly caught Katoyis and how happy he felt as Katoyis made his getaway with the basket that held the elk's song. Now the elk could once again signal the coming of winter and remind the other animals to prepare.

*****

The fire had burned down again, and as he watched the glowing embers, he thought about all the things that had gone through his head, this night. He tried to see into the shadow world again, but it was gone.

About that same time in a penthouse in New York.

CHAPTER 2

"What the hell!" Daniel said, sitting up in his bed, blinking his eyes and shaking his head as he came out of a deep sleep. His T-shirt, wet with sweat, his heart beating fast. He looked at the clock. 4:45 am.

He had been running from something, but what? He never saw it. There was only a deep, phwoof… phwoof… phwoof… and what sounded like snapping branches, just behind him, as he ran through a tangle of small trees. Whatever it was always gained on him every time he looked over his shoulder, but when he focused on running, a strange voice, some sort of foreign language, would somehow help him gain ground.

Daniel laid back and let out a deep breath. He tried to think what movie he had seen or what he'd eaten recently that might have triggered such a nightmare. He couldn't think of anything. His alarm went off. It was 5:00 am. He got up and went to take a shower.

He was still thinking about the dream, as he rinsed the shampoo out of his hair, it ran in his eyes and he squeezed them tight. The darkness, suddenly turned into bright blue sky with snow covered mountains off in the distance. Then a big tree, flashed into view. The top was dead, but a lower branch had turned straight up and had become the new top.

A few hours later…. Daniel was grinding some coffee beans and pouring a pot of water in the coffee machine in his office. He walked over to his desk and sat down to watch as the sun climbed above the New York skyline, turning the entire sky a golden orange. He realized he couldn't stop thinking of the strange dream from last night or the mountains and tree, he had seen in the shower. He wondered if they were connected; and then realized he was analyzing his dreams like some damned Psychiatrist. He hated to say anything to them. He didn't like the way they tried to get in peoples' heads and then think they knew all about them in twenty minutes.

His adopted mother had suggested it might be helpful, when he started asking questions and wondering about his place in the world. She told him it had helped her, when the doctors had told her, that she would never be able to have children of her own. He knew she only wanted the best for him and was worried about him. His father, his adopted father, had passed away several months earlier. They had been so close. Daniel had taken it very hard.

As Daniel poured a cup of coffee, he remembered when he was little, standing next to him in this office looking out at the city. He could still hear him saying, how he could have never asked for a better son.

After he had attended Columbia Grammar & Preparatory School and graduated with honors from Harvard Law School; he started working at his father's law firm as an Associate and then made Partner. Everything was going as they had always planned; and then one day his father had a heart attack and two days later, he was dead.

The suddenness of everything had started Daniel thinking about life and how the things that happen, can affect what will happen. He had found himself wondering about his birth parents more and more. He tried on several occasions to talk to his adopted mother about Montana and she'd always start by recalling the day they brought him home.

*****

"It was love at first sight. When the Child Services Lady led you into the room with us; Howard scooped you up, set you on his knee and told you not to worry, and that everything was going to be fine. You sat there the whole time we signed the papers…. You didn't know what to think about the elevator the first few times you rode on it. You would hold your stomach and look up with wide eyes and say 'OH.' It didn't take long though, and you would stand by our door and say 'GO,'" she'd tell him and then look at him and smile.

 Then one day, she told him that a friend of Howards had reached out to them and told them a terrible car accident, had killed a young couple, and left a small boy behind. She also told him, that he said, the man killed in the accident had once saved his life on a hunting trip. She said when he told Howard he wasn't sure what was going to happen to the boy, Howard said he would contact the Adoption Agency in Browning, Mt. and he did. She said they got a letter from a Law Firm in Kalispell, Mt. shortly after Daniel had come to live with them, that said the man had passed away in his sleep.

"If it hadn't been for him, we would have never known about you," she said.

Daniel wondered about that for a minute. One phone call had set it all in motion. But what had prompted the call…. There was something said about the man in the accident saving his life… was the man repaying a debt? Daniel thought about the details. He suddenly felt such an emptiness, that he wondered how it could ever be filled.

Daniel couldn't stop thinking about where he had come from and why he had become who he was. Who would he have been if things had been different? He took a sip of his coffee. Then there was a knock at the door.

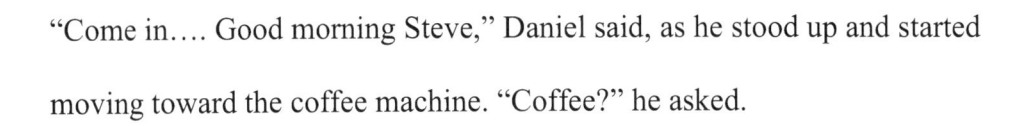

"Come in…. Good morning Steve," Daniel said, as he stood up and started moving toward the coffee machine. "Coffee?" he asked.

"Please," Steve replied.

Daniel poured some coffee for him and refilled his own cup.

"Thanks," Steve said.

"I'd like to talk to you about something," Daniel said, as he walked over to the conference table and sat down. "Since Dad died, I've been doing a lot of thinking about things…. Things like how one's circumstances mold one into whom they become, and what one does with the time they are given and… just… who am I?"

"You are the son of Howard and Evelyn Williams, an excellent Attorney, and an important part of this Law Firm," Steve said, trying to be supportive.

"That's just it. I am who I am, because of circumstance. I can't help but wonder who I would have been if my birth parents hadn't been killed. Who would I be?"

"I've been watching something eat away at you for a while, I wanted to say something, but I knew you'd talk, when you had something to say. How can I help?" Steve said, and then took a sip from his cup.

"I think I need to take some time off… go find whatever it is I can find out about where I came from. All I know is my birth certificate lists Browning, Montana as the place of my birth. My birth parents were members of the Blackfeet tribe. Mom told me they were killed in a car crash. But why wasn't I with them? Where was I? Do I have relatives back there? Why didn't they keep me?"

Steve brushed his hand through his goatee and took a deep breath and let it out. He glanced down at the table and then looked at Daniel. "I think some time off is exactly what you need. You go and do whatever you need to do. I'll hold down this corner of the world. You go conquer another part. This will all be here when you get back," he said, reassuringly.

Daniel was about to share his dream with him. But just then there was a knock at the door.

"Come in," Daniel said.

"Good morning…. Excuse me, Steve, your 10:00 o'clock is here, he's a little early, but he looks pretty shaken up, I have him in the Green Room with a cup of coffee," the young woman said, stepping just inside the door.

"Thanks Kathy," Steve said, getting up. He looked at Daniel and said, "If I can help you with anything, just let me know."

"Thanks Steve, I'll keep you in the loop," Daniel said, as he walked with him to the door and then went back to his desk and sat down. He typed, Browning, Montana, on his key board. A colorful title page appeared on his computer screen. He had discovered the site, one day while surfing the net. He liked scrolling through its pages, it was somehow soothing.

'Home of the Blackfeet Indians,' it read, above an image of painted teepees along a stream. The Plains Indian Museum and the Charlie Russell Exhibit came up as bullets. Browning was home to a large art gallery featuring Native American Art, a Charlie Russell exhibit and dinosaur bones.

Great Falls was the closest city with an airport and car rental. He decided to fly to Great Falls and drive to Browning. That was about as far as Daniel could plan, from that point on it would be an adventure. One as big as the country he was heading for.

CHAPTER 3

The past four weeks had gone by in a blur, and as if all he had to do to get ready for the trip wasn't enough, the same strange dream, where something was chasing him, had become reoccurring and started waking him up every morning at 4:45.

There was another dream that he also remembered having more than a few times. He seemed to be sitting in the back of an old SUV, maybe a jeep, looking forward and a woman sitting sideways in the front seat, talking to the man that was driving and looking back at him every few minutes. Every time she'd turn her head to look at him, several strands of hair would blow across her face and she'd smile, as she wiped them away. It was odd because, he didn't recognize the vehicle or the woman and it seemed to come in just brief flashes.

*****

The flight had required a stop in Salt Lake City, Utah, before heading on to Great Falls, Montana. When the plane took off on this last leg of the journey, a big weight seemed to lift from Daniels shoulders, it felt like, when the judge walks in the court room, and the bailiff says, 'Everyone rise.'

The final touchdown in Great Falls went smoothly. Daniel was amused by the small airport, because there were only two gates; but he was impressed that he arrived on time and his luggage hadn't been lost. He had reserved a car through Avis and so he made his way to the Avis counter. He stepped up to the desk and introduced himself.

"You have any ID," a man in his sixties asked, as he looked Daniel up and down.

Daniel produced his driver's license.

"Do you have another form of identification?" the agent said, after examining it.

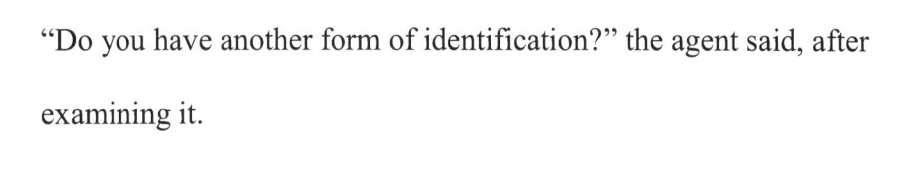

Daniel produced his passport, something he hadn't figured he'd need, but had brought anyway.

"Says here a Cadillac Escalade, pretty fancy ride for an Indi…. You sure that's what you want?" the agent said, after hitting a few keys on his keyboard and keeping his eyes on the screen.

"Yes I'm sure, thank you," Daniel replied.

"How would you like to pay for it?"

"I believe that's been taken care of," Daniel said, looking straight at the agent, his New Yorker radar picking up an 'asshole signal.'

"Says here, Williams, Williams and Johnson Law Firm. Do you have any identification that ties you to them?"

Daniel opened his wallet and handed him a business card. His look must have made the agent think twice about messing with him any further.

"Well, you can't be too careful with all that identity theft, that's out there," the agent said, looking down his nose at Daniel, as he handed him back his driver's license and passport. He printed an invoice and turned it around for Daniel to sign. The agent looked at the signature and pushed the keys across the counter.

Daniel put them in his pocket and waited for a copy of the receipt. He turned without saying anything and picked up his luggage. "Who the Fu** does he think he is?" Daniel said, to himself as he made his way to the parking lot.

The lot attendant saw him coming and hustled over to the door after dropping the big sponge he had been using to wash cars, back into the bucket. His long hair blew in the wind as he pulled the door opened. Daniel reached into his pocket and handed the attendant the keys.

"Your vehicle is right this way, sir," the young man said, leading the way to the SUV and opening the back doors for his luggage.

Daniel noticed the guy was a Native American, maybe 10 years younger than himself. His shoes and pants were wet from washing cars, but he seemed happy. He certainly knew about customer service. "What a joy it must be working with that jackass at the counter every day," Daniel said, under his breath. "Thank you," Daniel said, and held out a $10 bill as he got in.

The young man looked a little surprised and seemed almost reluctant to take it. But he did and tucked it in his pants pocket and closed the driver's door.

"Thank you. Drive safe," the Attendant said, bobbing his head as he smiled and waved.

Once off the lot, Daniel pulled over and googled motels in the area. There was a Gran Tree Motel that was 5.4 miles north on Interstate 15. He pulled out into traffic.

"I could get used to this," he said, to himself as he drove along. He had never driven a vehicle that sat as high as this before.

A sign just ahead read I- 15 north, with an arrow that pointed to the right lane. Daniel changed lanes and got onto I-15. A few minutes later there was a Gran Tree Motel sign on his right and he took the exit that lead to the frontage road and pulled into the parking lot. Daniel put his bags on one of the beds and pulled back the curtains. His room was on the third floor. It felt like the ground floor to him, but since there were few buildings taller, he could see across miles of open country and off in the distance a line of snowcapped mountains, like the ones he'd seen in the shower. He took off his suit coat and walked over to hang it up and then came back to the window and took in more of the view. He kicked off his shoes and put his hands together above his head and stretched back and then forward, slowly, touching the floor. He did this several times. The stretching helped relax his tight back. He put his hands on his hips and twisted right, left, right, left. He widened his stance and shifted into a shorter fighting stance. He stepped forward and back to stretch his legs. He had been involved in martial arts as far back as he could remember. He could take care of himself in a tight spot; though he'd been taught good character and self-confidence were the true fruits of his training. He could feel his muscles loosening up.

As his mind cleared, he let go of all the pressing thoughts that had accumulated throughout the past few weeks. The snowcapped mountains in the distance, reassured him that he was on the right track to finding the answers to his questions.

The mind and body now collected in the present. Daniel went through a series of defensive and offensive moves in a formal training exercise known as a Kata. It begins with the first assailant grabbing his shirt. Daniel reacts by putting his right arm over the attackers left and then under his right. With an upward thrust he breaks free from the attacker's grip. Then he pivots his hips, left to right and delivers a left punch to right kidney. He pauses a moment and then brings his right foot back and even with his left. With his hands together in front of him, right fist resting lightly on his left palm, deep breath in, slowly out. Daniel snaps his head to his right, responding to another attacker. His right arm comes up to block a punch, as he steps in with his right leg. He looks over his left shoulder and pivots his hips, putting his weight on his right leg and blocks a kick to the upper torso with his left arm and then delivers a front kick with his right leg, he recoils and then pivots 90 degrees to his right and then bringing his feet together, hands together in front of him, a deep breath in, and lets it out slowly and finishes with a shallow bow.

He twists his torso right to left and then stretches his neck side to side and moves his arms in circles. He takes another cleansing breath, then moves to his bags and puts them on the luggage rack, takes out his shaving kit, and goes into the bathroom. He felt a little tingle of excitement as he put his shirt and jacket back on. He smiled as he checked his hair in the mirror and picked up his keys.

He thought he'd drive around town and see what it had to offer. He headed south on the frontage road, and found himself skirting the airport and heading for the business district from the East. The route gave him sort of a panoramic view of the city. As he entered the downtown area, he noticed that most of the buildings didn't have more than four or five stories. It made even the center of the city seem open.

It was six o'clock; Daniel thought how impossible it would be to navigate the streets of New York at this time of day. Here traffic flowed smoothly. As he drove he noticed several places to eat: Perkins, Applebee's, Burger King, Pizza Hut, and a Dairy Queen and then before he knew it, he was at the edge of town. He pulled into the large Albertson's parking lot; which appeared to be a grocery store, and headed back into town.

Daniel decided on Applebee's and pulled up close to the entrance in the corner of a parking lot it shared with Wal-Mart. He thought it would be fun to see if it was any different from the one back home.

 He was seated right away. This amused him. There was almost always a wait for a table, no matter where you ate in the Big Apple. The Hostess took him to a small table off to the side of the restaurant and seated him. While he waited for his waitress, he looked around. There were pictures and posters of local sports teams on one wall and of cowboys riding bulls and bucking horses on another. A big picture of a rodeo clown helping a cowboy up, while a rather angry looking bull barreled toward them, caught Daniel's eye. Another wall had pictures of wildlife with snowcapped mountains in the background. The mountains made him think of the ones he'd seen from the window in his room.

He glanced around at the other patrons: a few families with children, several elderly couples, a table with four men who appeared to have just come in off the range, the first "cowboys" Daniel recalled ever seeing, not counting the 'singing cowboy' back home. He suddenly was aware that he might be slightly over dressed. He made a mental note to do something about it.

The waitress came and took his order. He sipped his water and observed a young couple with three children. The husband looked like he worked in retail sales and was in his thirties. His wife maybe a little younger was pretty. Daniel noticed she looked tired, as she divided her attention between the baby in a carrier to her right on the floor and a toddler in a booster seat on a chair, to her left. The man kept the oldest child, a boy, occupied by helping him color a picture on his place matt. In a booth, off to Daniel's far right, along the wall with windows, four young ladies sat together. They had noticed him too and as they talked, each seemed to take turns glancing his way and smiling. He smiled politely, but hoped his food would come soon so he could disengage. It wasn't that he didn't find them attractive; he just wanted to stay focused on his mission. He remembered his father saying to him when he was in college, "Don't let the girls distract you, Daniel, there will be time for that after you graduate."

His food arrived and as he ate, he went back to thinking about his clothes. A shopping trip might be in order.

It had been a long day and Daniel was starting to feel it. He took off his shirt and pants, and then turned down the blankets on the bed closest to the window. He thought the bed felt good and reached over and turned out the light. He lay on his back and thought about his day: The airplane ride, the airport here in Great Falls, Applebee's. He rolled over and was soon fast asleep.

The next morning Daniel woke up as the sky was just turning light blue. Except for the dream of going shopping, and walking out of the store dressed like he just stepped out of a western movie, he had slept soundly and thought it was a relief not to be awakened by something chasing him.

He was thinking about the Starbucks just down the street, while he took a hot shower and got dressed. In no time at all he had gone through the drive through and was sipping a large black coffee. He liked the height of the Escalade at the drive through window.

"I really could get used to this," he said, to himself, as he drove south out of town along the Missouri River. The open space seemed to go on forever and he pondered the phrase 'Big Sky Country,'… it certainly was. He noticed a historical marker ahead and pulled up near it. With his coffee in hand, he got out and read about Lewis and Clark and their eighteen- mile portage to avoid the waterfalls of the Missouri river.

CHAPTER 4

Daniel stepped out of the laundromat with his freshly washed 'Montana clothes' and took them to his SUV. He was anxious to wear them, but wanted to get something to eat first. He looked back at the little strip mall. Besides the laundromat, there was: A Hallmark store, a liquor store, H&R Block, a hardware store and a grocery store. Daniel walked down to the grocery store and went inside. There was a deli off to the right. He thought about the 2nd Street deli in the East Village, back home. "Looks like we're not in Kansas anymore," he said, under his breath.

One of the ladies behind the counter noticed him and stopped what she was doing and picked up a towel to wipe her hands as she stepped toward her side of the case.

"Can I get something for you?" She asked. She was short and fat, but had a friendly smile.

"Yes, please, I'd like a half pound of the seven-layer salad and three chicken strips."

She scooped some salad and put the chicken strips in a bag, "anything else?"

"No, thank you."

On his way to the checkout he walked passed a cold drink case and grabbed two bottles of water, labeled Montana Treasure, and then got in the one checkout line that was open. As he waited, he noticed the lady ahead of him. She was an older Indian woman, and had her grey hair in a braid that ran down her back. It rested on a beautiful leather vest.

The vest was almost white and looked very soft. A row of fringe hung down across the back. Below the fringe was a thought provoking embroidered scene, made with tiny beads. In the background was a building with two floors, four windows on each floor and a cross attached to its roof. Several small stick figure people were lined up like they were heading for a door under the cross. To the side of the line stood a larger, more detailed figure of a man holding a book in one hand and a cross on a chain in the other. Daniel studied it with fascination. He was so distracted by it, that he hadn't noticed what was going on in front of him.

"I will have to get those things the next time I'm in town," the old woman said, pointing to a couple of items, after the clerk had rung everything up.

Daniel opened his wallet, took out a twenty-dollar bill and discreetly dropped it in front of him, then bent down and came up holding the money.

 "Excuse me, you dropped this," Daniel said, holding out the money. The grey haired woman looked at him for a moment.

"I saw you drop this," he said, to her.

"Nomohtah sitaki," (thank you) she said, taking the money, not knowing what else to say, she knew she hadn't dropped it.

Daniel smiled at her. Their eyes locked for a moment. It felt like she was looking into his soul. Then she turned to the checkout clerk and handed the money to him. He handed her the change and bagged the groceries. She smiled at Daniel, again, took her three bags and walked out.

****

Daniel had just opened the door to the Escalade when he heard a voice. It was the old woman.

"Excuse me! excuse me!"

Daniel put his lunch on the seat and turned to face her. She walked with a limp, but kept a steady pace.

"I want to thank you, sir," the woman said, holding something in her hand. It was a medallion about the size of a silver dollar, decorated with tiny beads. White beads covered the entire surface and in the center was a red stick figure man holding a black spear as if he was about to throw it. "This is for you," she said, holding it out to him. "When I looked into your eyes I could see you have come a long way. You are searching for something. This will help you. 'Aakattsinootsiiyop'," she said, smiled a nearly toothless smile, then turned and walked away.

Daniel watched her make her way back to the passenger door of an old station wagon and get in. He looked at the necklace in his hand for a minute and then at the car as it drove away. His eyes shifted back to the medallion. It was beautiful. He tucked it in the inside pocket of his jacket, for safe keeping, and climbed into the big black SUV. As he ate his lunch, he thought about what the old woman said. He opened a bottle of water and took a drink. He tried to repeat the phrase, "'Aakattsinoot...sii...yo'p."

Closing his eyes, he saw the woman in his mind's eye. He could hear her saying it again. He had no idea she had told him, 'they would meet again.' He gathered his trash and took it to the garbage can, up near the Laundromat. It was time to try his new clothes on.

"But first a cup of coffee," he said, to himself.

There was a different barista, this time, Daniel was glad, since it was his third cup this morning.
"Sixteen - ounce Americano, please," he said and then glanced over at his new boots while he waited, thinking the snakeskin looked pretty cool.

The young girl returned with his coffee. Daniel handed her a five-dollar bill and put the coffee in the cup holder. "Thank you," he said, as he pulled away.

Back in his hotel room, he took off his shirt and went to get one of the new ones. As he passed the mirror he stopped to look at how he looked in his new jeans, they looked good, he thought. "They're a little stiff, I guess they'll soften up," he said, to himself. It had been awhile since he had worn a pair of jeans. He stood in front of the shirts, and picked the blue one with black sleeves and black collar and slipped it on. He snapped the snaps and tucked it in and then looped the belt through the belt loops and fastened the elk horn buckle. He thought of the medallion and got it out of his jacket. He went back in front of the mirror, opened his top button and tied the strips of rawhide together. The beads and design seemed to fit right in with his new clothes. He thought about the old woman again and the phrase she had spoken in her native language, as he tucked the medallion in his shirt. "'Aa'katt'sinoot'sii yop'," he said out loud. It seemed a little eerie, the way she had looked into his eyes. He wished he knew what it meant. It sounded so profound. He walked over and picked up his coffee and took another sip, and looked out the big window, at the snowcapped mountains off in the distance. He wondered how far away they were, maybe 50 miles? How endless this part of the country seemed? It made him feel like doing a little exploring.

****

On his way out of town, he stopped and filled up the Escalade at a gas station.

"Fuel on pump three and these," Daniel said, setting two bottles of water on the counter.

"That's ninety dollars and sixty cents, please," the girl behind the counter said.

Daniel handed her a debit card. She ran the card and looked back at him and smiled as she waited.

"Here ya go Hun," she said, flashing a big smile and giving him a good looking over, as she held out the receipt.

"Thank you," he said.

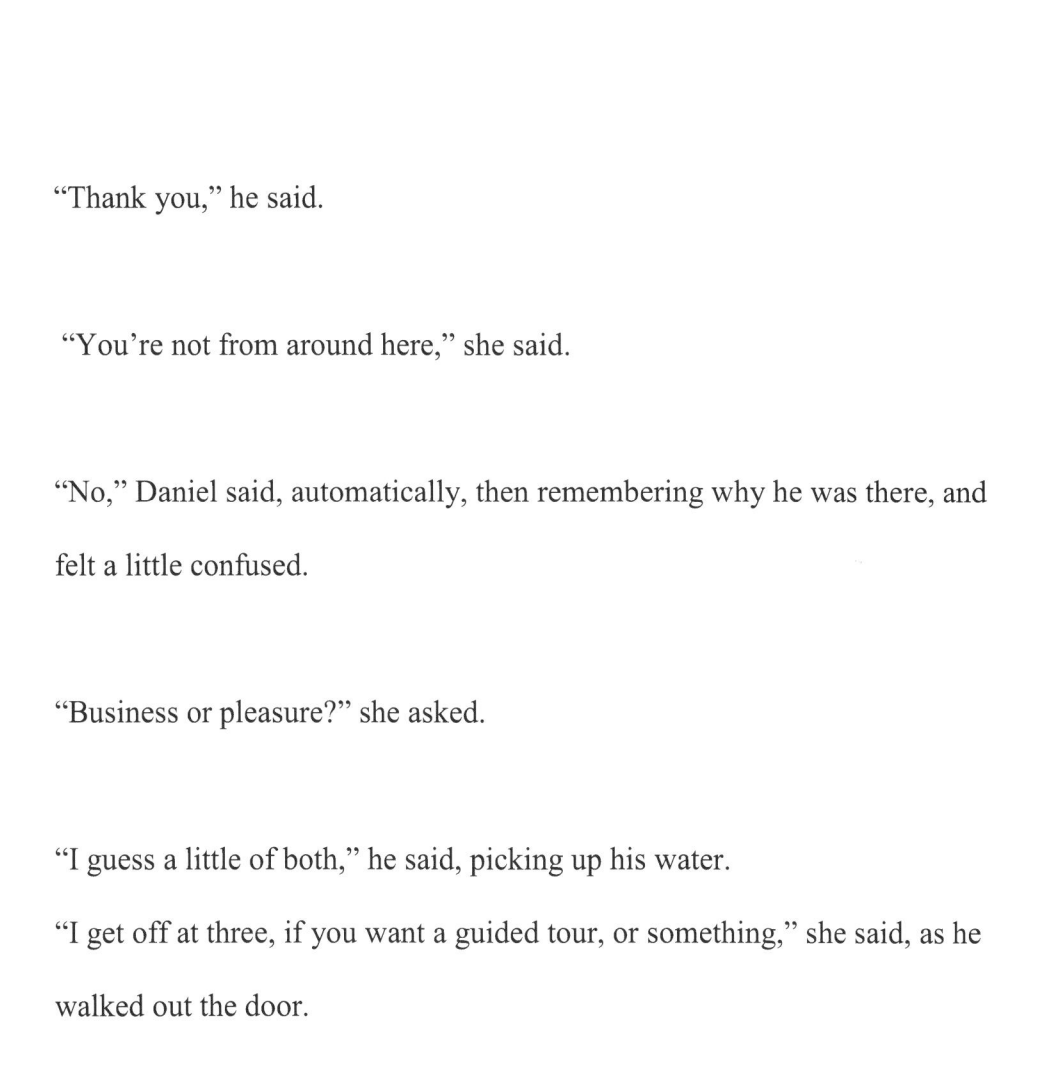

"You're not from around here," she said.

"No," Daniel said, automatically, then remembering why he was there, and felt a little confused.

"Business or pleasure?" she asked.

"I guess a little of both," he said, picking up his water.

"I get off at three, if you want a guided tour, or something," she said, as he walked out the door.

"I guess if I hadn't been adopted, she could have been Mrs.??? What would my last name have been? He said, suddenly going from chuckling about possible marriage prospects to thinking about the fact that he didn't really know what his last name was. He noticed a stop light coming up and turned right. He drove a couple blocks, turned around, and parked.

He pulled up Google Maps and saw, I-15 headed north to Shelby and then north into Canada and that Highway 2 ran across the top of the state through Shelby and west to Browning. He could go that way or take US Hwy 89 from Great Falls to Browning. It seemed to be about the same number of miles.

"It might be faster on the interstate," Daniel said, and then decided on US 89.

The highway rolled along and except for a couple small towns with only a gas station and a few homes, there wasn't much other than open land and blue sky. He followed the road into Browning and passed an old gas station, now used as a second hand store. A little further down the road was an old rundown motel with a couple of old cars parked in front of the rooms.

Daniel wondered if it was more of a long term living situation than a motel, on account of the lawn chairs and grills.

As he continued on, he could see most of the houses were in need of paint and some repair. He noticed a larger building coming up on the right. The sign said Museum and Art Gallery, looking a little farther, he saw the Museum of the Plains Indians, and drove down and parked in the large parking lot, then went inside. He wandered through each room, looking at all the artifacts: bows and arrows, pottery, clothes. He was impressed by the bead work on some of the dresses and shirts and read about the different styles of beading done by the different tribes. When he came to a display of pipes and leather pouches he noticed one of the bags had the same design as on his medallion. He touched one of the strands of beads that hung from his medallion and thought of the old woman.

He continued on, completely immersing himself in what he saw. When he finally circled back to the entrance, Daniel felt a sense of peace and calmness. As he walked back to his car, he reflected on everything he'd seen. He got in and drove to the art gallery, he had passed earlier.

****

A huge T-Rex skull was in the foyer to the left, as he stepped inside the door, a small ramp led up to another area where a Jurassic exhibit had several outstanding pieces on display. Daniel walked through the exhibit and was surprised to learn that the most complete T-Rex skeleton ever found had been found in Montana. He circled back to the ramp and continued up the gradual incline that led to the art gallery, walking slowly so he could examine the pieces of art hanging on the wall, along the way.

At the top of the ramp, he went through a door that opened up to a room with a maze of glass cases filled with: Handmade jewelry, dolls, carvings made from wood and antlers, knives and leather goods. Daniel worked his way around the room, noticed some paintings on the opposite wall and made his way toward them. There was one of a young girl with piercing coal black eyes and long braids. The painting was titled "Haunting Glance." The young girl's eyes did indeed catch the viewer's attention. She seemed to be not only projecting her thoughts but those of all her people from the beginning of time.

Daniel thought of the old woman back in Great Falls and how she had looked at him. As he examined the painting, he looked at the bead work on the girl's buckskin dress. It was made with the same tiny beads his necklace was made of. He thought about all the work that must go into such a project: the planning of the design, stringing the little beads, which seemed to be strung in groups of seven and then sewn to the leather, like on the clothes in the museum.

His eyes shifted to another picture and followed the tracks in the snow to a small band of Indians wrapped in buffalo skins and their travois being pulled by dogs, all looking tired but determined to make their way to the rugged mountains in the distance.

Daniel wondered why they were traveling in such weather and where they going?

He suddenly became aware of someone standing next to him, saying something. Daniel turned to his left, looking a little surprised.

"It's called, Following the Herd," the woman said, smiling at Daniel, as she repeated herself, realizing the first time hadn't registered with him.

"The herd?" Daniel said, with a questioning look on his face.

"'iinisskimm,' the buffalo," the woman said.

Daniel was instantly mesmerized by her long black hair and how it framed her face, accentuating her high cheek bones, and sparkling dark brown eyes. "A wonderful painting," he said, after what seemed like several seconds of trying to think of something to say, and then feeling awkward.

"It was painted by one of the local artists," she said.

"It really is striking," Daniel said, returning his gaze back to the painting.

"Can I help you with anything?" the woman asked.

"What's the story behind that one?" Daniel asked, motioning with his hand, toward the painting of the young girl staring out at them.

"'Bewitching Glance' by Karen Thayer, she's an Artist from Hillsboro, Oregon. Isn't she amazing?" the woman said, adding, "She's one of my favorites. I met her, at a Pow wow, a few years ago. We were talking about the beautiful day and when I mentioned my sunglasses had broken that morning, her husband Dave wanted to see them, and he took them back to his car and fixed them. When he handed them to me he said, looks like 'I've made a spectacle of 'em.' Karen told me he was an Optician and never left home without a repair kit the size of a suitcase. They were sure a nice couple."

"It's as though she is looking right into your soul," Daniel said, as he looked at the print.

"Her expression does make you wonder what she would say if she could speak. Mrs. Thayer used one of the local children as a model. She said, the little girls' eyes seemed to have the look of a very old soul…. Would you like to see some of my other favorites?" the woman asked.

"Yes, I would," Daniel answered, still somewhat distracted by her charms.

"I'm Summer," the woman said, holding out her hand.

"Daniel," Daniel said, extending his hand and holding hers a second longer than he normally would have. He caught himself and released it, hoping she didn't notice.

Summer smiled, she too, felt a little tingle when their hands touched. She turned and led him to another alcove, where a large painting of an Indian village, with several smaller prints, hung on the back wall. The larger painting showed several colorful Teepee's with pictures of horses and buffalo painted on them. A woman sat in front of one of them, sewing. Near another, two women cooked over a fire. Two men off in the back ground were skinning a deer and in the foreground, there were three young children playing with a dog, along a creek. The smaller paintings around the larger one were close- ups of the people in the bigger picture. The painting showing the two women cooking, revealed an older woman whose face was wrinkled with age and a life of wind and sun, her grey hair pulled back into a tight braid. A younger woman stood next to her and seemed to be watching intently, perhaps learning what the older woman was doing. Her hair was dark and unbraided. Daniel thought she looked like Summer.

"The detail is magnificent," Daniel said.

"The bright blue sky and short shadow on the back side of the Tee-pee's gives me the sense it is late morning, almost midday. The color of the grass and leaves on the trees tells me it is early fall," Summer said, showing a deep passion for the art work.

Daniel noticed how the light danced in her eyes. He found her voice enchanting. It was soft, but clear and confident. The words she used were eloquent in a simple and direct way. He hoped she wouldn't notice, but it was hard to keep his eyes off her. He thought she would be an excellent model for one of Karen Thayer's paintings. Then the phone rang.

"Excuse me," Summer said.

Daniel continued to browse, and found a collection of old photos; one of them was of an old man sitting on a buffalo skin holding a long pipe, a leather pouch next to him. Daniel looked into the face of that old man. His eyes were only slits and his leathery skin was cracked with deep wrinkles. The old man's expression was a knowing look that held neither joy nor despair.

Another photo showed an old man sitting on a wooden bench with his back against the outside wall of a shack. He was dressed in a thread barren shirt and pants that seemed two sizes too big. His somber face, like the one in the other photo, was a testament to the changes he'd seen. A deep furrowed brow concealed some of the last eyes to witness a way of life that his people had known for thousands of years.

Next to it, another photo, a young girl holding a rag doll in the crook of her arm, she looked tired, her smudged face, void of joy. Daniel thought of the pictures of his friends' children back in New York and the smiles on their faces and excitement in their eyes. There was none of that in the old photos that hung on the wall in front of him.

Summer returned after hanging up the phone, and stood next to him, she looked at the old photos, and then at him, she could see they touched his heart.

"They were the last of 'The Old Ones,'" she said.

They looked at each other, as their smiles turned to tightly drawn lips.

"Would you like to see some of the handmade jewelry?" Summer asked, trying to lighten the sudden down turn in mood.

"Okay," Daniel said, sensing her efforts and wanting to oblige. He gave the pictures one more look, before he turned away, and then walked over to the glass display case near the register.

"These necklaces are made from Amber," Summer said, as she held one with three cylindrical shapes hanging from it. The golden brown, almost, transparent substance, looked like hard polished honey.

"What is Amber?" Daniel asked.

"It's fossilized resin that was formed in the pockets and canals of trees from ancient forests during the Cretaceous period," Summer explained, and held out an amber necklace with a bug trapped inside the resin. "This one is from the Hell Creek formation."

He was impressed by her knowledge.

Inside the glass case next to some turquois bracelets and necklaces where beaded medallion necklaces, like the one he was wearing. He recognized one with the same pattern as his.

"The lady that made these, is from Browning," Summer said. "She is my grandmother, but you have already met her," she added, with a little smile. She had noticed the necklace around Daniels neck when they had first met and she recognized it as her grandmother's work. The phone call had been her grandmother calling to tell Summer, that she had made it home from Great Falls and that she had met a wanderer. Summer picked up the medallion.

"Katoyis (Blood Clot Boy), he wanders the earth slaying monsters and seeking truth," she said. "Grandmother told me that you did something nice for her. She said, when she looked into your eyes she could see you were looking for something. She also said you were wearing a nice suit," Summer looked at his shirt and boots and gave him a slightly questioning look.

"I had just bought these clothes and had just finished washing them, when I met her. I went back to my room and changed," Daniel explained, and reached in his shirt, pulling out his medallion. "She said it would help me find what I was looking for," he went on to say.

"Grandmother is always right about those things. What are you looking for?" Summer asked and gave him a smile.

Daniel felt his face getting a little warm. Being a New York lawyer, it wasn't often he was caught speechless. It wasn't that he didn't want to tell her. It was the whole thing of meeting the old woman, some 120 miles away, having her give him a necklace, telling him it will help him find what he is looking for and three hours later be identified as, Katoyis, in search of something; before he even gets to where he was going. It was all very ironic and exciting. Was it just a coincidence or was it a matter of destiny?

"Well, it's a rather long story. How about I tell you over dinner?" Daniel said, through a growing smile as he found his voice again.

Summer looked at him, as she considered the invitation. "My sister is watching my son. I need to pick him up after work," Summer replied. "There isn't much besides the Tasty Freeze or the Seven Eleven in town, if you don't want to risk getting into a fight. How would you like to come over to my house? We can have Dinner there."

"Alright," Daniel replied, a little surprised at the return invitation.

"It's 5:30," Summer said. "We stay open until 6:00. Why don't you go down to the coffee shop and wait while I get things wrapped up here," Summer suggested.

"Okay," Daniel said. "I'll go look at some more of those Dinosaur bones and meet you by the Coffee shop."

****

Shortly after 6:00, Summer came down the wide hall and stood alongside Daniel, who was standing in front of the T-Rex skull.

"My, what big teeth you have," she said.

"The better to eat you with, my dear," Daniel replied, as he turned to look at Summer. "Can you imagine being around, when those things were running wild?" Daniel asked.

"I think it would definitely add a little extra excitement to picking berries. Are you ready?" asked Summer.

"Sure," Daniel said.

"Well, I called my sister and she said Billy could stay over at her house tonight. She has a son named Tommy. They are about the same age. They're like brothers. So it's just us. Is that okay?" Summer said, as she flashed a little smile, and attempted a little humor as a way of hiding the flutter of nervousness she felt. It had been a long time since she had been on a date and this guy wasn't your typical date in Browning. "Do you like spaghetti?" she asked.

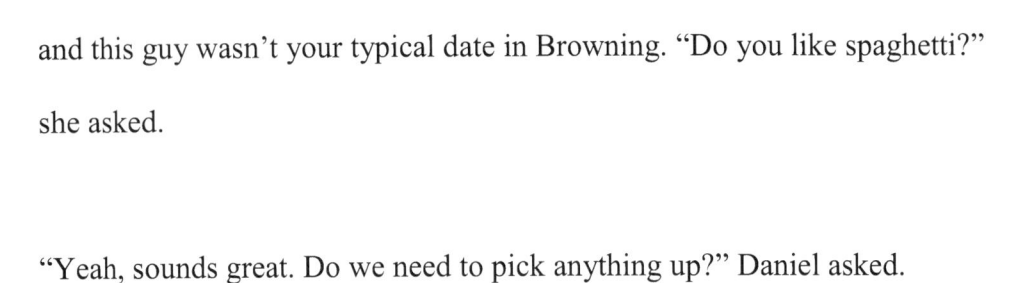

"Yeah, sounds great. Do we need to pick anything up?" Daniel asked.

"We could stop at the store and get some French bread or something like that," Summer suggested.

"Let's go. I'm parked out front. Where's your car?" Daniel said.

"I walk when the weather is nice," Summer said.

They walked out the front door and Daniel pointed to his SUV. He opened the passenger door, Summer got in and Daniel went around to the driver's side.

"The store is down this way." Summer said, as she gestured with her hand. "It's just a couple of blocks and on your left."

Daniel saw the small convenience store he had passed on the way into town. There was a cartoonish Indian with a silly expression on his face, painted on the side of the building. He was barefoot and wore baggy pants with fringes, no shirt, but a leather vest that looked two sizes too small, and an eagle feather in his hair. Under him it read, 'The Buck stops here.'

Daniel gave Summer a questioning look.

"It's owned by Indians. I guess that makes it okay," she said, looking at him, and shrugged.

"Hey Summer," a big man with a braided ponytail said, from behind the cash register, as they walked in.

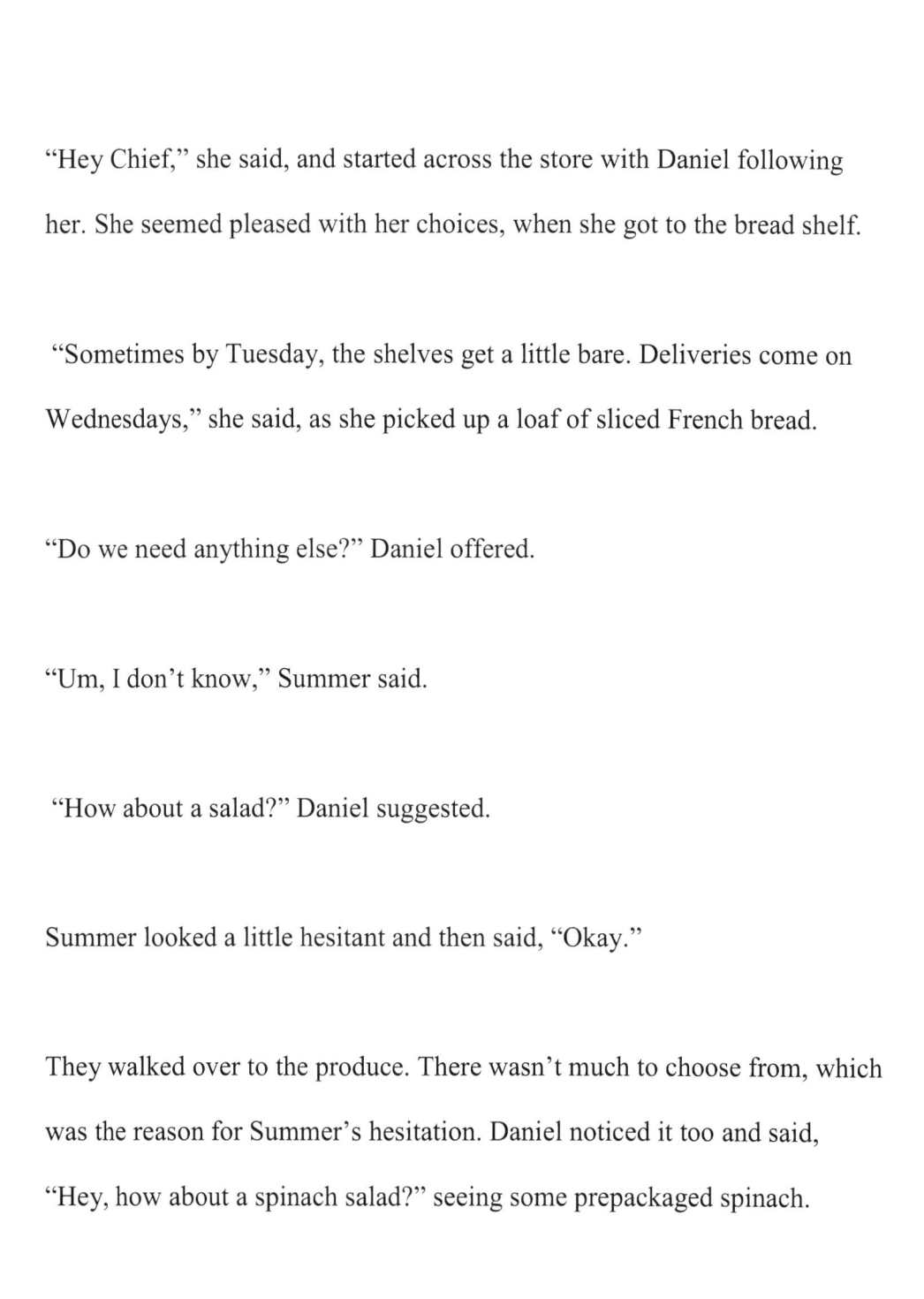

"Hey Chief," she said, and started across the store with Daniel following her. She seemed pleased with her choices, when she got to the bread shelf.

"Sometimes by Tuesday, the shelves get a little bare. Deliveries come on Wednesdays," she said, as she picked up a loaf of sliced French bread.

"Do we need anything else?" Daniel offered.

"Um, I don't know," Summer said.

"How about a salad?" Daniel suggested.

Summer looked a little hesitant and then said, "Okay."

They walked over to the produce. There wasn't much to choose from, which was the reason for Summer's hesitation. Daniel noticed it too and said, "Hey, how about a spinach salad?" seeing some prepackaged spinach.

Summer nodded. Daniel grabbed a package and said, "All we need now is some dressing and croutons."

"This will make a nice Supper," Summer said.

"I'm looking forward to it. Oh, and a bag of ice," Daniel said, grabbing a gallon of spring water as they made their way to the front of the store.

 The big Indian rang up their items and put them in a plastic sack and gave them a paper bag for the ice, which was outside in the freezer. "Fifteen twenty…. Bread and water and rabbit food. Pretty light dinner, if you don't catch that rabbit," he said, smiling. "They served better food in the joint," he added, as he handed Daniel his change. "Have a nice evening," he said, as they walked out.

"Was he serious about being in prison?" Daniel asked, once they were back in the suv.

"Chief?" Summer said, and smiled. "He's a nice guy. I don't think he was ever in any trouble. He told me once that he was too damn big; nobody dared to give him any shit. Besides he's a traditionalist. He helps the elders with the ceremonies at the Pow Wow, and makes sure if someone needs to get to Great Falls, they get there. He is very involved with the community. I think he was just talkin' smart.

My house is down 2 blocks and then left and then down two blocks," Summer said, gesturing with her hands, as Daniel started to back up.

He drove down two blocks and took a left. The houses were small and looked alike. Nobody seemed to own a lawn mower.

"That's it up on the right. The blue one," Summer said.

Daniel pulled in the drive way and parked behind Summer's car, an older Subaru station wagon. They walked up to the house; Summer led him to the kitchen. She set the bag on the counter top and washed her hands, then opened a cupboard and took out two glasses and a strainer.

"If you'll get some water for us, I'll wash the spinach," she said.

Daniel washed his hands, filled the glasses with ice and poured the water, then set them on the table.

"If you want you can take the ice and put it in the freezer, out on the back porch," Summer said.

When he opened the freezer, he noticed it was full of small white packages. They were marked: elk, buffalo and deer. He put the ice on top of them and went back in. Summer was just finishing washing the spinach and put the bowl in the refrigerator.

"Should we sit awhile or should I start cooking?" Summer asked.

"Let's sit awhile," Daniel said.

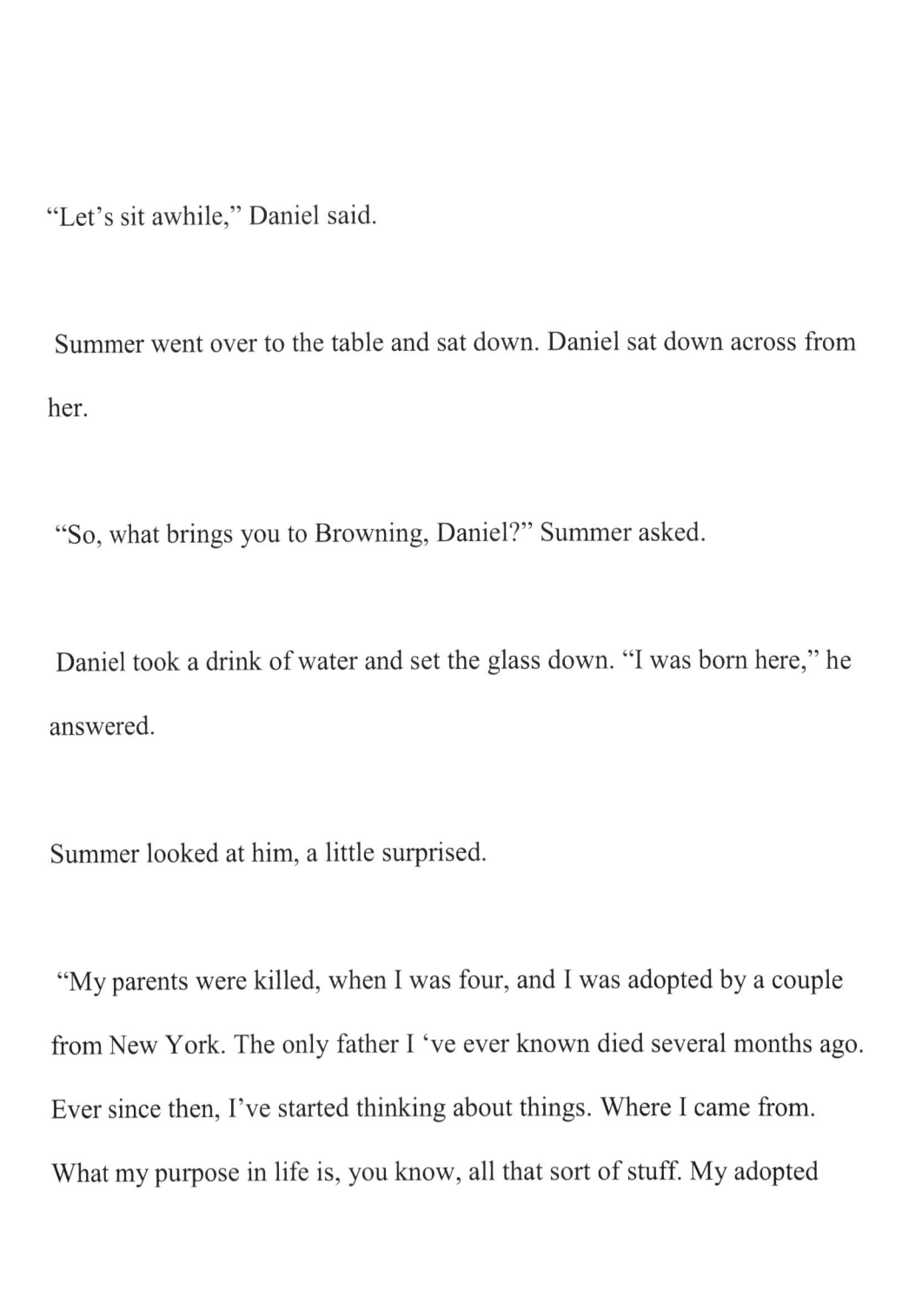

Summer went over to the table and sat down. Daniel sat down across from her.

"So, what brings you to Browning, Daniel?" Summer asked.

Daniel took a drink of water and set the glass down. "I was born here," he answered.

Summer looked at him, a little surprised.

"My parents were killed, when I was four, and I was adopted by a couple from New York. The only father I've ever known died several months ago. Ever since then, I've started thinking about things. Where I came from. What my purpose in life is, you know, all that sort of stuff. My adopted father was the senior partner in a law firm in Manhattan. I became a lawyer and part of the firm. It's a very good life. I just started wondering, what it would have been like if my birth parents hadn't been killed."

"You'd have probably ended up working at that little grocery store we just left, or the gas station down the street from the art gallery, or maybe you'd be in jail or even …. You've been here a couple of hours and already seen most of what's here," Summer said, in a slightly sharp tone. It was apparent that although she seemed to be making the best out of how life had worked out for her, she was aware of the lack of opportunity.

Daniel smiled at her, "you are probably right. I don't mean I'm not grateful for everything. I am. I couldn't have wished for a better life. But it's like something is drawing me here. I've even been having these strange dreams.

"Maybe we should start dinner," Summer suggested, and got up to put some water in a pot for the noodles. She then went to the refrigerator and took out a package wrapped in white paper. "One of the things you probably missed out on was elk meatballs," Summer said, as she washed her hands and then opened the package and started rolling out meatballs.

"What can I do?" Daniel asked.

"You can put the salads together if you want to," replied Summer.

Daniel got up and got the spinach from the refrigerator.

"The bowls are in there," Summer gestured with her head, as she buttered the bread and put some seasoning on it, before putting it in the oven. "Hey, I didn't mean to come down on you like that," she said, looking into the frying pan and turning the meatballs as they browned.

"You have every right," Daniel said, as he put some spinach into the two bowls and then put the rest back into the refrigerator, grabbing the dressing from inside the door as he closed it.

"It's just I tried my best to escape from here and I'm still here. You escaped and came back. It just doesn't make much sense to me," Summer said, trying to control her emotions. "Dinner won't be long," Summer said, after checking the noodles and stirring the sauce. "Can you grab a couple of plates, please?" she asked, as she took the garlic toast out of the oven and set it on a hot pad and then drained the noodles, in one fluid motion. "I think we are ready to eat," she said, and smiled at Daniel.

"Looks great," Daniel said, as he put sauce over his noodles.

"What do you think of the meatballs?" Summer asked, after watching him take a few bites. "Have you ever had elk?"

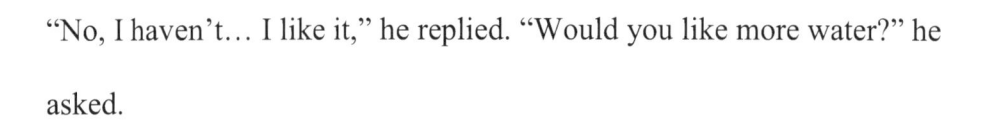

"No, I haven't… I like it," he replied. "Would you like more water?" he asked.

"Yes please," she replied, noticing his attentiveness.

****

"That was very good," Daniel said, as he finished his meal and sat back in his chair.

"Best Italian restaurant in town," Summer said, smiling as she got up and took their plates to the sink. As she started to rinse them, Daniel started clearing the table. "You don't have to do that," Summer said.

"I want to," Daniel replied.

Summer smiled at him, thinking how easy he was to be around, as she put the leftover spaghetti in a bowl and put it in the refrigerator.

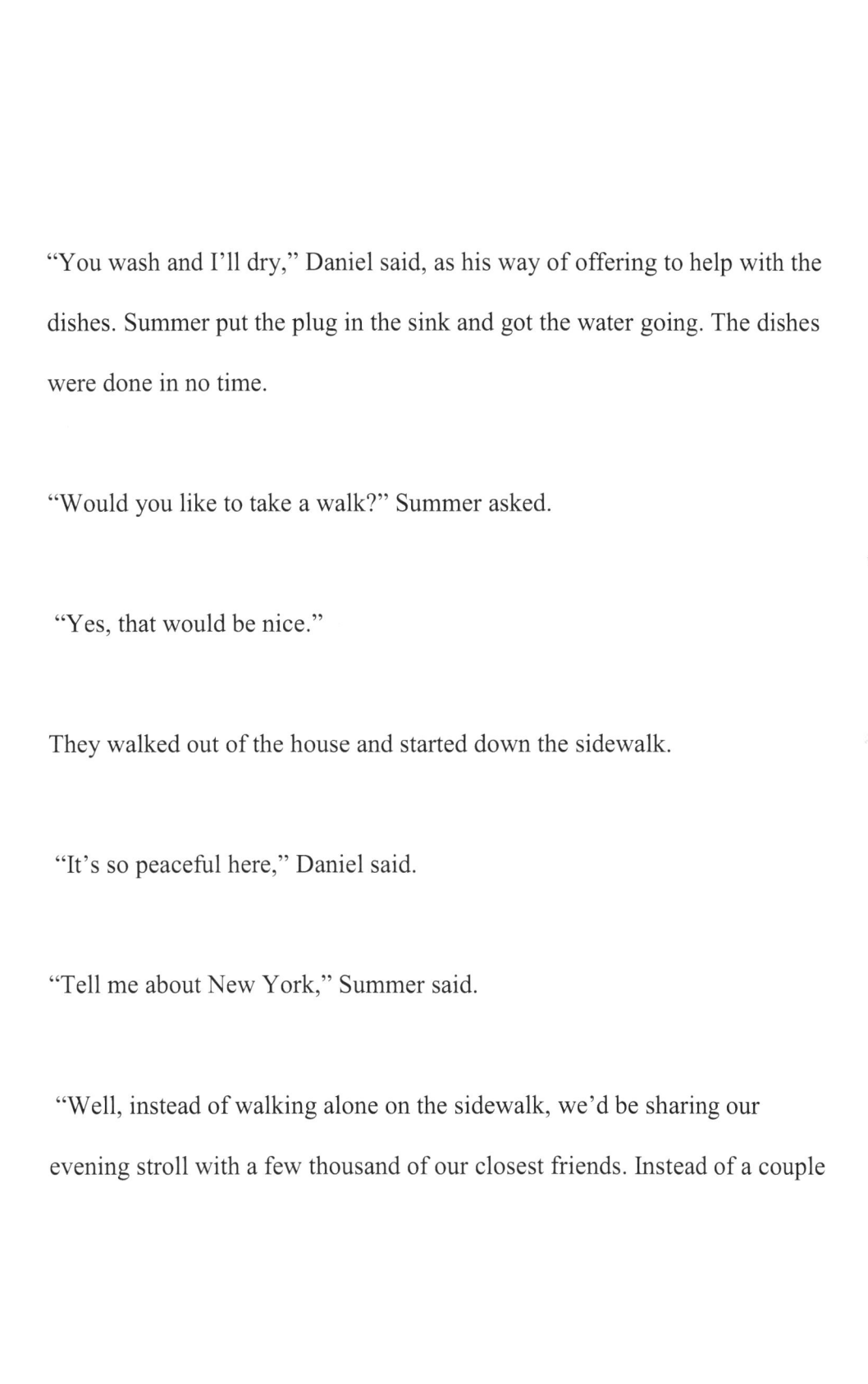

"You wash and I'll dry," Daniel said, as his way of offering to help with the dishes. Summer put the plug in the sink and got the water going. The dishes were done in no time.

"Would you like to take a walk?" Summer asked.

"Yes, that would be nice."

They walked out of the house and started down the sidewalk.

"It's so peaceful here," Daniel said.

"Tell me about New York," Summer said.

"Well, instead of walking alone on the sidewalk, we'd be sharing our evening stroll with a few thousand of our closest friends. Instead of a couple voices coming from the backyards, there would be buses and taxies honking."

They walked along, Summer thinking of the hustle and bustle of the big city and Daniel enjoying the fresh air and quietness of the small town.

"I noticed your freezer is full of wild game. Do you hunt?" Daniel asked.

"Everybody here goes hunting. I like to get out and enjoy nature, see the changing seasons. I shot that elk," she said, proudly. We all share with family. The buffalo meat came from the Pow Wow last fall. The tribe kills several from the herd that we manage and members of the council make sure everyone gets some. It keeps the traditions alive," she said. "What do you do when you're not being a big city lawyer? She asked with a big smile.

"I belong to a health club. I play racket ball, two afternoons a week and help teach a martial arts class two afternoons."

"What style of karate do you train in," Summer asked.

"Shotokan," replied Daniel, a little surprised at the question.

"I took some karate classes in college," explained Summer. "I teach a women's Self Defense Class, Wednesday nights. I have a couple of women that come regularly and some that come and go depending on how their men behave." She smiled when she said it, but it was the truth. "We change it up some. We'll do Self Defense one week and aerobics another. We have some weights and exercise equipment. I guess it's Browning's version of a women's day spa," she said and laughed.

Daniel was thinking what a nice laugh she had. He was also aware it hid a lot of pain.

They walked several blocks and took a right for a block and then another right. Daniel could see a loss of hope throughout the neighborhood. But he did find it quiet and peaceful in a way.

"This house is the one behind mine," Summer motioned with her head. "Sometimes you can hear them arguing, but not too often," she said, as they took another right and ended up back at Summer's house.

"More water?" Summer asked.

"Yes," Daniel said, and followed her out to the freezer.

"Are those from the elk you shot?" Daniel asked, looking up at a pair of horns hanging on the wall.

"Those are deer horns," Summer said, looking up at the large 5x5 mule deer rack, as she filled two glasses with ice. "It's better than average and the guys from town gave me plenty of crap about it being beginner's luck… which it probably was. A couple of guys even said, I found it dead. They were just jealous."

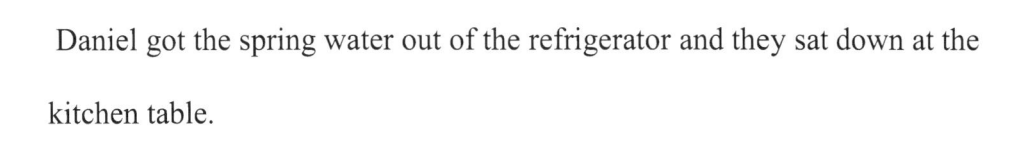

Daniel got the spring water out of the refrigerator and they sat down at the kitchen table.

"I think we should go see grandma tomorrow. She may remember something," Summer said.

"That sounds like a good idea…. I should probably get back to my room. I'll be back in the morning," Daniel said.

"That doesn't make a lot of sense. Its 120 miles back to Great falls and then you just have to turn around and come back in the morning. You can have Billy's room. I'll get some clean sheets."

"Are you sure?" Daniel asked. "You really don't know me," he added. He heard himself and thought; 'Now she probably thinks I'm gay.'

Summer made a noise with her lips. "Are you forgetting I'm the one with guns in my room. Besides Grandma thought you're okay."

"How can I refuse an invitation like that?" Daniel said, and went to get some clean clothes from his car. When he came back in, he found Summer changing the sheets on Billy's bed. "Thanks for letting me stay and taking me to see your grandmother tomorrow," Daniel said.

"It's considered poor manners not to help, Katoyis, if he comes," Summer said. "I'm going to get ready for bed. Do you need anything?" Summer asked, as she stretched her back.

"No, I think I'm good, thanks again for everything," Daniel said and took his bathroom kit and towel to the bathroom. When he came out, the house was dark. He could hear Summer in her room. The door was shut and light was coming from under it. "Good night, Daniel said, as he stepped across the hall to his room.

"Good night," Summer replied.

Daniel closed his door and as he lay on his back, he heard Summer's door open and then a couple of footsteps and then the bathroom door close. It had been an interesting day. He thought about everything that had happened. He thought about Summer. She seemed so smart and she was very beautiful. As he turned on his side, he wondered if her grandmother would be able to help. He fell into a sound sleep almost immediately. He slept through the night and was awaken by the sound of running water. He rolled onto his back and stretched. As he laid there, he recalled a strange dream he had during the night. The water had turned off and he heard the bathroom door open and footsteps going past his door. He could hear noises coming from the kitchen and soon he could smell coffee. He got up and got dressed and went into the bathroom. Then he made his way to the kitchen and found Summer sitting at the table with a cup of coffee.

"Good morning… coffee?" she said.

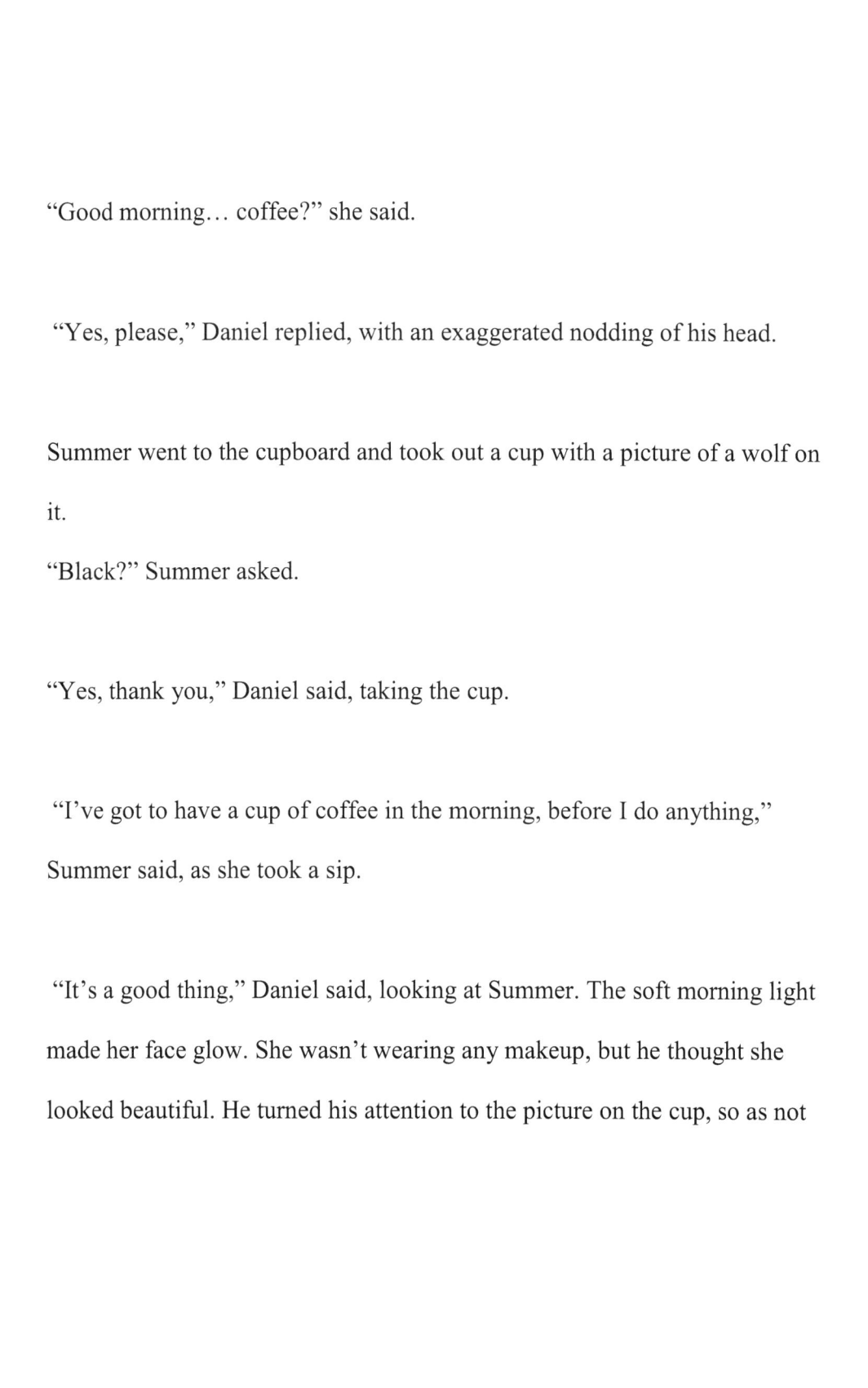

"Yes, please," Daniel replied, with an exaggerated nodding of his head.

Summer went to the cupboard and took out a cup with a picture of a wolf on it.

"Black?" Summer asked.

"Yes, thank you," Daniel said, taking the cup.

"I've got to have a cup of coffee in the morning, before I do anything," Summer said, as she took a sip.

"It's a good thing," Daniel said, looking at Summer. The soft morning light made her face glow. She wasn't wearing any makeup, but he thought she looked beautiful. He turned his attention to the picture on the cup, so as not to stare. The wolf's big grey head with yellow eyes looked straight out. "I had a dream about a wolf last night," Daniel said.

Summer looked at him, "Oh."

"It stayed just ahead of me, but always in sight. It was like it wanted me to follow it."

Summer gave him a little smile and said, "The Old Ones would say 'kayissta'pssiwa' (it was a spirit) trying to show you the way. Grandmother will want to hear more about this dream…. More coffee?"

"Yes, please."

"We'll have some breakfast in a little bit and then go get Billy. He likes to go to Grandmother's house. How does a couple of eggs and toast sound?"

"Great. Can I help with anything?

"Just drink your coffee, I'm fine," Summer said, as she got up to start breakfast. "It's considered good manners to bring something to the Elders when you seek their council. We'll stop at the store. Okay?"

"Of course," Daniel said, getting up to pour more coffee.

"Only half a cup… please, it stays hotter," Summer said, as he started to pour some in her cup.

"Yeah I think so too," he said, giving himself half a cup as well, and then went back and sat down. "Looks good, thanks," Daniel said, as she put a couple of eggs on his plate, just as the toast popped up.

After they finished breakfast and straightened up the kitchen, Summer said, "Well, are you ready to go meet my sister and get Billy?"

"Ready," Daniel said.

"Let's stop at the store first," Summer said.

As they walked in, the same guy that had been working there last night greeted them.

"Good Morning," Chief said, with a knowing grin. "Catch that rabbit?"

"Morning Chief," Summer said, ignoring the question, as they walked passed him.

"The customary things are salt, flour and sugar," Summer said, as Daniel grabbed a basket.

"What else?" Daniel asked.

"Coffee," Summer suggested

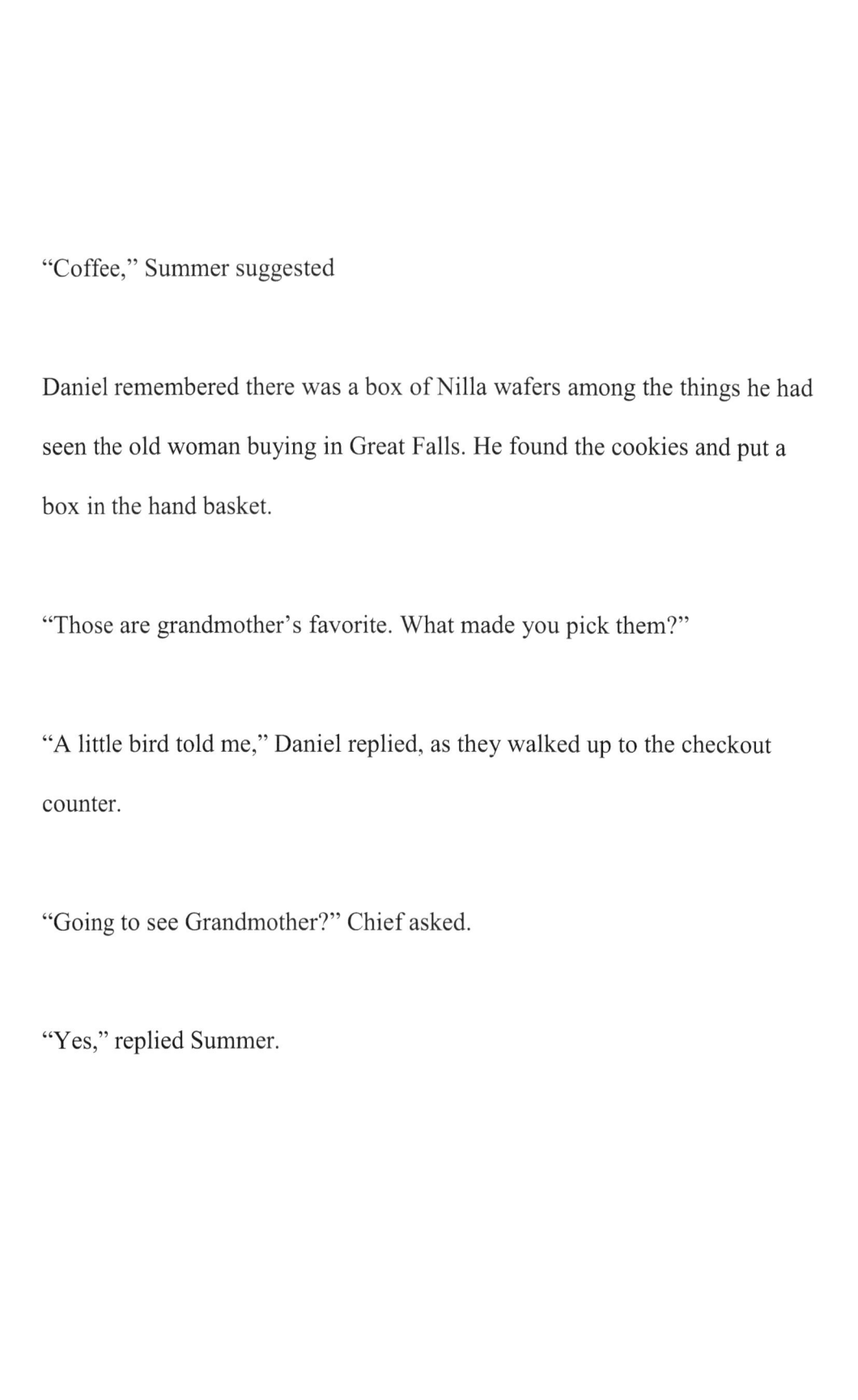

Daniel remembered there was a box of Nilla wafers among the things he had seen the old woman buying in Great Falls. He found the cookies and put a box in the hand basket.

"Those are grandmother's favorite. What made you pick them?"

"A little bird told me," Daniel replied, as they walked up to the checkout counter.

"Going to see Grandmother?" Chief asked.

"Yes," replied Summer.

"Good choice on the cookies," Chief said, giving Daniel a nod. "Say hello, for me and tell her, I'm going to Great Falls, again, next Friday," Chief said to Summer and gave Daniel a wink.

*****

"Mommy, Mommy, we had blueberry pancakes!" Billy said when he saw Summer coming through the door. Then he saw Daniel come in behind her. "Hi," he said, in a shy tone.

"Billy, this is Daniel, Daniel this is Billy."

"Hi, Daniel," Billy said.

"Hi, Billy," Daniel replied.

A woman came out of the kitchen, wiping her hands on a towel.

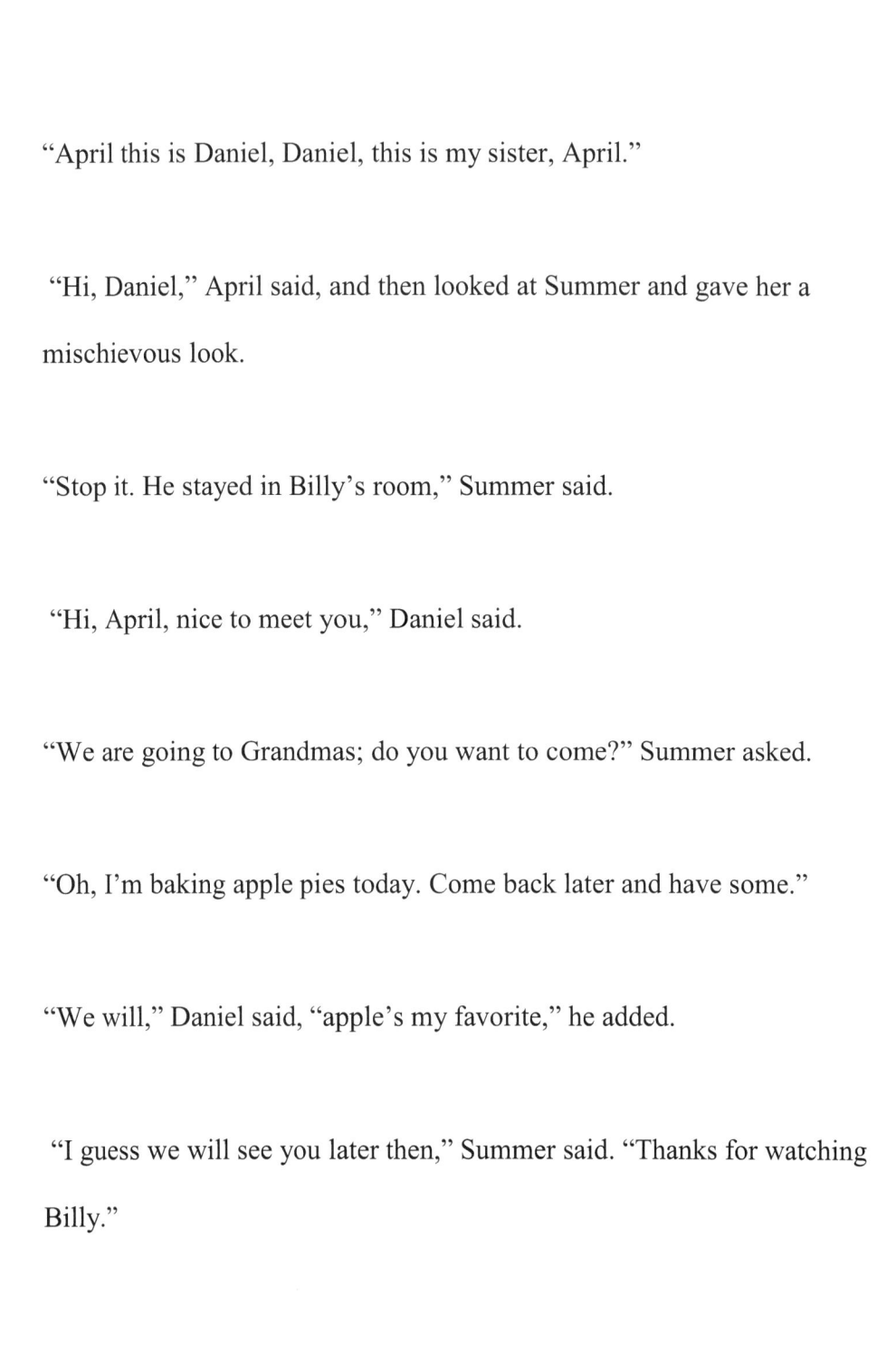

"April this is Daniel, Daniel, this is my sister, April."

"Hi, Daniel," April said, and then looked at Summer and gave her a mischievous look.

"Stop it. He stayed in Billy's room," Summer said.

"Hi, April, nice to meet you," Daniel said.

"We are going to Grandmas; do you want to come?" Summer asked.

"Oh, I'm baking apple pies today. Come back later and have some."

"We will," Daniel said, "apple's my favorite," he added.

"I guess we will see you later then," Summer said. "Thanks for watching Billy."

"I'll see you later," April said

CHAPTER 5

Thirty minutes later they pulled in front of an old house in the middle of nowhere. There on the porch was the woman Daniel had seen in Great Falls, she was sitting in a rocking chair sorting through a bowl of green beans she had just picked from her garden.

"'I'taamikskanaotonni'," (good morning) Summer said, as she got out of the SUV.

"Grandma!" Billy shouted as he ran to the old woman.

Daniel carried the bag of groceries and followed them.

When the old woman saw Daniel, she took the bowl of green beans and set it on the table next to her and stood up. "Okinapi, (hello friend)" she said.

"Hello," Daniel said, not knowing what she had just said, and thought about the last time they had met.

 The old woman said something else to Summer, in their native language and Summer answered. Daniel looked at Summer with a surprised expression on his face. She gave him one of those raised-eyebrow looks along with a tight lipped smile.

"We meet again. Welcome," the old woman said, attempting to redirect the conversation by adding, "I like the new look."

"It's nice to see you again. This is for you," Daniel said, handing her the bag.

"Thank you. Come in," the old woman said, as she led them into the house.

The doorway opened into the kitchen. An old rectangular metal table, with a faded red Formica top, was pushed up against the wall with three red chairs around it.

"Sit down," the old woman said, as she set the bag on the counter. They watched as she put things away. She turned to Daniel and with a smile said, "Nilla wafers, very traditional." Then she took the can of coffee to the refrigerator, put it inside and took out the opened can.

The refrigerator was old. It reminded Daniel of the one Indiana Jones had taken shelter in; in one of the `Rader's of the Lost Ark` movies. She put some water and coffee in the coffee maker and then came and sat down at the table with them.

"How have you been? Grandmother," Summer asked.

"I have been good for an old woman," she said…. "I had a dream last night," she continued. "I dreamed I was a wolf. I was trying to get back to my pack. A pup was following me. It wasn't mine, but I felt like I should watch over it. I kept waiting for it to catch up…. The Old Ones say when you see yourself as a wolf in a dream, you are preparing for a journey." She looked down at her old wrinkled hands and then at Summer and forced a smile. "I 've been canning pickles and green beans this week… an owl has landed on top of the shed every morning, for the past three days and watched me, as I sort through the beans on the porch. Yesterday, when I came in, I went to the sink to rinse the pickles. I smelled your Grandfather's pipe. When I turned around, I could see him sitting there. He smiled at me and then he was gone."

"You'll be with us a long time, 'Grandma," Summer said, putting her hand on her Grandmother's.

"We all die, Honey. It's the end of one journey and the beginning of another."

"You'll be missed, 'Nah-ah'," (Grandmother) Summer said softly.

"That will be my final honor," the old woman said, and put her hand on top of Summers.

"You have found your way to my home," the old woman said to Daniel. "When we first met, I could see you were like `Katoyis`, on a quest. What is it you are looking for?" she asked.

Daniel felt the necklace with his right thumb and index finger. He gently rubbed it.

"Katoyis," he brought you to me. You seek truth. What can I do to help you?" she asked.

"I was born here in 1977. My parents were killed when I was 4 years old. I was adopted by a couple from New York and I'm trying to find out about my roots," Daniel said, looking straight into the eyes of the old woman. He thought he recognized a light that flickered in them. His dream! The wolf's eyes in his dream! The old woman seemed to see something too, as they held each other's gaze.

"I had a dream last night, too," Daniel said. "I was following a wolf along a creek. I could hear a woman's voice, it was calling out, Jimmy! Jimmy! as I was making my way through a thick forest and across a field. But I don't think I know a Jimmy."

 "We should have coffee. It's ready," the old woman said as she rose from her chair. "1977…. Thirty years ago." Her gaze went far beyond the view from her window over the kitchen sink. Her thoughts transported her back in time. Back to when she was younger. Back to when her husband was still alive and her bones didn't ache with arthritis. She returned to the present, as if she had only been searching for her words.

"1977… that was a long time ago." She brought two cups of coffee and set one in front of Daniel and one in front of Summer and then went back to the counter. "I was forty-five," she said, returning to the table and sitting down. "My husband, Ray Crow Wing, was still alive. He was a hunter. All the local men wanted to go hunting with him. He would take them, but only after he had gotten an elk or enough deer to get us through the winter. He always said 'hunting was between him and the animals, and should only be seen by the Creator.' Ray believed that was how the Creator decided the direction of your next journey. There was one man, he did like to hunt with. Joe Standing Bear. Joe and his family lived west of town, out in the foothills. They were very much traditionalists. They seldom came to town. Once their business was done, they left. Back home they went. Joe and his older brother, John, had almost every animal there is, as a pet at one time or another. Ray said that is why they were such great hunters. They knew the ways of all the animals. They even brought home a grizzly cub one spring. Some of the people say that was the beginning of the end for the Standing Bear Clan. Others say it was a sign from Naapi (Old Man,) that they would one day become legend.

It began one spring. The brothers had been out looking for shed elk antlers; when they saw an avalanche on the south facing slope across the canyon from them. They went over to look at the damage the snow had done. When they got to the lower end of the slide they could hear a noise. They said, it was like a person calling out. They started poking their walking sticks in the snow trying to pinpoint the sound. They hit something and started digging. The sound grew louder as they dug, then they found a sow Grizzly, dead, and a little cub still alive tucked between her front legs. John reached down and picked the bear up, it clung to him so tight, its claws left permanent scars on his neck and chest.

They took the cub home. Their father said that they were damn fools. They should not have been there in the first place and they should have left the cub with its mother. It would die anyway.

But it didn't die. It grew into a healthy young bear and caused all sorts of trouble. It would pull clean wash off the line and get in the garden.

One time we went to visit, and there was Sally chasing this 400-pound grizzly with a broom, and those two guys on the porch yelling, 'don't hurt her, she didn't mean to do it.'

When it killed some of their chickens and got into the smoke house, and finished off most of a pig, their father finally told them it couldn't stay any longer. They took it deep into the back country. But she found her way home. They took her farther the next time, and stayed until it was time to hibernate. Those boys would go back each spring and camp. The bear would come and stay with them. They would hunt and live together as bears. Some of the people thought the brothers were strange because they would rather spend time with the bear than other people. They thought people were the strange ones."

The old woman stopped talking and drank her coffee. She let the story simmer like a kettle of soup.

"John and his wife had a son. He loved the mountains and the animals as much as his father and uncle. He married a young girl and they had a child. They died in a car accident… that was many years ago."

The old woman looked at Daniel, as she finished the last part of the story and said, "Maybe you should talk to Joe Standing Bear."
They finished their coffee in silence.

"Ray was an artist. Would you like to see some of his work?" the old woman asked, after several minutes.

"Yes," Daniel said.

They went out on the porch and down the steps. The old woman led them around the house and down an overgrown trail. She stopped and pointed to a lilac bush. A figure of a coyote, cut from metal and welded to re-bar looked out at them. "'Aapi'si'," (coyote) he was the first to notice the Human

Beings," the old woman said. She turned and took a few steps. "Hidden in the long grass are other figures, too. They are arranged in a circle to honor the seasons. In the middle is a warrior. Ray would come out and turn him to face each of the figures during their season. I am getting too old to tend to the Spirit garden like we once did," she said and smiled as she turned to look at Summer with Daniel at her side.

Daniel walked out to the center of the garden and stood next to the warrior. "Where should he be facing?" he asked.

"To the south… toward the Sun figure…" Summer said, and pointed.

Daniel freed the pin that anchored the warrior and turned him to face the Sun figure and then put the pin in place to hold him there. Ray had used a coffee can, filled with cement, as a base for the figure and then buried it. The warrior could rotate and a pin could be placed in one of the four holes, evenly spaced long the edge. This would point the warrior in the direction opposite the anchor pin. He came back and stood next to Summer. She looked at him approvingly.

"Ray is glad you came here today. I am glad, too. It has been a long time since the warrior has sung to the Spirits."

They walked back to the house. Billy was sitting on the porch playing with the kittens. He had a black and white one on his shoulder and two tabbies on his lap. The black and white one was on its hind legs and playing in Billy's hair with its front paws. Billy had his shoulders hunched up because of the kittens' sharp, little claws. He was laughing as he watched the two tabbies using the inside of his legs as a wrestling arena. He looked up at Daniel and said "Get this one off me!" as the little kitten started scrabbling up the side of his head. Daniel picked the kitty from Billy. It squirmed in his hands.

"Hold it close to you," Summer said.

Daniel brought the little ball of fur closer to his chest. He shifted the kitten into the palm of his left hand and playfully wiggled his right index finger at it. The kitten flipped onto its back and bit the tip of it. He had never held a little kitten. It was so soft and yet, acted so ferocious. Its little teeth and claws were so tiny and still so sharp. When he looked up, Summer and the old woman were looking at him.

"`Soka'pii mosskitsipahpi` (good heart)," the old woman said.

Summer nodded at her.

"Your visit today was much appreciated," the old woman said. "You must come again."

"Time to go, Billy," Summer said.

"Okay," he replied but kept playing with the kittens a minute longer. He finally stood up.

"Bye, Grandma," he said and he gave her a big hug, then Summer helped him into the SUV.

"`Aakatt'si'noot'sii'yo'p, (we will see each other again)" Summer said.

The old woman returned the phrase, and then said, "Go and see Joe Standing Bear. He will be able to help you;" as Daniel circled around the yard and waved to her.

What was that you said to each other, as we were leaving? Aakatt'si'…." Daniel asked, as he drove along.

"Aa'katt'si'noot'sii'yo'p, that's Blackfeet for, we will see each other again," Summer said.

"She said that to me the first time we met," Daniel said.

CHAPTER 6

April was putting her last two pies in the oven, when Summer and Daniel walked through the door.

"Hey! How 'bout some pie," she asked, reaching for two plates and cutting into one of the pies on the counter, without waiting for an answer.

"Oh, we just stopped in to tell you that we were heading…" Summer started to say, when Daniel cut her off.

"Sure!" he said and smiled at Summer.

"Heading where?" April asked, as she put a warm piece of pie on a plate and handed it to Daniel.

"Joe Standing Bears house. Grandma thought he might be able to help Daniel," Summer said.

"Oh, I haven't been up there in years. Take a pie with you," April offered.

"I bet he'd like that. Why don't you and Tommy come too," Daniel said, after taking a bite of pie.

"It will be at least another hour before we could leave. You'll be late enough coming back as it is," April said.

"She's right. It's only twenty miles from here, but once we turn off the highway, the road gets pretty rough in spots, we could end up camping out, if we got stuck," Summer said.

"We could get an early start in the morning… after breakfast?" April suggested, attempting to sweeten the deal with more of her cooking.

"If you think we should wait, then we'll wait," Daniel said, looking at Summer. He didn't want to put anyone in danger. He also saw it would mean something to April, if she and Tommy could come with. "And if her breakfasts are as good as her pie…" he playfully thought to himself. "It's probably better if we get a fresh start in the morning," he said.

"We could go grab some things to take up there and maybe go for a ride," Summer suggested.

"Sounds good," Daniel agreed, noticing the smile on Aprils face.

"Go do that and come back later for dinner…. Elk meatloaf," April offered.

"Deal!" Daniel said, giving Summer a wink.

The next morning, after breakfast, he watched as everyone got settled in and then looked to Summer for directions.

"Down to the stop sign, take a right," she said.

Once they got through town and had been traveling west on Hwy. 2 for a little while, Daniel began to try and remember the last time he had felt this relaxed, when he realized he thought he smelled something. He had always had a diminished sense of smell; his parents had taken him to several specialists, none of which had been able to explain it. He opened his window a little and took a deep breath. He let it out and then took another and held it for second, before letting it slowly slip out from between his lips. He glanced at Summer and caught her looking at him. They both smiled.

"We need to make a right turn on, Blacktail Creek Road," Summer said, as they passed a sign that read Glacier Park 40 miles, Kalispell 90 miles. "A little past that curve, up ahead, she said, making a gesture with her hand....

"There it is," she said, several minutes later.

Daniel slowed down and turned onto the forest service road. It was slow going and Daniel did his best to avoid the large pot holes, as they gradually made their way up the mountain.

The road wiggled like a big snake, as it made its way down to the bottom of the next draw. They crossed a small wooden bridge and then continued up the east side of another mountain. About half way up, the road got steeper and turned into more of a two track trail, which had partially washed out during spring runoff. It was difficult to keep from high centering.

"If you put it in 4-wheel low, you'll be able to keep the left tire between the ruts and the right one to the side of the trail. It will make it easier going," Summer said, trying to be helpful.

"How do I do that?"

"That's a good question. The older ones had a lever to pull… just push that button, I guess," Summer said, after looking at the dash board for a minute.

Daniel looked at her as he felt the SUV crawl along, he felt like he was driving a tank. At the top of the ridge, the road forked.

"Stay to the right," Summer directed. From here on out it'll be flatter going. I'd put it in 4- wheel high," she said, smiling.

Daniel looked at the dash and pushed the button again, until the light indicated 4- wheel high.

The narrow road curved around to the west side of the mountain and then gently sloped down through a patch of Quaky Aspen and out into a clearing, dotted with big stumps. The road turned into a widened out area, it reminded Daniel of a cul-de-sac.

"It was built for loading logs onto trucks," Summer said, reading his inquisitive look, as he pulled around and stopped in front of a small white house with a rusted metal roof. An old man sitting on a wooden chair watched them from the porch as they got out.

"Oki tsa niita'pii wa, (hello, how is everything)" Summer said, after stepping out of the SUV.

"Oki tsa niita' pii wa," replied the old man.

"I am Summer Morning Star, Mary Crow Wing is my Grandmother," she said, identifying herself, and then opened the back door. This is my son Billy, my sister April and her son Tommy." She reached inside for the box of groceries and started toward the house, with Billy and Tommy right behind her, followed by April carrying her pie.

"No moh tah sit' aki, (Thank you)," the old man said, as he took the box. "To what do I owe this honor?" he said to Summer, and then his focus shifted, as Daniel stepped from around the vehicle and came toward the house.

"This is Daniel Williams. He is from New York. Daniel, this is Joe Standing Bear," Summer said.

The old man stood there silently, starring at Daniel.

"Grandma said, he should come and talk to you. She thought you might be able to help him," Summer said, suddenly feeling a little awkward.

 "I will help, if I can. Come and sit," Joe said, as he made his way up the porch stairs.
He set the box on the little table next to his chair and pointed to the other chairs.

"This is for you too," April said, handing him the pie, before sitting down.

The old man took a long look at Daniel and then took the pie into the house. When he came back, Daniel told him what had brought him to Montana. The old man's eyes never left Daniels face the whole time he spoke. When Daniel had finished, the old man stood up and went inside. He returned holding a black and white picture of a young man standing next to an old Ford Bronco, and handed it to Daniel. The young man in the picture was tall and lean. He had a big smile on his face. His long black hair hung down behind his shoulders. Except for the long hair, it could have been a picture of Daniel. Daniel noticed the printed date on the picture, Oct. 15, 1975.

"That is a picture of my Nephew. His name was Eddy. He bought that Bronco in Kalispell with the money he earned guiding Hunters. He was very proud of it. He married that pretty girl sitting in the passenger seat, that next spring. There was a baby born a year later. His name was Jimmy. His parents brought him to visit many times. He was staying here a few years later, the day his parents were killed. They were coming home from Christmas shopping in Kalispell. It was the second week of December… it had been snowing lightly all day. Just before evening, a black cloud suddenly covered everything. I lit the lamp on the table and stepped out onto the porch. I couldn't see more than 10 feet. I had never seen anything like it…. Jimmy suddenly started crying and John brought him out to show him there was nothing to fear. Jimmy pointed out at the storm and acted like he had seen something that scared him. The Freezing mist hung in the air and squeezed in like a hand making a fist…. Then there was a bolt of lightning, it hit the tree. In the flash, I thought I saw someone standing next to it. There was another flash… that time I saw no one… They must have just reached the top of the pass about then…. A semi-truck heading west, jack-knifed and crossed the center line. The driver of the truck told the sheriff, he drove into a white out, just as he reached the top of the pass. He said there was a terrible wind gust and didn't even know the Bronco had gone under the trailer, until he got out of his truck. It took the top completely off. The

Coroner said it killed them both instantly," the old man said, and then fell silent as his gaze shifted from the picture in Daniels hand to the mountains off to the West.

Daniel continued to study the picture. He was amazed by how much he looked like the man in the photo. The woman was so pretty and looked so happy, as she smiled for the camera. It must have been windy, because several strands of hair had blown across her face. Then suddenly he realized it was the woman from his dream! The Bronco was the SUV they were riding in. The dream was part of a memory he had from when he was little. He looked up and out from the porch. The Bronco would have been parked just behind where he had parked the Escalade. There was a tall skinny tree in the back ground of the picture. A rather impressive cedar stood there now. The top was burnt, but several feet under the dead area; a branch had grown out and turned straight up, making a new top. It was the tree Daniel had seen in his visions!

"You were four years old. The People all told me 'Joe Standing Bear, you and John, have raised every kind of animal that lives in the forest, but a boy needs a mother.' Your Grandmother had died from the Flu just that spring and so it was only John and myself. The lady at the adoption agency said a couple on the east coast wanted to give you a good home. She said they knew the man from Kalispell that Eddie had taken hunting several times," Joe paused as big tears started to fill his eyes. They were tears of joy. "It was one of the hardest things we had ever done. Your Grandfather woke up crying every morning for many years after you left. Every morning we would go out on the porch and look at the tree. Every morning he'd say 'Nits'o'kan' (his dream) and think about what Naapi (Old Man) had told him many years ago. He always believed you would return. I have been asking 'The Old Ones' to wake the bear inside you and bring you home. You have come, it is good."

The old man took a deep breath and smiled, as he looked at Summer and April.

"Nipowa(Summer,) Matsiyikapisikisoom(April,) I saw you both with your Grandmother at the Pow Wow, last year. How is she doing?"

"Good, she's keeps busy with her garden, still canning all those green beans and pickles. Billy keeps me busy, when I'm not working. Grandma says you and Grandpa Ray would go hunting sometimes."

"Yes, besides family, he was the only man I ever liked to hunt with. He understood the animals like 'The Old Ones' did. He heard their voices and honored their spirits. He saw them as fellow beings and gifts from Naapi (Old Man,)" Joe said and smiled, as he thought of days gone by, then he looked at Daniel. "I knew you as Jimmy. I will try to call you Daniel, in honor of your adopted parents… I had given you a name too. It was, 'Akai aazist awa' (Many Rabbits.)"

"Many Rabbits?" Daniel repeated and smiled.

Uncle Joe chuckled as he got up and went back inside. When he returned, he was carrying an old black top hat. He tipped the hat over, it appeared empty. Then holding it by the brim with his left hand, opened end up, he waved his right hand over it a couple times and then reached inside and pulled out a homemade stuffed rabbit. He waved his hand over the hat again, reached in and pulled out another stuffed rabbit. His audience was impressed and clapped their hands. He held up his hand, as a sign to hold the applause. A third time, he waved his hand over the black hat and reached inside and produced another rabbit. He then put all three rabbits back in the hat, gave it a little shake and turned it over, nothing came out. They all looked at Uncle Joe, a little surprised. Uncle Joe reached inside and pulled out a rabbit. "Velcro," he said, smiling. "Sally made it for you many years ago, your Grandmother," Uncle Joe said, as he handed the magic hat to Daniel. "You never got tired of it. 'Bits, Bits, Bits,' you would say holding the hat out. I'd do the magic show and then do it again and again. Then you'd take it to someone else and watch as they did it. So you became known as 'Akai Aazistawa' (Many Rabbits.)"

Daniel looked in the hat, then turned toward Summer. She could see by the look in his eyes that he was a little overwhelmed. She reached out and took his hand and flashed a little smile. That seemed to help center him. He had so many thoughts racing around in his head: Jimmy Standing Bear, Many Rabbits, Daniel Williams! How could he be all of those people?

"When mom first took me shopping, she said I went over by a display of men's hats. She said I stood there pointing at them, they thought I wanted to try one on. I took it off and looked inside and said, 'Bits, Bits, Bits.' They thought I was panhandling and trying to say two-bits, two-bits. They actually called me two-bits for a while. But it didn't stick. My father didn't like it. He said there was nothing 'two-bit' about his son." There was silence.

"It is good you are here again, 'Akai Aazistawa (Many Rabbits.) Naa' pi' (Old Man) has seen to it that we walk down the same path together, again."

Daniel looked at the old man. Uncle Joe smiled a knowing smile. Daniel thought about the strange dreams he had before he left New York and the one the other night. He wondered about the 'Spirits' that might be guiding him. Where would they lead him? What did Uncle Joe mean when he said, awaken the bear inside him? He smiled back, something inside told him everything would be alright.

Billy came over and looked in the hat at the stuffed rabbits. Daniel picked up the hat, shook it, and turned it over, nothing came out. Then he reached in and pulled out a rabbit.

"How does it work?" Billy asked.

"Magic," Daniel said.

They all laughed, as Billy and Tommy looked at each other with their mouths slightly opened.

"Would you like some sun tea? I put some in the root cellar yesterday," Uncle Joe said.

"Will you show me your root cellar?" Daniel asked.

"You have been to the root cellar many times, maybe seeing it again will help you remember something. Let's go."

They followed him behind the house to a small shed with firewood stacked along one side; then down some narrow steps that went under the floor of the building. It was noticeably cooler down there. The light coming down the stairs illuminated the wooden shelves along the back wall. The top shelf had several rows of glass jars, each full of tomatoes. The lower shelf had rows of jars filled with meat. Burlap bags with potatoes and onions hung from the floor joists above. Daniel looked around trying to remember something about the root cellar.

The old man held his arms out and said, "here we are!" He could see Daniel was searching for memories. "I once told you a story about a bear. You called this, the cave and always wanted to come and see if the bear was here.

Daniel thought a minute, then, let out a little sigh, "I can't remember anything."

Let's go have some tea, it still may all come back," Uncle Joe said, as he picked up one of the two big pickle jars of sun tea and handed it to Daniel. He then took a metal pail and put two jars of tomatoes, 2 jars of meat, several potatoes and an onion in it. "I might as well do all my shopping, since I'm here," he said with a smile.

Daniel and Summer turned to go back up the stairs. Uncle Joe followed and closed the door behind him and they walked back to the house.

****

Uncle Joe set the metal pal on the counter and took the tea from Daniel and poured several glasses. Daniel looked around the room, he noticed the sink had no faucet and drained into a five-gallon bucket. There was no refrigerator. An oil lamp on the table seemed to be the only source of light. The stove was an old wood cook stove which doubled as the source for heat. Daniel realized there was no electricity or running water.

"Let's go back out on the porch. It's too nice to be indoors," Uncle Joe said. They returned to the chairs on the porch and sat down. "What are your plans now that you have found the answers to your questions?" Uncle Joe asked.

Daniel thought for a moment. He really didn't know. He hadn't planned that far ahead, how could he have. "I'd like to see a little more of this part of the country," Daniel answered, thinking on his feet.

"I'd be willing to bet Summer would be happy to show you around. You won't find anyone better." Uncle Joe said, watching for a telling sign from either of them. He sensed a spark between them and thought it would be right if the granddaughter of his friend, Ray Crow Wing and his brother's grandson could be together. I hope you will come and see me again. We have much to talk about."

"I'd like that," Daniel said, glancing out at the snowcapped mountains. They did have many things to talk about, but no one felt compelled to say anything more, just then. Oddly enough, for people who barely knew each other, they all felt very comfortable together.

CHAPTER 7

As the hot water from his hotel room shower ran off his head and down his back, he thought about Uncle Joe and how he lived in the mountains his whole life without running water or electricity. He thought how different his life would have been if he'd been raised by his Grandfather and Uncle Joe. He was surprised at how much had happened in the short period of time he'd been in Montana. It was like this whole other life was out here waiting for him. He had only needed to follow his inner voice. That had set everything in motion.

He thought his father would be proud of him, he thought about that, both of them. Now he had tracked down the story of his birth parents, met a great uncle and Summer. He had asked her if she and Billy would like to come and spend a couple of days with him in Great falls. He had made it clear that they would have their own room. He thought they could enjoy the indoor pool and do a little exploring. She had said yes, but said she had to work the next two days and then teach the Self Defense class, Wednesday evening. She had suggested they could come Thursday afternoon and stay until Sunday. So he had been on his own for a couple of days. It had been a little strange. He felt like something was missing. He came out of the bathroom, found his other pair of jeans and put one of his new shirts on. He picked up the medallion Mary had given him and put it on. He couldn't help but think of her and Uncle Joe. They lived such simple lives and seemed so happy. He smiled at himself in the mirror. He liked his new look and wondered if he could fit into a quieter life style. Maybe someday, but now he was ready for a cup of coffee and he wanted it now, so he grabbed his keys and drove to the drive -through at Starbucks. Ten minutes later, he was sipping his coffee and headed out of town. He had decided to drive around and do a little exploring, so he headed east on Hwy. 87.

It wasn't long and he felt like he was in the middle of nowhere. He passed a sign that read, Havre 75 miles. He didn't have any destination in mind, he just wanted to see the country, and so he just kept driving and sipping. He started to think about New York. It was 11:30 mountain time, 1:30 eastern time. When Daniel saw a historical marker sign with a little parking area, he pulled in to read what it had to say. The view seemed endless and he just sat there a few minutes enjoying the breeze as it blew through the windows, it was so relaxing, he momentarily forgot why he stopped; then he picked up his phone and called the office.

"Good Afternoon, Williams, Williams and Anderson law office," a woman's voice said.

"Betty! This is Daniel."

"Daniel! Hello, how are you?"

"I'm fine…. Yes, Montana sure is big open country. How's everything back there? Good, good. Is Steve available? Thanks, Betty."

"Daniel! How are things out there in big sky country?" Steve said, when he came on the line.

"I can see why they call it that... everything's fine. I'm trying to blend in. I traded my grey suit for jeans and snakeskin cowboy boots." Daniel said pausing for a reaction.

"Some.... What!" Steve said.

"Some Snakeskin boots."

"If that's what it takes to blend in… and you're having a good time. Have you made any discoveries?"

"Yes, I have. I met a great uncle. He showed me a picture of my birth parents, 6 months before they were married and I met a woman."

"You Dog!" Steve said jokingly.

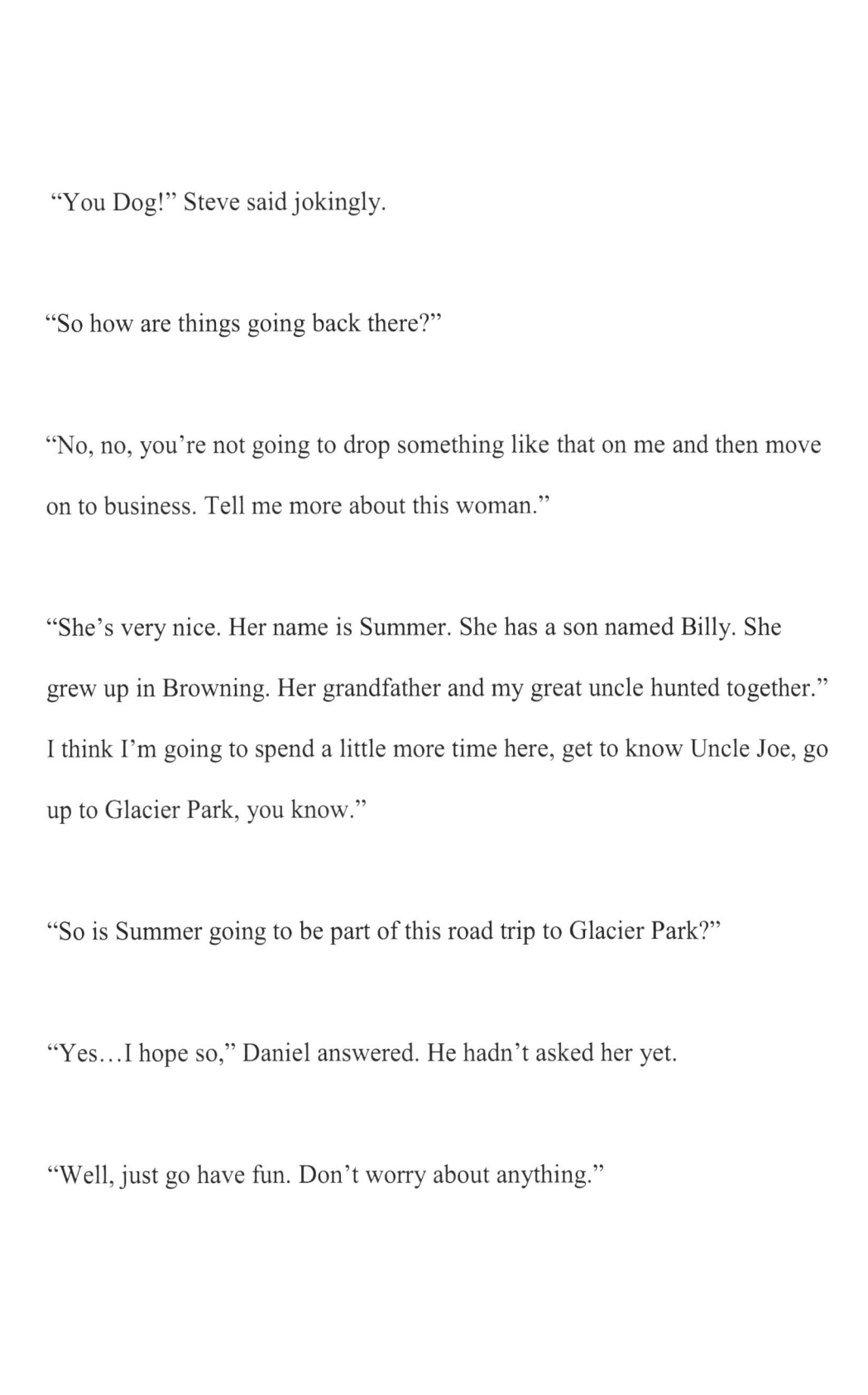

"So how are things going back there?"

"No, no, you're not going to drop something like that on me and then move on to business. Tell me more about this woman."

"She's very nice. Her name is Summer. She has a son named Billy. She grew up in Browning. Her grandfather and my great uncle hunted together." I think I'm going to spend a little more time here, get to know Uncle Joe, go up to Glacier Park, you know."

"So is Summer going to be part of this road trip to Glacier Park?"

"Yes…I hope so," Daniel answered. He hadn't asked her yet.

"Well, just go have fun. Don't worry about anything."

"Okay, I will, thanks," Daniel said and then turned off his phone. He looked out at the wide open space and then headed back to Great Falls. He thought he should eat something, so he pulled into the drive- through at Wendy's and ate a hamburger on the way back to the motel.

When he got back to his room, he took off his boots and turned on the TV. The History channel had something on about mining in Montana and the richest hill on earth, but he couldn't focus on the program, all he could think about was Summer. Then the room phone rang. Summer was on the house phone in the lobby. He went down to meet her.

CHAPTER 8

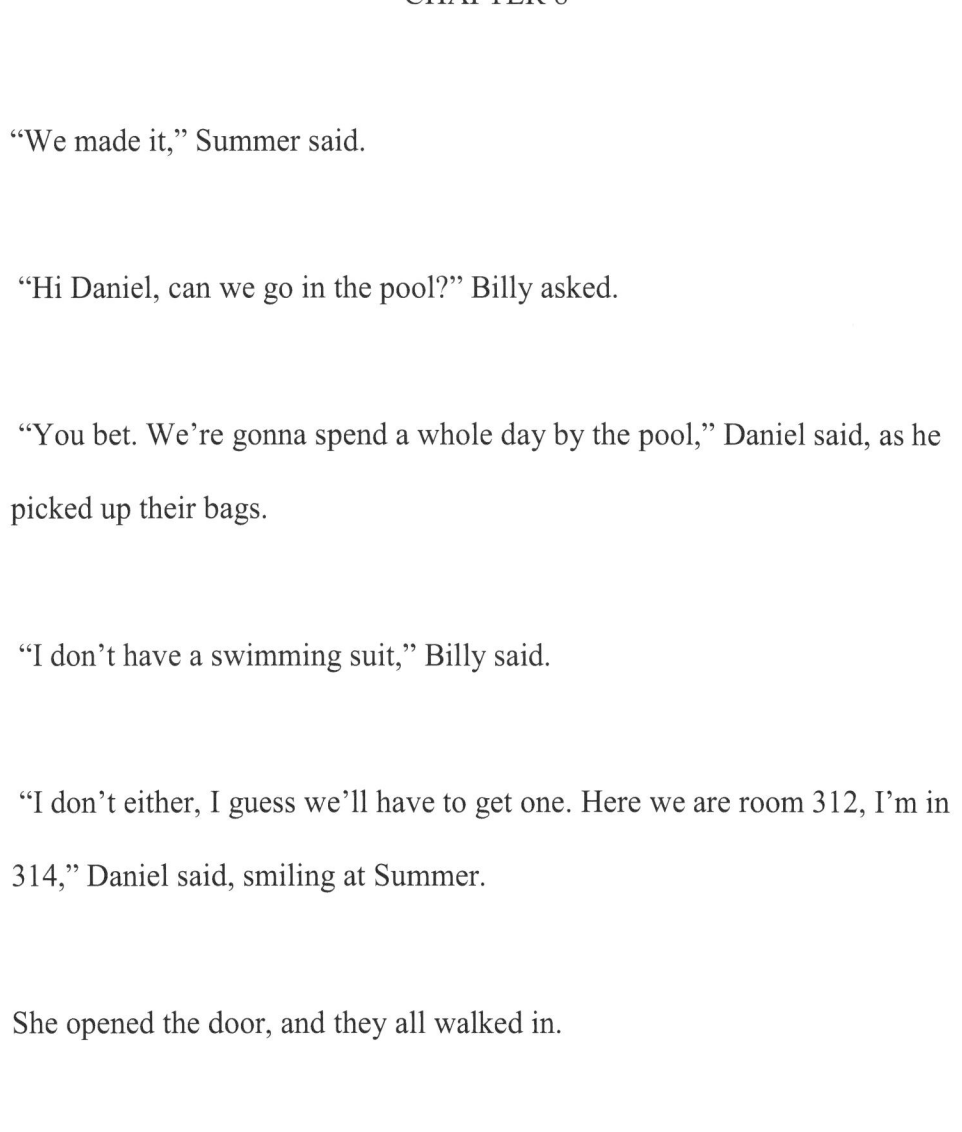

"We made it," Summer said.

"Hi Daniel, can we go in the pool?" Billy asked.

"You bet. We're gonna spend a whole day by the pool," Daniel said, as he picked up their bags.

"I don't have a swimming suit," Billy said.

"I don't either, I guess we'll have to get one. Here we are room 312, I'm in 314," Daniel said, smiling at Summer.

She opened the door, and they all walked in.

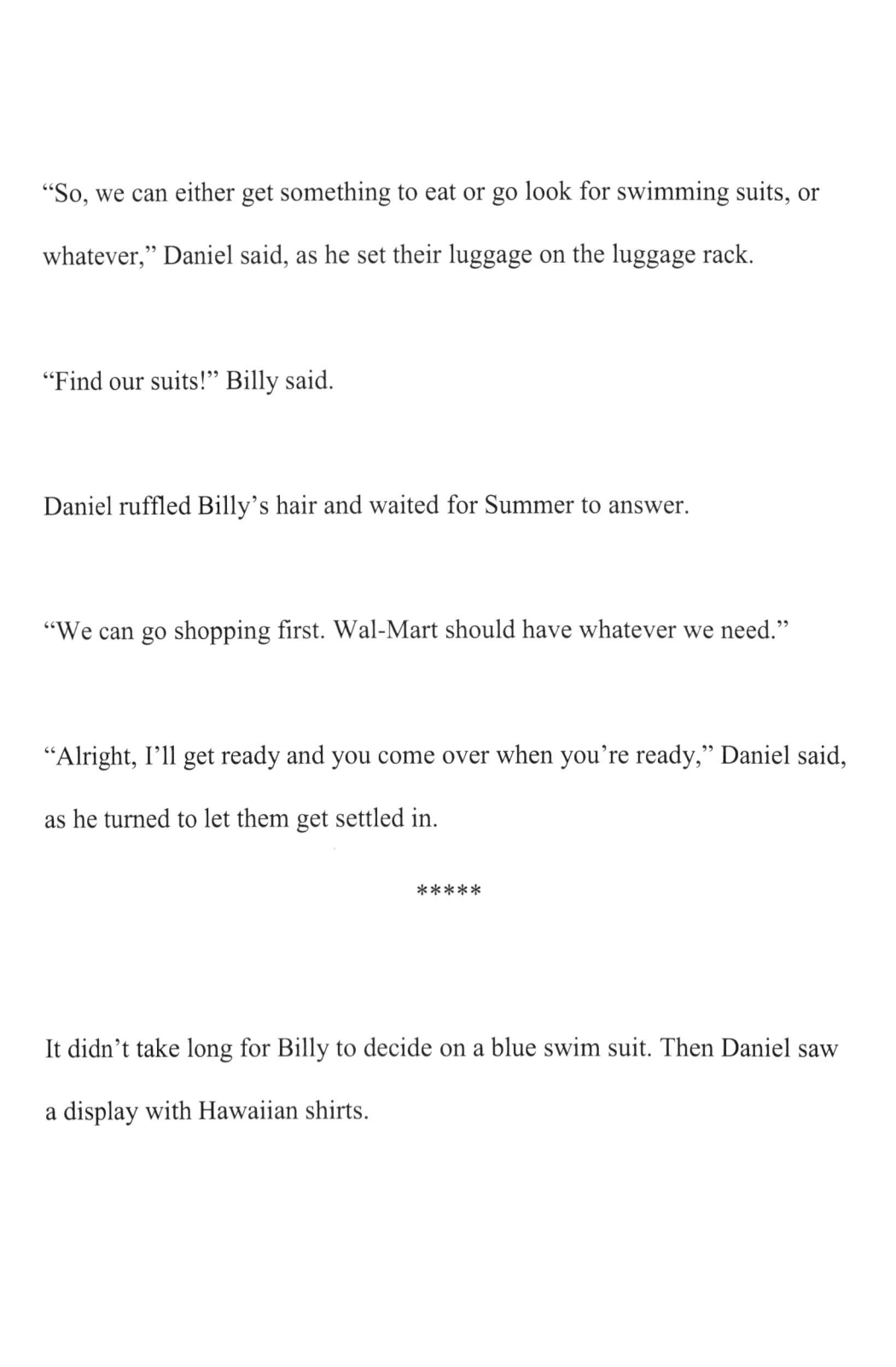

"So, we can either get something to eat or go look for swimming suits, or whatever," Daniel said, as he set their luggage on the luggage rack.

"Find our suits!" Billy said.

Daniel ruffled Billy's hair and waited for Summer to answer.

"We can go shopping first. Wal-Mart should have whatever we need."

"Alright, I'll get ready and you come over when you're ready," Daniel said, as he turned to let them get settled in.

*****

It didn't take long for Billy to decide on a blue swim suit. Then Daniel saw a display with Hawaiian shirts.

"Let's check it out," he said, to Billy.

"Okay," Billy said, and followed Daniel.

"What do you think of this one?" Daniel said, holding out a blue shirt with red and yellow Sponge Bob Characters on it.

"Yeah," Billy chuckled.

"I think your mom needs a suit too, don't you Billy?" Daniel said, looking at Summer with a twinkle in his eyes.

"Oh, you think so, do you?" Summer said.

"Let's go pick one out for her," Daniel said.

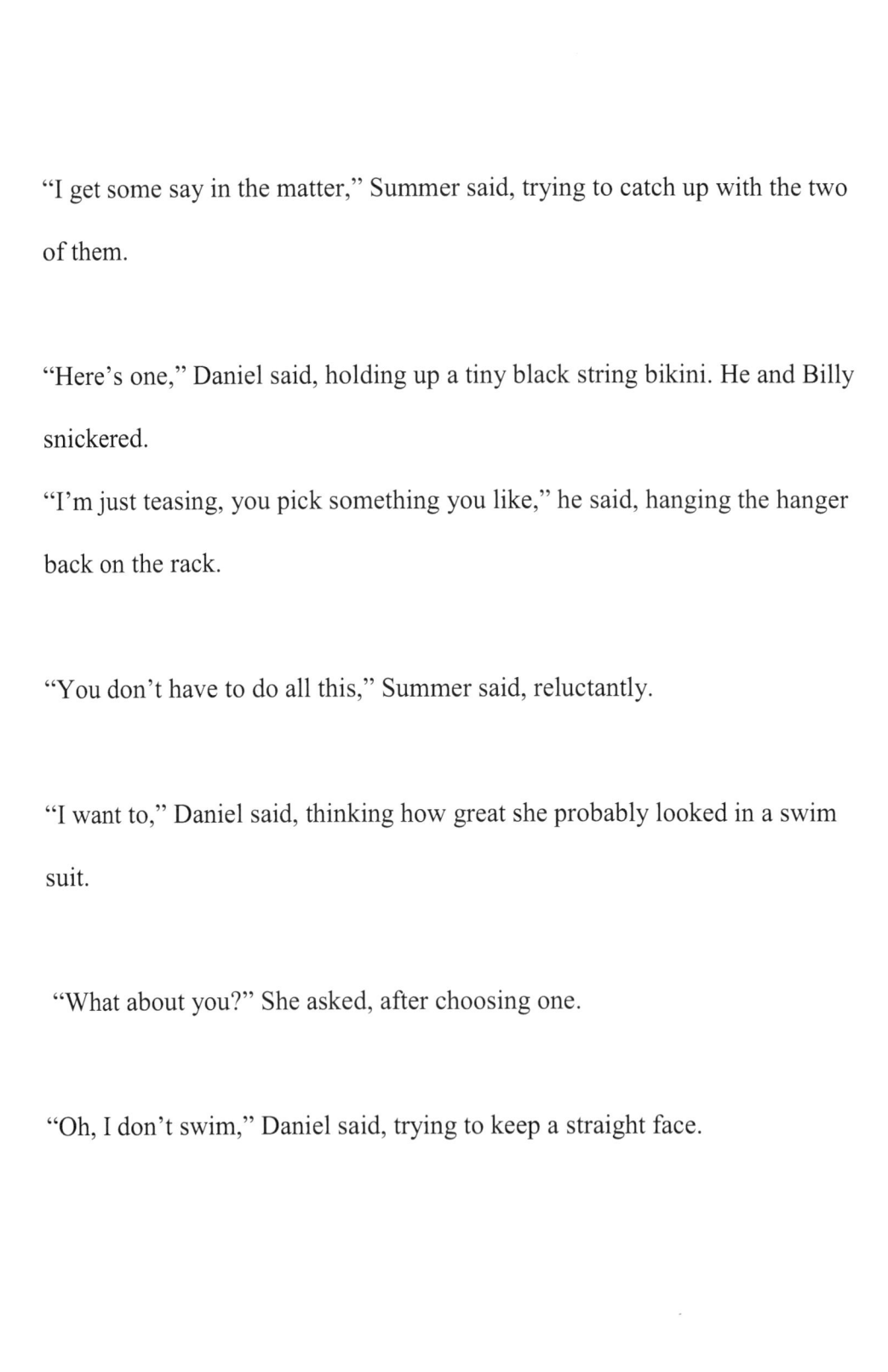

"I get some say in the matter," Summer said, trying to catch up with the two of them.

"Here's one," Daniel said, holding up a tiny black string bikini. He and Billy snickered.

"I'm just teasing, you pick something you like," he said, hanging the hanger back on the rack.

"You don't have to do all this," Summer said, reluctantly.

"I want to," Daniel said, thinking how great she probably looked in a swim suit.

"What about you?" She asked, after choosing one.

"Oh, I don't swim," Daniel said, trying to keep a straight face.

"Oh no, come on Billy let's go pick a suit for Daniel. We can't have all the fun, can we?" She said, giving Daniel a cheesy smile, as she took Billy's hand and headed for the men's dept... "How about this one?" she said, holding up a tiny red Speedo, mocking Daniel's choice of suits for her.

"I don't think so," Daniel said, feeling his cheeks turn warm. "How about this one?" He held up a charcoal grey, surfer style suit.

"Chicken," Summer said.

After Daniel found one, he said, "Let's go check out some pool toys."

As they were walking toward the SUV with their packages, Summer looked at Billy and said, "What do you say to Daniel?"

"Thanks for the swim suit. Thanks for the shirt. Thanks for the flip-flops. Thanks for the goggles. Thanks for the diving rings. Thanks for the ball."

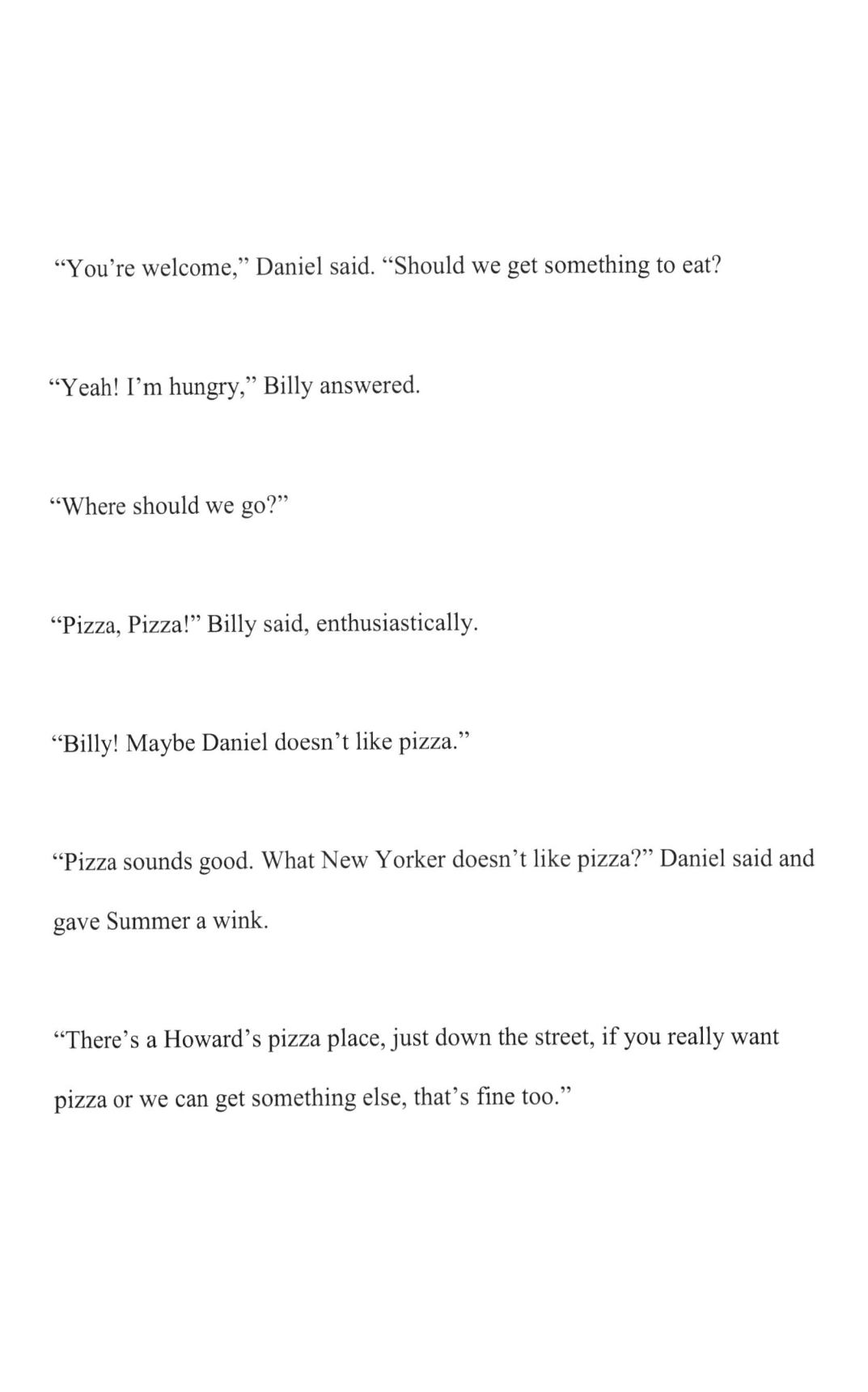

"You're welcome," Daniel said. "Should we get something to eat?"

"Yeah! I'm hungry," Billy answered.

"Where should we go?"

"Pizza, Pizza!" Billy said, enthusiastically.

"Billy! Maybe Daniel doesn't like pizza."

"Pizza sounds good. What New Yorker doesn't like pizza?" Daniel said and gave Summer a wink.

"There's a Howard's pizza place, just down the street, if you really want pizza or we can get something else, that's fine too."

"Howard's sounds great," Daniel said, as he helped Billy get into the back seat and opened the passenger door for her.

Later that Evening Daniel was watching the local news, when a knock on the door caught him by surprise. He got up and looked through the peep hole. It was Summer.

"Hi, is everything okay? Where's Billy?"

"I arranged for a sitter for a couple of hours," she said, and smiled at him.

Daniel noticed she had her new robe and flip-flops on. Summer noticed him noticing.

"Did you want to go down to the pool?" Daniel asked, pretending to be naive.

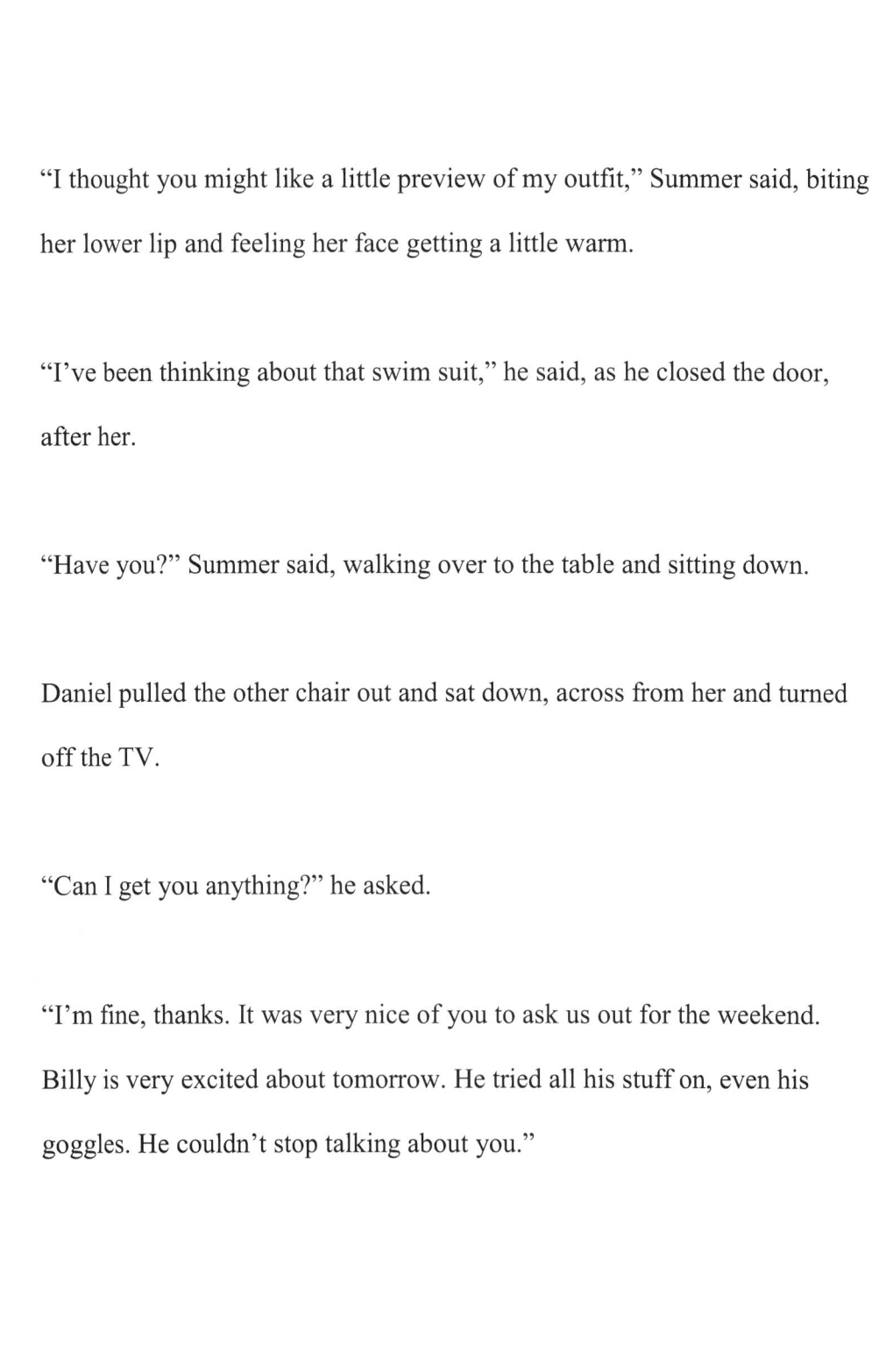

"I thought you might like a little preview of my outfit," Summer said, biting her lower lip and feeling her face getting a little warm.

"I've been thinking about that swim suit," he said, as he closed the door, after her.

"Have you?" Summer said, walking over to the table and sitting down.

Daniel pulled the other chair out and sat down, across from her and turned off the TV.

"Can I get you anything?" he asked.

"I'm fine, thanks. It was very nice of you to ask us out for the weekend. Billy is very excited about tomorrow. He tried all his stuff on, even his goggles. He couldn't stop talking about you."

"I think he's a great kid," Daniel said. He paused for a second, then said, "I'd like to go to Glacier Park. Maybe if you and Billy have fun this weekend, we could all go?"

"Maybe, I'll have to see if I can get time off from work," she said, glancing down at the floor, trying to gather up her nerve. Then she stood up and untied her robe and let it fall to the floor. She stepped in front of Daniel, "Well, what do you think?"

"I think you're beautiful," Daniel said, as he looked at her long legs and curves.

"I meant the suit!" she said, innocently.

"I think it's great too," Daniel said, as he stood up. He put his arms around her and gently pulled her close to him. He reached up and touched her hair. It was so black and shiny. He looked into her eyes and kissed her. He could feel her curves, as she put her arms around him and pressed closer to him. They looked at each other as their lips met again, this time, a little longer. They sat down on the edge of the bed. Daniel kissed her neck, as he took in her scent. She touched his face with her left hand, as they lay back on the bed.

CHAPTER 9

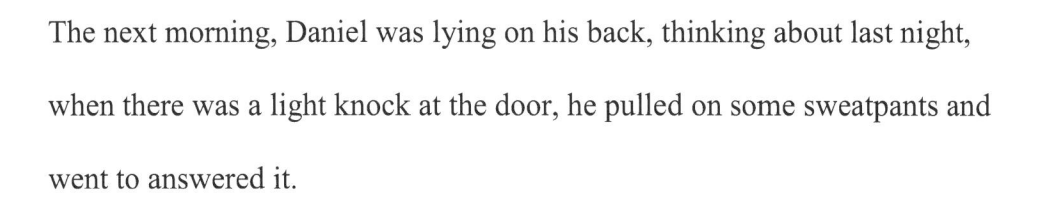

The next morning, Daniel was lying on his back, thinking about last night, when there was a light knock at the door, he pulled on some sweatpants and went to answered it.

"Morning," Billy said.

"Morning… does your mom know you're here?"

"Yeah."

"Come on in, you can watch TV while I get ready. Daniel turned on the TV, and got Billy settled in one of the chairs by the table. "Let's see what's on," Daniel said, flipping through the channels.

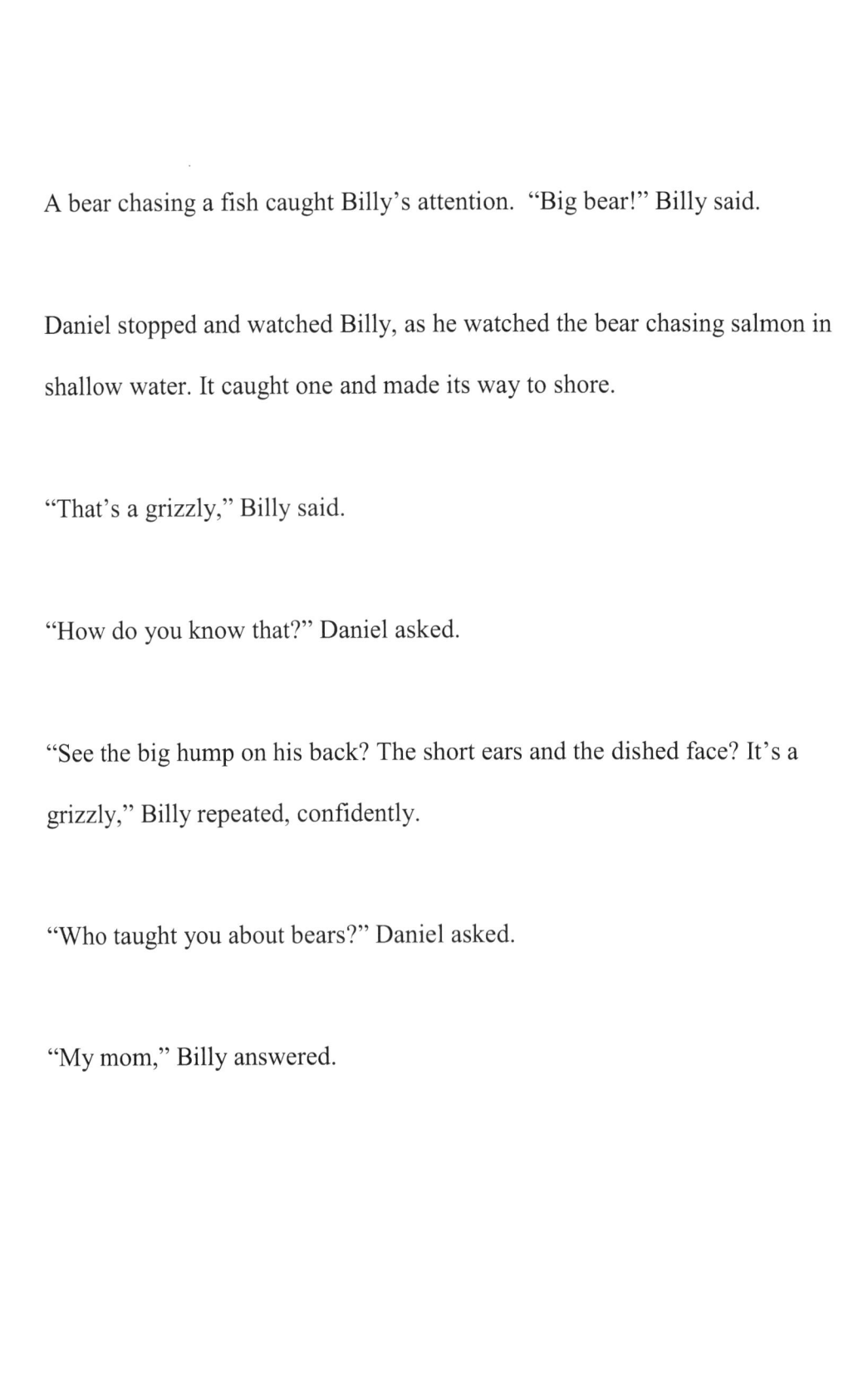

A bear chasing a fish caught Billy's attention. "Big bear!" Billy said.

Daniel stopped and watched Billy, as he watched the bear chasing salmon in shallow water. It caught one and made its way to shore.

"That's a grizzly," Billy said.

"How do you know that?" Daniel asked.

"See the big hump on his back? The short ears and the dished face? It's a grizzly," Billy repeated, confidently.

"Who taught you about bears?" Daniel asked.

"My mom," Billy answered.

They were watching as another bear and three cubs came down to the water's edge to fish and how she had to leave the cubs unattended while she competed with bigger male bears for the best fishing spot, when there was a knock at the door. Daniel got up and went to answer it. It was Summer.

"Good morning. Is Billy …?"

"Hi mom."

"I said; watch TV while I took a shower."

"We are," Billy said.

"We're watching bears on TV…I guess we lost track of time," Daniel said, realizing he was still wearing sweatpants. They smiled at each other.

Summer could see Daniel and Billy were getting along well and she was glad, but irritated that he had left the room.

"Come and see the little bear," Billy said.

"I'll get ready," Daniel said, taking some clothes into the bathroom.

Summer went over and sat with Billy.

"Me and Daniel were watching TV," Billy said, trying to defend his actions. "I think he's nice," Billy added."

"I like him too," Summer said, and gave Billy a hug.

Daniel came out of the bathroom wearing a pair of jeans and T-shirt. He sat on the edge of the other bed, while he put his boots on and then jumped up, chose a shirt and went back into the bathroom. Summer and Billy looked at each other and smiled. "Well, are you two loafers ready to go, or are you going to watch TV all day?" Daniel said.

"Yes!" Billy said, jumping up and running to the door.

Summer turned off the TV, and walked over to Daniel. She stopped in front of him and took hold of his hands and looked him in the eyes. "Hey, handsome," she said, and kissed his cheek.

"Hey," Daniel said, keeping hold of her right hand, as they headed toward the door.

*****

"We should go have a look around town," Daniel said, as he took a bite of his omelet.

Summer was about to say something, but just then, the waitress came by with a warm up.

Daniel picked up his cup and took a sip, "Looks like it's going to be a beautiful day," he said.

"Yes, it does," Summer said, wondering what he was up to.

"I'm done," Billy said, putting the last bite of French toast in his mouth.

"Drink some more water, and sit still while we finish our coffee," Summer told him, and gave him one of those 'I mean business looks.' There was a moment of silence.

"What do you want to go look at?" Billy asked.

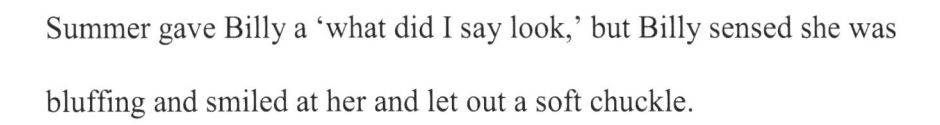

Summer gave Billy a 'what did I say look,' but Billy sensed she was bluffing and smiled at her and let out a soft chuckle.

"Oh, I don't know, I just thought we could look around," Daniel said.

Summer looked over her cup at him. She had the feeling he was planning something. Daniel smiled as he took a sip from his cup.

"That was very good, thank you for breakfast," she said, as she discreetly nudged Billy's leg with her left hand.

"Thank you for breakfast, it was very good," Billy parroted.

"You're welcome… are you ready?" Daniel asked, Summer.

"Yes, if you're ready."

"I'M READY!" Billy said, a little loud.

Summer looked at him and Daniel let out a chuckle.

"Well let's go," Daniel said, as he stood up.

"I saw some pretty cool stuff at the Ranch and Home store, when I was in there, wanna go check it out?" Daniel asked, trying to make it sound like he just thought of it, and then pulled out of the parking lot, without waiting for an answer.

As they made their way through the store, they walked past a display of framed prints. One in particular caught Daniels attention. It was a picture of a herd of Buffalo being hazed off a cliff by a group of Indians. He stood there a minute, looking at it and then gave Summer a questioning look.

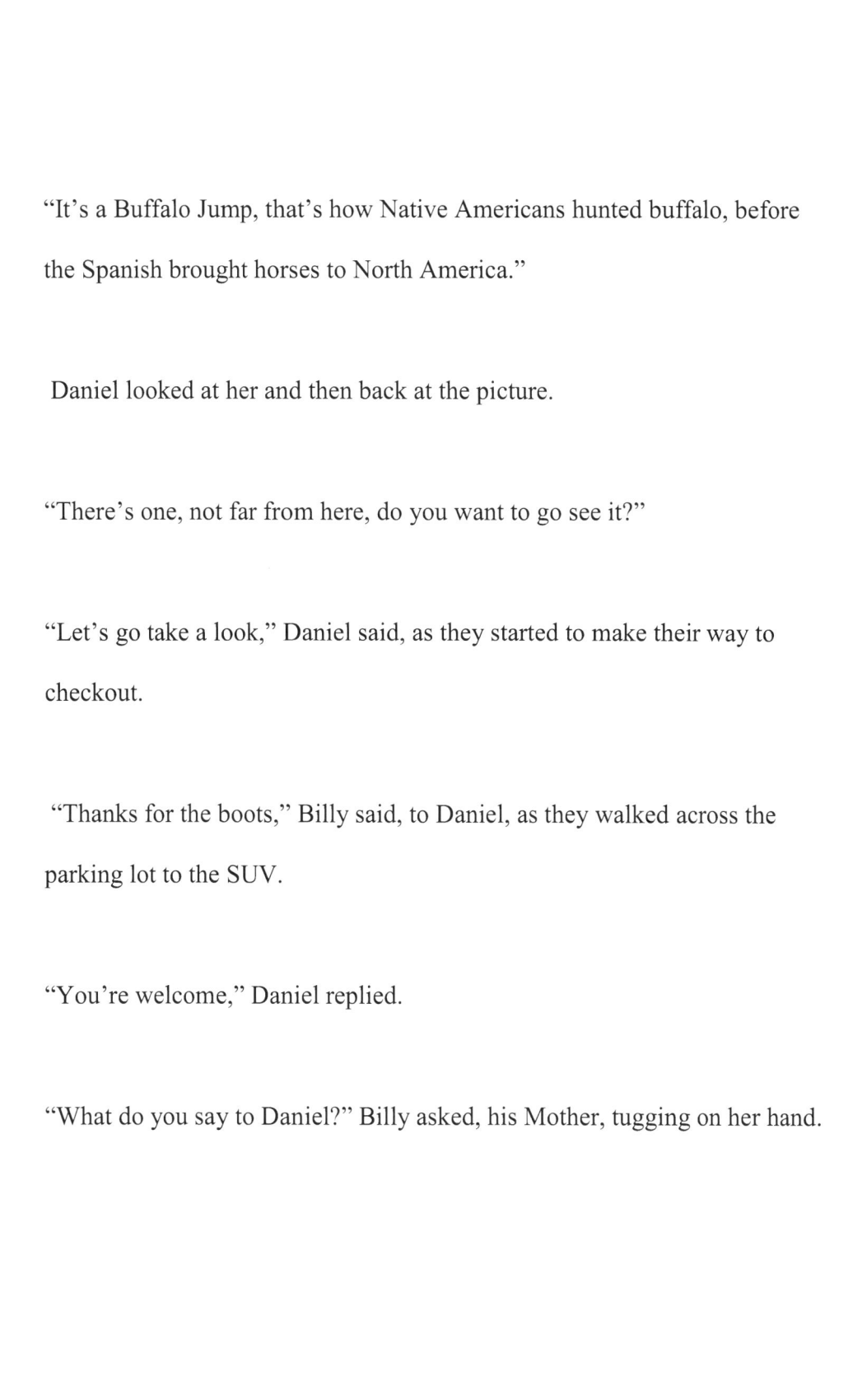

"It's a Buffalo Jump, that's how Native Americans hunted buffalo, before the Spanish brought horses to North America."

Daniel looked at her and then back at the picture.

"There's one, not far from here, do you want to go see it?"

"Let's go take a look," Daniel said, as they started to make their way to checkout.

"Thanks for the boots," Billy said, to Daniel, as they walked across the parking lot to the SUV.

"You're welcome," Daniel replied.

"What do you say to Daniel?" Billy asked, his Mother, tugging on her hand.

Summer looked over at Daniel who saw what was going on and smiled, at her.

"Thank you for the boots," she said, trying to hold back a smile. "They're very pretty," she added.

Daniel looked down at Billy and mouthed the word 'PRETTY.' Billy made exaggerated big eyes at him, and then wrinkled up his face. When they reached the SUV, Daniel helped Billy in. Summer opened her door, set her new boots on the floor and then put her arms around Daniels waist and kissed him. Daniel looked into Summer's eyes, she was so pretty and so confident, he thought as he kissed her.

"Thank you for inviting us up here, I'm glad we came," Summer said.

"I'm glad you did too."

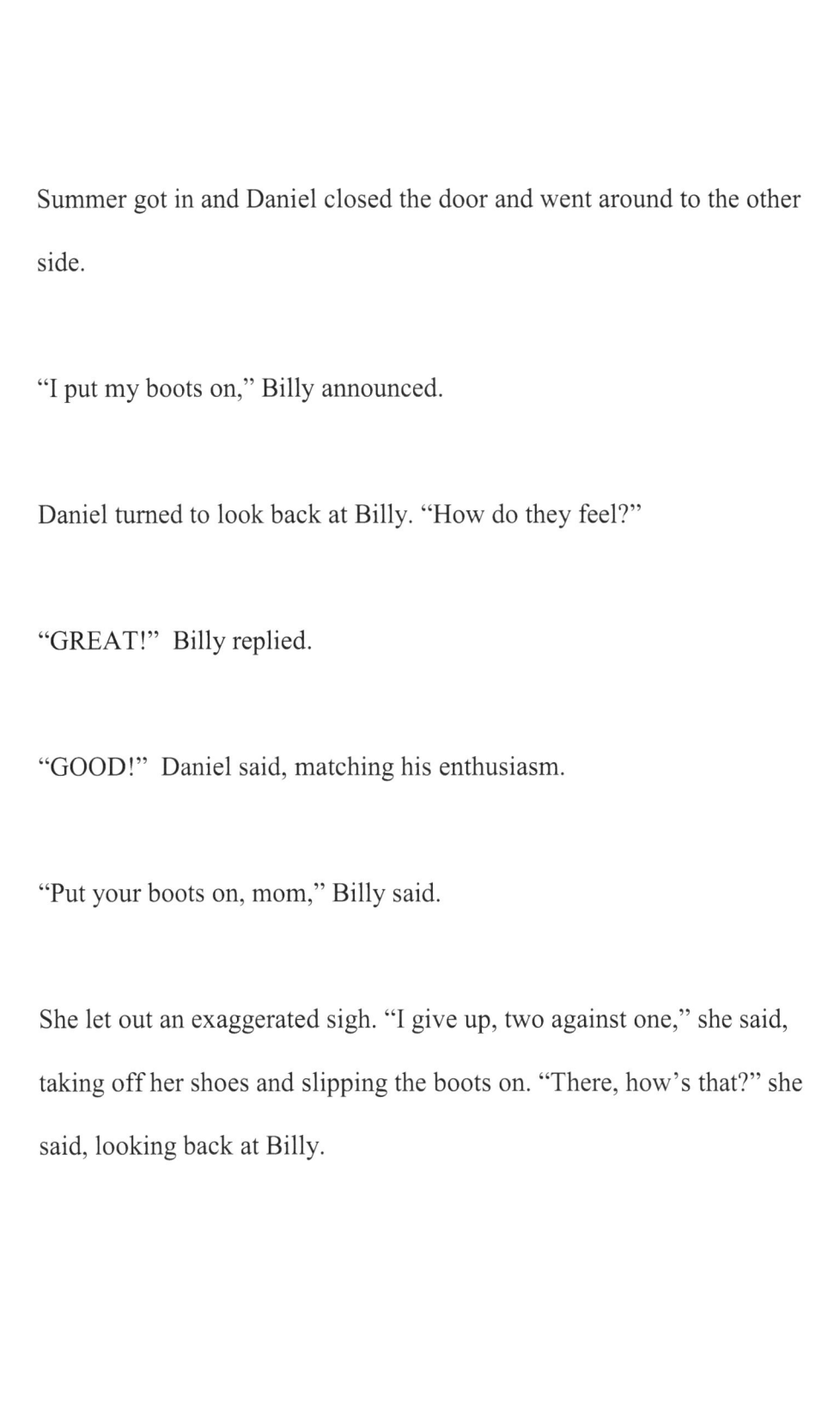

Summer got in and Daniel closed the door and went around to the other side.

"I put my boots on," Billy announced.

Daniel turned to look back at Billy. "How do they feel?"

"GREAT!" Billy replied.

"GOOD!" Daniel said, matching his enthusiasm.

"Put your boots on, mom," Billy said.

She let out an exaggerated sigh. "I give up, two against one," she said, taking off her shoes and slipping the boots on. "There, how's that?" she said, looking back at Billy.

Billy lifted his left foot and said, "cool mom."

CHAPTER 10

"First People's Buffalo Jump State Park, five miles ahead," Summer said, as they passed a sign.

Several minutes later Daniel slowed down and turned right. They followed the gravel road as it led them across what looked like a seemingly endless prairie, but then it dropped down unexpectedly into a valley and ran parallel to the ridge for several miles as it skirted the valley floor.

"During the last ice age, a glacier moved through here and cut through the prairie to form this valley," Summer said, as a large brown and gold sign came into view. "We're here," Summer said, pointing toward the cliff.

Daniel pulled into the parking area and went around and stood next to Summer, she was looking up at the cliff in front of them, while she waited for Billy, who had walked over to the tall grass to pee.

"There it is," Summer said, pointing to the ridge. A gravel trail led up to a pavilion, which offered an excellent view.

"Should we walk up and check it out?" Daniel asked, when Billy joined them.

They followed the trail to the Pavilion, a stone structure with large wooden beams supporting the roof, providing shelter from the sun and rain. A long wooden bench anchored in the cement provided a perfect place to look out over the site. Several plaques explained the history of the buffalo jump and how different tribes would use the area at different times throughout the fall to procure meat and hides for the winter. Another depicted how the buffalo were herded to the cliff by people wearing wolf pelts and then lured into jumping off, by boys wearing buffalo hides. The boys then sought refuge under a small outcropping of rocks and watched as hundreds of buffalo fell like rain to the rest of the tribe below.

"That's like what we saw back at the store," Daniel said.

"The buffalo were the focal point of the plains Indians existence. They provided everything: food, clothes, shelter and religion," Summer said.

They stood in silence, looking up at the cliff as the wind blew through the long grass and juniper bushes. It seemed to whisper that this was sacred ground. Billy walked over to the bench and sat down. He swung his legs, looking at his boots. Daniel turned and looked at him.

"What do you think of the Buffalo jump?" he asked Billy.

"Pishkun," Billy said.

Summer turned toward Daniel and said "The Sik'sik'awa' (Blackfeet) name for Buffalo jump"

"How do you know that, Billy?" Daniel asked.

"Mom told me."

Daniel looked at Summer and said, "She's pretty smart isn't she?"

"Yep," Billy said.

Summer went over and sat down next to Billy, put her arm around him and pulled him in close.

"Are you ready to go swimming?" Daniel asked.

"Yeah!" Billy said, as he hopped off the bench.

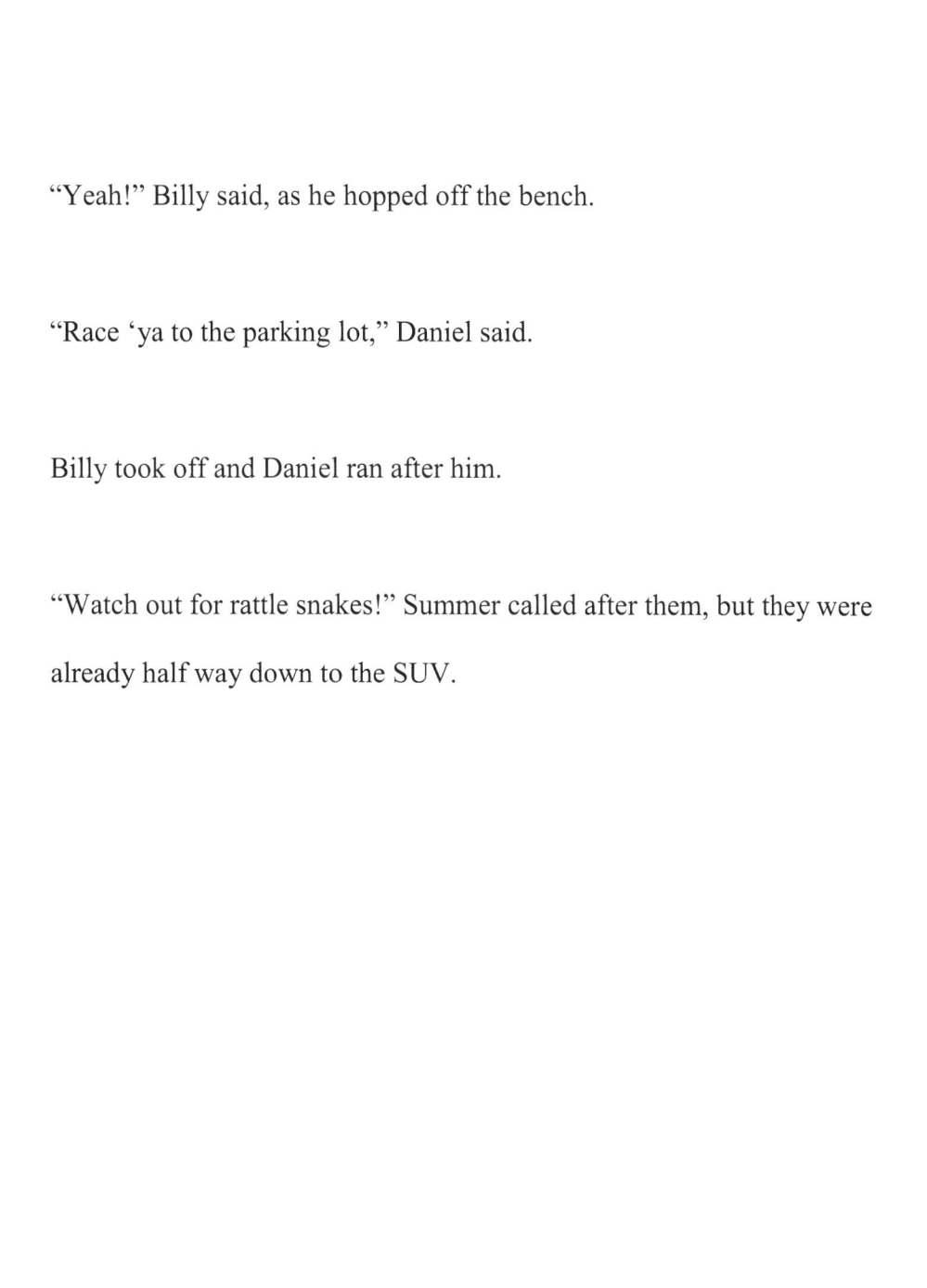

"Race 'ya to the parking lot," Daniel said.

Billy took off and Daniel ran after him.

"Watch out for rattle snakes!" Summer called after them, but they were already half way down to the SUV.

CHAPTER 11

They had the pool area to themselves. It looked clear and inviting. Daniel was just about to sit down at a table next to Summer, when he felt Billy grab his arm.

"Come on, Daniel!" Billy said.

Daniel looked at Summer. She looked amazing in that white bikini. He could have sat there all day, holding hands and talking, taking in her charms.

"Come on, Daniel, let's go in the pool!" Billy said.

Summer looked at Daniel. She seemed to know what he was thinking and made a little face, as if to say, "now what are you gonna do?"

"Let's go!" he said, giving her one of those, 'I got this,' looks and walked with Billy to the edge of the pool and dove in. He came up and turned to look at Billy. Billy tossed him the ball and then jumped in.

"Are you a good swimmer?" Daniel asked, as they tossed the ball back and forth.

"Pretty good," Billy said.

"Can you do a side stroke?"

"A what?"

"Like this," Daniel said, as he swam passed Billy. You pull the water in with your right hand, and push it away with your left. Pull with your right hand and grab and push with your left, extend your right arm and glide. Daniel repeated this fraise as he swam to the far side of the pool and back.

"Now you try it, pull with your right hand and grab with the left, extend your right arm, that's right. Good! Good!" Daniel said, as he swam alongside Billy. "That's good. Can you float on your back?"

Billy laid back and flapped his arms to keep his face above water.

"Just relax and breathe normally. Good, now reach over your head with your right arm and pull it under and around to your side, now you're left arm. That's right, good. Right, left, right, left. That's called a back stroke."

They did the back stroke together across the pool, and stopped in front of Summer.

"Good job, Billy!" Summer said as she came to the edge of the pool, holding the mask and diving rings. "Do you want to play with these?"

"Yeah! Thanks."

"We'll watch you swim for a while, okay? We'll be right there at the table, okay?" Summer said, as Daniel got out of the pool. She handed him a towel and then took his hand, as they walked back to the table and sat down facing the pool. Summer had ordered some ice tea and the young man from the lounge was just bringing it over to the table.

"Here ya go. I'll be back to check on you in a little bit," he said, setting the glasses down.

"You're really great with Billy," Summer said, as she sipped her ice tea through a straw.

"I think he's a great kid," Daniel said, his eyes never leaving Billy.

"He really likes you."

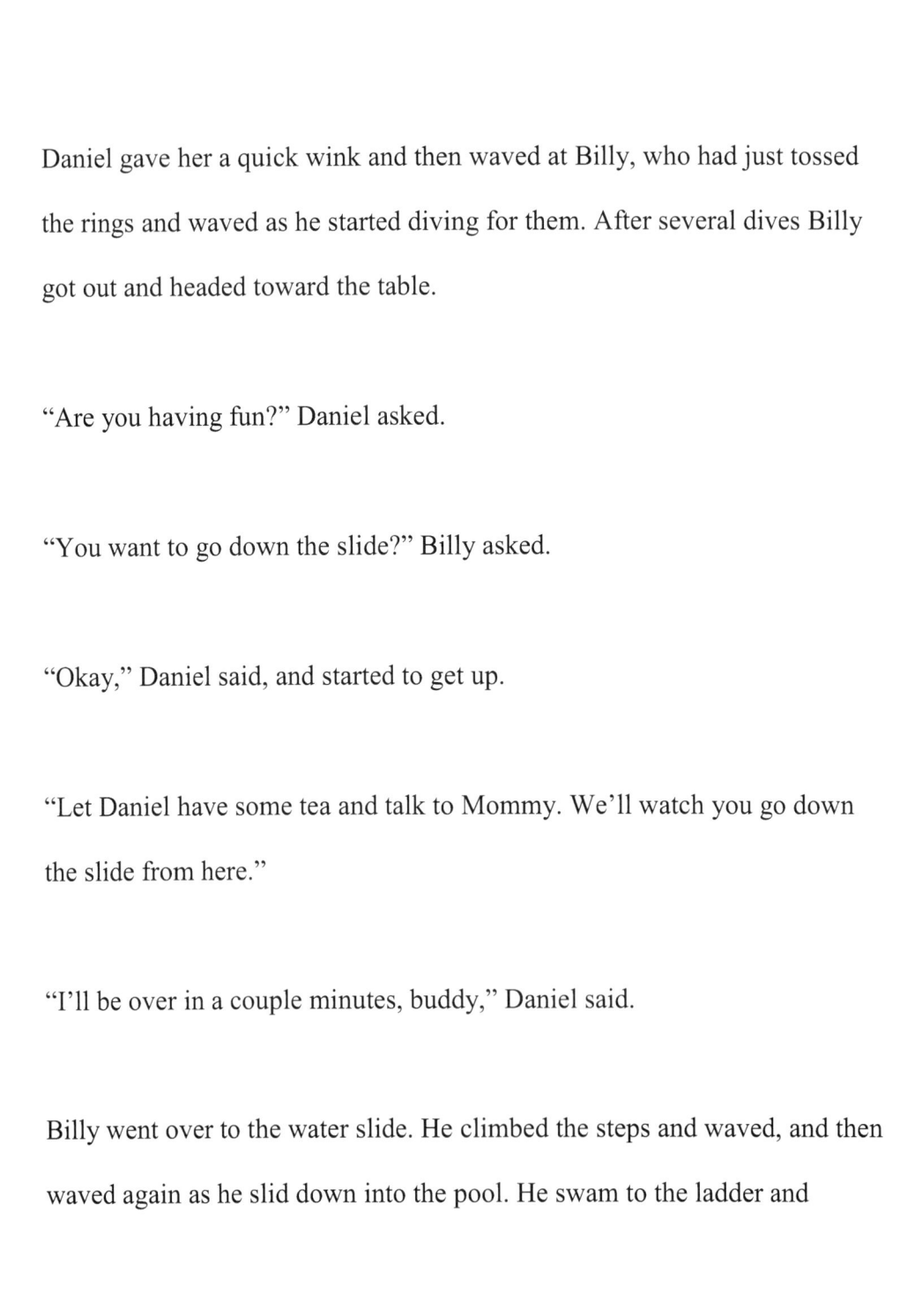

Daniel gave her a quick wink and then waved at Billy, who had just tossed the rings and waved as he started diving for them. After several dives Billy got out and headed toward the table.

"Are you having fun?" Daniel asked.

"You want to go down the slide?" Billy asked.

"Okay," Daniel said, and started to get up.

"Let Daniel have some tea and talk to Mommy. We'll watch you go down the slide from here."

"I'll be over in a couple minutes, buddy," Daniel said.

Billy went over to the water slide. He climbed the steps and waved, and then waved again as he slid down into the pool. He swam to the ladder and climbed out. He waved to them, again, as he went back and climbed the ladder to slide down again.

"I think we both should go over and try out the slide," Daniel said.

"Oh, you do? I think you just want to see what happens when this suit gets wet," she said, as she let her eyes wonder down Daniels chest. "Let's go," she said in a mischievous tone, as she stood up.

They walked over to the ladder and met Billy as he got out of the pool. Then they all walked over to the slide and followed Billy down. After they swam around a little bit, Billy got out and grabbed the ball, then climbed the steps and threw it as he came down the slide. When he popped up Daniel tossed the ball at him and hit him in the head.

"Hey!" Billy said, as he went for the ball. He threw it at Daniel, but it fell short. Daniel grabbed it and turned toward Summer.

"Leave me out of it," she said, turning her back, but that was all Daniel needed and he fired the ball at her, bouncing it off her shoulder.

"It's on now!" she said, as she grabbed the ball and hurled it at Daniel, hitting him in the head. It turned into a game of dodge ball, their laughter echoed off the ceiling and walls.

"That's enough for me," Summer said, after a while. "We'll watch you for a bit, okay?"

"Okay," Billy said.

They went back to the table and watched him practice the different strokes. Daniel couldn't help but steal a few glances at Summer. The wet suit clung to her and revealed a bit more of her charms. Summer kept her attention on Billy, but was aware of Daniels growing interest. He saw her noticing and shifted in his chair. She gave him a wink and then returned her full attention to Billy, who was tired of swimming alone and was heading back over to the table.

"Would you like something to drink?" Summer asked.

"Can I have a Coke?"

"Yes," Summer said.

"Go over to the counter and ask that man," Daniel said.

"Okay," Billy said, and walked over to the concession counter.

Daniel watched Billy as he went over and gave a little wave to the young man, when he looked in their direction.

****

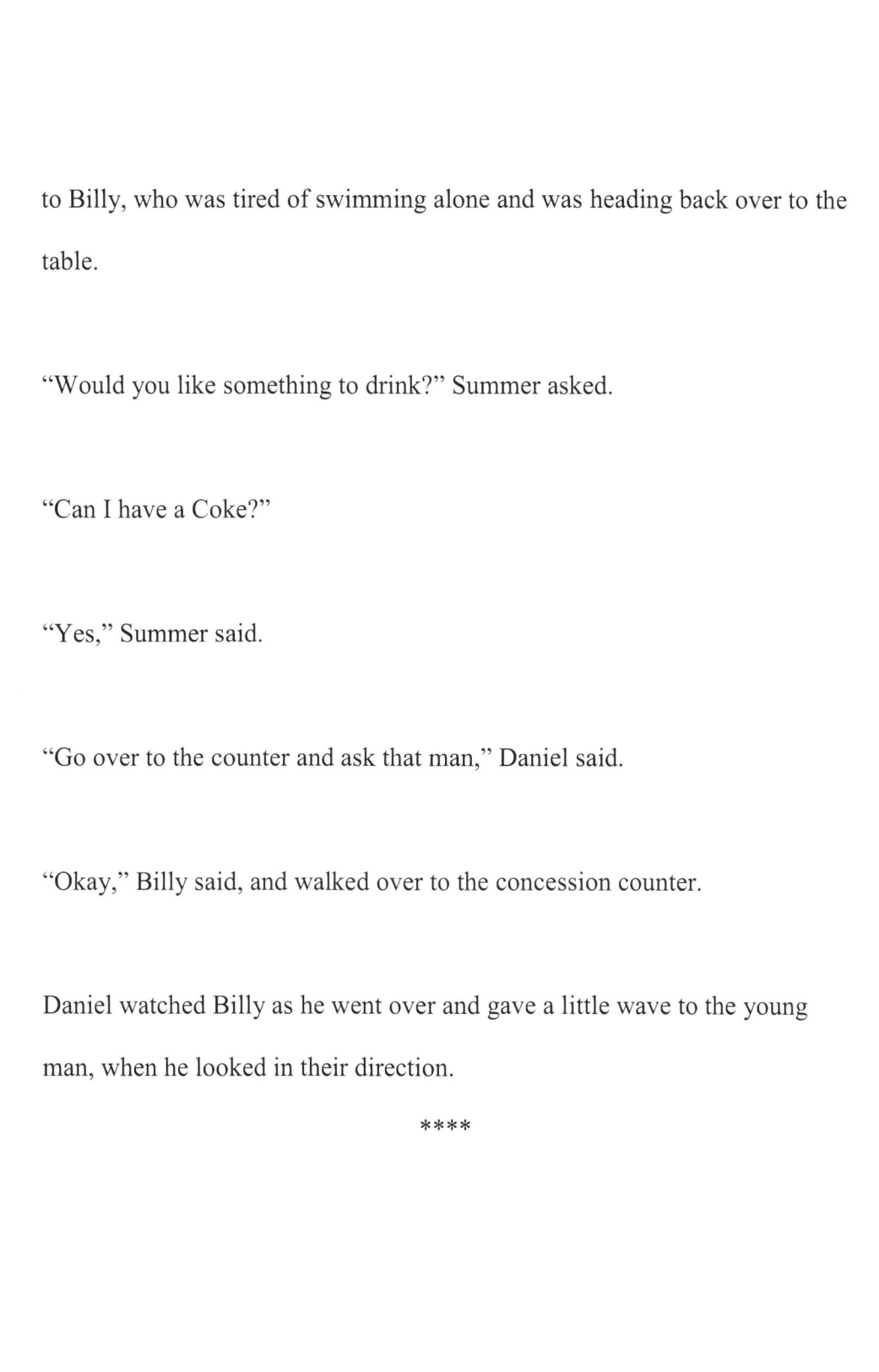

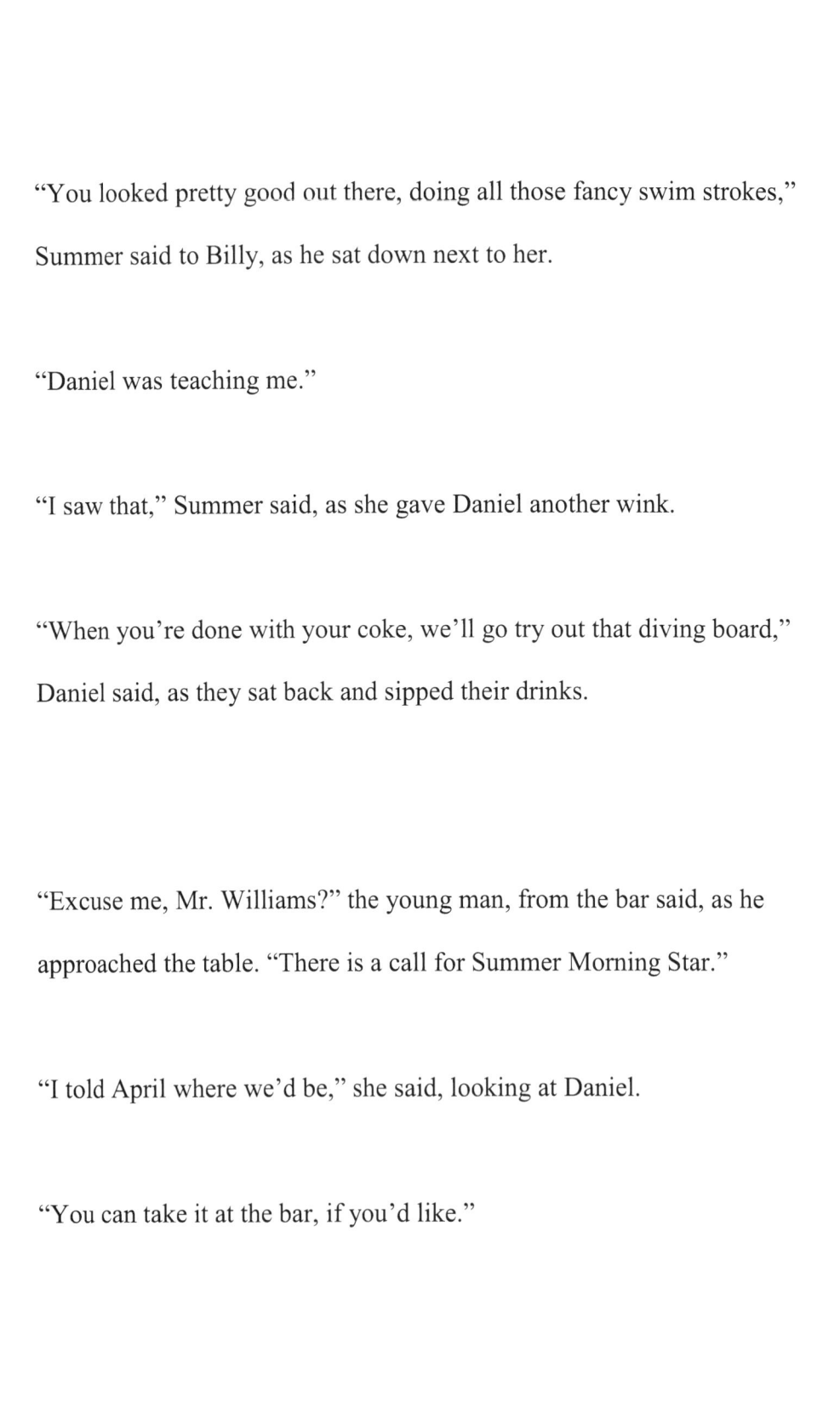

"You looked pretty good out there, doing all those fancy swim strokes," Summer said to Billy, as he sat down next to her.

"Daniel was teaching me."

"I saw that," Summer said, as she gave Daniel another wink.

"When you're done with your coke, we'll go try out that diving board," Daniel said, as they sat back and sipped their drinks.

"Excuse me, Mr. Williams?" the young man, from the bar said, as he approached the table. "There is a call for Summer Morning Star."

"I told April where we'd be," she said, looking at Daniel.

"You can take it at the bar, if you'd like."

"Thank you," Daniel said.

Summer followed the man back to the bar, while Daniel stayed at the table with Billy. Several minutes later Summer came back to the table. She was crying and used her towel to blot away the tears as she sat down.

"Grandma had a heart attack… April found her in her chair this morning, when she went out to visit her. The Coroner said she had been there overnight."

Daniel went over to her and put his arms around her as he bent over her.

"I'm so sorry," he said.

"Grandma thought you would make quite a catch."

Daniel looked across the table at Billy who was just looking at them.

"Grandma died," he said, as he came around the table with big tears rolling down his cheeks and put his head on Summer's chest.

"I should go back home," Summer said.

"Of course, we can pack and be on the road whenever you like."

"Thank you… and we were having such a nice time… Poor Grandma!" she said, and leaned her head against his right arm and put her hand on his.

CHAPTER 12

Daniel pulled in behind Summer, as she parked in her driveway and walked over to her, as she got out. "Go on in. I'll get your things," he said. "Billy, you wanna give me a hand?"

When Daniel and Billy came in, Summer was talking to April on the phone. "We just got home, a few minutes ago. How are you doing? We'll be over in the morning, then. Okay. Good night," she said, and hung up the phone.

"I'm gonna go, get a couple of my things," Daniel said, setting her bags down.
When he came in, he found Summer leaning against the counter in the kitchen, just looking at the floor. The tea kettle was whistling, but Summer seemed to be a million miles away. He went over to her. She buried her face

in his chest. He could feel her shake as she wept. He held her. After a couple of minutes, they sat down at the table.

"What a terrible ending to a perfect weekend," Summer said, as her eyes filled with tears. "It's just me, April and the boys… that's all that's left."

Daniel got up, filled two cups with hot water and brought them to the table. Summer dunked her tea bag up and down a few times and then got up, went to the counter, took out a package of instant hot chocolate and a mug.

"I'll be right back," she said, setting the spoon on the counter after stirring.

Daniel sat there a few minutes after drinking his tea, then got up and refilled his cup. Billy must be taking it hard, he thought. It made him think about his own losses.

The old woman would be missed, she was a person of strong character and was respected in her community, now that she had passed to 'The Other World' as she called it, she would live on in the memories of her grandchildren and great grandchildren. Daniel thought about the trip out to her house and her premonitions of being with her husband once again, before too long. He recalled his dream, the night before their visit and how when their eyes met, there had been some recognition between them. It was as if they had known each other for a long time.

Summer returned to the kitchen and attempted a smile as she sat down. She picked up her cup and took a sip. The tea had cooled and she made a little face. She got up and walked over to the counter, poured the tea into a glass and put it in the refrigerator, then, she poured hot water into her cup and returned to the table. She dunked the tea bag a few times and watched, as the water turn color.

"How's Billy doing?" Daniel asked, as he put his hand on hers.

"He'll be fine…. He knows Grandma is watching over him…. I don't want to be alone tonight."

"I'm here for you."

"No, I mean, I want to be with you tonight. I talked to Billy and explained to him that I have special feelings for you and that you would be here when he got up tomorrow morning."

"What did he say?"

"He said he was glad and that he likes you."

Daniel looked into Summer's eyes, she was truly amazing. He had never met anyone like her.

"Let's take our tea into the living room?" she said.

Daniel put his left arm around her as they got settled on the couch, and she snuggled in next to him. They drank their tea in silence. When Summer was finished, she put her cup on the coffee table, stood up and held out her hand. Daniel put his cup next to hers and she led him to her room.

CHAPTER 13

It had been two weeks since Mary had passed away. They had spent the last couple of days out at the old place, with April and Tommy, getting everything ready for the gathering to celebrate Mary's life and ask Naapi (Old Man) to guide her safely to the Sand Hills.

Daniel was sitting on the porch, in the chair she had spent her final minutes and thought of their chance meeting at the grocery store and the role it had played in everything. Would Summer have been as curious about him, if he hadn't been wearing the medallion? If she hadn't been, he might have never seen Mary again and might have never met Uncle Joe. He was watching the shadows, the clouds made, move across the rolling hills, when Summer came out of the house and sat lightly on the arm of the chair.

"Grandma loved it here," she said.

"It's easy to see why. It's so peaceful," Daniel said, putting his hand on her knee.

She was about to say something, but the sound of a vehicle coming up the gravel road, interrupted her. After a few minutes they saw, an older pickup truck slowly approaching. "That's Chief's truck," Summer said, as it pulled in the yard and parked by the shed.

They watched as Chief came around and opened the tail gate for the people riding in the back. The passenger door opened and Uncle Joe stepped out, he tucked something under his arm and started toward the house, holding his hand up when he saw Daniel on the porch. Daniel got up and made his way to the guests.

"Oki' nik'so'ko'ik'si'," (hello, my relatives) Uncle Joe said.

"Welcome," Daniel said, to the small group as they stood silently looking at him. Summer made her way to Daniel's side.

"It is good to see you again," Uncle Joe said, to both of them.

"Oki," (hello) Chief said.

"Oki," (hello) Summer said, returning the greeting.

"I am sorry to hear of your Grandmother's passing. We are here to remember the good times we shared and see her off, on her new journey," one of the women said.

"I baked some apple pies. Mary and Ray would always see that I never needed meat and I would make them pies, from apples, I picked from my trees. Mary would always say 'now I'll have to bring you more meat,' and I'd always say 'then, I'll have to bake more pies.' Ray would laugh and say,

'I guess I'll have to shoot more deer and eat more pie, all is good.' We thought it was funny, because we all could remember harder times when you couldn't always get sugar and flour," the woman next to her said.

"Come inside," Summer said, and led the way.

Daniel offered Uncle Joe the rocker. He sat there looking out at the rolling hills for several minutes, as if he was seeing it through Daniels eyes. Then he looked at Daniel.

"I remember one fall," he began, his eyes shifting to the shed. "Ray and I had gone hunting. We were hanging up the deer we had killed that day. Mary came out. She touched each one of them and thanked them for their gift to us," Uncle Joe said. He took a slightly larger breath and let it out. "Remember, 'A'kai' 'Aa'zist'awa', (Many Rabbits) life can be short or long. It is what happens while we are here that determines what will be in the next life. Mary was prepared for this next journey. She is with Ray.

They are together with 'The Old Ones', and with your parents and my parents, my brother and his wife. They all sit around the fire and wait for us. She will reassure them that you walk the Red Road. All is good," Uncle Joe said. "Katoyis (Blood Clot Boy,)" he said, pointing at the medallion around Daniels neck. "One day I will have to tell you and the boys about the boy who went to slay monsters and wicked people."

Then Uncle Joe got up and took him to join the others standing at the other end of the porch. Chief was leaning against the house as he talked with the two other men. They fell silent as Uncle Joe and Daniel approached.

"This is my great nephew, Daniel," Uncle Joe, said proudly.

Daniel noticed their eyes settle on the medallion around his neck. They didn't say anything, but nodded their heads slightly in acknowledgement. Chief gave Uncle Joe a strange look, but Uncle Joe ignored him and said, "We should finish the preparations for the ceremony."

"We'll get some wood," Chief replied and motioned for the two men to follow him.

Uncle Joe and Daniel made their way behind the house, and stood next to the Spirit Warrior.

"Ray was quite an artist. I remember when he finished the garden. We stayed out here all night and danced around the fire until the sun came up. We sang all the old songs. We were much younger," he said, as he looked around. "Aka'ista'ao' (This is a place of many ghosts)" he said, and then knelt down and untied the strip of leather around the bundle he carried. He laid the hide out in front of him and placed several items on it: A red clay pipe with a long wooden stem, an old leather pouch with long fringes and intricate bead work and a rattle made with part of a deer's leg and a turtle shell. He stood up and walked around the Spirit Warrior, shaking the rattle and singing an old song. Chief and the other two men came with their arms loaded with wood. They set the wood down and watched Uncle Joe until he had finished and then went back for more wood. Uncle Joe returned to where he had spread out the bundle, and then sat down with his legs crossed. He motioned for Daniel to sit next to him on his left. Uncle Joe looked at Daniel and smiled. "I am glad you have returned to us, 'A'kai' 'Aazistawa' (Many Rabbits). It is good that you see the ways of your people."

Chief and the other two men returned with more wood and put it on the pile. Daniel watched as Chief thoughtfully arranged some of it, in the ring, in front of the Spirit Warrior. He put a small ball of grass inside the arrangement and lit it with a match. He tended to it like it was a living thing, until there was a blazing fire. Then he came and sat on the other side of Uncle Joe. A few minutes later, the other two men returned with another arm load of wood. They tossed it on the pile and then joined the others around the deer hide.

"It is good we are together today," Uncle Joe said, as he reached for the pipe. He held it up and said "Oki' napi'awa,' Aa'katt'si'noot'sii'yo'p (hello friends, we see each other again.) We ask Naa'pi' (Old Man) to help us make our way along the Red Road. We ask Naa'pi' (Old Man) to light the shadow world so Mary can find her way to her new lodge, in the Sand Hills, where the others wait.

He rested the pipe on his lap and put some dried leafy material he had taken from another small pouch in the bowl. He lite the pipe and drew a puff from it. He handed the pipe to Chief. Chief drew in a puff and handed it back to Uncle Joe. Uncle Joe passed it to Daniel.

"Na'wak'osis, (herb given to the Siksikawa from the medicine Beaver)" he said, as he made two fists and held them out in front of him.

Daniel reluctantly took the pipe and drew in a puff. The smoke expanded in his lungs and it was all he could do to keep from coughing. He handed the pipe back to Uncle Joe, and got a nod of approval. Uncle Joe refilled it and lit it again, he handed it to the man sitting next to Chief, who smoked from it and handed it back to Uncle Joe. Uncle Joe then handed it to the other man. He smoked from it and handed it back. They smoked in this way three times. As Daniel took in the smoke for the third time, his head felt a little strange and his eyes seemed to be drawn to the fire. When he looked up at Uncle Joe, he couldn't believe what he was seeing. Uncle Joe's head had turned into that of a great grizzly bear. When he looked at Chief, he saw, he too had undergone a transformation. His head was now that of a bull buffalo. He quickly looked at the other two men, whose heads were now those of Aapi'si'(coyote). They all seemed to be looking at him, too. Uncle Joe set the pipe down, picked up the rattle and shook it at each man, just as the sun set. Off in the distance, a coyote howled and another one answered. Uncle Joe began to speak in the words of the Siksikawa (Blackfeet.)"

As Daniel listened, he realized he understood what was being said. Then the words grew faint and his eyes returned to the fire. When he heard singing, he looked up. The women were coming down the trail, with Summer and April leading the procession. They seemed to float along the path as they sang an old song. He couldn't take his eyes off Summer, she sang with such conviction and expression, her hands moving fluidly, telling the nonverbal version of the tale. They formed a circle around the fire and holding hands, they sang another song, as they danced around it. Daniel wished he understood the words. When it was over, Summer silently led the women back to the house.

Uncle Joe walked over to the fire and let something slip from his hand, as he passed it over the flames, causing them to flare up with a poof. He then came back to the group of men, gathered his things, rolling them up into the deer skin and then walked back over to the fire in front of the Spirit Warrior. He stood next to the figure, looking out in the same direction it was pointing for a moment, and then followed the path back to the house. After several minutes, Chief rose and subtly motioned for Daniel to do the same, and they walked back to the house. The other two men stayed behind and stirred the coals of the fire. When Daniel and Chief reached the house, the women were standing in the kitchen, eating some of the food they had brought and talking.

Summer smiled at Daniel, as he and Chief came through the door. "Would you like some coffee?" she asked.

"Yes, please," Daniel said.

"Thank you for coming. Please have something to eat," she said to Chief, handing him a cup.

"It was a good ceremony. Mary and Ray are together again. Their spirits can rest," he said. Then he went out on the front porch and waited for the other men.

Summer turned to Daniel and said, "Uncle Joe is in the front room. He's waiting for you."

Daniel went into the other room and sat next to Uncle Joe.

"Good coffee," Uncle Joe said after a few minutes.

"Yes," Daniel responded, not quite knowing what to say. He sensed Uncle Joe had much more on his mind than the coffee and wanted to hear what it was.

"A long time ago, when The First People came into the world, they were cold and hungry. Da' animals took pity on them. They looked into 'The People's hearts. In the hearts of the Plains People, the buffalo saw great strength. In the hearts of the Mountain People, the great bears saw they feared nothing. The animals said, as long as The People honored them, they would never be hungry or come to harm."

"I saw you turn into a bear!" Daniel said.

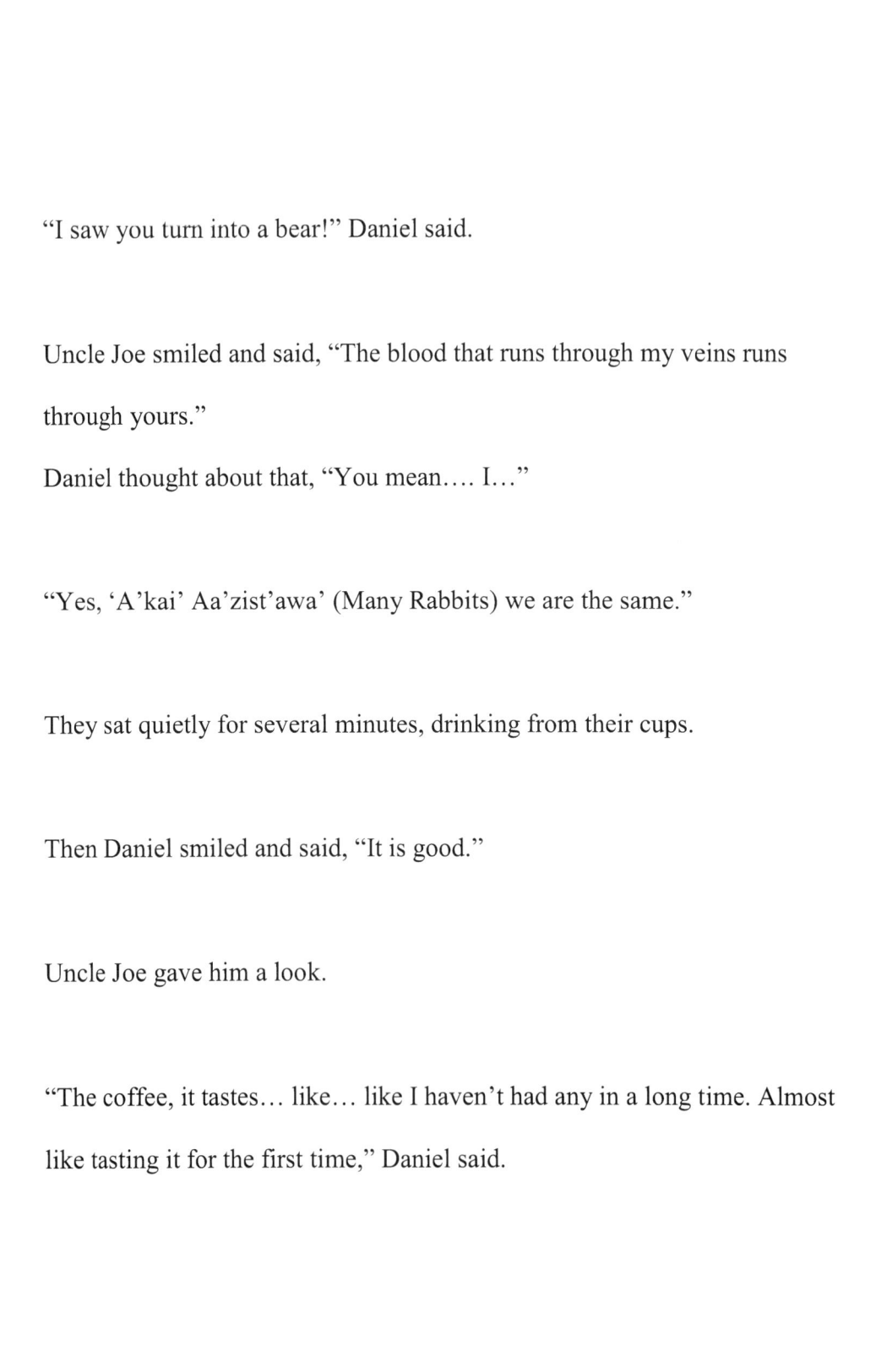

Uncle Joe smiled and said, "The blood that runs through my veins runs through yours."

Daniel thought about that, "You mean…. I…"

"Yes, 'A'kai' Aa'zist'awa' (Many Rabbits) we are the same."

They sat quietly for several minutes, drinking from their cups.

Then Daniel smiled and said, "It is good."

Uncle Joe gave him a look.

"The coffee, it tastes… like… like I haven't had any in a long time. Almost like tasting it for the first time," Daniel said.

Uncle Joe understood and nodded his head.

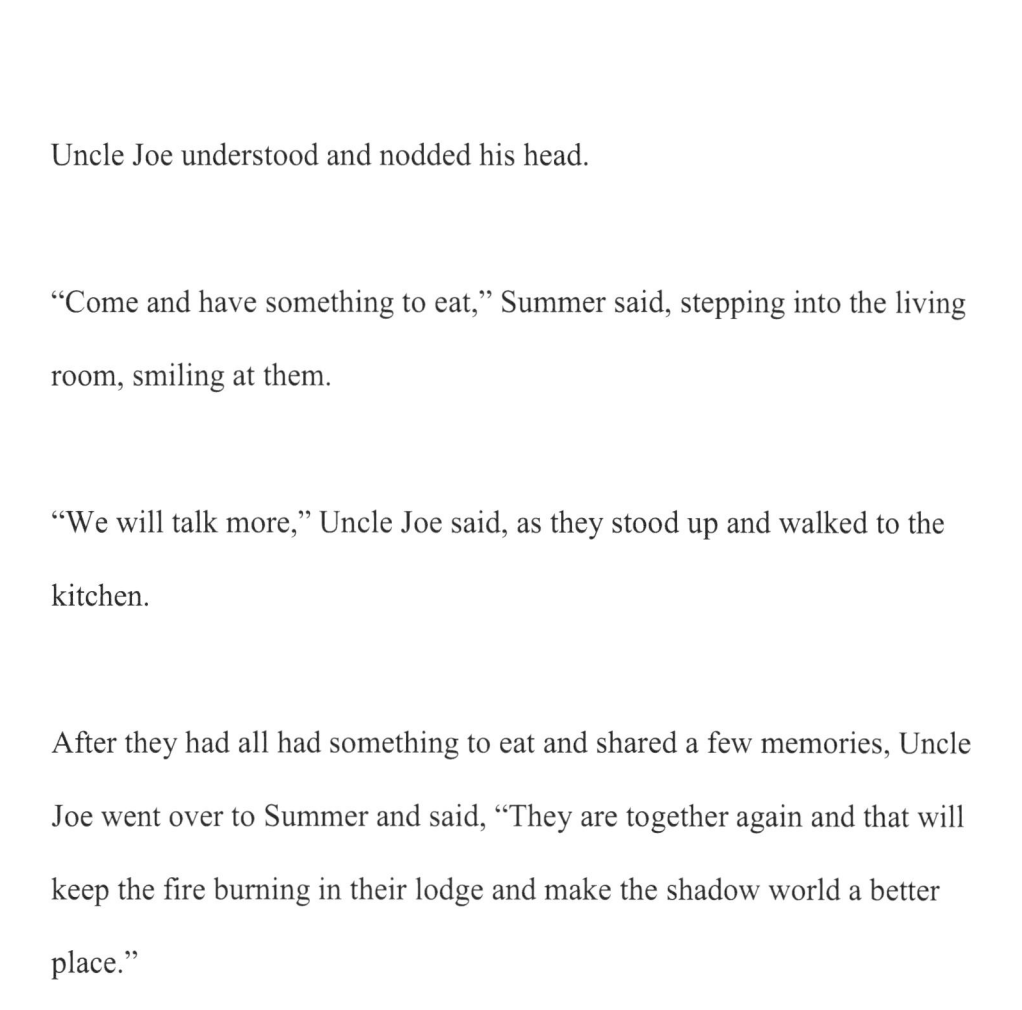

"Come and have something to eat," Summer said, stepping into the living room, smiling at them.

"We will talk more," Uncle Joe said, as they stood up and walked to the kitchen.

After they had all had something to eat and shared a few memories, Uncle Joe went over to Summer and said, "They are together again and that will keep the fire burning in their lodge and make the shadow world a better place."

"I will miss them," Summer said.

"Remember they will always be with you… here and here," he said, pointing to his head and heart. Then he said, "It is late. We must go."

CHAPTER 14

The next morning, Daniel felt the breeze from the open window on his face and arms, as he rolled over on his back, slowly waking up. He had noticed the days started out cool and ended cool, much different from the humid, muggy feeling back home, where hot days lingered into the night and sometimes even greeted you the next morning. Here, each day, felt like a new beginning.

He could hear some birds singing and listened for a few minutes, then the smell of coffee won out, and after going to splash some water on his face and comb his hair, he walked out into the kitchen and found Summer and April sitting at the table.

"Good morning," they both said, simultaneously.

"Coffee?" Summer asked.

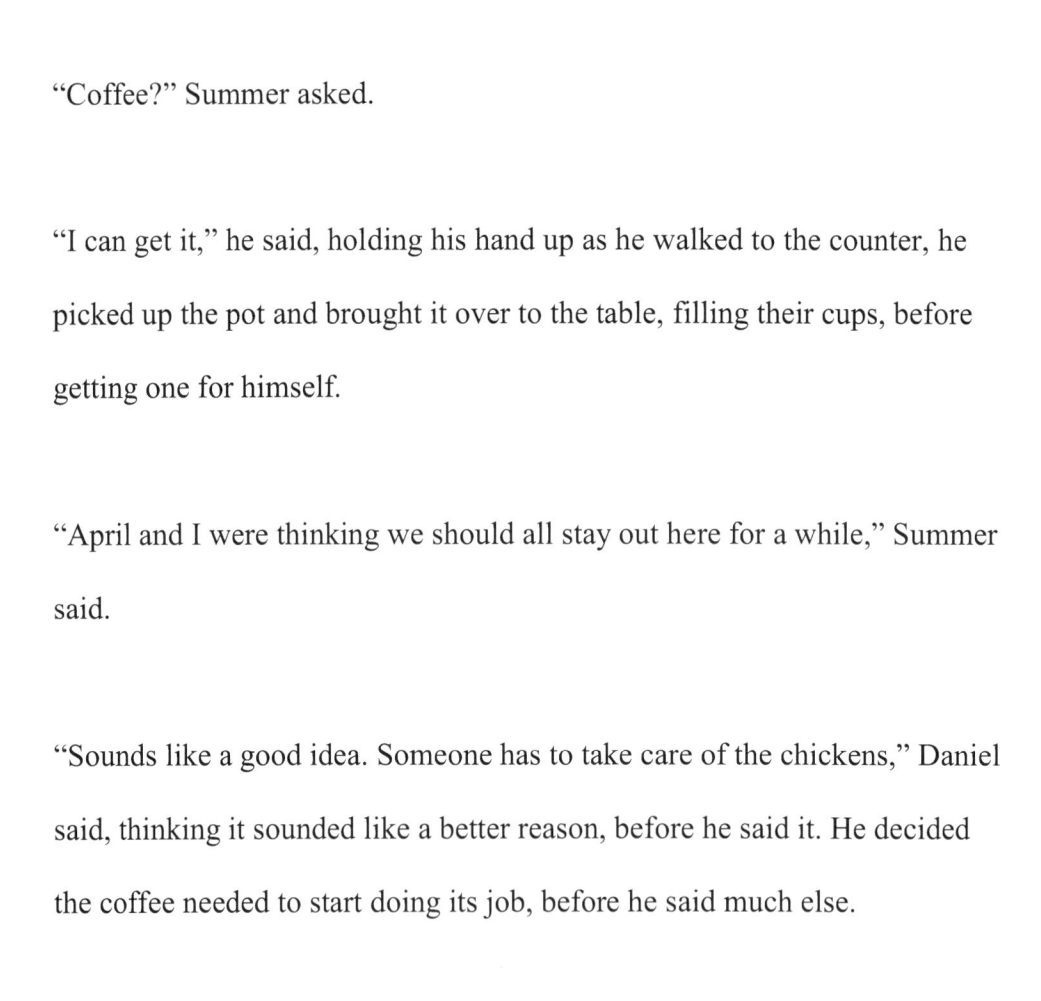

"I can get it," he said, holding his hand up as he walked to the counter, he picked up the pot and brought it over to the table, filling their cups, before getting one for himself.

"April and I were thinking we should all stay out here for a while," Summer said.

"Sounds like a good idea. Someone has to take care of the chickens," Daniel said, thinking it sounded like a better reason, before he said it. He decided the coffee needed to start doing its job, before he said much else.

"I'll make some eggs and toast," April said, getting up.

"Where's Billy and Tommy?" Daniel asked.

"As soon as they finished breakfast they went outside. They think it's great out here," April said.

****

After he had eaten, Daniel went looking for the boys and found them in the shed next to the chicken coop.

"Morning," Daniel said.

"Morning… look at these big mule deer horns," Billy said, as he and Tommy each held out a pair of antlers twice as wide as they were.

"How do you know they're from a mule deer?"

"See how they fork off the main beam, they're from a mule deer," Billy said confidently.

"I suppose your mom taught you that?" Daniel said, as he watched Billy, as he admired the antlers. It made him think about the morning in the motel, when Billy came over to his room and they watched the bears on TV. He certainly knew all about animals. Daniel wondered for a second, if he would have known those kind of things, if… if…. He smiled and realized with having an uncle like, Uncle Joe and from his description of his birth father, he probably would have.

"Yep," Billy said with a big grin on his face.

"There sure is a lot of cool stuff in here, isn't there!" Daniel said, looking around.

Grandma said we should come in here and play," both boys said at the same time.

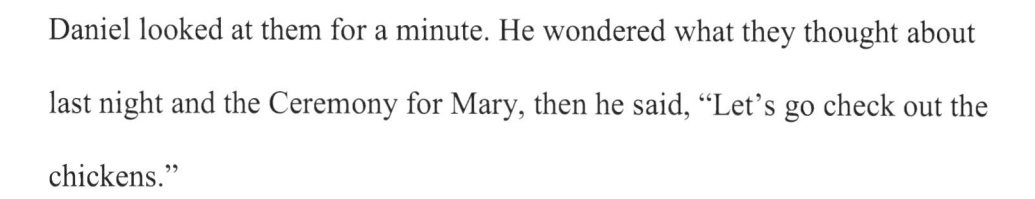

Daniel looked at them for a minute. He wondered what they thought about last night and the Ceremony for Mary, then he said, "Let's go check out the chickens."

"Okay!" they said, putting down the antlers and racing out the door.

Daniel followed them, after taking another quick look around the shed.

The boys were waiting in front of the wire pen, watching several large brown chickens scratching the ground, as he walked up to them.

"Let's go inside and get the eggs," Tommy said.

"You think we should?" Daniel asked.

The boys looked at him kind of funny, then, opened the door. Two mice ran across the floor and down a small hole that led under the building. The boys chased after them, but they were long gone.

"Come on in," they called out to Daniel.

He had never been inside a chicken coop before, it wasn't what he had expected and wondered if he'd ever eat eggs again, as he watched Billy reach in a nesting box and pull out an egg and then hand it to Tommy, who wiped a little chicken poop off it and then pulled the bottom of his tee-shirt out and dropped the egg inside the make-shift basket. Billy checked the other boxes, handing off the eggs as he went.

"Let's take these in the house and come back and try to catch those mice," Tommy said to Billy and headed for the house.

Daniel followed behind them after shutting the door.

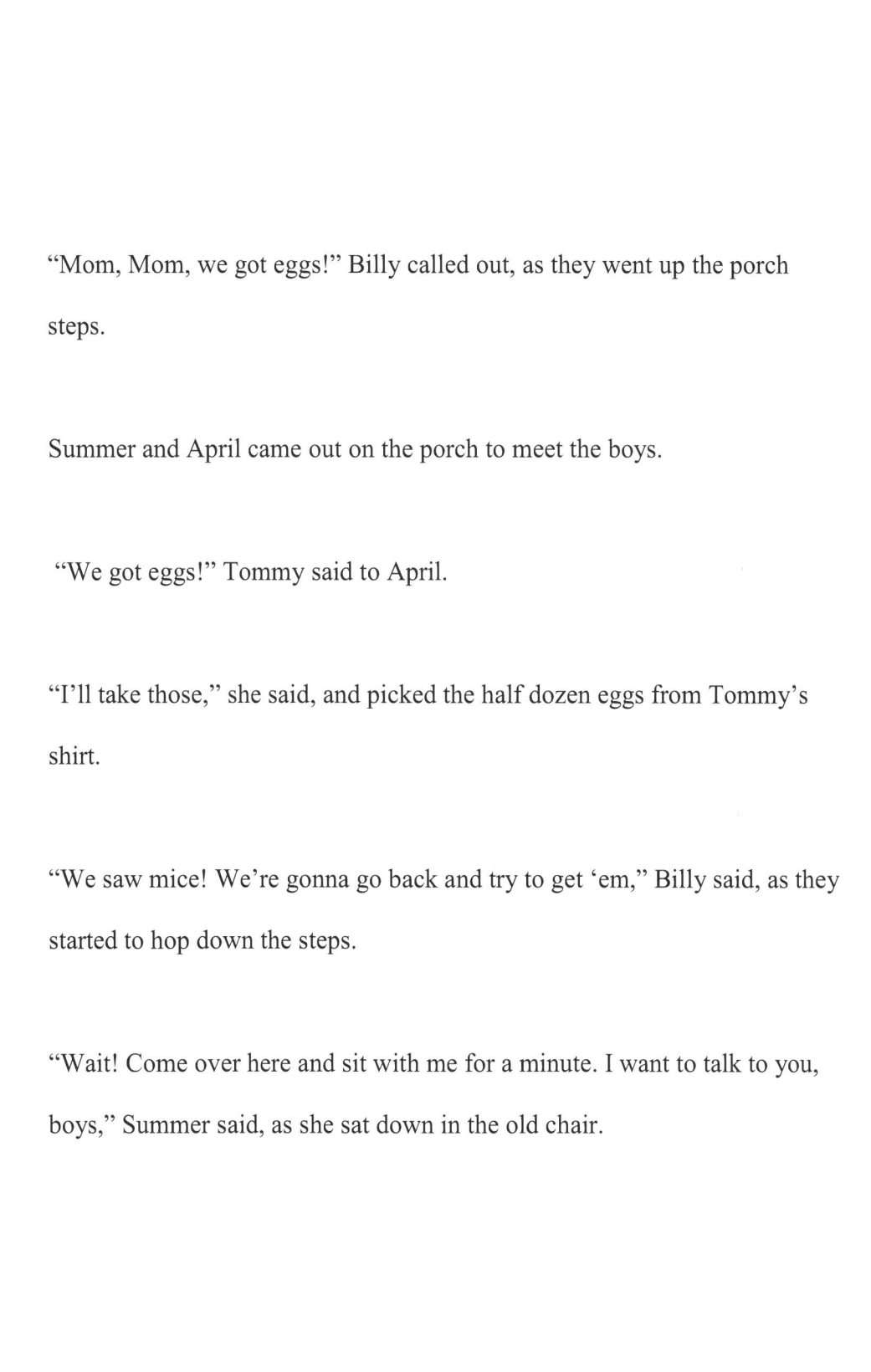

"Mom, Mom, we got eggs!" Billy called out, as they went up the porch steps.

Summer and April came out on the porch to meet the boys.

"We got eggs!" Tommy said to April.

"I'll take those," she said, and picked the half dozen eggs from Tommy's shirt.

"We saw mice! We're gonna go back and try to get 'em," Billy said, as they started to hop down the steps.

"Wait! Come over here and sit with me for a minute. I want to talk to you, boys," Summer said, as she sat down in the old chair.

The boys sat on the wooden porch floor in front of her.

"I know you are both excited to be here and are having fun. But we must respect the animals around us. Even the mice. We all live in this world the same."

The boys looked at each other and then back at her.

"The Blackfeet people do not kill mice," she said.

"Why?" they asked at the same time.

"This is the story I was told by my mother, who was told by her mother, who heard it from her mother," Summer began. "A long, long time ago, 'Naa'pi' (Old Man) grew tired of listening to the animals argue about who was in charge. He told them they needed to choose a chief. He showed them a game that would help them decide who should be chief. It came down to the buffalo and the mice. The mice won, but they said, they were too small to be the chief. They said, Man should be chief and from then on the Blackfeet People said they would never kill mice."

"The cats catch mice. Does that make them bad?" Tommy asked.

"No, that is their way…. That's enough for now, go and play, but remember what I have said."

The boys got up and went down the porch steps. The kittens swarmed around their ankles. They each picked up two and started for the chicken coop. Daniel came up on the porch and smiled at Summer as she watched them.

"I remember coming out here when I was their age. I never wanted to go home. I would spend hours out behind the shed, exploring. Once, I picked a handful of flowers and brought them to Mary. She took them and put them in a glass with some water. Two days later they were wilted. She took them out of the water and then asked me to show her where I had picked them. We walked out behind the shed and I showed her. She laid them down on the spot. She wasn't mad at me and said she understood that I was trying to bring her happiness, but happiness at the expense of another is not a good thing. 'These flowers still had living to do, they would have produced seeds and those seeds would have grown into flowers and made seeds of their own and they would have grown into flowers. We only take what we need from the earth. Think of the flowers as your mothers' hair, so pretty, you wouldn't pull out your mothers' hair. Leave the flowers and go to visit them, in that way, no matter where you are, you can think of them and they will always bring you happiness,'" Summer said, forcing a little smile and fighting the small tears that were forming in her eyes.

"Let's go take a look," Daniel said, and took her by the hand, as they went for a walk.

Daniel put his arm around Summer as they stood looking out at the wild flowers. He tried to think of something to say, but instead thought of Mary's words and let nature's beauty comfort her.

Later that evening, Daniel walked behind the house to the Spirit Garden. He sat in the old metal chair facing the Spirit Warrior. As he looked at the figure, he thought about the ceremony the night before. Then his thoughts turned to the boys and how they said Mary had told them to look in the shed. He was thinking about some of the stuff he had seen inside it; when across the Spirit Garden, a white wolf suddenly appeared. It stood there for a long time looking at him with its big yellow eyes. Then it walked closer and closer. It circled around him and then let out a deep howl.

A sudden gust of wind came from nowhere. The pin that kept the Spirit Warrior figure in place flew out of its hole and the warrior spun around wildly, causing Daniel to turn in that direction. When he looked back to the wolf, Mary was sitting in the chair next to him.

"O'ki, A'kai Aa'zist'awa (hello, Many Rabbits)," she said. She looked pale, almost translucent, but peaceful. "You have seen the nature of your inner self. You must walk the Red Road," she continued.

Another gust of wind spun the spirit warrior, again causing Daniel to look at it, when he looked back at the chair where Mary had been sitting, a magpie now sat and then suddenly flew off.

 The 'Red Road,' what was this Red Road and where did it led? Daniel thought about it for several minutes and then went to find Summer to see what she could tell him. He found her sitting with April in the front room. They were going through some of Mary's things and sorting them into different boxes, so they could be distributed to those who could use them.

"You look like you've seen a ghost," April said.

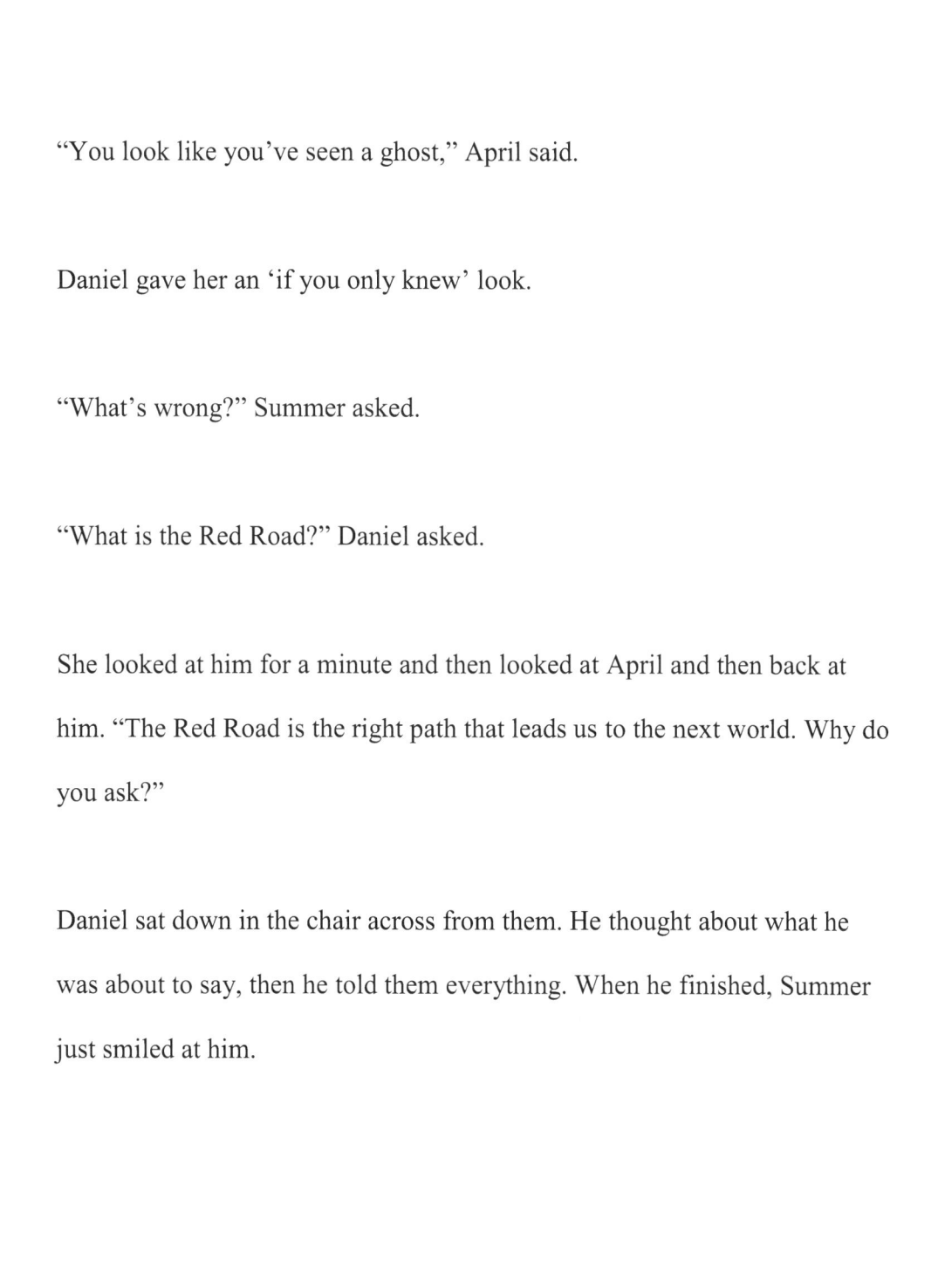

Daniel gave her an 'if you only knew' look.

"What's wrong?" Summer asked.

"What is the Red Road?" Daniel asked.

She looked at him for a minute and then looked at April and then back at him. "The Red Road is the right path that leads us to the next world. Why do you ask?"

Daniel sat down in the chair across from them. He thought about what he was about to say, then he told them everything. When he finished, Summer just smiled at him.

"Grandma was right. You are a Ni'namp-skan, (medicine man.) You should go and spend some time with Uncle Joe, he could tell you a lot more."

CHAPTER 15

As he crossed the wooden bridge, Daniel recalled his first trip to Uncle Joe's house and his introduction to four-wheel drive. When he got to where the road ran along the ridge line, he looked down at the lake and thought about the Ceremony for Mary, the transformation of people into animals and the apparition of Mary in the Spirit Garden. He had so many questions.

*****

"A'kai Aa'zist'awa! (Many Rabbits) Uncle Joe called from the porch, when Daniel stepped out of the suv. "Aakattsinootsiiyop (we see each other again.) It's good to see you my son," he called out in a voice that clearly showed he was excited to see Daniel.

"I have come for a visit," Daniel said, as he opened the cargo door and reached in for the supplies he had picked up at the store.

"It is a great honor," Uncle Joe said, as he stood holding the door opened and waited for Daniel to pass through. He pointed to the counter and after he put things away, gave Daniel a tour of the small house. "This is your room," Uncle Joe said, and left him to settle in.

Daniel tossed his bag on the bed and looked around the room. Someone had drawn several animals and mountains on the wall with a black crayon, next to an old dresser. He kneeled down for a better look. It appeared to be the drawings of a child. Daniel stood up and opened the top drawer, inside, neatly folded were tiny t-shirts, underwear and socks. He closed it and went to find Uncle Joe. He sat down in the chair next to him and they looked out at the wilderness and watched as the sun started to set.

"I have some questions," Daniel said, as he watched a magnificent display of clouds, change from orange to shades of red and grey.

"We should have a fire. Come we will get some wood," Uncle Joe said.

They went around the house to the wood pile and each took an arm load and then walked out near the big cedar.

"Whether you make a fire at home or in the bush, the rules are the same. The first thing is to organize your materials. First gather plenty of wood, enough to last you all night. You don't want to have to go looking for wood in the dark. Second, find some small sticks and dry leaves and grass. Once you have everything. Build a small tee-pee with the sticks and stuff the dry leaves and grass inside. Then, one match," Uncle Joe said, handing Daniel a book of matches and motioned for him to start the fire, while he went back to the house.

Daniel put everything together, then lit a match and held it to the dry grass. It started smoking. He got down low and gently blew into the smoldering grass, until the small sticks started burning, like he had seen Chief do. He fed it slightly larger pieces and soon had the beginnings of a nice fire. He watched with satisfaction, as the flames danced. He had lost track of time, and felt relaxed, when Uncle Joe returned and sat next to him.

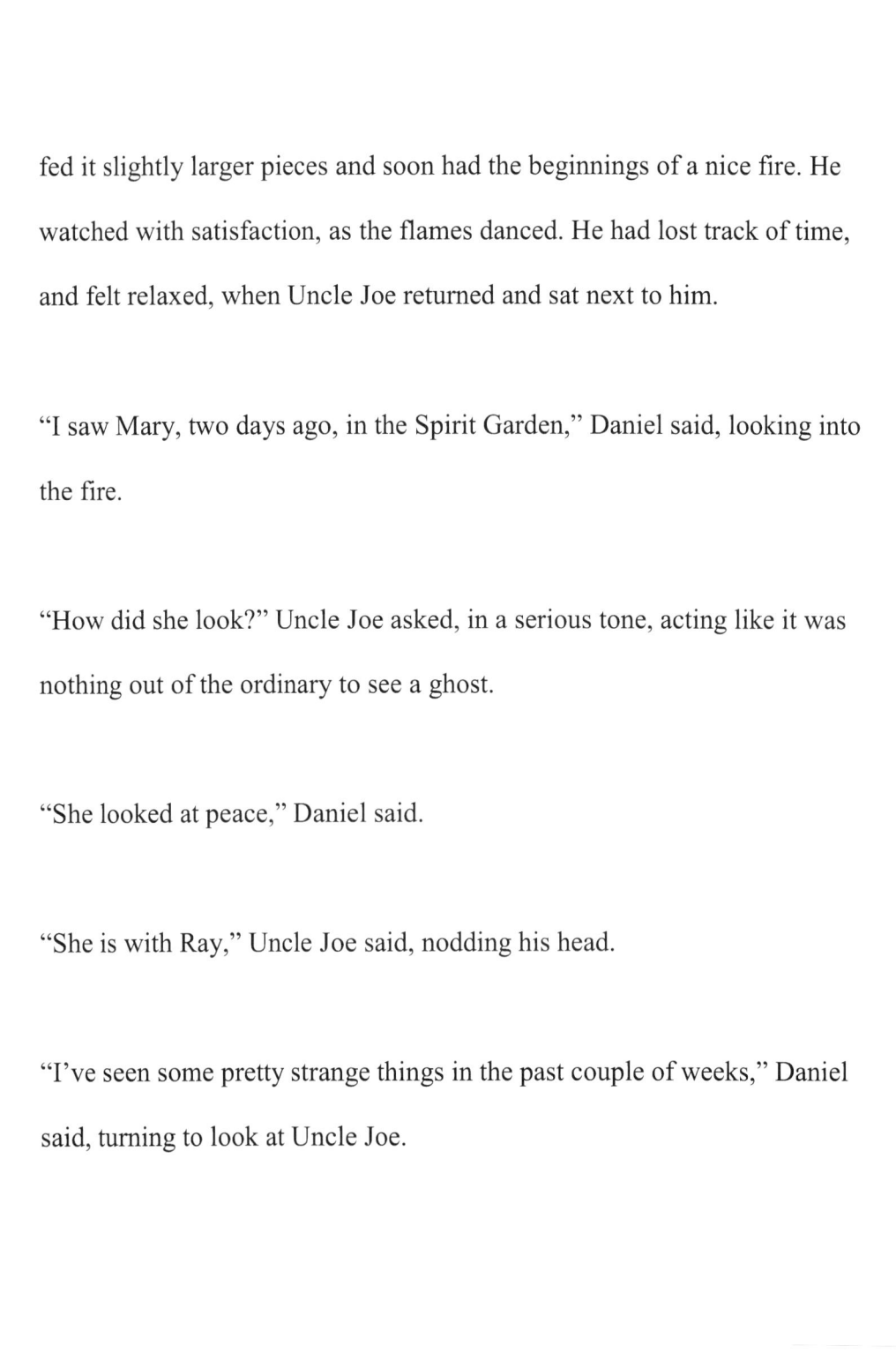

"I saw Mary, two days ago, in the Spirit Garden," Daniel said, looking into the fire.

"How did she look?" Uncle Joe asked, in a serious tone, acting like it was nothing out of the ordinary to see a ghost.

"She looked at peace," Daniel said.

"She is with Ray," Uncle Joe said, nodding his head.

"I've seen some pretty strange things in the past couple of weeks," Daniel said, turning to look at Uncle Joe.

"They are not so strange; you are just not accustomed to seeing them."

"Not accustomed! You're right! I am not accustomed to seeing ghosts! I'm not accustomed to seeing people turning into animals!" Daniel said slightly unraveled.

"A'kai Aa'zist'awa, (Many Rabbits) it is alright, it is nature's way. You were just removed from it. Naapi' (Nah-pee, Old Man) sent you on a journey and has now brought you home to see the ways of your people. It will be alright," Uncle Joe said, trying to be reassuring.

He unrolled the deerskin bundle, held up the pipe and spoke a few words in Siksikawa (Blackfeet.) He set the pipe down. Picked up the leather rattle and shook it at the fire and at Daniel. He reached into the larger pouch. He brought out the little tobacco pouch and put some Na'wak'o'sis' (herb from the Medicine Beaver) in the pipe and lit it with the end of a small twig, after sticking it into the fire.

He drew in, tilted his head back and sent a stream of smoke toward the Sky People. He handed the pipe to Daniel, nodding encouragingly. Daniel took it, recalling last time, he reluctantly lifted it to his lips and drew in a mouthful of smoke, then released it into the night sky, he handed the pipe back. They smoked in this fashion two more times.

Daniel felt tingly, like he had the night of the ceremony in the Spirit Garden. Uncle Joe reached into the other small leather pouch. He tossed a pinch of its contents into the flames. The fire flared up with a flash and a poof. Daniel looked at Uncle Joe and wasn't surprised to see his head had turned into that of the giant grizzly. He could see his reflection in the bear's eyes. He too was a bear.

Uncle Joe started to speak in Siksikawa(Blackfeet.) He began by telling Daniel of the Above Sky People and how they were the ones who were the creators of the Great Spirit, Apistotoke (ah-piss-toh-toh-kee.) He explained how everything in this world was sacred and connected, like a circle. He talked about the world today and how people no longer honored the Earth.

"It is not completely their fault. The people in Washington tell them it is their right to use all of what Mother Earth has, with no concern of the consequences. It will not be until the last tree is cut down and the last fish is caught, that Human Beings will realize they are not the center of the web of Life, only a small strand."

He explained how Naapi' (Old Man) was responsible for helping shape the world and told Daniel how he frequently helped people, but that sometimes his actions seemed cruel. He assured Daniel that he too, was part of the circle and Naapi' had his reasons for sending him away and one day it would all be revealed. Uncle Joe got up and put some more wood on the fire. Embers leaped into the air and smoke curled up, as it made its way to the Above Sky People. He smiled at Daniel.

"Nit'tak'ki'tsi'ni'ki (I will tell a story,)" he said.

"I was eleven that spring we found A'sita'pi aa'kiim (Young Sister.) Our mother gave her that name, when she saw the scratches on Johns' neck and chest. She said, 'now you will see what having a A'sitapiaakiim would have been like. Your days of running free are over.' My father didn't say anything, but he seemed very angry. I saw him give John, that look; I could see it said more than, 'You are older, you must watch over him.' But he seemed to soften up after a while, he enjoyed having her too. It was only as he neared death, that he told us why he was so angry, that day we brought A'sita'pi aa'kiim (Young Sister) home from the mountain. He could no longer walk and asked us to take him to the fire pit. We got the fire going and carried his chair from inside the house down to it. We made a travois, laid him on it, and took him down and when we got him settled; he asked us if we remembered the story of how our family came to be called Standing

Bear. We told him, we remembered. Then he said there was part of the story he had left out."

*****

"It was a few days after the Warrior had stood up to the pack of wolves to protect the bear cub. Naapi went to his camp and saw the cub following him around, like a dog. He told the man it was not right, and said, 'I made a man to be a man and a bear to be a bear.' When the man tried to explain, how everything had come about, Naapi grew even angrier, he said, 'A man isn't supposed to have the madness to roar, as you did that day, no man should be able to kill five wolves with only a knife; it was the bear inside you that raised up, it is not your fault, it is mine. I am not as angry with you, as I am with myself,' Naapi told him. 'It was I that threw the rock that started the avalanche that killed the cubs' mother. I too, have my moments of weakness… I had sent the wolves to return the cub to its' mothers' side. The Chief of the wolves asks, if you are Man or Bear. He says the wolves were confused in the fight and did not know how to fight you. I have come to test you,' Naapi told him.

The Man stood up straight and looked at Naapi, and said, 'I am as you made me, no test will say it is not so.'

At that same moment the little cub, got up on its' hind legs and stood next to the man. Naapi' saw that their auras over lapped, and realized they were connected.

'You share the same light. What happens to one of you will happen to the other. The fate of your children and of your children's children, will forever be tied to 'Otah'ko'i'ssk'sisi Yooh'kiaayo (grizzly bear,') Naapi told the Warrior and then turned and disappeared into the timber, like a wisp of mist."

*****

Uncle Joe was silent for a moment. His eyes were looking into the fire. But the expression on his face was blank and it was clear that if he saw any flames at all they were from a fire that burned many years ago. Then he looked at Daniel. "After our father told us this, he said he heard the words of Naapi in his head, that day we brought A'sita'pi aa'kiim (Young Sister) home. He said he feared it was the beginning of the end for his family… When she was three years old, our Father finally said she could no longer live with us. He said even her mother would have sent her off by now to make her own way. He said, we should take her back to be with other bears. So we went back to where we had found her. We camped there for four weeks. We built a small cabin, out of small logs and stayed until A'sita'pi aa'kiim found a den. We followed her in and pet her and told her to sleep good and that we would be back when she woke up. It was the second spring she came out with two cubs. She showed them we were her family and even left them with us to go on short hunts of her own. There were two other litters, she would bring them to our camp each spring and show them we could be trusted.

…. I remember, the year she died. We had gotten an elk, packed up what we could carry and started for home. A'sita'pi aa'kiim claimed the rest for herself, we figured whatever kept her out of our fathers' hair, was good. We returned two days later, to do more hunting. A'sita'pi aa'kiim (Young Sister) was waiting for us at camp. She had been torn up pretty badly. There wasn't much we could do. For two days she laid with her head on his lap. John didn't move, for anything, nothing. When her breathing stopped… we both died a little, that day. After we buried her in her den, we went down to where we had killed the elk. The sign was six days old, but we could see a much larger bear had tried to take over the carcass. He said he was gonna send that bear to hell. He smoked Na'wak'osis' (herb from the Medicine Beaver) for two days, the whole time singing an old war song, over and over; as he worked on a five-foot pole, shaping it like a spear and hardening it with fire; then he broke off the handle of his knife and fitted the spear with the blade. He took off all his clothes and painted his body for war and asked me to stay by the fire and ask the 'Above Sky People' to help him.

Three days later he returned, a giant paw hanging around his neck. When we made it back to the house and our father saw the bear paw and heard what had happened, he said, 'now one of ours would pay the price.' John said one of us had already been killed. Our father screamed, A'sita'pi aa'kiim (Young Sister) was not one of us and said, that if his son thought she was, then he was more bear than man and should go live with the bears full time. John spent the winter out there, somewhere. In the spring, father asked me to go and get him. I found him and I spent a week with him, but he did not want to come back with me. Finally, just before the snows of the second winter, he came home. He later told me, Naapi (Old Man) had come to see him and that they had talked. He said, Naapi had told him that there would be hard times ahead, but that it was not his fault and that whatever happened was part of something that started a long time ago. He said Naapi also told him that the Standing Bear Clan would one day do great things for the Siksikawa (Blackfeet.)

"He believed that for the rest of his life," Uncle Joe said, as he wiped a tear from the corner of his eye. "I believe, the death of your parents and the things you learned on your journey when you went to live with your adopted family, was all a part of Nits'o'kan (his dream) to help 'The People.' I believe Naapi (Old Man) used your dreams to return you to us and those good things will soon come to be for our People.

CHAPTER 16

It had been five days since Daniel had returned from his visit with Uncle Joe. He was working in the chicken coop, cleaning out the nesting boxes and removing the dirty straw that covered the floor, replacing it with cedar shavings. He was deep in thought as he raked out the shavings and when the chicken coop door suddenly opened, it surprised him. Summer stood in the doorway with a shocked look on her face.

"There's been trouble. Chief wants us to meet him in town."

Daniel could tell by the urgency in her voice and the look on her face that it must be pretty bad. He set the rake in a corner and followed her to the house. Several minutes later they were speeding toward town.

Chief was waiting for them outside the market. "Some son of a bitch shot up the buffalo," He said to Daniel, through the drivers' window, noticeably upset.

"Let's go take a look," Daniel said.

Chief climbed in the back seat and gave Daniel directions to the ranch where the tribe kept the buffalo. They pulled off the tar road and started on a two- track that led across the open prairie.

"There, head that way," Chief said, when he spotted a vehicle off in the distance.

When they pulled up to the pickup, Daniel noticed it was the two men that had been at Mary's ceremony. They were sitting on the tail gate. Chief got out and went over to them. The two men told Chief they had come out to shoot gophers and found the buffalo dead. They pointed to the coulee in front of the truck. Chief walked quickly to the rim of the coulee. There in the bottom lay 10 large shapes.

"NO! NO! OH! NO!" Chief yelled as he started down to the dead buffalo.

Daniel and Summer could hear him crying, as they made their way down to him. His sobbing turned into an eerie chant as he knelt next to one of the slain animals. Daniel and Summer came around the front of the animal and stood next to Chief. There to the side of the dead cow buffalo was a smaller buffalo. It had been skinned out.

"This was Nits'-o-kan', (His Dream), the white buffalo calf. She symbolized the promise that one day, the buffalo would return and the land that was taken from us would be ours again," Chief said as he stood up and wiped his arm across his face. He turned and looked at each of the fallen animals and then walked back up the hill. Daniel stood for a minute and looked at the carnage; then looked at Summer and saw tears rolling down her checks.

"What happened here?" Daniel asked, looking at the dead animals.

"The Cattlemen don't want the buffalo here. They carry brucellosis, it causes pregnant cows to abort their calves and that affects their bottom line, by limiting trade with other countries, if they don't have a brucellosis free status. They won't be happy until they are all gone."

Daniel did not know what to say. He had seen plenty of the ugly side of humanity in his legal career. His father's law firm handled corporate law and so Daniel was no stranger to selfishness and greed. He had learned to never be surprised at what a man would do for power and wealth. Still, he could not understand how a person could be driven to destroy these magnificent animals and leave them to rot. The lawyer inside Daniel rose to the surface as his blood started to boil. "I'll get to the bottom of this! Come on, let's go talk to those men and see if they can shed any light on what happened."

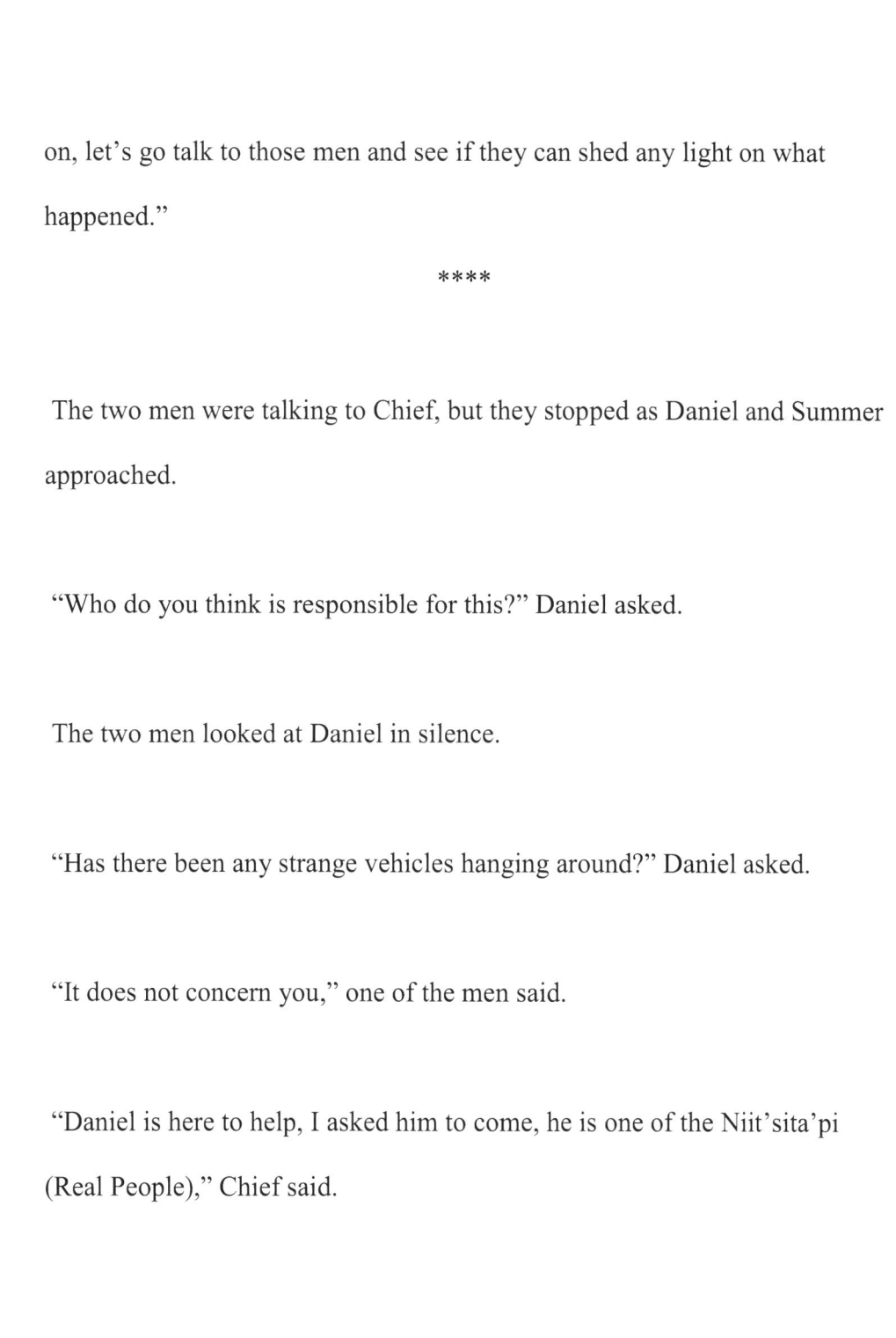

****

The two men were talking to Chief, but they stopped as Daniel and Summer approached.

"Who do you think is responsible for this?" Daniel asked.

The two men looked at Daniel in silence.

"Has there been any strange vehicles hanging around?" Daniel asked.

"It does not concern you," one of the men said.

"Daniel is here to help, I asked him to come, he is one of the Niit'sita'pi (Real People)," Chief said.

"He is not one of us! He is one of them!" The man who had said very little up until then, snapped.

"He was born here, just like the rest of us. He had no say in what happened to him. Maybe Naapi (nah-pee, Old Man) chose him to go and become someone who could help his people. Joe Standing Bear says it is good that he has returned," Chief said.

But the men refused to listen.

Chief turned toward Daniel and said, "I'm sorry… distrust of outsiders and hatred for the white man's law, is the way of the Rez."

"I understand. I'm not going to take it personally. I will get to the bottom of this," Daniel said to the two men as they got into their pickup and drove off; spinning their wheels in the sandy topsoil and creating a cloud of dust as they went. Daniel, Summer and Chief stood there for a few minutes, in awkward silence.

The gentle breeze that was making the prairie grass wave back and forth suddenly changed to a strong wind, making an eerie sound as it channeled through the contours of the land. Daniel looked out over the open country and for an instant, he thought he heard the voices of a large group of people rushing past him. He looked at Summer; she gave him a knowing look.

"What was that?" Daniel asked.

"You heard them?" Chief asked.

"Heard who?" Daniel asked with a puzzled look.

"The 900," Chief said, then turned to look at Summer, as she started to explain.

"A long time ago, there was a village not far from here, the U.S. government, sent a group of soldiers to ask them to move, when the elders refused, the General in charge offered them 'gifts' to help persuade them. Those gifts included blankets that had come from white settlers that had died from the small pox. An entire band died from the pox. The General got a medal for 'removing' so many savages without losing any of his men. It is said the spirits of those villagers still refuse to leave what is theirs and the wind carries their voices," Summer said.

The drive back into town was a quiet one. Daniel's mind was trying to process the gruesome images at the crime scene. Summer could see the wheels turning and decided to quietly watch the scenery as it passed by. Daniel parked in front of the grocery store, and turned toward Chief.

"I need to make a few calls. I'll be in touch," he said, in a professional tone.

"Thank you," Chief said, as he got out and closed the door.

****

"I'd like to learn more about the dynamics of the Tribe. The Tribal Council, its lawyer. Can you help me?" Daniel asked Summer, after several minutes of silence.

"Of course," Summer replied.

"Tell me more about the Stock Growers Association," Daniel asked, changing topics as he began thinking of something else.

"They are a very powerful group of landowners and ranchers, some families going back several generations. They have deep pockets and lobbyists in Washington, who convince the politicians to see things their way," Summer said.

"How much does the Department of Natural Resources have to do with making the actual policies concerning wildlife in the state?" Daniel asked.

"The Fish, Wildlife and Parks… they are like any other government agency, run by a political agenda. They try to strike a happy medium between ranchers and hunters and maintain a healthy population of game animals so the state can generate income," Summer replied.

"I think a road trip to Great Falls is in order. I'd like to speak with the FWP," Daniel said, turning onto the dirt road that led to Mary's farm….

"Hey Boys," Daniel said, as he and Summer got out of the suv.

"Hi," they both said together.

"Hey," April said, as she came out on the porch to meet them. She could tell something terrible must have happened and followed them into the house, saying "You boys stay outside for a little while, okay."

Daniel and Summer sat down at the kitchen table. April brought them some ice tea.

"What happened?" April asked.

Summer glanced at Daniel, he nodded his head.

"Several buffalo were killed out at the ranch…. They skinned Nits'-o-kan' (His Dream,)" she said.

April's mouth dropped open, and her eyes welled up with tears.

"What are we going to do?" she asked.

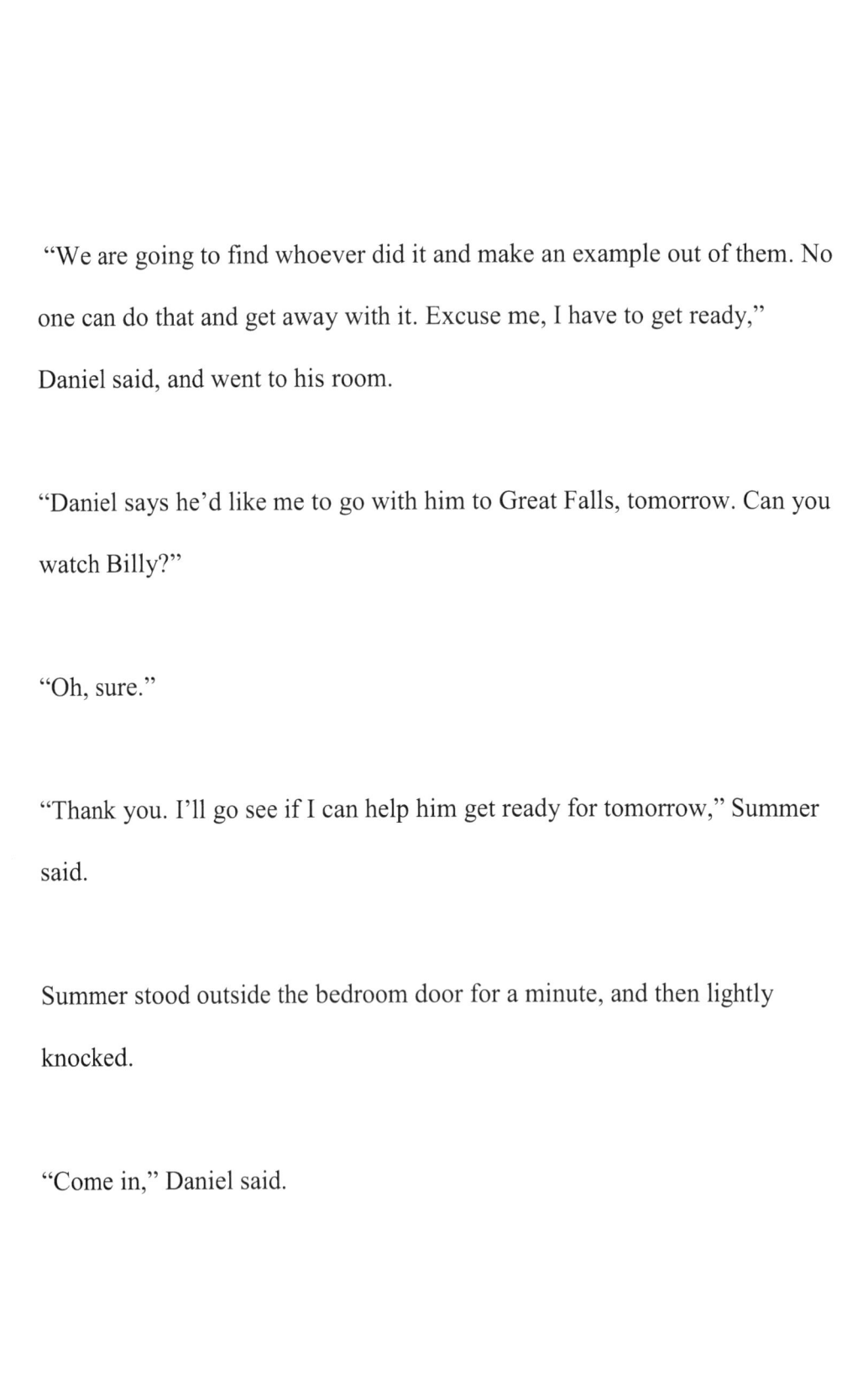

"We are going to find whoever did it and make an example out of them. No one can do that and get away with it. Excuse me, I have to get ready," Daniel said, and went to his room.

"Daniel says he'd like me to go with him to Great Falls, tomorrow. Can you watch Billy?"

"Oh, sure."

"Thank you. I'll go see if I can help him get ready for tomorrow," Summer said.

Summer stood outside the bedroom door for a minute, and then lightly knocked.

"Come in," Daniel said.

"I asked April if she could watch Billy tomorrow. It's all set," she said.

"Good," Daniel said, rubbing a shoe with a little cloth like it was a magic lamp. It was something his adopted father had taught him. "'Shoes… shoes are the first thing they see. Show 'em polished shoes. It's a good time to think about what you're gonna say and how you're gonna say it,' he'd always say that," Daniel said.

Summer looked at Daniel's suit hanging on the closet door and then at Daniel.

"I haven't had any real need to update my wardrobe for a while," Summer said, feeling her face getting a little warm.

Daniel stopped polishing his shoe and stood up, "Of course…we should plan on doing a little shopping."

"I wasn't asking for…" Summer started to say.

"Summer, I need your help. This is going to be an uphill battle. We are going to take on whoever the hell gets in our way! We have to look like we mean business. Besides, it's tax deductible," Daniel said, and smiled at her.

Summer's eyes sparkled a little. She closed the door behind her and stepped toward him, putting her arms around his waist. "Does that mean I'll be working for you?" she asked.

Daniel thought about it and said, "I guess it does." Then he kissed her.

"Isn't that grounds for sexual harassment or do you kiss everybody you work with?" she asked.

"Well not everybody… I'm sure Steve wouldn't be as receptive as a few of the paralegals might be," Daniel replied, acting naughty.

"Oh… that's how it is? Then this ought to be worth a raise," she said, as she pushed him back on the bed, putting her index finger to her lip

CHAPTER 17

Summer was trying on her new dress and Daniel was on his lap top, as they relaxed in their motel room after a day of traveling and shopping.

"Change in plans," Daniel said, as he closed his laptop and sat back. "I think we should go in, way under the radar. I'm not going to wear my suit. I'm going to wear my jeans and boots." As he was saying this, he looked at Summer in her new dress.

"Oh," she said.

"You can still wear that, it looks great," Daniel said, seeing the look on her face.

"No, it would look kind of funny, I'll wear jeans, too," Summer said.

"I'll make it up to ya,'" Daniel promised and walked over to her.

*****

The next morning, as they walked through the doors of the Department of Fish Wildlife and Parks building, in Great Falls, they saw a stocky middle aged woman dressed in green pants and a light brown shirt waiting on the other side of the counter to greet them.

"How can I help you?" she asked.

"Who would I talk to if I had a few questions about policies that govern the large animals in Montana," Daniel said.

The woman gave him sort of an odd look and then said, "I'll see if Mr. Rose is available, can I tell him your name?"

"I'm Daniel Williams," he said, with a friendly smile.

The woman disappeared down a narrow hall and returned a few minutes later. "Mr. Rose will be with you shortly," she said, with a smile and then returned to her desk.

A few minutes later, a tall man dressed in the same green and brown uniform came from the narrow hall.

"Hello, I'm Jim Rose. How can I help you?"

Daniel extended his hand. "Hi, I'm Daniel Williams; it's nice to meet you. This is Summer Morning Star. It's my first time in Montana and Summer has been showing me around. I've seen: deer, elk, a wolf, and a moose, but when I said, I hoped to see a wild buffalo, she said, that wouldn't probably happen until we reached the National Bison Range, are they treated differently than other animals?"

"Oh... well... let's go back to my office," Jim said, and gave the woman at the desk, a look. "Follow me," he said, and led them back down the hall. "Please, have a seat," he said, gesturing to two chairs, as he sat down behind the desk in his small cluttered office and folded his hands. "You have questions concerning bison?" he asked, with a puzzled look on his face.

"Yes, why are they treated differently than other wild animals?" Daniel asked.

There was a moment of silence, as Jim shifted nervously in his chair and thought of a reply. "Bison are large animals that can be aggressive. They can cause a lot of damage to fences, crops and people, if not managed," he said.

"Managed? Do you mean confined to specific areas? Are bison more dangerous than grizzly bears? I watched the 'Night of the Grizzlies' documentary on PBS, the other night. It seemed like the people were hunted, like prey. Why are we allowed to hike the back country of Glacier National Park and not the bison refuge? Is it to keep the Public safe or to keep the buffalo out of the Public consciousness? Daniel asked.

"The policies governing bison are very complicated," Mr. Rose said.

Daniel smiled and said, "I see." It took some self-control to fight back the urge to say, "Yeah, well I'm a lawyer, go ahead and try."

"Some people would like to see the return of the old west. Others aren't so sure there is a place for bison in the modern world…."

"There must be a place for them, they aren't… dinosaurs," Daniel said, with a slight smile, referencing a statement made by a Montana State Senator, that he had read on the internet, last night.

Jim suddenly looked very uncomfortable. He had that 'deer in the headlights' look, as he tried to think of something to say.

"How many buffalo were around when the First Peoples Buffalo Jump was still being used?" Daniel asked, deciding not to make him squirm any longer. He wasn't ready to show his hand yet.

"Some estimates are more than 50 million," Jim said, more at ease with that type of question. "Nearly a thousand Jumps have been identified across the great plains, 300 in Montana alone. There is a wonderful topographical map of the state in the conference room; would you like to see it?" Jim asked, as he got up and walked to the door, before getting an answer.

"Yes, that would be great," Daniel said, rolling his eyes at Summer, as they stood up and followed Jim to the conference room. Daniel listened to him explain how it is believed the Indians used the contours of the land to funnel the buffalo through miles of country before they lured them over the cliffs. It all sounded so 'canned.'

"Well, I'm sure you are very busy and I appreciate you taking the time to talk with us," Daniel said, after taking as much as he could.

"It's been a pleasure talking with you, I hope you enjoy the rest of your visit to Montana," Jim said, leading them back to the lobby, obviously relieved the meeting was over.

Daniel and Summer walked out of the building to their SUV.

"Coffee?" Daniel asked as he climbed in behind the wheel.

"Sure," Summer replied.

A few minutes later, he pulled up to the window at Starbucks and said, "Two medium black coffees, please." Then he turned to Summer and said, "I'll bet we got Mr. Rose's wheels turning. I wonder what sort of bugs will come crawling out of the walls."

"What's next?" Summer asked, sipping her coffee as they pulled away from the building.

"I was thinking we could take a long drive, then go someplace nice for dinner and head back tomorrow.

"What? I meant what was next with FWP…. We can't stay another night! April will be expecting us.

"We'll give her a call and make sure it's alright," Daniel said. "We can look for something nice for her, to show our appreciation," he added, handing her his cell phone. He drove down to the river, parking so they faced the water.

It made him think of the Hudson in a strange sort of way, and he wondered if it had looked something like this before its banks became part of one of the largest cities in the world.

After several minutes, he heard Summer say, "Okay, we'll see you tomorrow, love you, bye," She held the phone out to Daniel. "There, I did your dirty work."

"So?" Daniel said, pretending not to know the answer.

"She said it was fine," Summer said, indulging him.

"So…let's go to that Western Supply store," Daniels said.

"Why?" Summer asked.

"We could look for something for April, the boys… Uncle Joe," Daniel said.

"Nobody expects anything. It even makes some people feel… bad… like it reminds them, they don't have money. I remember in grade school. It felt weird if you got a new pair of shoes or some new clothes. Your mom and dad would wear their clothes until they were rags, but wanted you to look nice for school. You were sure proud of your new things, but besides feeling a little guilty for having them, you got picked on by the other kids, because they didn't have anything nice. I remember one boy came to school one day wearing new jeans, new shirt and new tennis shoes. During recess, a bunch of boys he played with every day started pushing him around, it turned into a real frenzy. By the time the teacher could break it up, his shirt was all torn, and he was missing a shoe," Summer said, looking down at her snakeskin boots.

"I don't want anybody to feel bad. I just want to do something nice for the people I care about. Whenever my mom would take me shopping, we'd always get dad a new tie, she said it showed we were thinking about him and wishing he could be with us," Daniel said, as he reached over with his right hand and touched Summers arm.

Later that evening, they stood looking out their motel room window at the lights of Great Falls.

"Not quite the Skyline of Manhattan," he said, as a way of masking the silence, while he rehearsed, one more time, how he was going to say what was on his mind.

"Do you miss the Big City?" Summer asked, smiling at him.

"That sounds like a leading question, did I tell you how terrific you look in that black dress?" Daniel said, in a playful attempt to redirect.

"I withdraw the question, counselor, but I object; your attempts to redirect are leading me to believe your motive is to manipulate this witness," Summer said, playing along.

"You sound like a big city attorney," Daniel said, smiling,

"I've watched a few episodes of 'The Good Wife,'" Summer said.

"I guess, I never thought of living anywhere but New York. It seemed my life was just as it should be. But now that I'm here in Montana… I feel so much more alive! I feel… I feel like I'm falling in love with you!" Daniel said, as he turned toward her, taking her right hand and bringing it up to his lips.

Summer stepped closer to Daniel and slipped her arms around his waist. "I feel the same way," she said, "But how could it work? My life is here. I want to raise Billy here, among his People, for whatever successes or failures it brings…. Once I thought moving away from all the dysfunction would solve the problem, it didn't. In school, it seemed okay, but under the surface, I was still an Indian in Missoula, and in Browning I was treated a little 'whiter,' I really didn't fit into either group. After I came back to take care of Mom, and had Billy, something changed. I saw the people I grew up with, making all the same mistakes their parents made, and some of their children already following the same path. I started thinking, maybe, instead of trying to escape to another culture, I could bring some change and repair some of the damage done to this one, but old habits die hard and for many it is a daily struggle to choose not to fill the emptiness with drugs and alcohol…. Me and Billy don't have a lot, but we've got more than we need. And there's April and Tommy. Who would they have if I…."

Daniel touched her cheek, her hair brushed against the back of his hand and he felt a tingle go up his arm. "I know we haven't known each other very long, and it sounds funny to say it, but, I have never met anyone like you…

I can't say I understand how you feel; I didn't experience what you did. I guess growing up in a place like New York and being in the middle of everything, where everybody looks different, you just come to accept people are different. You… you even get suspicious of the ones that come off too buddy, buddy. Sure different neighborhoods have their own ethnic influences, but they sort of balance each other out. That's what makes it work, people living too close together, to worry too much about who is what. Most people thought I was Italian when I was growing up. I do understand family, maybe even more so, after losing my Dad and finding out what I have about my birth parents…. All I know is there's a voice inside me screaming 'WOW!' and I don't think I could ignore it and go on with my life if I wanted to. I'm not going to try and rip you and April apart, I'm just thinking how great it would be for you to meet the other people in my life and show Billy all the things I'd seen by the time I was his age."

"Billy can't miss school!" Summer said, as a million things starting to swirl in her head, as she tried to think of reasons they couldn't go.

"I don't know if I can get off work," she said.

"I thought you worked for me?" Daniel said. "Think of it as a business trip for you and a field trip for Billy."

Summer could see she wasn't going to win this one. Not that she really wanted to, anyway.

Daniel sensed she wanted to say yes, but her self- installed safety buttons were firing. He took her by the hand and led her over to the bed.

"Are you tired?" Summer said, acting innocent.

Daniel made a kind of snorty sound in his throat, as he gently pulled her to him and kissed her.

"It seems like you've been doing a lot of thinking," she said, running her hand over his shoulder and down his arm; as he pressed against her.

Daniel smiled at her, as they laid down on the bed.

CHAPTER 18

The next morning, they ate breakfast, smiling the whole time, like a couple of teenagers.

"Do we need anything before we head home?" Daniel asked. As he heard the word, home, it gave him a sense of peace.

"When we come to Great Falls, we usually bring a cooler, and make a stop at Wal-Mart, for milk and vegetables, our little store is okay for some stuff, but it saves some money, if we stock up. Did you know, you can freeze milk and it will stay fresh for a long time. Strawberries and broccoli are easy to freeze too, it just takes a little planning," Summer said.

"So, we'll pick up a cooler and get a few things," Daniel said.

****

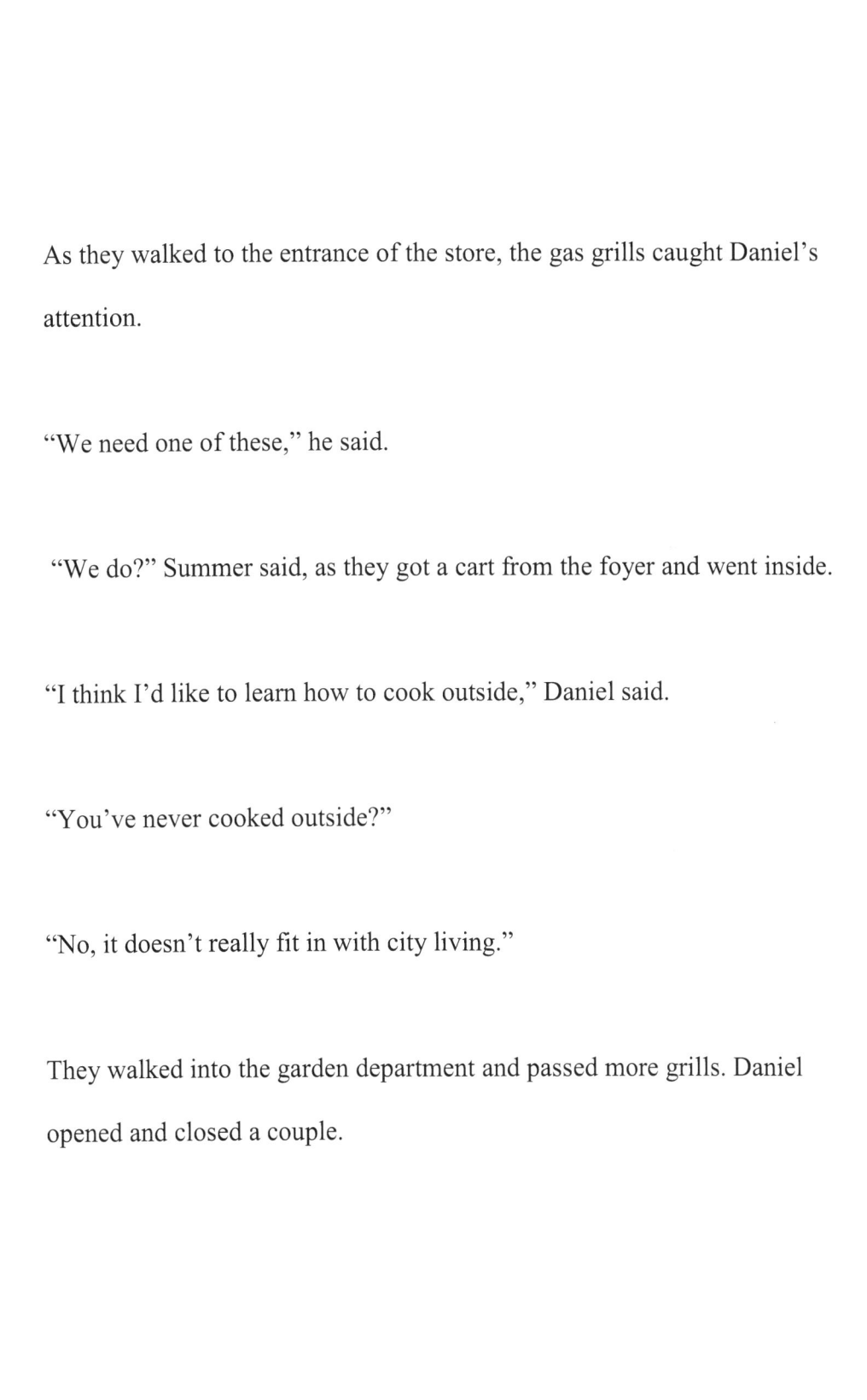

As they walked to the entrance of the store, the gas grills caught Daniel's attention.

"We need one of these," he said.

"We do?" Summer said, as they got a cart from the foyer and went inside.

"I think I'd like to learn how to cook outside," Daniel said.

"You've never cooked outside?"

"No, it doesn't really fit in with city living."

They walked into the garden department and passed more grills. Daniel opened and closed a couple.

"What do you think of this one?" he asked.

"I think it's very nice," Summer said, watching as he went to find someone to help him. "I'll take the cart and get the food and ice," she said, not sure if he had heard her, and thinking he looked like a kid in a toy store, as she watched him walk away.

****

They talked and held hands, the entire way back to Browning. The trip seemed to take no time at all; but as they turned off Hwy2 and drove through town, Daniels thoughts shifted and he moved his right hand back to the steering wheel.

"Ever see the movie, 'Dead Man?'" he asks, looking from one side of the street to the other, as they drove along.

"No," Summer said.

"It was filmed in black and white. Johnny Depp plays a character, William Blake, like the poet; anyway there's a scene where he walks through a Makah village, while in a critically delirious state, after being shot… there are flashes of buildings, totem poles, children, old people…." Daniel said, as they pass several more buildings with signs still in the window from the last failed business that tried to make a go of it there.

Daniel did notice, that although most houses needed a basic paint job, many had designs painted somewhere on them or a totem pole or metal sculpture in the front yard, along with a pile of wood and a junked car. He wondered about the people that lived in those houses and the complex mixture of pride, persecution and poverty that surrounded him.

Summer seemed aware of Daniels shift in focus. She too seemed to be brought back to reality, as they passed the Art Gallery. She realized her life was about to change. It was exciting and scary, all at the same time.

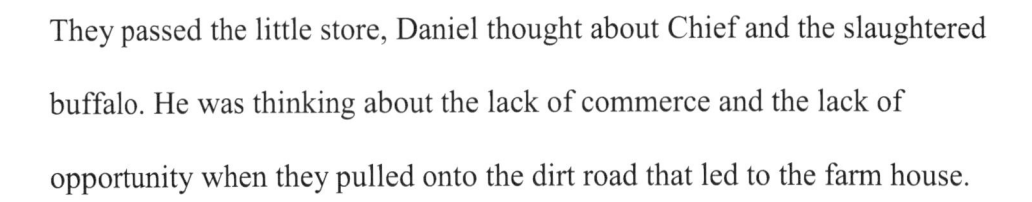

They passed the little store, Daniel thought about Chief and the slaughtered buffalo. He was thinking about the lack of commerce and the lack of opportunity when they pulled onto the dirt road that led to the farm house.

"Where does this road become private?" Daniel asked.

"I never really thought about it," Summer said, with a furrowed brow.

"I'd like to check into that," he said, offering only a little smile.

Summer was still thinking about it, as the house came into view. She waved to Billy and Tommy as they came running from behind the house.

"The partiers have returned," April called out to Summer, from the porch.

"We were working," Summer said, making a little face at her.

"And when we weren't working, we were grocery shopping," Daniel chimed in, as he opened the back of the SUV.

"That's quite a haul! Did you make a clean getaway? Or are the police coming out to get us?" April said to Daniel, jokingly. "What is all this?" April asked Summer quietly, as they walked around to the back of the vehicle.

"Hi, Mom," Billy said, as the boys came over, he put his arms around Summers waist. "You look really pretty."

"Thank you, Sweetie," Summer said, and kissed the top of his head. "Will you boys take these," she said, handing them each a couple bags of groceries and a couple bags to April and then helped Daniel with the big box that had the grill inside.

"Come into the living room," Summer said, as she came through the door, to April who was just finishing putting away the last of the groceries.

Summer reached down for a bag and said, "Daniel found a couple of cool shirts for you guys."

"Thanks!" they both said.

"They're just like yours!" Billy said.

Tommy took his shirt off and put one of the new ones on. "Look, Mommy," he said to April.

"I see! Very nice!"

"We also got you a couple pair of jeans," Summer said to the boys, as she pulled four pair of jeans out of another bag.

"Thanks," they said, both looking very pleased.

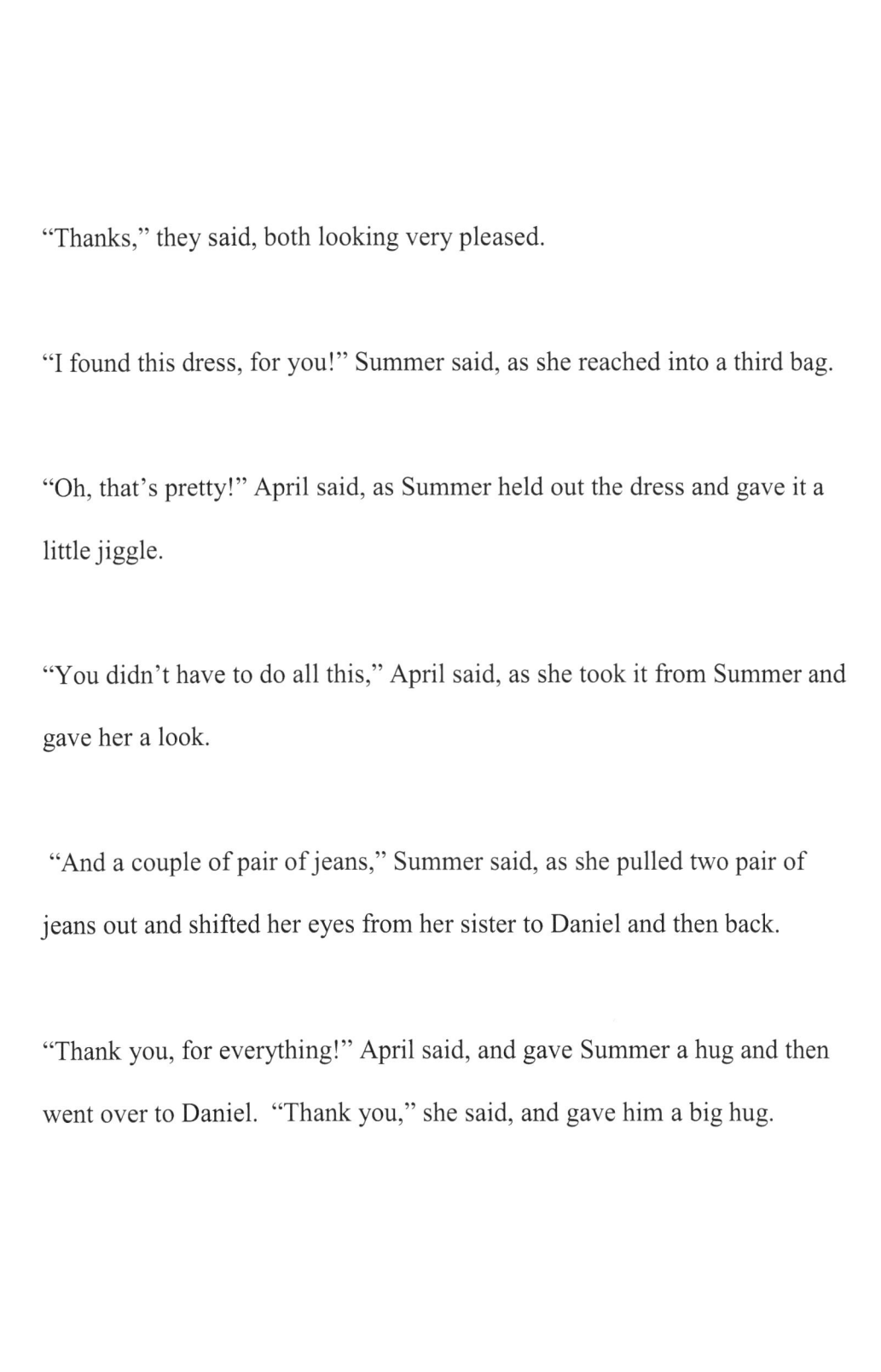

"I found this dress, for you!" Summer said, as she reached into a third bag.

"Oh, that's pretty!" April said, as Summer held out the dress and gave it a little jiggle.

"You didn't have to do all this," April said, as she took it from Summer and gave her a look.

"And a couple of pair of jeans," Summer said, as she pulled two pair of jeans out and shifted her eyes from her sister to Daniel and then back.

"Thank you, for everything!" April said, and gave Summer a hug and then went over to Daniel. "Thank you," she said, and gave him a big hug.

"You're welcome," Daniel said, looking over her shoulder at Summer.

"Let's see how that dress fits," Summer said, and they went upstairs to April's room.

After changing his clothes, Daniel stepped out on the porch, looked down at the grill and then across the yard to the chickens. Two of them started to make a fuss over the same worm and it reminded him of the new feeder and water tank, so he took them over to the coop. He was just finishing filling the water tank, when the boys came out of the house and over by him.

"Wha'ch ya doin'?" they both asked, at the same time.

"Filling the new water tank for the chickens," Daniel said. "Wanna grab the feeder?"

Billy picked up the feeder and Tommy went to open the door for them. Daniel set the watering tank down in the center of the coop and Billy set the feeder next to it.

"Get that bag of feed and fill it up," Daniel said, as he stepped out and watched the boys through the screen door. They got along so well. Daniel had often wondered what it would have been like to have a brother. "Let's go take a look at that grill," he said, as the boys came out. Daniel noticed Tommy was careful to latch the door behind him and he waited a second so they all could walk up to the house together.

The three of them stood in front of the big box and looked at the picture on the side.

"Is that what it looks like?" Billy asked.

"Wow!" Tommy said.

"That's it. Looks like we need: a knife, a screw driver, a pliers and a wrench, think there's some tools in the shed?" Daniel asked.

"Yep," they both said at the same time.

"Let's go take a look," Daniel said.

He walked through the partially open double door and immediately noticed a good sized bird, sitting on a red tool box. It looked directly at him. It was like a wood pecker, but bigger. Its body and head were brown with black spots and the undersides of its wings and tail feathers were orange. It looked down at the tool box and then flew out the broken window. It had startled Daniel at first and then he thought about how the Blackfeet People believed the dead sometimes returned as animals. He found himself wondering if that could have been Ray. He realized he felt okay with that. It felt comforting, somehow.

He looked at the boxes piled along the side walls and the cluttered bench against the back wall, then walked over to the tool box and opened it. Inside he found a good selection of hand tools. He could tell Ray must have been pretty handy. He pulled the top shelf out and noticed a leather sheath with a folding knife. He moved a couple of other things around and soon had the wrench, pliers and screwdriver that he needed. As he turned to leave, a box on the lower shelf caught his attention. He set the tools down and picked up a piece of wood with a big bear drawn on it. The wood had been chiseled away all around the bear, giving it a raised look, there was also wood removed along the bears midsection to define the front leg and shoulder muscles. Pencil marks outlined details of the face, suggesting more areas where Ray had planned to work. It's too bad it never got finished, he thought as he gently put it back where he found it.

"Come on, let's go put that grill together," he said to the boys, picking up the tools again and headed toward the door. As he stepped through the opening, he stopped to see what prevented the door from closing and saw the top hinge had lost two screws. "We should fix that," he said, as they all walked back to the house.

Daniel set the tools on the ground next to the box and took the folding knife out of the leather sheath; it made a loud click as the blade locked into position and made a clean cut through the heavy cardboard. After reading the instructions, it didn't take long and the grill was together.

"Good to see seven years of college, didn't go to waste," he said, stepping back and admiring his handy work.

The boys took the card board to the burning barrel and Daniel took the tools back to the shed and put them back where he had found them. He looked at the leather sheath that held the knife for a minute and then, undid his belt and slipped it through the loop in the sheath and fastened his belt back together, and then walked back to the house.

The boys were checking out the grill. "We can cook hot dogs outside!" Billy said.

"We can cook all sorts of stuff," Daniel said.

"Come and see the grill!" the boys called to their mothers.

April came out wearing her new dress. Summer noticed Daniel looking at her and said, "Doesn't she look nice?"

"She looks great!" he replied.

"Thanks," April said, as they came down the steps.

"Looks like you got it put together… looks good," Summer said, lifting the lid.

"Can we make hot dogs?" Billy said.

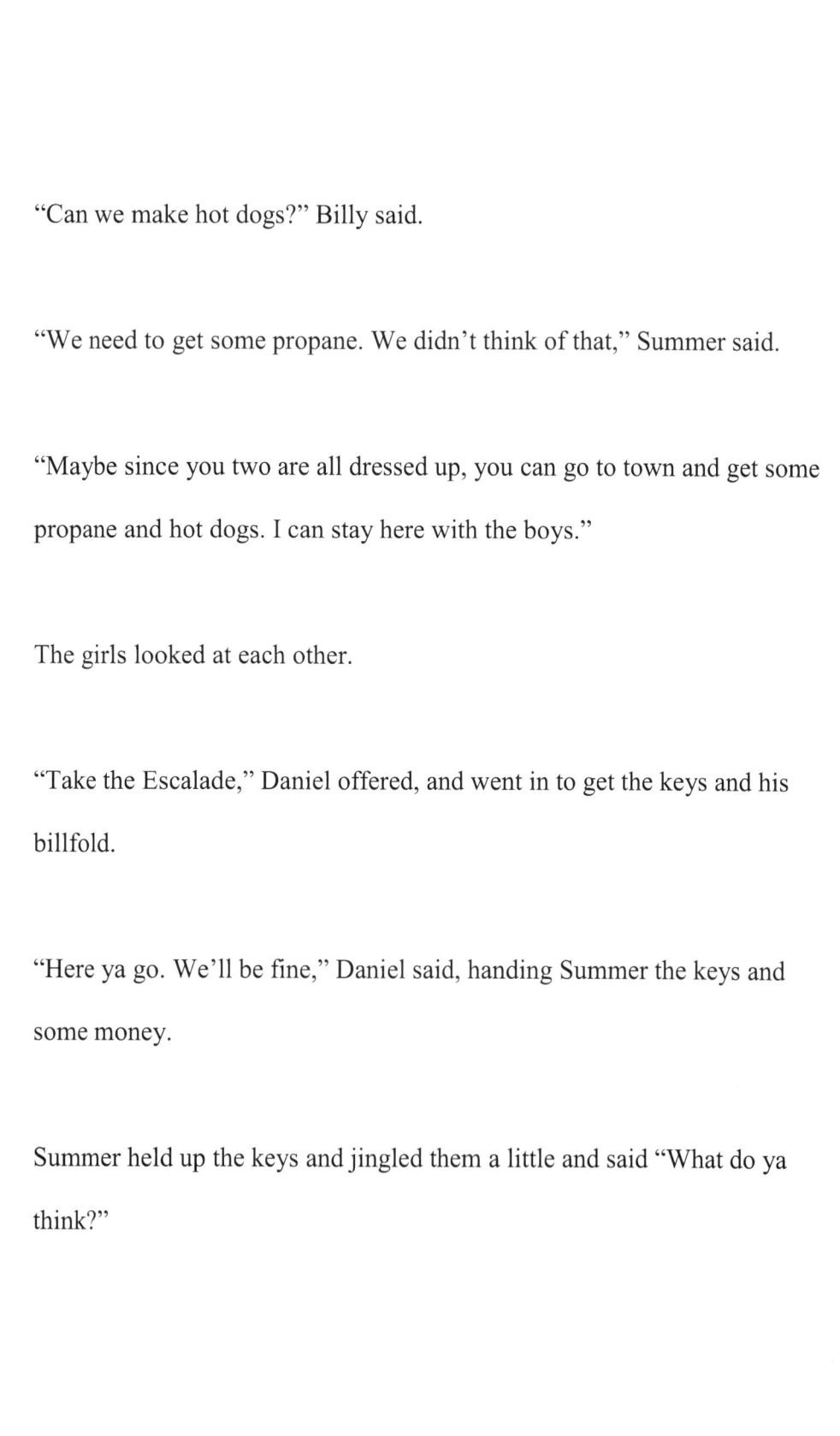

"We need to get some propane. We didn't think of that," Summer said.

"Maybe since you two are all dressed up, you can go to town and get some propane and hot dogs. I can stay here with the boys."

The girls looked at each other.

"Take the Escalade," Daniel offered, and went in to get the keys and his billfold.

"Here ya go. We'll be fine," Daniel said, handing Summer the keys and some money.

Summer held up the keys and jingled them a little and said "What do ya think?"

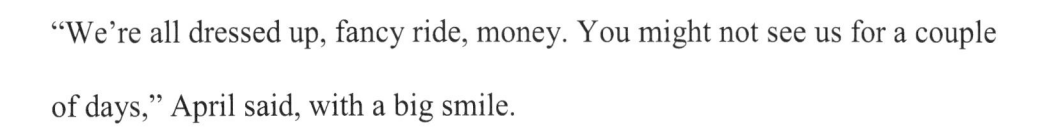

"We're all dressed up, fancy ride, money. You might not see us for a couple of days," April said, with a big smile.

"We'll just have to manage," Daniel said, shrugging his shoulders and playing along.

"Be good for Daniel," April told Tommy, as she opened the door and stepped up to get in.

Summer started the engine and they were off.

Daniel watched them drive off. He stood there for a few minutes and then wondered what he could get into. He decided to go back to the shed and take another look at the doors. As he stepped through the opening, there was a whir of wings, the bird had apparently returned as soon as Daniel had left.

"Stop that!" Daniel shouted, startled, even though it had happened earlier. "Maybe, I'd better fix that window too!" he threatened, but then thought, if it was Ray, it was his shed and so who was he to keep him out. He turned toward the doors and lifted the one that was broken. He discovered both hinges had missing screws. He found a couple small blocks of wood and propped the door on them to keep it where it needed to be. Daniel could see the wood around the screw holes had deteriorated. There just wasn't enough there to support the weight with screws.

He walked over to the work bench to see what he could find and found a coffee can nearly filled with different size nuts, bolts, screws and nails. After picking through the assorted hardware he found six bolts with nuts and several washers that looked like they would do the job. He wondered what Ray had salvaged them from, and if he had intended to use them on the garage doors. The bolts were going to have to have a hole drilled all the way through the door. He needed a drill, then, he realized there wasn't any power out there. He looked in the tool box again, and pulled out something that he'd seen in a museum, once. A hand drill, he remembered the old man next to him at the exhibit, talking about it. What did he call it? A brace? Now he needed a bit. There were several in the first drawer he pulled out. He took his tools over and sat down on the ground. The hand drill made a hole through each of the old screw holes in no time, once he figured out how to push and turn at the same time. It was awkward, trying to get it started from a sideways position, but once he did, it was easy going, partly because of the condition of the wood, but it was an impressive tool.

After he drilled all the holes, he put a washer on each bolt and stuck them through the hinge and door. Then he went to the inside of the door, slipped another washer and nut on it, and tightened it as much as he could. He'd have to get one of the boys to hold the head on the other side to really tighten it down. He repeated this for the other two holes on the top hinge and the three for the bottom hinge. He swung the door. It would be perfect, once everything was tight! He took the tools back to the tool box and closed the lid.

He looked under the workbench at the slab of wood with the bear on it, again, and wondered what other cool things he might find. He started looking through some of the boxes along the side walls. They were filled with pieces of wood and scraps of metal, many of them had pictures of birds and animals drawn on them. He found an old metal folding chair and sat down for a closer look.

He seemed to be able to see Ray's creative process as he went through each of the boxes and was so fascinated with everything, that it took the sound of a vehicle to break the spell. It was the girls returning from town. He must have been in there for a couple of hours. He stood up and went to the door. Summer gave him a little wave as she passed the shed. She parked and let April and the boys take the stuff from town into the house and walked over to the shed.

"What'cha doin'?" she asked.

"I fixed the door so it closes better," Daniel said, pleased with his handy work.

"Handy and handsome, I like it," she said, and came in close enough for a kiss.

Daniel didn't let the opportunity pass him by and pulled her closer. Their lips touched and she put her arms around his waist. They held each other for several seconds.

"What made you fix these old doors?"

"I just thought I'd try to keep the weather out. There's a lot of cool stuff in there," Daniel said. "Here, hold the bolts, out there while I give these nuts a couple more turns," he said, giving her the pliers while he went inside with the wrench. "There!" he said, when they had tightened them all, and swung the door back and forth to demonstrate the quality of his repair.

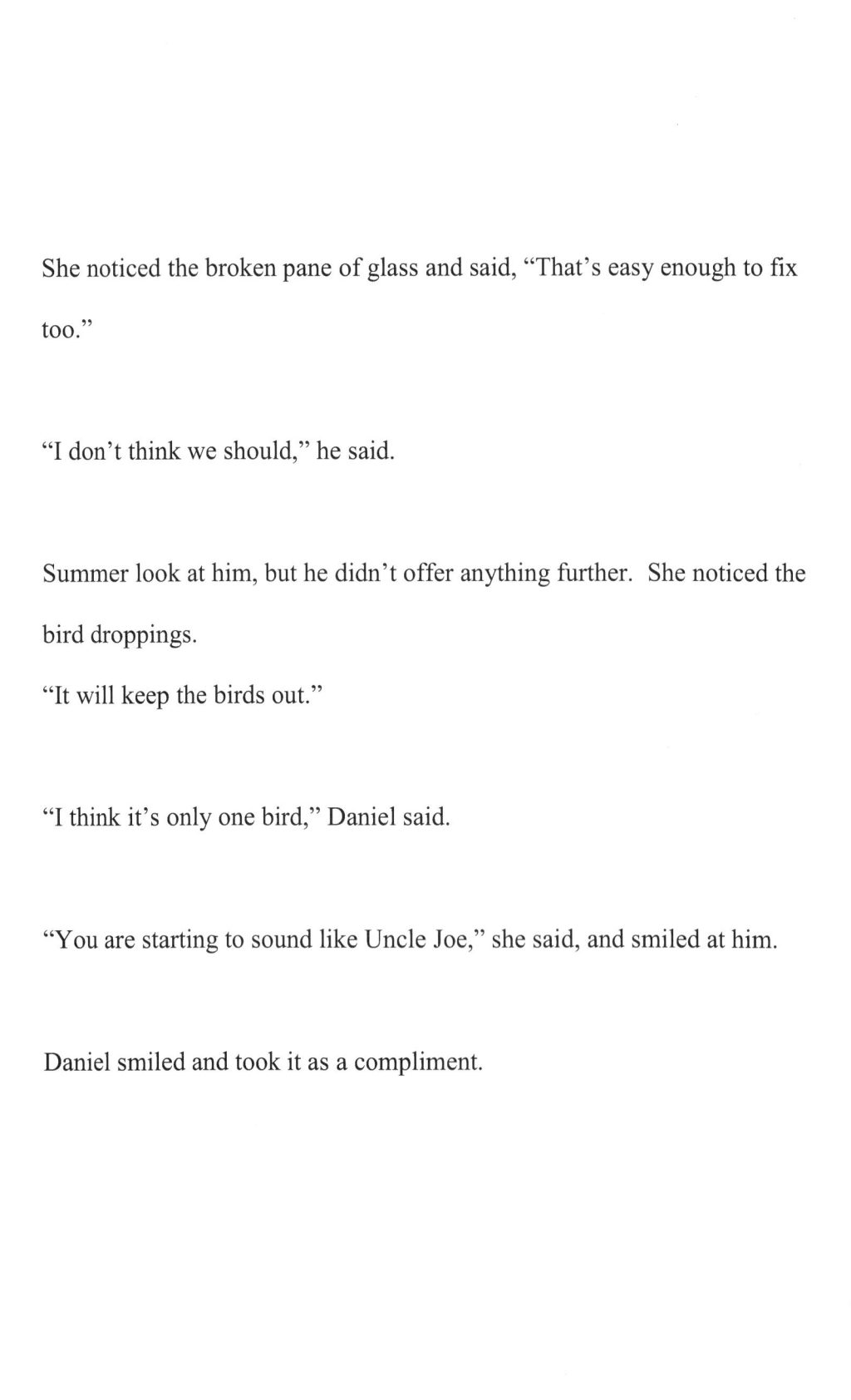

She noticed the broken pane of glass and said, "That's easy enough to fix too."

"I don't think we should," he said.

Summer look at him, but he didn't offer anything further. She noticed the bird droppings.

"It will keep the birds out."

"I think it's only one bird," Daniel said.

"You are starting to sound like Uncle Joe," she said, and smiled at him.

Daniel smiled and took it as a compliment.

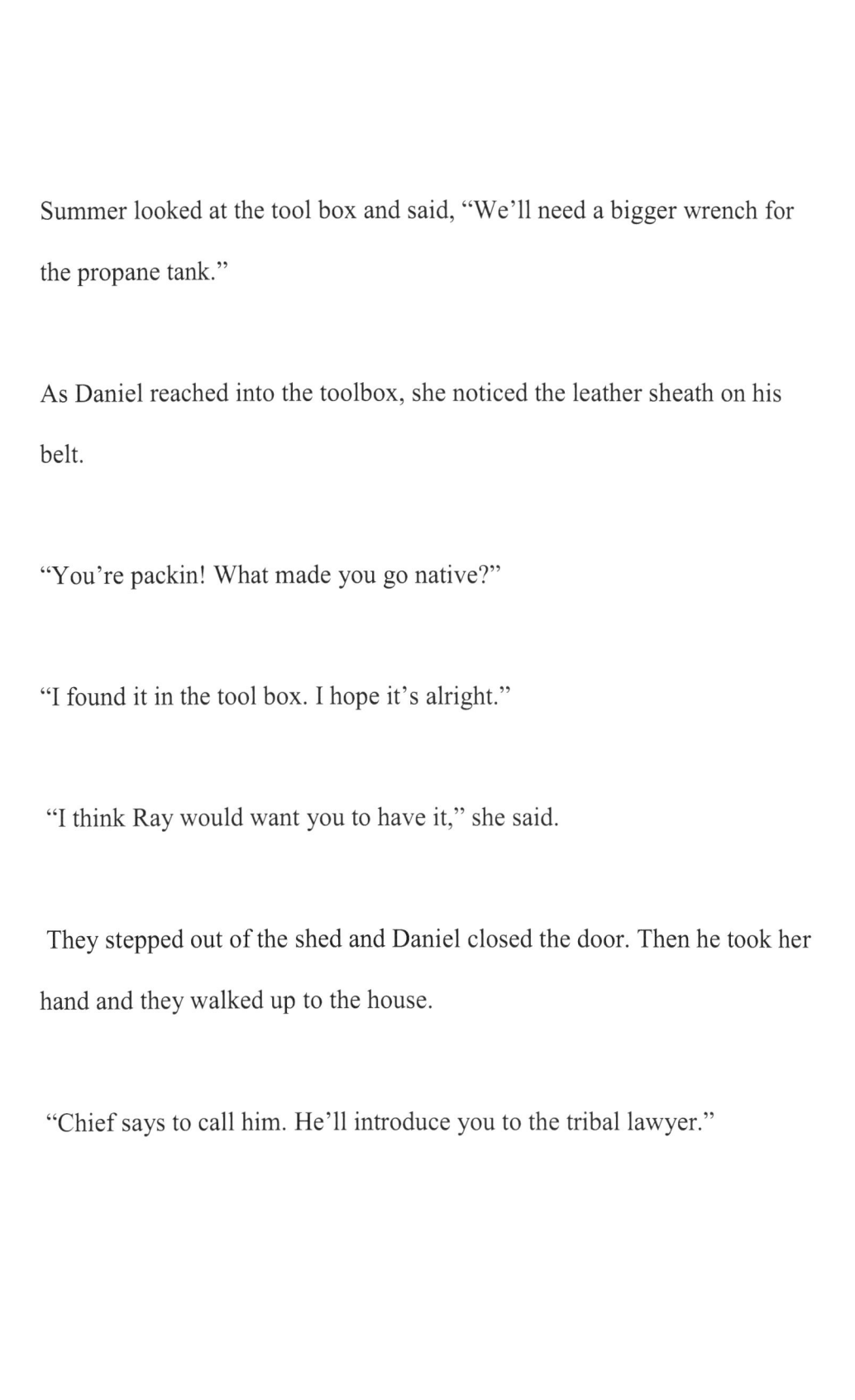

Summer looked at the tool box and said, "We'll need a bigger wrench for the propane tank."

As Daniel reached into the toolbox, she noticed the leather sheath on his belt.

"You're packin! What made you go native?"

"I found it in the tool box. I hope it's alright."

"I think Ray would want you to have it," she said.

They stepped out of the shed and Daniel closed the door. Then he took her hand and they walked up to the house.

"Chief says to call him. He'll introduce you to the tribal lawyer."

"Alright," Daniel said, as he stood up after installing the propane tank.

"Is it ready?" the boys asked together, as they came down the steps.

"Yep!" Summer said.

They ran back in the house to tell April.

"This is how you start it, at least the first six or seven times, that's about how long it lasts," Summer said, referring to the ignition button, as she pushed it a couple of times, creating a flame and adjusting the burners. "I'll go and get some meat and you can start grillin'," she said, and left to go inside.

Daniel lifted the grill top and looked at the flames and then closed it. Then he looked back at the shed. He thought it looked much better. He'd never really done any home repair stuff before, but liked how it felt to do something with his own hands. Then he looked at the house with that DIY look. There were more than a few shingles missing and it could use a coat of paint. He thought it might be fun.

Summer came out carrying a plate with two large sirloin steaks and four hot dogs on it. She set the plate on the side table and said, "There you go! Man, Fire, and Meat."

Daniel smiled and opened the grill.

"Use the brush to wipe off the rack, that'll get rid of the rest of whatever might have been on it from the factory," Summer said.

Daniel gave it a good brushing and then stuck one of the steaks with the oversized fork and put it on the grill. It made a sizzling sound as it touched the hot grill. He stabbed the other one and tossed it on. Then he put the hot dogs off to the side.

"You want to use a fairly high heat and let the steaks cook really good on one side and then turn them over. The hotdogs you want to roll them around and let them brown a little and then put 'em on the top rack," Summer instructed, and then took the plate back in to wash it and help April who had some potatoes already boiling and was making a salad.

The aroma of the meat started to fill the air and the boys came and stood next to Daniel. He opened the lid and they looked in.

"Are they ready?" they asked.

"It's getting close," Daniel said, turning the steaks and giving the hotdogs another roll. The boys ran to the house for a plate.

*****

"That was excellent! Medium rare. Good job!" Summer said, as she set her fork on her plate.

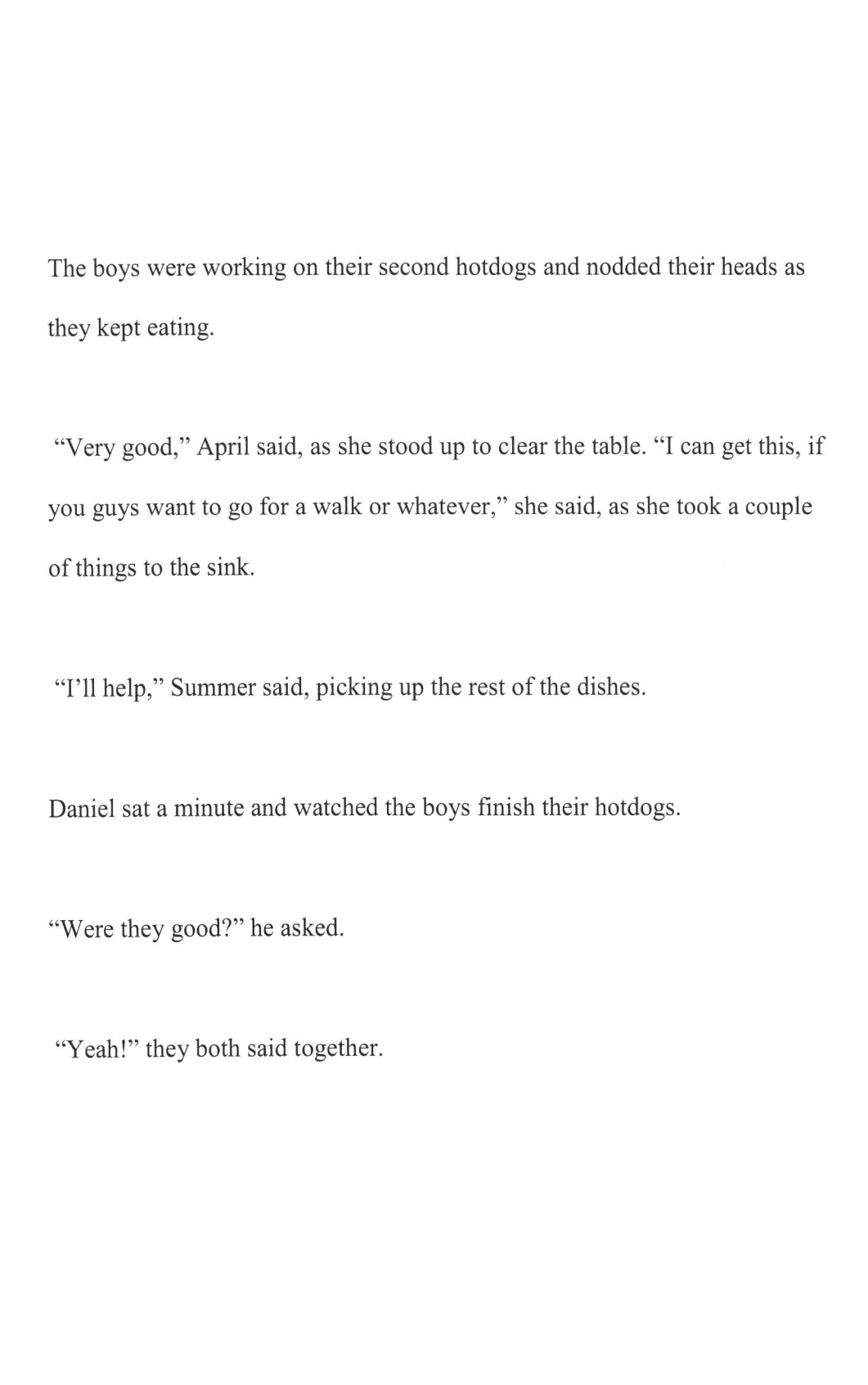

The boys were working on their second hotdogs and nodded their heads as they kept eating.

"Very good," April said, as she stood up to clear the table. "I can get this, if you guys want to go for a walk or whatever," she said, as she took a couple of things to the sink.

"I'll help," Summer said, picking up the rest of the dishes.

Daniel sat a minute and watched the boys finish their hotdogs.

"Were they good?" he asked.

"Yeah!" they both said together.

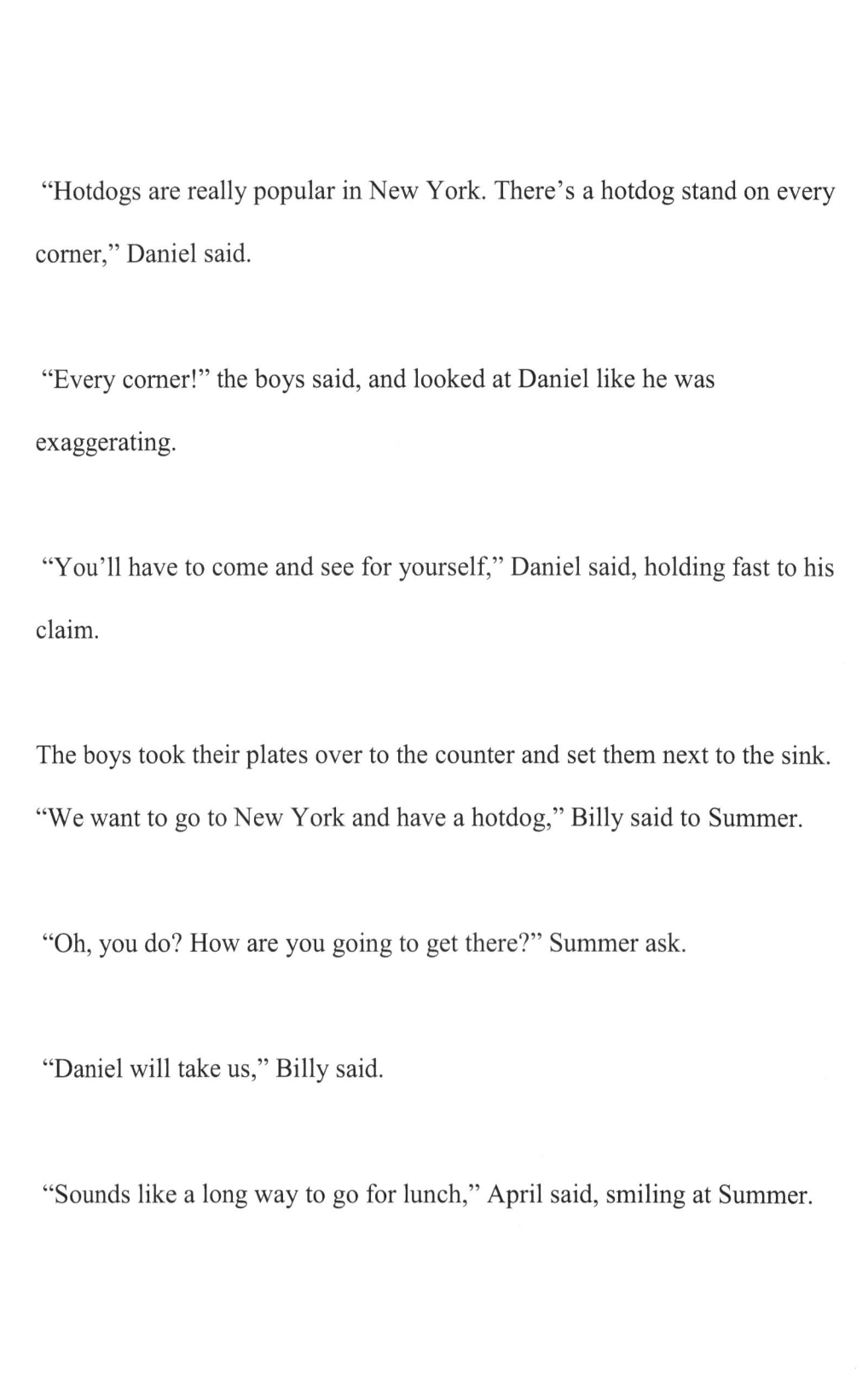

"Hotdogs are really popular in New York. There's a hotdog stand on every corner," Daniel said.

"Every corner!" the boys said, and looked at Daniel like he was exaggerating.

"You'll have to come and see for yourself," Daniel said, holding fast to his claim.

The boys took their plates over to the counter and set them next to the sink. "We want to go to New York and have a hotdog," Billy said to Summer.

"Oh, you do? How are you going to get there?" Summer ask.

"Daniel will take us," Billy said.

"Sounds like a long way to go for lunch," April said, smiling at Summer.

Summer looked over at Daniel, he had been watching what was going on and tried unsuccessfully to hide the grin on his face. She gave him a pretend scowl. It only made the twinkle in his eyes more intense.

CHAPTER 19

"Come on in," Daniel said, as he gave the door a push and flipped the light switch.

"Wow!" Billy said, opening his eyes wide for a minute and then struggled to keep them open.

"Wow is right! It's beautiful," Summer said.

 "I bet you'd like to see your room," Daniel said to Billy, and led them across the living room and down a hall way. "Here we go," he said, as he turned on the light.

"That's a big bed!" Billy said.

"Yes, it is," replied Summer, smiling at her son.

"The bathroom is in there," Daniel said, as he pointed to the door on his right.

"I'll put him to bed and be out in a few minutes," Summer said.

"Good night, Billy," Daniel said, as he walked out of the guest room and down the hall to his bedroom.

The Master bedroom ran the entire width of the suite and vertical blinds covered the windows that ran along the front wall. Daniel went into the bathroom and washed his face and brushed his teeth. He came out, just as Summer came through the bedroom door.

"He was asleep before his head hit the pillow," she said.

"We all had a long day," Daniel said, "There's the bathroom. I put some towels out for you."

"Thanks," Summer said. "It really is quite a place you have here," she added, a little nervously as she began to see the things Daniel was accustomed to… this fancy apartment, with its doorman and wall of windows that framed in the perfect view of New York and the town car that picked them up at the Airport… it was very different from Browning. "I'll bet you're glad to be home," she said, as her eyes danced around and then back to him.

"Would you like a tour?"

"Okay," she said, and took his hand as they walked back down the hall, through the living room and into the kitchen area.

The appliances and sink where along the far wall, with a countertop separating it from the living area. A formal dining room table and chairs, made of Cherry wood, sat in front of a sliding door that led out to a small patio.

Summer walked over and opened it. "You could have a grill out here."

"Against building code," Daniel said, walking over to her.

"Not much different than Great Falls," Summer said, looking out at the lights of New York.

"It is hard to tell them apart," he said, thinking back to the night in Great Falls, when he first told her, how much she meant to him. He put his arm around her and said, "we're gonna have a great time."

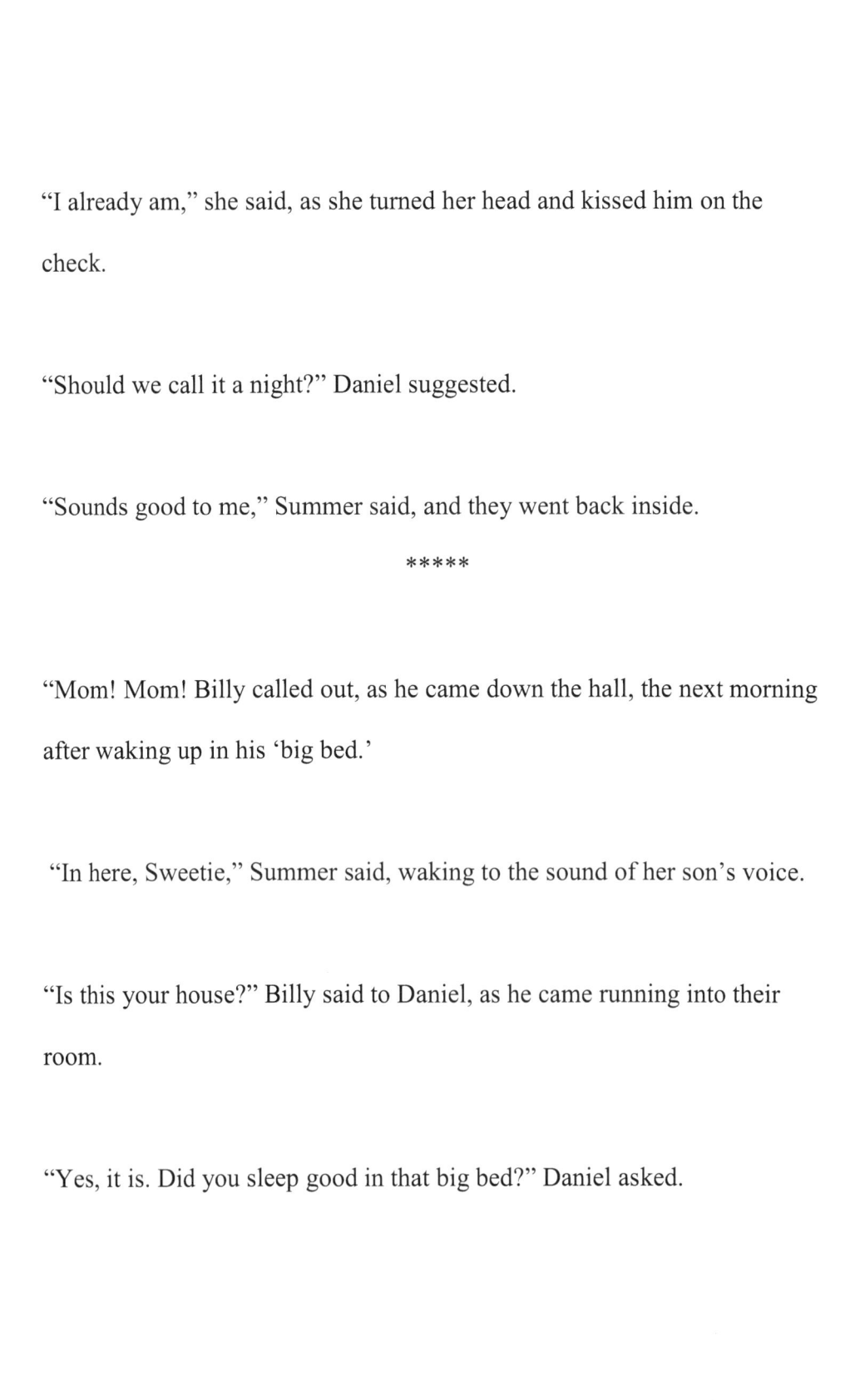

"I already am," she said, as she turned her head and kissed him on the check.

"Should we call it a night?" Daniel suggested.

"Sounds good to me," Summer said, and they went back inside.

*****

"Mom! Mom! Billy called out, as he came down the hall, the next morning after waking up in his 'big bed.'

"In here, Sweetie," Summer said, waking to the sound of her son's voice.

"Is this your house?" Billy said to Daniel, as he came running into their room.

"Yes, it is. Did you sleep good in that big bed?" Daniel asked.

"Yeah!" Billy said, chuckling.

"I've got a big screen TV. Should we see what's on?" Daniel asked.

"Yeah!" Billy said, enthusiastically.

"I'll start some coffee. If you want to shower, everything you need should be in there," he said to Summer, as he pulled on some sweatpants and took Billy out to the living room.

Daniel pressed the red TV button on the remote, as they sat down on the sofa. The 60" inch screen gave off enough light to illuminate the room. Daniel pressed guide and started flipping through the channels: Local channels, Home shopping network, TV land, Nickelodeon. "SpongeBob Square Pants is on next. Do you want to watch him for a while?"

"Okay," Billy said.

"I'm gonna go start some coffee," Daniel said, as he got up and went to the kitchen. He opened the refrigerator and took out the coffee beans, which was about all that was in there. He thought back to just before his trip out to Montana and how he'd cleaned everything out. Then he opened the freezer. "Oh, good," he said, and reached in for the can of orange juice and set it in the sink, while he ground some coffee beans and found a pitcher to make the juice. He poured two glasses of juice and went back to watch TV with Billy. "Here you go," Daniel said, as he handed Billy a glass.

"Thank you," Billy said.

They watched as a sponge wearing underpants went to the Moon with a Squirrel that lived underwater in a bubble.

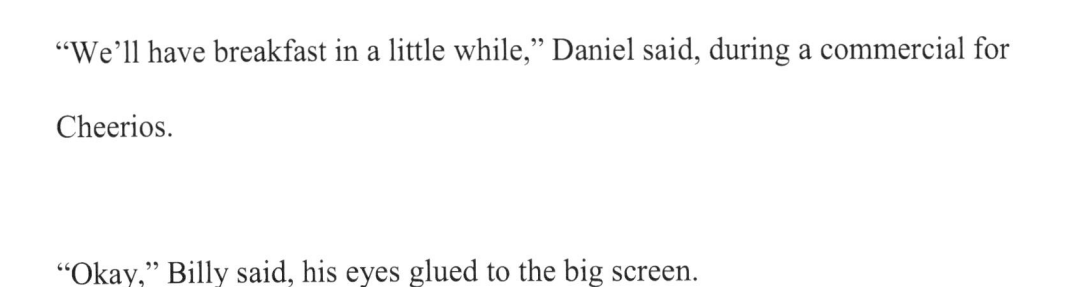

"We'll have breakfast in a little while," Daniel said, during a commercial for Cheerios.

"Okay," Billy said, his eyes glued to the big screen.

They sipped their juice and watched in silence. Another episode had started and Daniel was about to go check on the coffee, when Summer came into the room.

"Coffee?" Daniel asked.

"Sounds good," she said, and they walked back to the kitchen.

"I'll order some breakfast, there's a great restaurant just down the street that delivers the best French toast in the world," he said, as he poured two cups of coffee.

"Sounds good," Summer said, as she took her first sip.

After making the call, Daniel walked over and opened the vertical blinds a little, to let in the morning light. Billy got up and came over by him and looked out the glass wall.

"Wanna, check out the patio?" Daniel asked. They walked over to the sliding door and went outside. "What do you think?" Daniel asked, after a few minutes.

"That's a lot of big buildings," Billy said.... "The air smells funny," he added.... "And it's loud," he said, after further observation.

Daniel looked out at the city, and saw it a little differently than he did before his trip to Montana. He recalled the view from Mary's chair and thought about the endless sea of prairie grass, waving in the breeze and only the sounds the wind made as it went around the house and out buildings. "It does smell funny. It is noisy," he said.

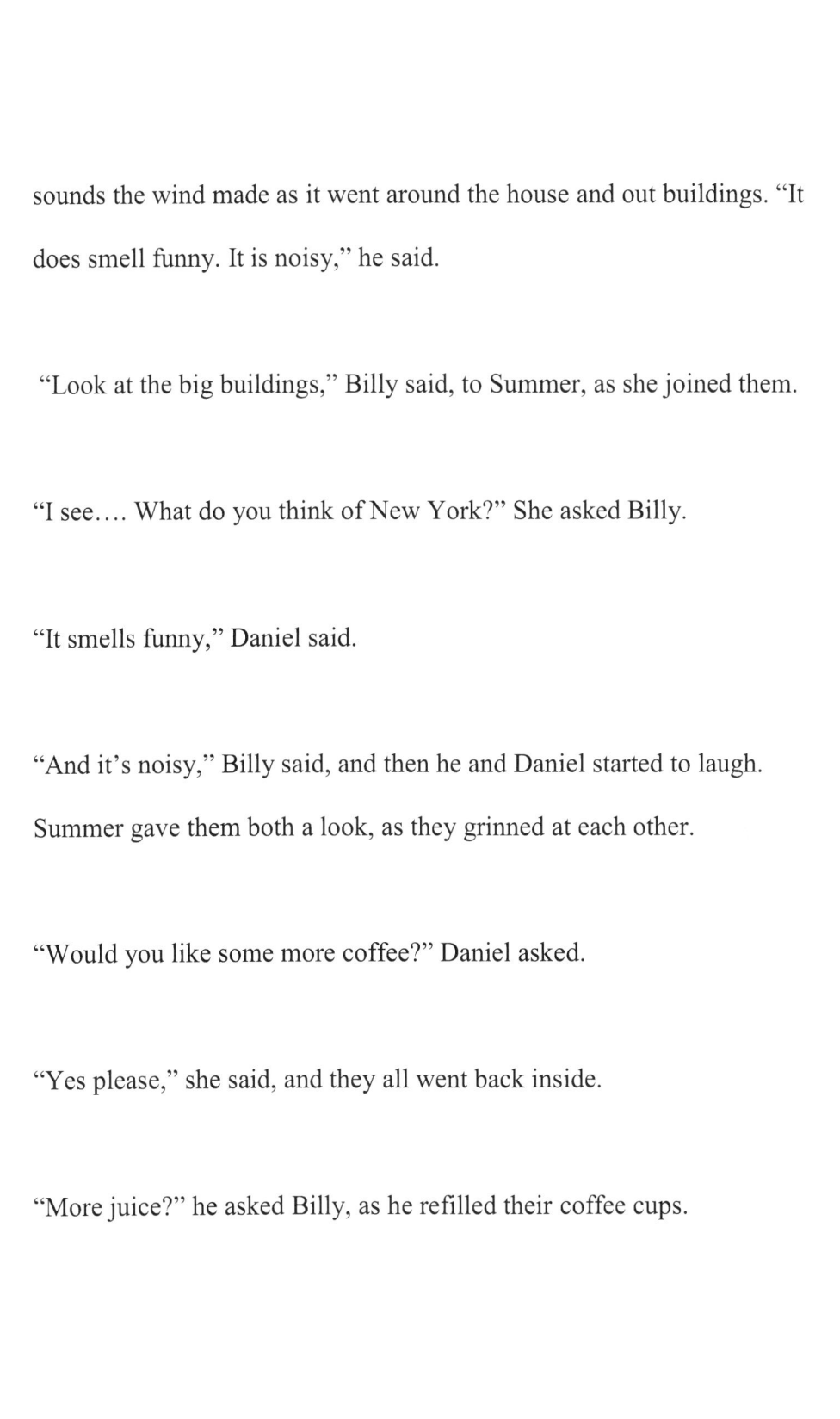

"Look at the big buildings," Billy said, to Summer, as she joined them.

"I see…. What do you think of New York?" She asked Billy.

"It smells funny," Daniel said.

"And it's noisy," Billy said, and then he and Daniel started to laugh. Summer gave them both a look, as they grinned at each other.

"Would you like some more coffee?" Daniel asked.

"Yes please," she said, and they all went back inside.

"More juice?" he asked Billy, as he refilled their coffee cups.

"Yes please," Billy answered, and handed Daniel his glass.

Summer gave her son a wink of approval, then, she said, "I see you are watching a documentary."

"It's SpongeBob Square Pants!" Billy said, chuckling.

"Go watch a little more and drink your juice and then we'll have breakfast," Daniel said.

"Okay," Billy said, and went over and sat on the couch.

Summer noticed how the two men in her life were interacting. She smiled at Daniel and said, "So how does it feel to be home?"

"It smells funny and it's noisy," he said, with some seriousness in his voice, but a smile on his face. He looked around the room, seeing it with a slightly different prospective.

"Food will be here in about 45 minutes. I'll go shower. Have some more coffee. Make yourself at home," Daniel said, as he took his cup and headed down the hall.

Summer took her coffee over to the couch and sat down next to Billy, as Elroy, from the Jetsons, was walking Astro on the dog walker.

"Is that how they walk their dogs here in the city?" Billy asked.

"You should ask Daniel," she said, with a little snicker. "Let's go shower and get ready for breakfast."

*****

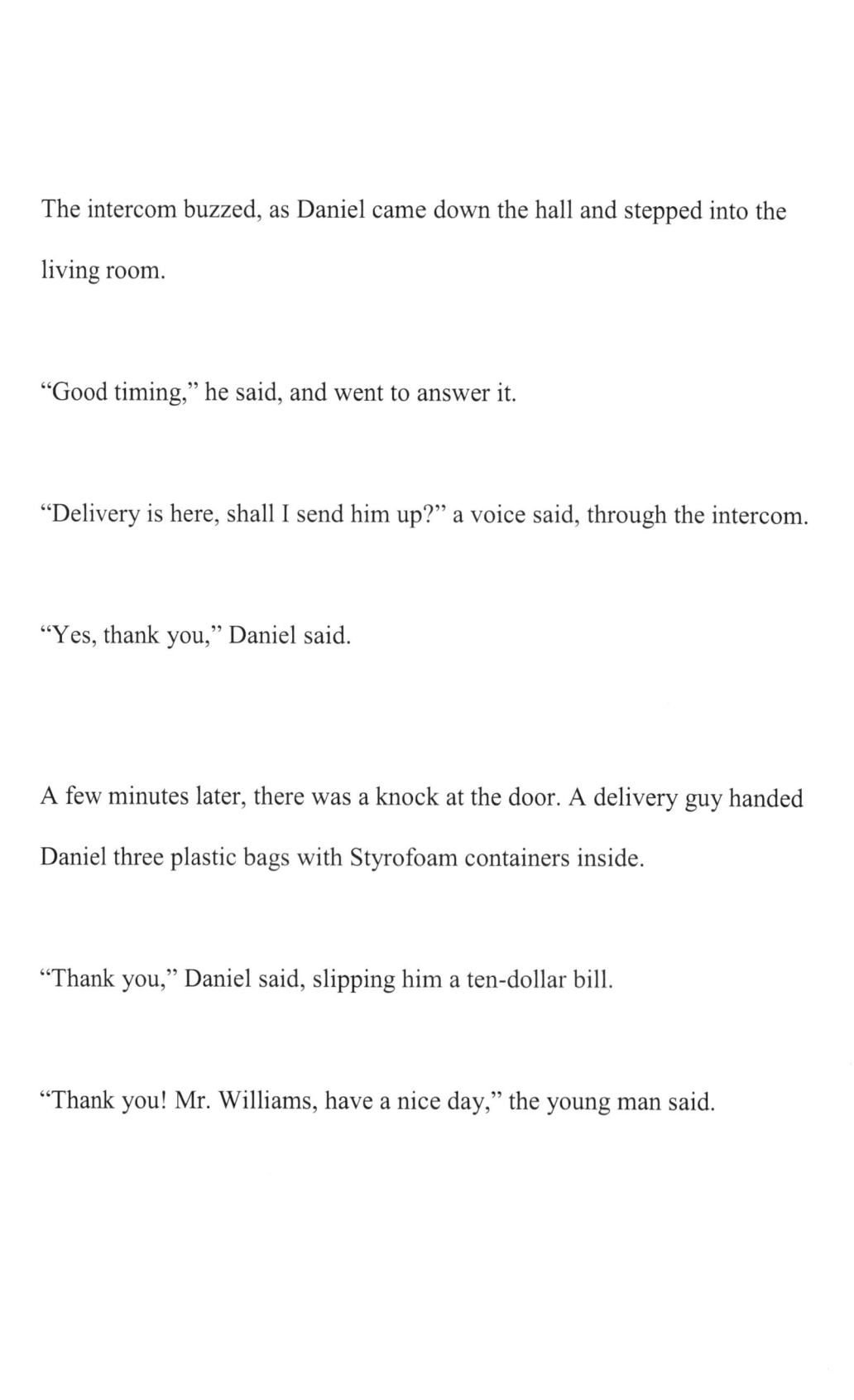

The intercom buzzed, as Daniel came down the hall and stepped into the living room.

"Good timing," he said, and went to answer it.

"Delivery is here, shall I send him up?" a voice said, through the intercom.

"Yes, thank you," Daniel said.

A few minutes later, there was a knock at the door. A delivery guy handed Daniel three plastic bags with Styrofoam containers inside.

"Thank you," Daniel said, slipping him a ten-dollar bill.

"Thank you! Mr. Williams, have a nice day," the young man said.

Daniel closed the door and took the food to the kitchen. He got some plates out and said, "Come and get it." "Dig in!" he said, presented them each with a plate of French toast, two eggs and bacon, as they sat down in the chairs across the counter from him.

"Wow!" Billy said.

"Wow, is right," Summer said.

Daniel came around and sat next to her. As they ate, he made some suggestions for their first day in the Big Apple.

"More coffee?" he asked, going around to the other side of the counter and holding out the pot.

"Maybe, just a half cup, I should go and get ready," Summer said.

He poured half a cup for each of them and put their plates in the dishwasher, then went over to the couch and sat down.

"Let's see what else is on," he said, and scrolled down the list of channels. The National Geographic channel had Horseshoe crabs coming to the Jersey Shore by the thousands to lay their eggs. "Do you want to watch the crabs, while we get ready to go out?" Daniel asked.

"Sure," Billy answered, and come over and sat next to him.

Daniel watched with him for a while and then went to get dressed and see how Summer was doing. She was just finishing at the sink and saw Daniels reflection in the mirror as he came through the door.

"Does this look alright?"

"You look great!"

"I don't look too native?"

"What?" Daniel said, giving her a funny look.

"People are going to ask you 'what you're doing with that Indian woman?'"

"Nobody is going to ask anything like that. Besides if they do, I'd tell them…." Daniel whispered in her ear.

She playfully slugged his arm and said, "Maybe later."

"Hey, how about if I wear my clothes I bought in Great Falls?"

"You packed those?" Summer said, surprised.

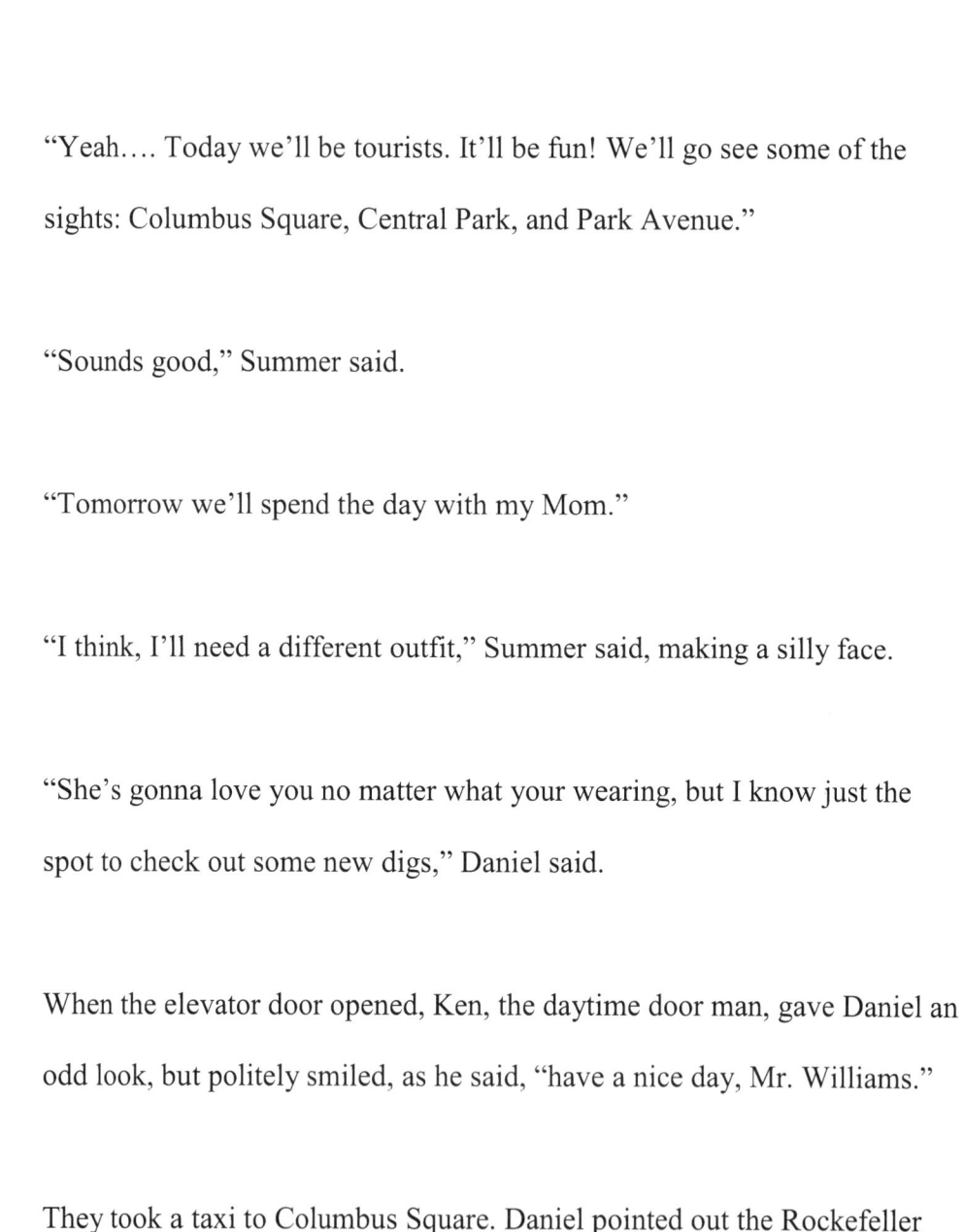

"Yeah…. Today we'll be tourists. It'll be fun! We'll go see some of the sights: Columbus Square, Central Park, and Park Avenue."

"Sounds good," Summer said.

"Tomorrow we'll spend the day with my Mom."

"I think, I'll need a different outfit," Summer said, making a silly face.

"She's gonna love you no matter what your wearing, but I know just the spot to check out some new digs," Daniel said.

When the elevator door opened, Ken, the daytime door man, gave Daniel an odd look, but politely smiled, as he said, "have a nice day, Mr. Williams."

They took a taxi to Columbus Square. Daniel pointed out the Rockefeller building and several other landmarks.

"Look! There's a hotdog stand!" Billy said.

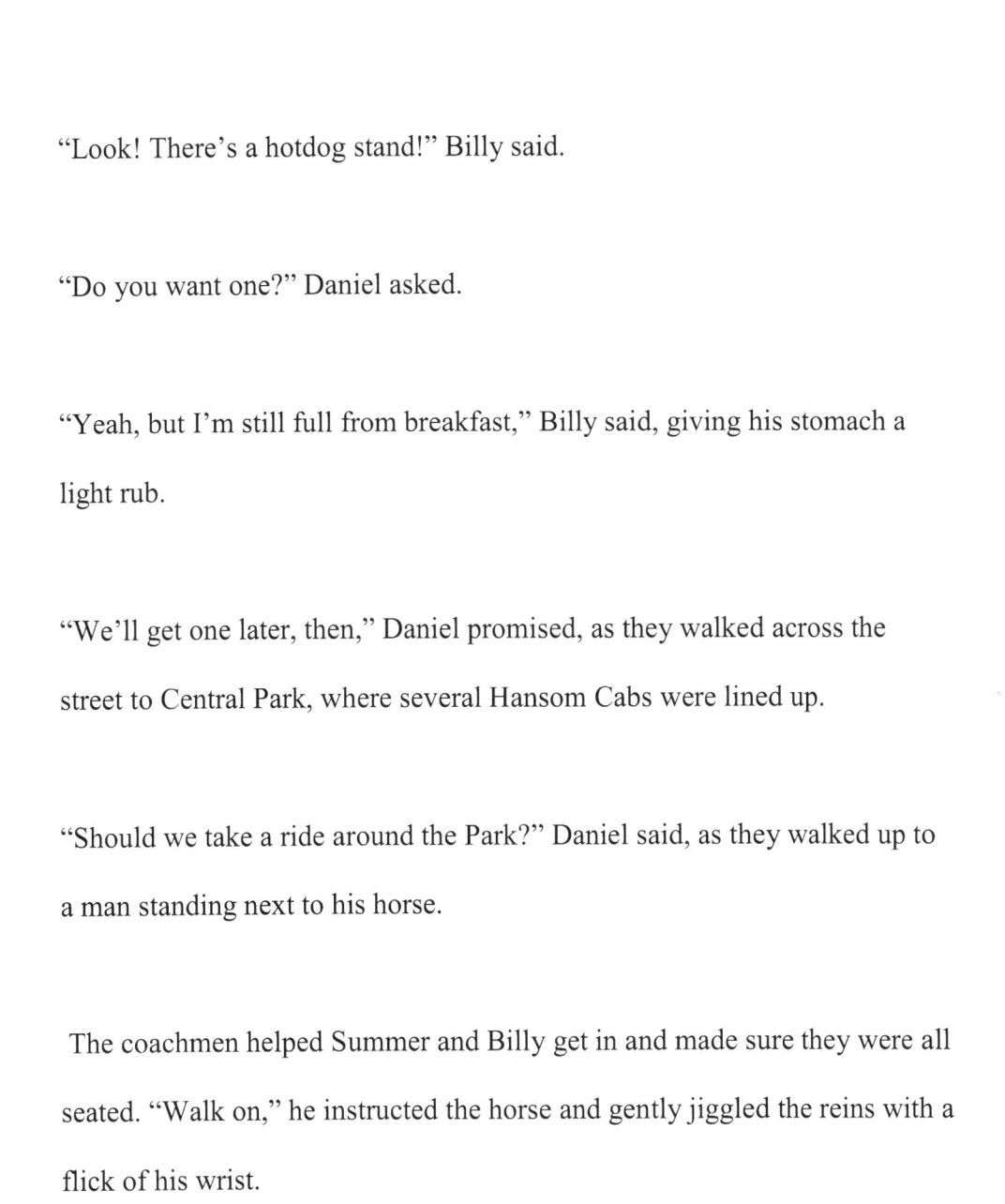

"Do you want one?" Daniel asked.

"Yeah, but I'm still full from breakfast," Billy said, giving his stomach a light rub.

"We'll get one later, then," Daniel promised, as they walked across the street to Central Park, where several Hansom Cabs were lined up.

"Should we take a ride around the Park?" Daniel said, as they walked up to a man standing next to his horse.

The coachmen helped Summer and Billy get in and made sure they were all seated. "Walk on," he instructed the horse and gently jiggled the reins with a flick of his wrist.

"We'll get off here," Daniel instructed the Coachmen, after they had gone about three quarters of the way around Central Park. They walked several blocks, people watching and looking in Department store windows as they went. Daniel stopped in front of a pair of revolving doors.

"This is mom's favorite store," he said, and led them in.

CHAPTER 20

"Breakfast is here!" Daniel said, as he made his way across the living room to the front door. He took the bags from the same delivery guy as yesterday and tipped him. The enterprising young man had quite a list of people that he had told his employer, had requested him as their guy.

"French toast and bacon! who's gonna eat that?" Summer said.

"I will!" Billy said, as he pulled the plate a little closer to him and dug in.

The other two orders were marked ham and cheese omelets. Summer put them on plates and Daniel tossed the take out boxes in the trash.

"The Car will be here at ten 'O clock. That gives us a little time after we eat to finish getting ready," he said, as they ate.

"I am ready," Summer said, trying to keep a straight face, sitting there still wearing her pajama bottoms and one of Daniels shirts.

"I like it," Daniel said, still in his sweat pants and old T-shirt. "I'll wear this, then."

"I'm going to wear my suit!" Billy announced as he finished his breakfast.

"And you are going to look so handsome! How about you watch a little TV, while you finish your juice and I'll help you get ready in a little bit," Summer said.

"Okay," Billy said, and went to the couch and turned on the big screen.

"I'll clean up here, you can… I guess, watch TV with Billy, until it's time to go. Since you're ready," Daniel said, wrinkling up his nose at Summer.

Daniel poured more coffee in her cup and she headed off to the bedroom. Then he rinsed the dishes and loaded the dish washer. He took a minute to sit with Billy on the couch. He noticed Bugs Bunny and Daffy Duck were arguing about what season it was.

"It's duck season!" Daniel said, as he sat down next to him.

"It's rabbit season!" Billy shot back, as the animated characters continue the debate, until Bugs, turns the table and Daffy ends up saying "DUCK SEASON!!" and gets blasted by a dozen hunters suddenly coming out of hiding.

Billy lets out a laugh and Daniel chuckled, remembering the cartoon from when he was little.

"We'll be out in a little bit and then I'll help you with your tie," he says, ruffling Billy's hair and starts down the hall.

Summer was standing in front of the mirror putting on a little makeup as Daniel popped his head in.

"You changed your mind?" he said, acting surprised.

"Do I look okay?" Summer asked, obviously stressing out. She was wearing the black and white dress with the big black belt and black high heels with white polka dots, she had gotten the day before.

"You look amazing!" Daniel said. "But now, I'll have to put something else on." Then he went to find the suit that matched Billy's, which he had intended to do from the start.

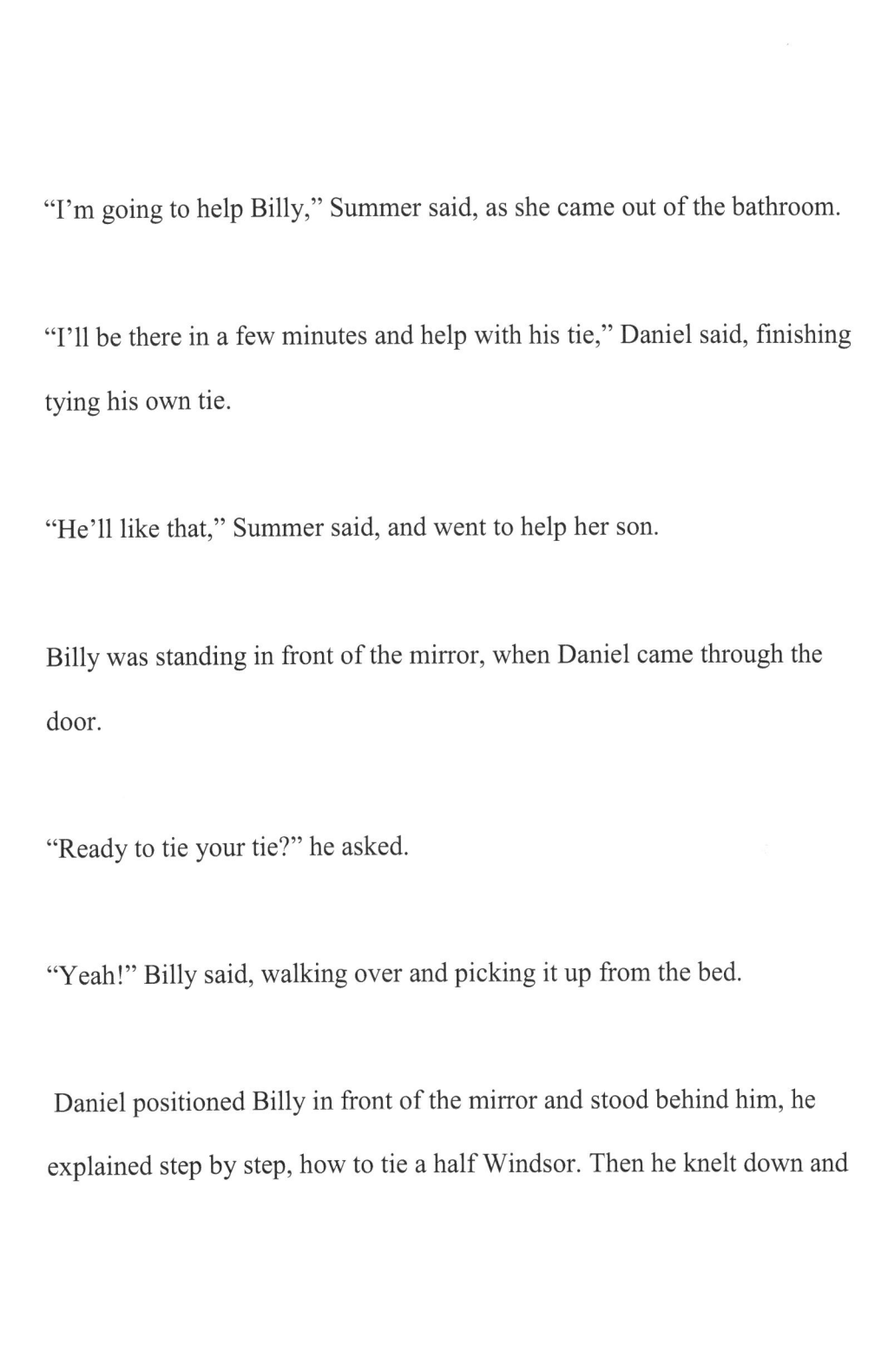

"I'm going to help Billy," Summer said, as she came out of the bathroom.

"I'll be there in a few minutes and help with his tie," Daniel said, finishing tying his own tie.

"He'll like that," Summer said, and went to help her son.

Billy was standing in front of the mirror, when Daniel came through the door.

"Ready to tie your tie?" he asked.

"Yeah!" Billy said, walking over and picking it up from the bed.

Daniel positioned Billy in front of the mirror and stood behind him, he explained step by step, how to tie a half Windsor. Then he knelt down and turned Billy, so he faced him. Daniel made a few final adjustments and helped him with his jacket.

"You look real sharp, Billy," Daniel said, and put his hand on his shoulder.

*****

"Well, I think we're ready," Summer said, making an exaggerated worried face, several minutes later as they stepped out of the apartment.

"She's going to love you," Daniel said, pulling the door shut.

CHAPTER 21

Two hours later, Daniel entered the four-digit code that opened the gate to a marina along the East River. They made their way past several rows of docks with very large boats, in fact, yachts, tied up along both sides of them. Daniel turned and started leading them down dock number ten.

"Which one is it?" Billy asked anxiously.

"The third one from the end, on the right," Daniel said.

It's beautiful!" Summer said.

"Dad bought it when I was about fifteen. We spent every 4th of July and New Years on her. He'd always wanted to be here for his birthday, too, he really loved the water."

A man in his mid- forties met them as they stepped on deck. "Good afternoon, Daniel, it's been a while," he said.

"Hello, Robert, it has. I think it was New Year's," Daniel said.

Robert had worked for his father on the boat since he'd bought it. He had started out as First Mate and had been the Captain now for five years. "Your Mother is on the aft deck," he said, gesturing with his left hand and watched as they made their way to the rear of the boat.

"Hi, Mom," Daniel said, and gave her a big hug. "This is Summer and her son Billy. Summer, this is my Mother, Evelyn."

"Welcome Summer, it's nice to meet you!" Evelyn said, and gave her a hug.

"It's nice to meet you too," Summer said.

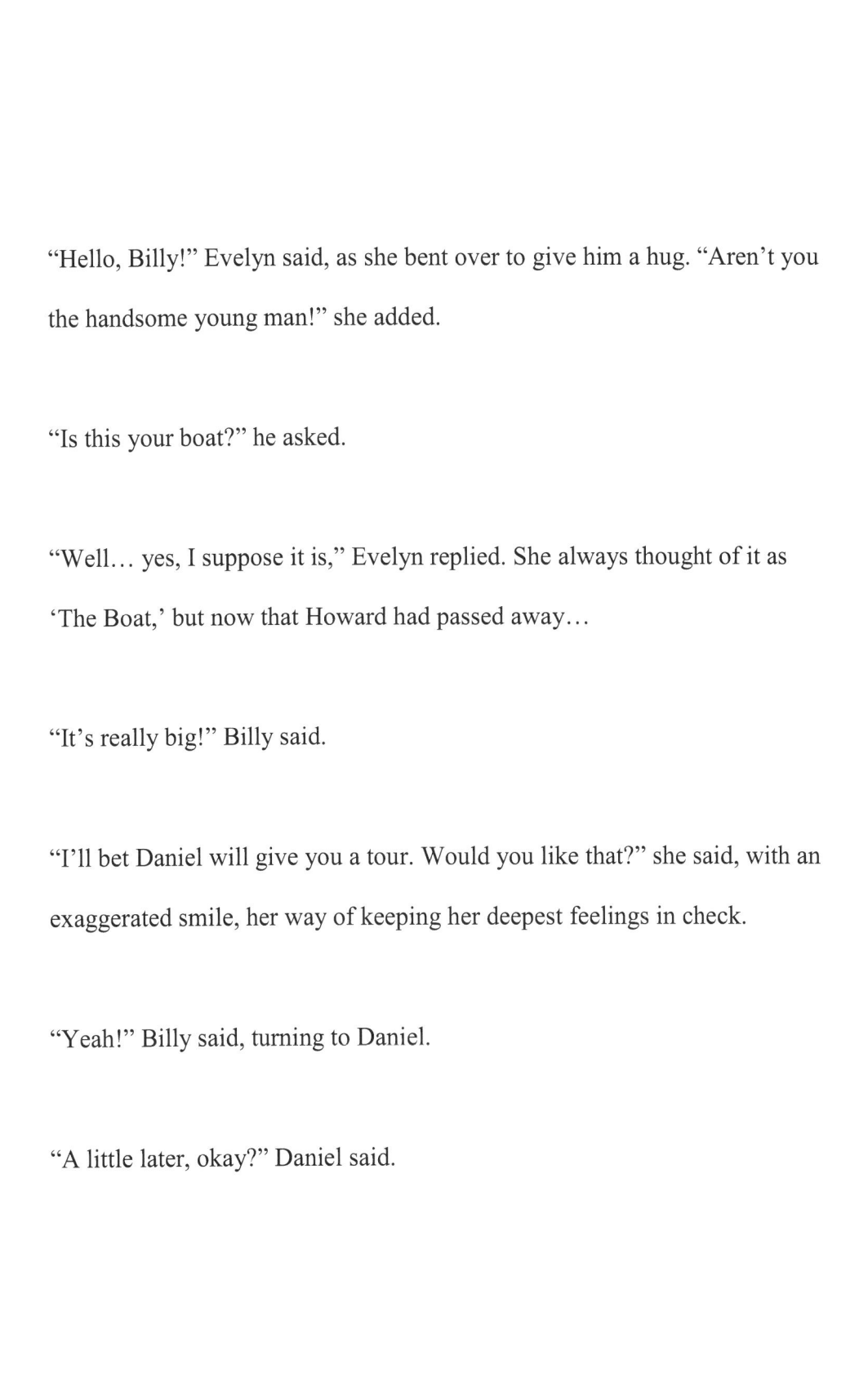

"Hello, Billy!" Evelyn said, as she bent over to give him a hug. "Aren't you the handsome young man!" she added.

"Is this your boat?" he asked.

"Well… yes, I suppose it is," Evelyn replied. She always thought of it as 'The Boat,' but now that Howard had passed away…

"It's really big!" Billy said.

"I'll bet Daniel will give you a tour. Would you like that?" she said, with an exaggerated smile, her way of keeping her deepest feelings in check.

"Yeah!" Billy said, turning to Daniel.

"A little later, okay?" Daniel said.

"Okay," Billy said.

"Come, sit," Evelyn said, and led them to a table and chairs. "Is this your first visit to New York?" Evelyn asked, Summer.

"Yes, it is," Summer replied.

"That's a very pretty outfit, Ralph Loren, from Bloomindales? That's my favorite store," Evelyn said.

"Thank you, we did a little shopping yesterday," Summer said, and smiled at Daniel.

"Well, you and I will do more than a little shopping, one day this week, when Daniel goes into the office… and we will have to take in at least one Broadway show," Evelyn said. She was eager to learn more about the lovely young woman that her son had brought home. "So, tell me a little about yourself," Evelyn said.

"Well, I was born in Browning. I grew up there. I graduated from MSU, in Missoula. I majored in art history. I moved back to Browning right after I graduated to help take care of my Mother. She had a heart attack, my junior year. I thought the move was only temporary. I started seeing a guy that I had dated in High School and well… I got pregnant. My Mother died a month before Billy was born. The week after he was born, my sister, April, found out she was pregnant. We help each other out. She watches the Boys. I work at the Art Gallery in Browning. That's where Daniel and I met," Summer said.

"So, Art! Well… we will definitely have to go to the Metropolitan Museum…. I can see right now, you'll have to extend your stay so we can get everything in," Evelyn said, and then looked at Daniel. He had a big smile on his face, as he held Summers hand under the table. Evelyn could see they were very happy together. She was happy for her son and could see why Daniel was so attracted to her. She thought Summer was absolutely charming. Evelyn looked at Billy sitting between her and Summer, he reminded her of Daniel at that age. He was so very well behaved. He sat there watching the boats, as they went up and down the river and the birds as they flew by, making a racket, as they swooped over the water. She discreetly pressed a call button on the edge of the table next to her hand. A few minutes later a young woman came to the table. "Connie, would you please bring a bottle of Champaign and … Billy what would you like? Evelyn asked.

"A Coke?" Billy responded.

"And a Coke," Evelyn said, with a smile.

"Yes, Ma'am," Connie said, and left to get the beverages. When Connie returned she poured three glasses of Champaign and opened the can of Coke, pouring some in a glass of ice.

"Thank you, Connie," Evelyn said, as Connie left with the tray. "I'd like to make a toast, to Daniels return and the wonderful treasures he has found," Evelyn said, as she raised her glass. They sipped from their glasses. There were a few minutes of silence, as they enjoyed the Champaign and took in the beautiful day on the water. As they started to discuss plans for the week ahead, Billy started to get a little restless.

"I have to pee," he said, trying to whisper in his Mothers ear, but saying it a little louder than he intended.

"I'll take him," Daniel volunteered, and took Billy inside.

Evelyn smiled at Summer and said, "He's a lovely boy. He reminds me of Daniel, when he was young.... Would you like me to show you around? I'll bet we find the Boys up on the Captains Bridge in about ten minutes."

"Yes, that sounds like fun," Summer answered.

Evelyn led Summer, through the Galley and lounge and then to the State Rooms. They could hear Billy asking Robert, what all the controls were for, as they made their way up steps to the bridge.

"I thought we'd find you up here," Evelyn said, to Daniel.

"I was showing Billy around," he said.

"Yes, I was giving Summer a little tour, too. We were thinking it might be nice if we all stayed on board tonight. You could go into the Office from here and we could get an earlier start on our day."

Daniel looked at Summer, as she gave him a look of approval. "Sure. Why not?" he said, realizing the decision had already been made and he was merely being informed

CHAPTER 22

The next morning Daniel got up and went to the Galley, he put some coffee on and then walked out onto the rear deck. He had always loved being on the water; this morning, however, as he took in the sights and sounds of the river, he noticed a funny smell. It made him think of Billy's comment. He took a closer look around the marina, and saw the oil and gas rings, floating around the docks. As he looked across the river at the towering buildings, he thought about all the people inside them and what a burden human beings put on the earth. He went back inside to get some coffee, as he poured a cup, Summer walked in wearing a pair of his pajamas.

"Coffee?" Daniel asked.

"Yes," she said, nodding her head, still a little sleepy. She followed him to the lounge and curled up next to him on the sofa.

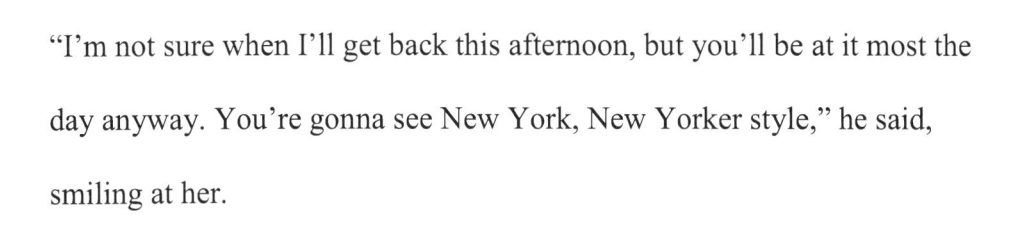

"I'm not sure when I'll get back this afternoon, but you'll be at it most the day anyway. You're gonna see New York, New Yorker style," he said, smiling at her.

"I thought that's what we did yesterday?" Summer said.

"That was nothing, compared to what you'll see today," he said, and smiled.

"I'm sure it will be fun, I like her," she said, and gave him a quick smooch on the lips

"Yeah, I saw the two of you concocting some sort of plan after dinner last night."

Summer tried to hide her smile behind her cup, but her eyes sparkled mischievously. It made him happy to see her so happy.

"The car will be here shortly, I'd better get going," he said, and leaned in to kiss her, just as his phone buzzed with a text, to say the car was waiting. The buzz from his phone, through his timing off and the kiss came up a little short; but he was already heading for the door, and said, "See you tonight!"

"So, now I know what it will be like when we're seventy-something," Summer said, teasingly about the less than passionate kiss.

"I'm sorry. I guess I was thinking about the office and everything. Come here," he said, and opened his arms. He gave her a more heart felt kiss on the lips. This time, he projected his love in a slightly more dramatic way.

"Alright. Now you're just being silly. Get out of here," she said.

It was nine-thirty, when the Town Car stopped to let Daniel out.

"Two hours just to get across the river, what a pain in the ass," he said, as he got out, remembering how easy it was to drive the Escalade in the streets of Great Falls.

He grinned as he looked up at the granite building and thought, 'what am I doing comparing the two cities? It's part of normal life here.' The word normal stuck in his mind for a second.

He made his way through the crowd to the elevator, and was one of the last to get on before the door closed. The elevator stopped on nearly every floor and it seemed the people getting off first, were the ones furthest back. Daniel thought it took forever to get to his floor.

"Welcome back!" Betty said, from behind the desk. "How was Montana?"

"Amazing! I think I could get used to all that open space…would you let Steve know I'd like to see him, when he's available," Daniel said, and started down the hall to his own office.

*****

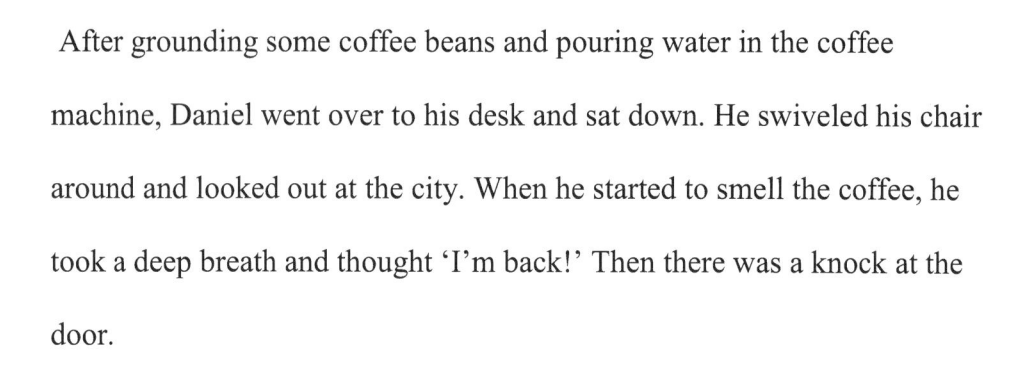

After grounding some coffee beans and pouring water in the coffee machine, Daniel went over to his desk and sat down. He swiveled his chair around and looked out at the city. When he started to smell the coffee, he took a deep breath and thought 'I'm back!' Then there was a knock at the door.

"Come in," Daniel said.

"Hey, welcome back!" Steve said, as he came forward and shook Daniels hand.

"It's good to be back," Daniel said, "Coffee?"

"Yes, please," Steve replied.

Daniel poured two cups and they went over to the conference table and sat down.

"This is exactly where we were about ten weeks ago," Steve said, "So how was it?"

Daniel looked at him for a second and wondered what Steve would think if he told him everything that had gone on. "It was unbelievable," Daniel said, finding a little irony in his response. "The openness, the mountains, the blue sky, it was all so peaceful."

Steve looked at Daniel and noticed something different about him. "So you told me, when we talked on the phone, that you had made a few discoveries," Steve said, trying to help the conversation along.

"Yes! I have a Great Uncle. He showed me a picture of my birth parents before they were married. I met Summer and her Son, Billy. I saw the town I was born in. I saw the

Reservation…" Daniel paused, "I wasn't prepared for the poverty and the lack of opportunity," he paused again, to take a sip from his cup.

Steve waited thoughtfully, he knew Daniel well enough to know that once he started talking, a flood gate would open.

Daniel told him about how he had met Mary and how she had turned out to be Summers Grandmother and how she had sent him to Uncle Joe. He knew he couldn't tell him everything. He knew Steve would think he was off his rocker, if he told him about seeing Mary's ghost and watching Uncle Joe's head turn into that of a bear. He heard himself telling Steve about the day they went out to where the Buffalo were found and how they were killed and left to rot. As he retold part of the legend of the White Buffalo and its significance to the Blackfeet People, he felt like someone else was talking and he was listening. He described the tension between the Indians and some of the Ranchers, who felt the range was theirs to control, and were using lobbyists to influence and pressure state legislators to restrict where buffalo were allowed to roam.

"I feel like I need to do something," Daniel said.

There was silence, while Steve considered what Daniel had said. He tugged on his whiskers for a minute, then, put his finger tips together and rested his forearms on the edge of the table. "Politics, Elected Officials, Lobbyists, Quid Pro quo," Steve said, as he sat back in his chair clasping his hands together behind his head. "I'm behind you all the way, what is it you'd like to do?"

"I want to bring the buffalo home! I want the symbol of the Blackfeet People restored, and I want to remind Washington that the Native Americans were here first and they are still here and their voice must be heard and their beliefs honored," Daniel said.

"So buy a ranch and get some buffalo, give it a colorful name, everyone will say, 'look there's some buffalo,'" Steve said.

"No, that's not it. I want them to be treated like any other native species, not restricted to this place or that place. Did you know buffalo are the only North American animal not allowed to roam free? And had it not been for Teddy Roosevelt and the Boone and Crocket Club, the last genetically pure herd would have been completely wiped out by the end of the nineteenth century. Even now, more than one hundred years later, their numbers are strictly regulated and they are subject to hazing and shipped off to slaughter, if they leave Yellowstone Park in search of food," Daniel said, starting to get a little defensive.

"What species are you talking about, again?" Steve said, beginning to do, what he does, in a manner, that shows why his time, commands six hundred dollars an hour.

"The buffalo!" Daniel said, then feeling his face get warm, because he had taken the bait.

"It sounded like you were talking about a group of people," Steve said. After a few seconds, he added, "I think you found something out there, something that was always deep inside of you. Something you needed to find for yourself. Do you remember what your Dad used to say?"

"If you don't have passion, you're just going through the motions," they both, said together."

"So let's use that passion I just saw to achieve the goal. You say, 'return the buffalo and give the Native Americans a louder voice.' I'm thinking, give the Native Americans a louder voice and return the buffalo…. So how are we going to get a louder voice?" Steve said.

"Money?" Daniel said.

"How are we gonna get the money?" Steve asked.

"The old fashion way, anyway we can," Daniel said, with a smile, glad to have Steve on his side.

"Sustainable energy! Now there's an idea. Create jobs by using natural renewable resources. I'm sure there are government grants," Steve said, nodding his head.

"Yes!" Daniel said, making the connection. There is so much in the Native American culture about treating the earth with respect. Getting involved with wind turbines or Solar panels sounded like an excellent idea.

"I have a client with some experience in renewable energy; he might have some ideas. I can talk to him about it," Steve said.

"Yes! That sounds great!" Daniel said, as he started to think of all the possibilities.

"I have to be in court this afternoon, but I'll make a call tomorrow and we'll see what I can come up with," Steve said.

"Sounds good. Thanks!" Daniel said, as they stood up.

"It's good to have you back," Steve said.

*****

As soon as Steve left, Daniel started researching wind and solar energy on his lap top. He was encouraged by how many different government grants and loans that were available as incentives to businesses.

Around two o'clock Daniel's cell phone rang. It was his Mother.

"Daniel, how are things going? I was wondering if I could make dinner reservations somewhere and you could meet us there straight from the office?" She said.

"Yeah, that's a great idea. I will wrap things up here in a little bit. Let me know. Love you, too," he said, as he turned his phone off and returned to the article on harnessing the sun and wind.

CHAPTER 23

Daniel arrived at the restaurant first. While he waited for the others, he looked around at the other tables. All the men were wearing jackets and ties. This was one of his Mothers favorite restaurants. It was where she liked to come for the 'Special Occasions.' It was where she and Daniel had dinner, just before he had left for Montana. She had told him, even though it was just the two of them, it felt like his father was there, with them. He wished he could be there with all of them tonight.

It wasn't long and he saw the host bringing the rest of his party to the table. Summer was wearing a beautiful dress and had her hair done differently. She smiled as soon as she saw Daniel. Daniel stood, as they reached the table and help her with her chair.

"You look absolutely beautiful! I like the hair. The dress is gorgeous." Then he noticed the jewelry: Diamond earrings, necklace and a ring. "It looks like you had quite a day," he said, quietly.

"We did a little shopping," Evelyn said, coming to Summers defense. "I never had a daughter to do things with. I think I could get used to it," she added, and gave Summer a little wink.

"How was your day? Billy," Daniel asked. "Good… Grandma says, she's gonna take me to see the Lion King!" he said.

"She did?" Daniel said, looking at his Mother.

"Yes, she did," Evelyn said, as she made a face that expressed her contentment with the new title. "We were thinking it might be nice if we all stayed on the boat, again, tonight," she added.

"All right," Daniel said, seeing the two of them had already discussed it.

Later that evening Summer and Daniel were in their room.

"You had a nice time today?" Daniel asked, as Summer changed into the pajamas she had worn the night before.

"Yes, it was probably one of the best days of my life…. I don't just mean all the beautiful things; it was hard to let her spend that kind of money on me, I don't make in a year what this necklace cost," she said, touching the diamonds that hung around her neck. It was how I was being treated. It was like having another Mother…. I'll be out in a minute," she said, as she closed the bathroom door.

Daniel took off his clothes and stretched across the bed in just his boxer briefs and T-shirt. The ceiling fan made him start thinking about wind turbines, and he was in the middle of something, when the bathroom door opened.

"Oh, are you tired? Maybe we should turn out the light and go right to sleep. It is eight o' clock," Summer said, in a patronizing tone.

"No, I was just thinking… we can watch some TV," he said, as he propped himself up on his left elbow, and looked at Summer, standing at the foot of the bed. Instead of the men's pajamas, she was now wearing a little black two piece, like you might get from Victoria Secret.

"Your mother said, we shouldn't forget about you, when we were out today, and kept an eye on Billy, while I went looking for something. But if your too busy thinking, or you want to watch TV," she said, as she walked over beside him. She stood over him for a minute, letting him get a look up the short top, then, she leaned over and kissed him.

"So you're not too busy or too tired? Are you sure, you aren't going to miss something on TV?" Summer continued playfully, as she crawled on top of him, pinning his arms to the bed. "But we can't get too wild. Your Mother and Billy are in the next room," she said, kissing him.

"Do you want me to just lay here then?" he asked innocently.

"Well! I guess we can blame some waves on rough seas," she said, as she let him flip her onto her back.

The next morning, Daniel woke up with his arms wrapped around her. He listened as she slept. He watched her shoulder, move up and down with each breath. The scent of her hair and the traces of perfume on her neck started to arouse him. He thought about last night. "You are incredible," he said softly, and moved in a little closer, feeling her heat.

She stirred a little and touched his hand, letting him hold her, as she woke up.

After a bit she reached around behind her and said, "Is this a stickup?"

"That's right and I'm not afraid to use it," Daniel said.

She turned toward him and kissed him on the lips, putting her arms around his neck and said "Yeah? Well I know a dozen ways to disarm you."

"Is Billy going to be okay or should we check on him?" Daniel asked.

"Do you think you should be walking around… in your condition?" Summer asked. "Your mother said, we should sleep in, she said, she'd watch Billy and make him breakfast," Summer added.

They melted into each other's arms as the world disappeared around them. Then, they fell into a contented sleep, at least Daniel did. Summer, laid there, with his arm over her shoulder; her mind was too busy thinking, but she did close her eyes, for a little while. She felt so relaxed, so happy, as she gently stroked his arm. After a bit, she carefully slipped out of bed and into the bathroom. She had managed to shower and get dressed without waking him and so, she quietly went to see how Billy was doing.

"Morning," Summer said, as she walked into the galley and put her hands on Billy's shoulders.

"Morning!" Billy said, sitting at the counter, with a big stack of pancakes in front of him. "Grandma made pancakes!" he said, with a slightly sticky face.

"I see!" Summer said.

Evelyn turned from the grill and said, "Morning! Coffee?"

"Yes, please," Summer said, and took a seat next to Billy. "Thank you," she said, as she took a sip, then let out a sigh of satisfaction.

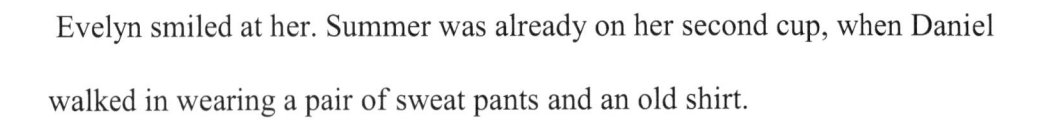

Evelyn smiled at her. Summer was already on her second cup, when Daniel walked in wearing a pair of sweat pants and an old shirt.

"Good Morning! Coffee?" Evelyn said.

"Yes, please," Daniel replied, and sat next to Summer.

Evelyn let him have his first cup in peace, and then, as she poured the second one said, "if it's alright, today, I'd like to take Billy to the Pier and then to The Lion King. Would that be alright?"

"Of course," Summer said.

"Would the two of you like any pancakes?" Evelyn offered, unable to conceal her excitement.

"Yes, please," Daniel said.

"Can I help?" Summer offered.

"No, you just relax. You're on vacation," Evelyn said, picking up the batter bowl, I'm doing just fine," she added, as she merrily, poured several scoops of batter on the griddle.

After breakfast Summer took Billy and got him ready. He picked his dark blue khaki pants and a light blue Polo shirt.

"You be good for Evelyn and stay close to her. Okay?" Summer said, standing behind her son, as she looked at him in the mirror.

"Grandma!" Billy said, turning and looking up at her.

"Okay! Grandma," Summer said, thinking of her own mother. It made her sad to think she never got to meet either of her grandchildren. They went back to the lounge. Daniel had gone to take a shower and Evelyn went to go put herself together, now that Billy was done.

"Can I have some orange juice?" Billy asked.

Summer got some juice for him and then they went out on deck and sat down.

"This is a nice boat," Billy said, looking around.

"Yes, it is," Summer said, as she looked at her son, wondering what he thought about everything and if he even realized the shift in status, that comes from being able to have the means to have a 'nice boat' and the crew to run it, or to have all the nice things, they were suddenly surrounded with. It was a little hard for her to adjust to all of this and hoped it wouldn't change him, too much.

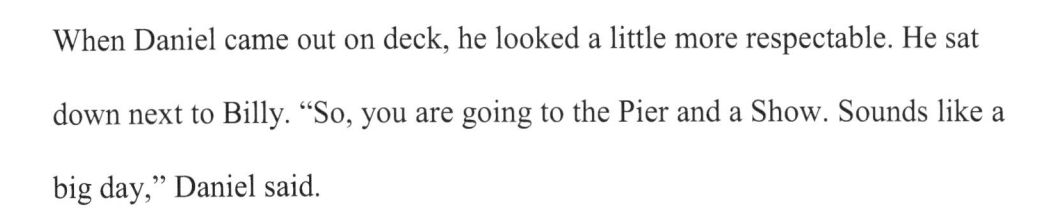

When Daniel came out on deck, he looked a little more respectable. He sat down next to Billy. "So, you are going to the Pier and a Show. Sounds like a big day," Daniel said.

"Yep," Billy replied.

"The Pier is a great spot to have a hotdog; some people think it's the best!" Daniel said.

Evelyn walked out on deck and over to them. "Are you ready to hit the town with Grandma?" she said.

Daniel noticed her eyes sparkling, as she said it.

"Make your own dinner plans, we'll be gone all day," she said.

Billy got up and took her hand.

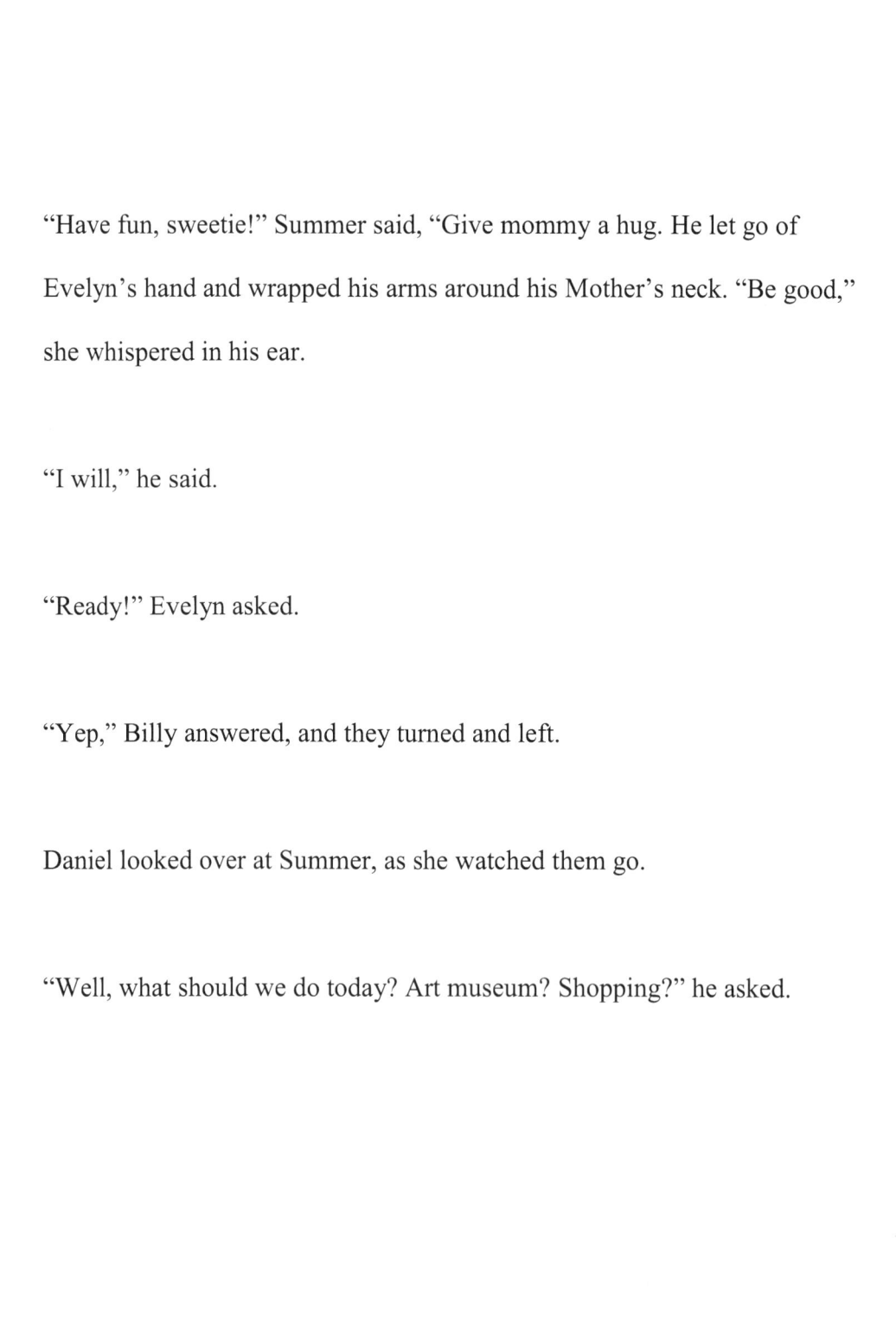

"Have fun, sweetie!" Summer said, "Give mommy a hug. He let go of Evelyn's hand and wrapped his arms around his Mother's neck. "Be good," she whispered in his ear.

"I will," he said.

"Ready!" Evelyn asked.

"Yep," Billy answered, and they turned and left.

Daniel looked over at Summer, as she watched them go.

"Well, what should we do today? Art museum? Shopping?" he asked.

Summer looked at him a moment, then; she got up and held out her hand.

Daniel stood up and she led him below deck to discuss their options.

Chapter 24

"How about a coffee break?" Daniel asked, as they circled back to the main lobby of the Metropolitan Art Museum. She nodded her head and they made their way to a concession area. "Penny for your thoughts," he said.

"It's just so amazing!" was all she managed to say, as she looked at him with glazed over eyes. "Being right here with some of the paintings and sculptures, I studied in college. And all the new exhibits… it's amazing," she said, and smiled, as she reached across the little table for his hand. "I can't believe I'm here. I'm so glad we came."

"Tomorrow we could go to Carnegie Hall or the Historical Society Museum or …" Daniel said, sounding like an ambassador for the city.

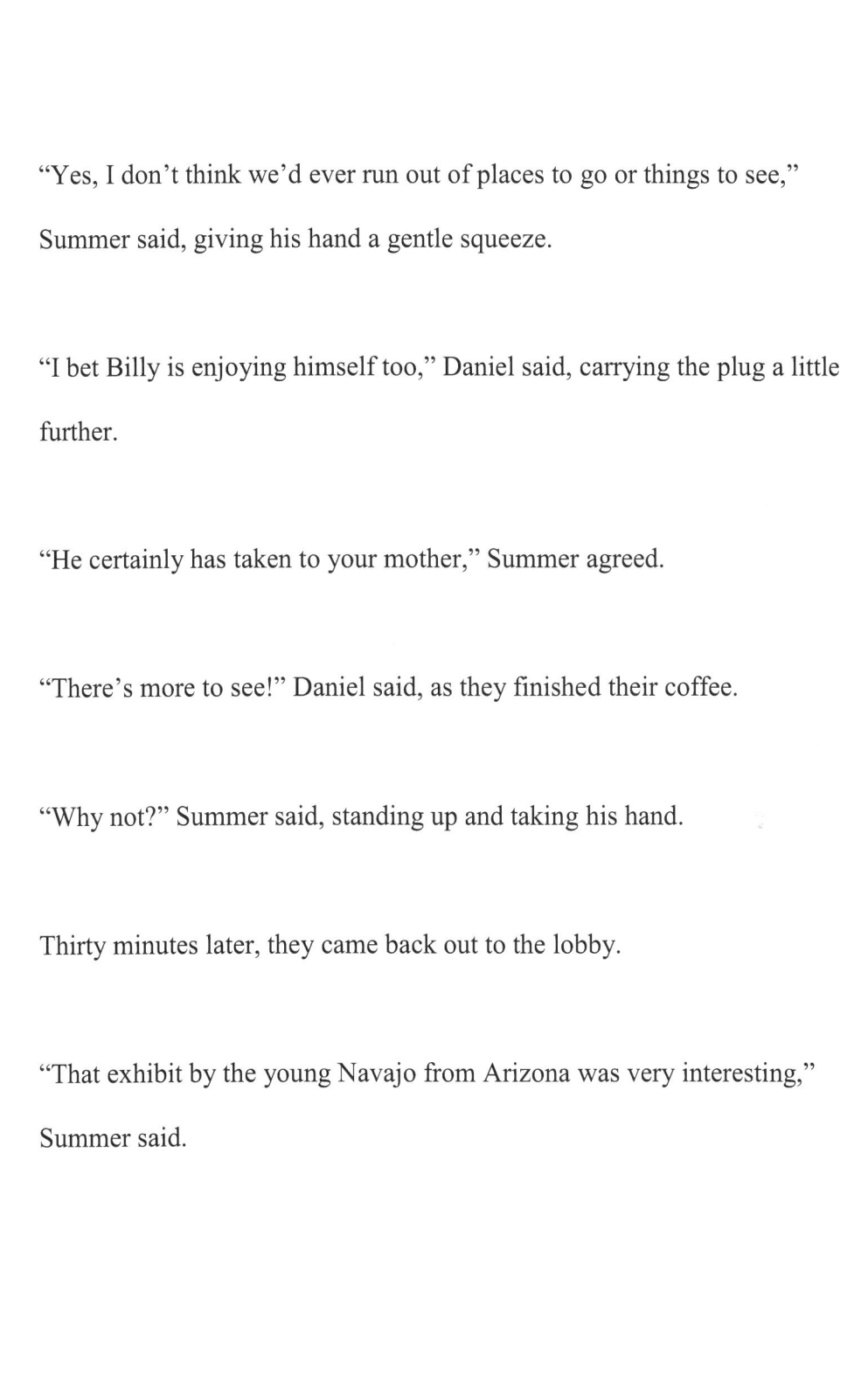

"Yes, I don't think we'd ever run out of places to go or things to see," Summer said, giving his hand a gentle squeeze.

"I bet Billy is enjoying himself too," Daniel said, carrying the plug a little further.

"He certainly has taken to your mother," Summer agreed.

"There's more to see!" Daniel said, as they finished their coffee.

"Why not?" Summer said, standing up and taking his hand.

Thirty minutes later, they came back out to the lobby.

"That exhibit by the young Navajo from Arizona was very interesting," Summer said.

"The one with the two big pictures and the smaller ones between 'em? Yeah, it really made you think," Daniel said. "I thought the big black and white photo with the model dressed in traditional Native American clothes, really looked authentic. The paper even looked old. She sure looked different in modern clothes," Daniel said.

"His arrangement of the smaller ones was interesting too," Summer said. "I liked how all the shots in traditional dress were getting progressively out of focus, as they got closer to the colored one, until they were almost completely blurred out. I think his way of showing how the past blurs, fades and then disappears, makes a very powerful statement. It really questions who any of us really are and that time is a veil that conceals the truth," Summer said.

"Yeah, they made me think about some of the things, Steve and I talked about yesterday," Daniel said.

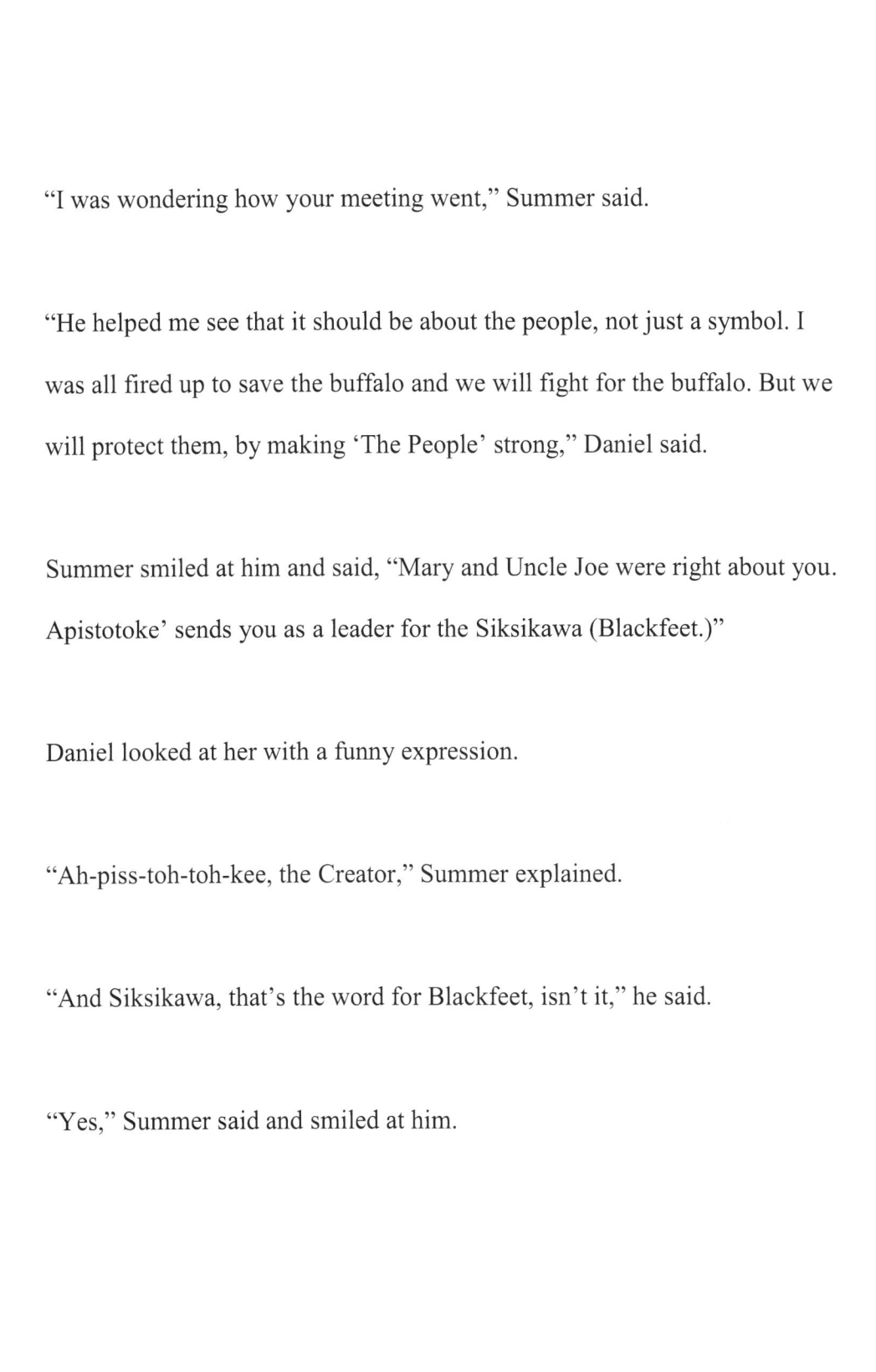

"I was wondering how your meeting went," Summer said.

"He helped me see that it should be about the people, not just a symbol. I was all fired up to save the buffalo and we will fight for the buffalo. But we will protect them, by making 'The People' strong," Daniel said.

Summer smiled at him and said, "Mary and Uncle Joe were right about you. Apistotoke' sends you as a leader for the Siksikawa (Blackfeet.)"

Daniel looked at her with a funny expression.

"Ah-piss-toh-toh-kee, the Creator," Summer explained.

"And Siksikawa, that's the word for Blackfeet, isn't it," he said.

"Yes," Summer said and smiled at him.

Daniel's smile broadened and then he said, "Behind every great man is a great woman. It looks like you have been chosen too…. I'm starting to get hungry. How about you?"

"Yeah, I'm ready to eat," Summer replied.

"I know of a place, several blocks from here. Should we walk?" Daniel suggested.

"We're getting our exercise today, aren't we," Summer said.

"We sure did," Daniel said, and raised his eye brows a couple of times.

"I meant all the walking!" she said, feeling her face get warm, seeing how he twisted her words.

Daniel smiled and gave her a little wink.

"Remember our walk in Browning, the day we met? We had the sidewalk to ourselves. The birds were singing," Daniel said, recalling their first date.

"Well… we have birds," Summer said, pointing to a flock of pigeons, flying overhead. "But I'm afraid we have a little more company," she added.

They walked a few more blocks and arrived at the restaurant. It was relatively early, so they were seated fairly quickly, although, it probably didn't hurt anything that Daniel discreetly slipped the host a twenty-dollar bill, as he stepped up to get on the list.

When they arrived back at the Marina, they found Evelyn and Billy in the lounge, playing a game on her laptop and eating pizza.

"We're back!" Daniel announced as they walked in.

"Did you have a nice day?" Evelyn asked.

"We went to the Met. and then had a bite to eat at Eleven Madison Park," Daniel replied,

"They have the best Cappuccino," Evelyn said.

"I told you," Daniel said, looking at Summer.

"We did have cappuccino after dinner. Daniel made it sound like it was one of the rules of eating there," Summer said, smiling at Evelyn.

"It should be…. We went to the Pier… went on a few rides, had a hotdog from Max's hotdog stand and salt water taffy from the Sugar Shack. The Lion King was excellent!" Evelyn said, with a big smile.

"Did you have fun today?" Summer asked, smiling at Billy.

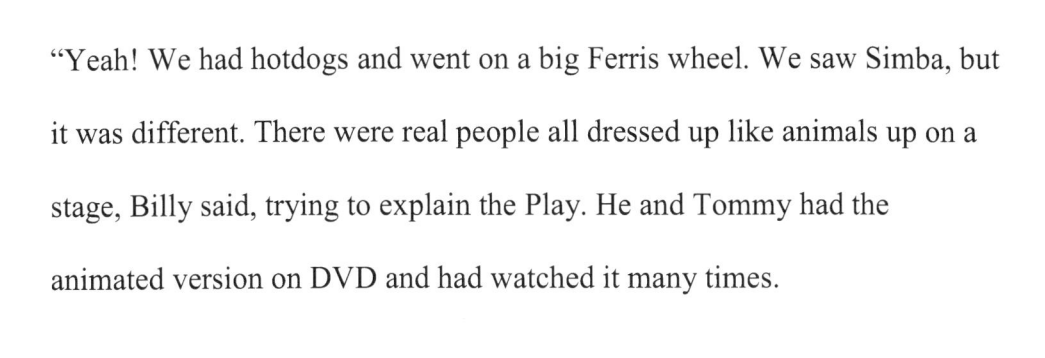

"Yeah! We had hotdogs and went on a big Ferris wheel. We saw Simba, but it was different. There were real people all dressed up like animals up on a stage, Billy said, trying to explain the Play. He and Tommy had the animated version on DVD and had watched it many times.

"You look tired. Should we get ready for bed?" Summer asked.

"Can we play one more game?" Billy asked.

"One more and then we'll turn in. Robert is going to be here early and take us for a ride on the river," Evelyn said.

"Okay," Billy said, obediently.

Daniel looked at his mother.

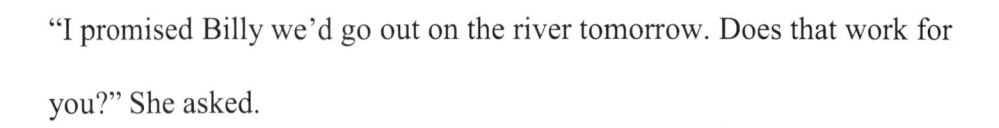

"I promised Billy we'd go out on the river tomorrow. Does that work for you?" She asked.

Daniel looked at Summer, who gave a little shrugged.

"I guess that would be fine," Daniel replied.

"Excellent! Connie will be here and have breakfast at eight. Robert will take us out after that. We'll have lunch afloat and dinner back here in the Marina," Evelyn said.

"Sounds like a plan," Daniel said, seeing how much his mother was looking forward to spending the day with them and all the preparations she had made to make the day special.

The next morning, Daniel awoke to a knock on their bedroom door. "Yes?" Daniel said.

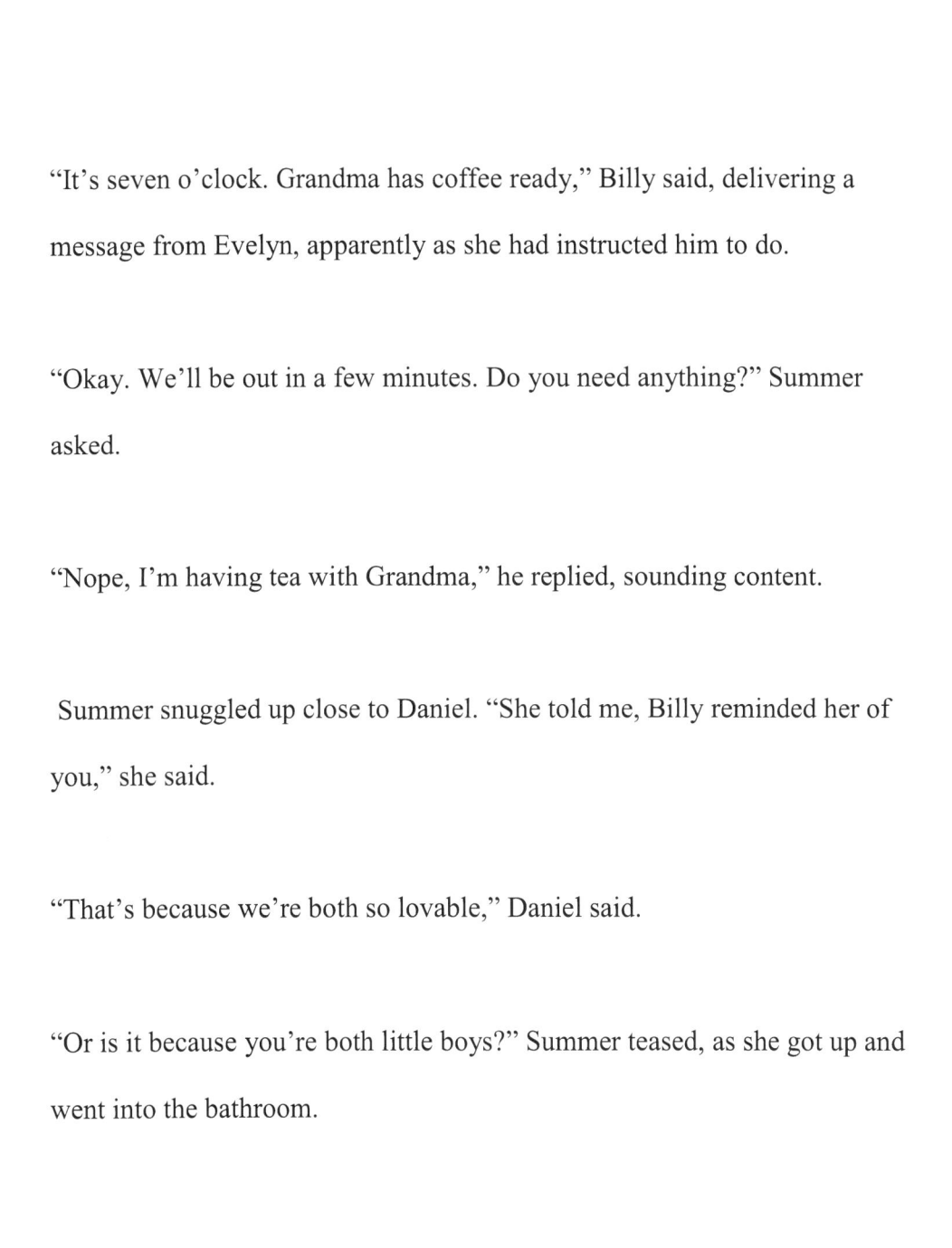

"It's seven o'clock. Grandma has coffee ready," Billy said, delivering a message from Evelyn, apparently as she had instructed him to do.

"Okay. We'll be out in a few minutes. Do you need anything?" Summer asked.

"Nope, I'm having tea with Grandma," he replied, sounding content.

Summer snuggled up close to Daniel. "She told me, Billy reminded her of you," she said.

"That's because we're both so lovable," Daniel said.

"Or is it because you're both little boys?" Summer teased, as she got up and went into the bathroom.

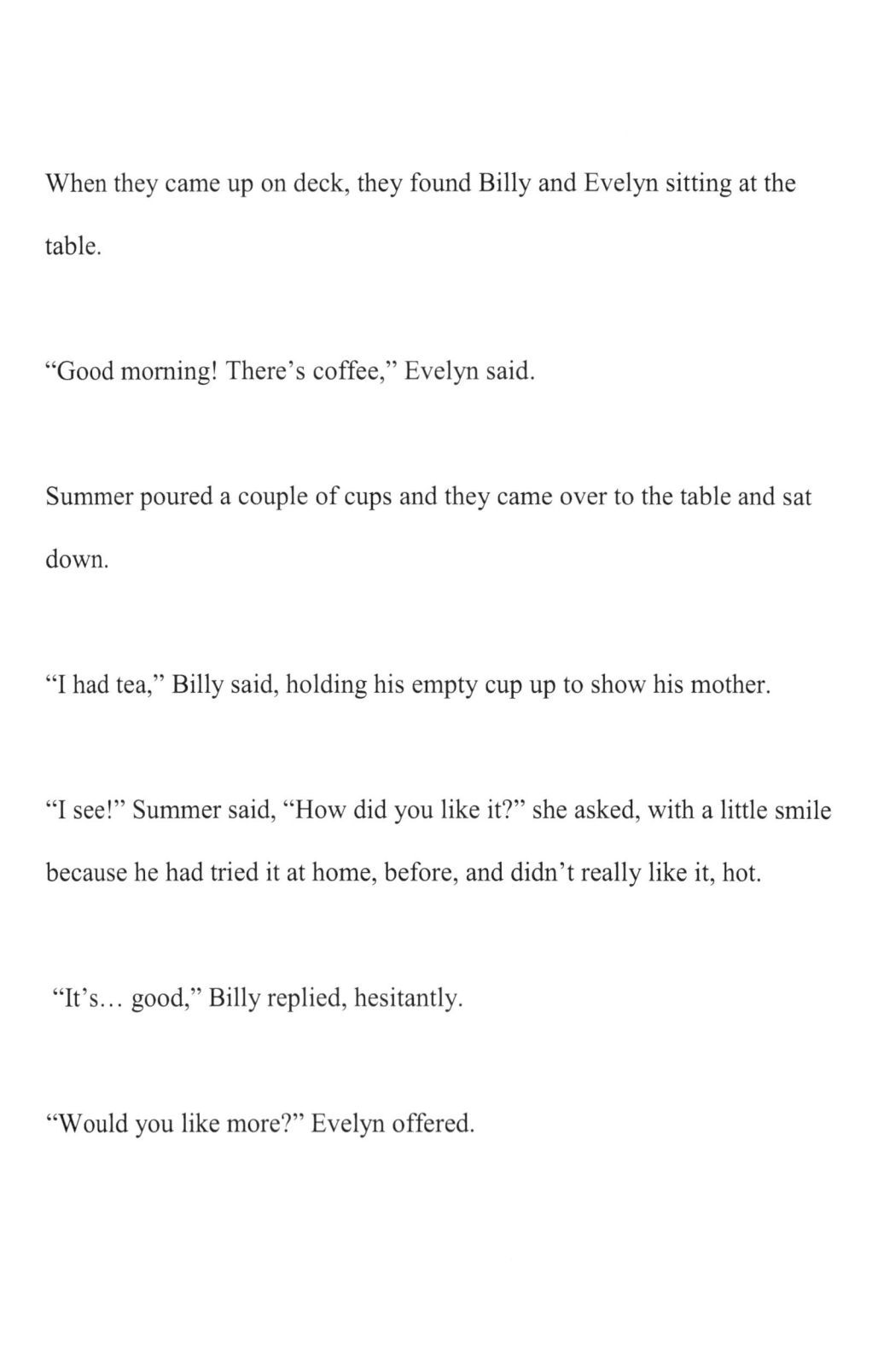

When they came up on deck, they found Billy and Evelyn sitting at the table.

"Good morning! There's coffee," Evelyn said.

Summer poured a couple of cups and they came over to the table and sat down.

"I had tea," Billy said, holding his empty cup up to show his mother.

"I see!" Summer said, "How did you like it?" she asked, with a little smile because he had tried it at home, before, and didn't really like it, hot.

"It's… good," Billy replied, hesitantly.

"Would you like more?" Evelyn offered.

"No thank you. Can I have some juice?" he asked politely

It wasn't long and they heard Connie come on board. "Good morning!" she said, as she appeared in the lounge and brought the coffee pot to the table. She poured Daniel and Summer another cup. She noticed Evelyn was having tea and asked, "More tea?"

"Yes please," Evelyn replied.

Connie returned a few minutes later with more hot water and a fresh tea bag. "Shall I start breakfast?" she asked.

"Yes, thank you," Evelyn said.

"I'm so glad everything worked out, so we could go out today. I'm so looking forward to it!" Evelyn said, looking at Daniel and Summer.

Daniel noticed that sparkle in her eyes, again, and wondered what she was up to. He smiled at her. Evelyn seemed to sense he suspected something and raised her eyebrows slightly as she lifted her cup to her lips.

The sunlight reflected off the surface of the Hudson as they cruised along. It was a perfect day to be on the water and the breeze blew through their hair, as Daniel and Billy stood on the back deck, throwing small pieces of bread, up in the air for the seagulls to catch. Evelyn and Summer sat facing the Manhattan water front. They could hear 'the boys' having fun.

"The two of them seem to get along so well," Evelyn said.

"Billy adores him. Daniel is so considerate," Summer said, "That was something I noticed about him when we first met," she added and smiled at Evelyn.

"Tell me about your Sister," Evelyn said.

Summer thought for a moment, then said, "April is two years younger than I am. We look a lot like. She has a son, Tommy, he is one year younger than Billy. We help each other out. She stays at home and bakes and cans, while she watches the boys. I help her with bills. We're close. It's just the two of us."

Evelyn touched Summers hand for a moment and then said "I understand family. My parents were the children of Italian emigrants. I remember sitting at the table with both my mother's and father's parents. They spoke English, but at home they preferred Italian. My grandmothers would be in the kitchen with my mother and her sister. The grandmothers would be asking, why they did something one way and then tell them how they used to do it.... That big house was so full of activity; you couldn't find a quite spot if you wanted to…. As the years past and those loved ones past away, holidays never seemed the same. After Howard past away…" Evelyn fell silent.

Summer squeezed her hand. Evelyn put her right hand on top of Summer's.

"I can see that you and Daniel are very happy together. We have just met, but I think you and Billy are wonderful. I don't want to seem like an over bearing mother, but I want you to consider something. Would you ever think of living here? I mean you, Billy, April and her son. We could be a family. Think of the opportunities. Think of the education the boys could have." Evelyn felt a lump start to grow in her throat. She swallowed. She wasn't used to showing all this emotion, she was a New Yorker, and perhaps that was what made her aware that she had a narrow window of opportunity to make her wishes known and to seize the moment before it slipped away.

"You have been so wonderful to us. I would be very lucky to call you family," Summer said.

"Well, that's settled. All we have to do is plan the wedding," Evelyn said, teasingly. "What do you say we enjoy this beautiful day and the gifts we are blessed with?" she said, as she stood up. "Let's go find the 'boys," she said, and started toward the rear deck. They found no one. "They're probably up with Robert," Evelyn said.

"Boys," Summer said.

They laughed and went back to their seats to wait for them to return. As Summer looked out across the water at the tall buildings, she thought about what Evelyn had said. She wondered what April would think of the idea of living in New York.

"I got to drive the boat!" Billy said, as he and Daniel came out on deck.

"You did?" Summer said.

Daniel winked at her.

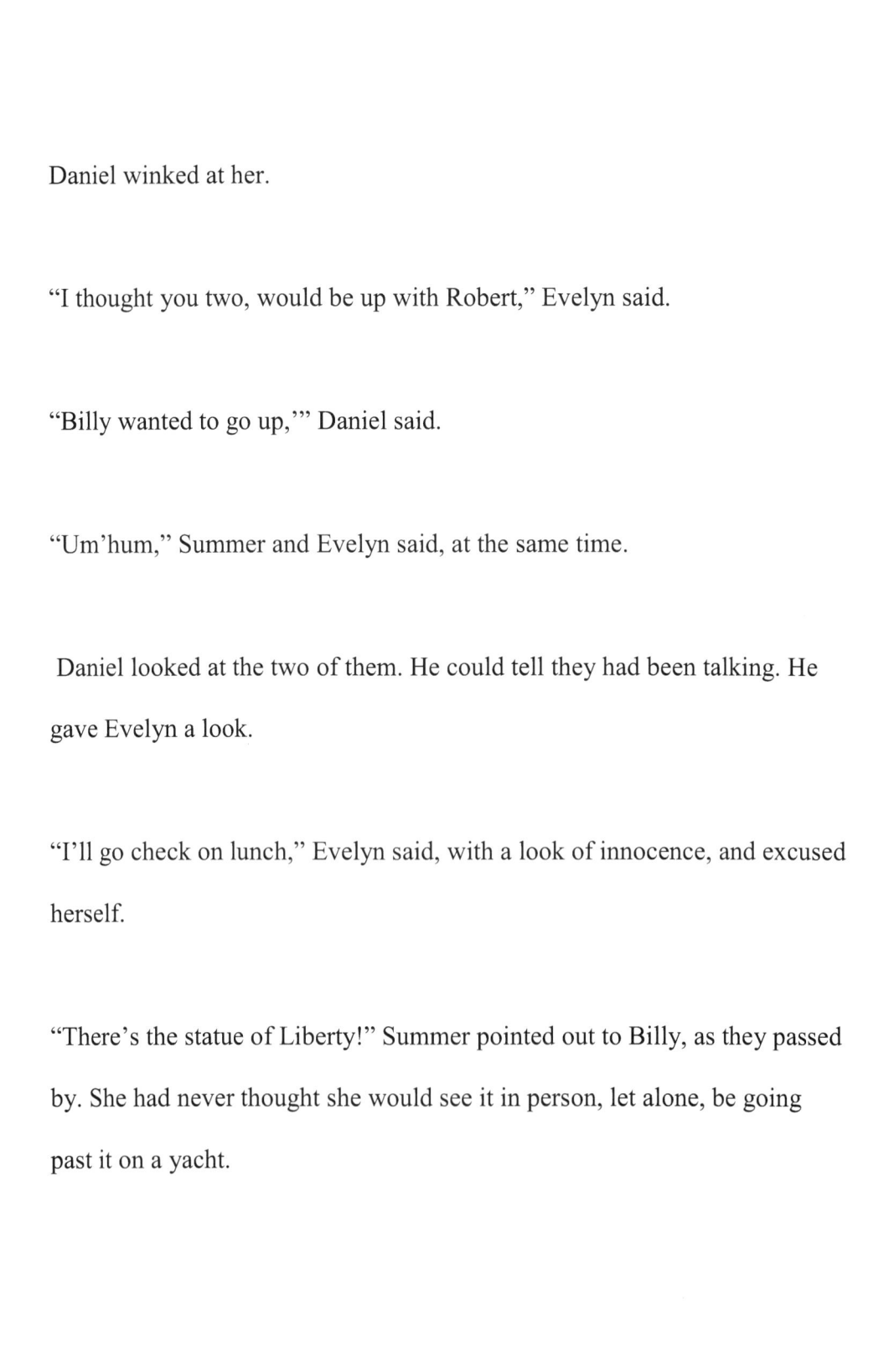

"I thought you two, would be up with Robert," Evelyn said.

"Billy wanted to go up,'" Daniel said.

"Um'hum," Summer and Evelyn said, at the same time.

Daniel looked at the two of them. He could tell they had been talking. He gave Evelyn a look.

"I'll go check on lunch," Evelyn said, with a look of innocence, and excused herself.

"There's the statue of Liberty!" Summer pointed out to Billy, as they passed by. She had never thought she would see it in person, let alone, be going past it on a yacht.

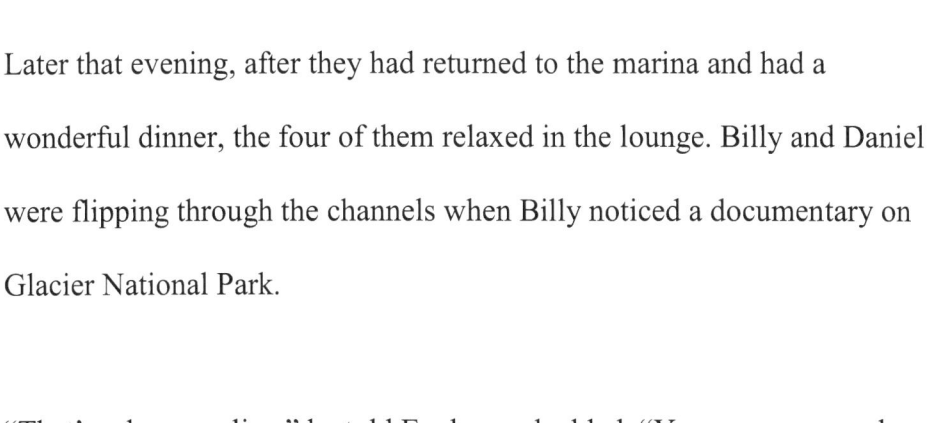

Later that evening, after they had returned to the marina and had a wonderful dinner, the four of them relaxed in the lounge. Billy and Daniel were flipping through the channels when Billy noticed a documentary on Glacier National Park.

"That's where we live," he told Evelyn and added, "You can come and see us."

"I'd love to," Evelyn said, as they watched the rest of the show. "It certainly is beautiful out there," she said, as the credits started to roll.

"Maybe you could come and live with us!" Billy said.

Evelyn smiled at him and said, "You never know."

Daniel gave her a funny look, but she pretended not to notice.

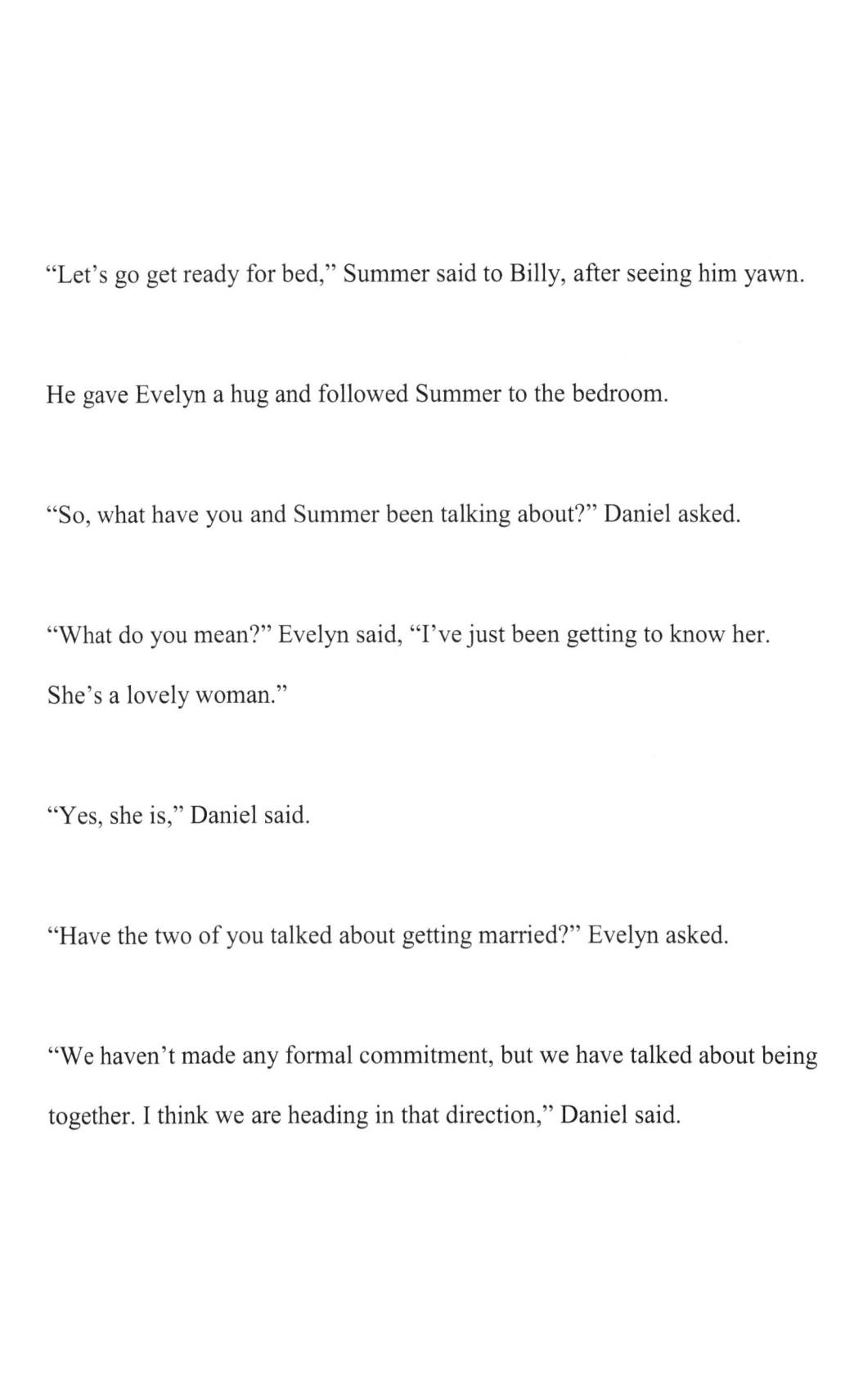

"Let's go get ready for bed," Summer said to Billy, after seeing him yawn.

He gave Evelyn a hug and followed Summer to the bedroom.

"So, what have you and Summer been talking about?" Daniel asked.

"What do you mean?" Evelyn said, "I've just been getting to know her. She's a lovely woman."

"Yes, she is," Daniel said.

"Have the two of you talked about getting married?" Evelyn asked.

"We haven't made any formal commitment, but we have talked about being together. I think we are heading in that direction," Daniel said.

"I think the two of you make a lovely couple and Billy is simply adorable," Evelyn said. "Have you given any thought, as to where you'll live?" she continued after a brief pause.

"Well… no… not specifically," Daniel said, trying to think of a way to explain Mary's old farm house and how the quiet, open country made him feel. He knew he would never be able to explain … explain what? Ghosts and transformations? He didn't understand it, himself. "There is a lot to work out yet," he said.

Evelyn looked at him. She never had trouble speaking her mind, but she found herself searching for words. "When are you going back to Montana," she said. But what she really wanted to say was "why are you going back."

"We are scheduled to leave Tuesday," Daniel said.

Tears formed in Evelyn's eyes, but she refused to let them fall and brushed them away, like a fly. "I want you to be happy. I did ask Summer if she would ever consider living here. I also opened my arms to her sister and her son, as well. Go back to Montana. Do whatever it is that you have to do. But remember your heart can have several passions and we have been blessed with the means to nurture more than one at a time," Evelyn said, and then smiled. "And I'm not going to forget that I have an offer to come and live with all of you."

Daniel was amused at the thought of Evelyn living at Mary's farm. "You will always be welcome, no matter where we are," he said. "Thank you for everything," he added.

Summer returned from tucking Billy in and sat down next to Daniel. "Thank you for taking us out today. Billy couldn't stop talking about it," she said.

"You're welcome. I enjoyed it very much, too," Evelyn said, "I was just trying to get Daniel to tell me what he had planned for the next couple days, so I could plan our next outing."

"I'm sure Billy and I could find something to do tomorrow, if the two of you wanted to do something," Daniel said.

"Well, what do you think? You and me, hitting the town tomorrow?" Evelyn said.

"Sounds great," Summer said.

"Well, I think we should get an early start. I'll have coffee on at six and arrange for a car to pick us up at seven, so, I think I'll turn in now. Goodnight. See you in the morning!" Evelyn said, and gave each of them a kiss on the cheek.

Daniel looked at Summer and smiled. He placed his hand on top of hers. "So Mothers got you on the fast track to becoming a New Yorker," he said, with a chuckle.

"She's a wonderful woman. She just doesn't want to be alone," Summer said. "She is a wise woman. Grandma would have liked her," she added.

Daniel thought about that for a moment. He agreed a conversation between the two of them would have been one worth overhearing. "Let's go out on deck," he said.

They got up and walked out. He put his arm around her, she nestled closer to him. They stood there for a few minutes and listened to the sounds of the city, all around them and then turned in for the night.

The next morning, Summer got up at four-thirty to get ready. Daniel pretended to still be sleeping, so she could do her thing, but kept an eye on the clock so he could see her off. About quarter to six, he got up and poked his head in the bathroom.

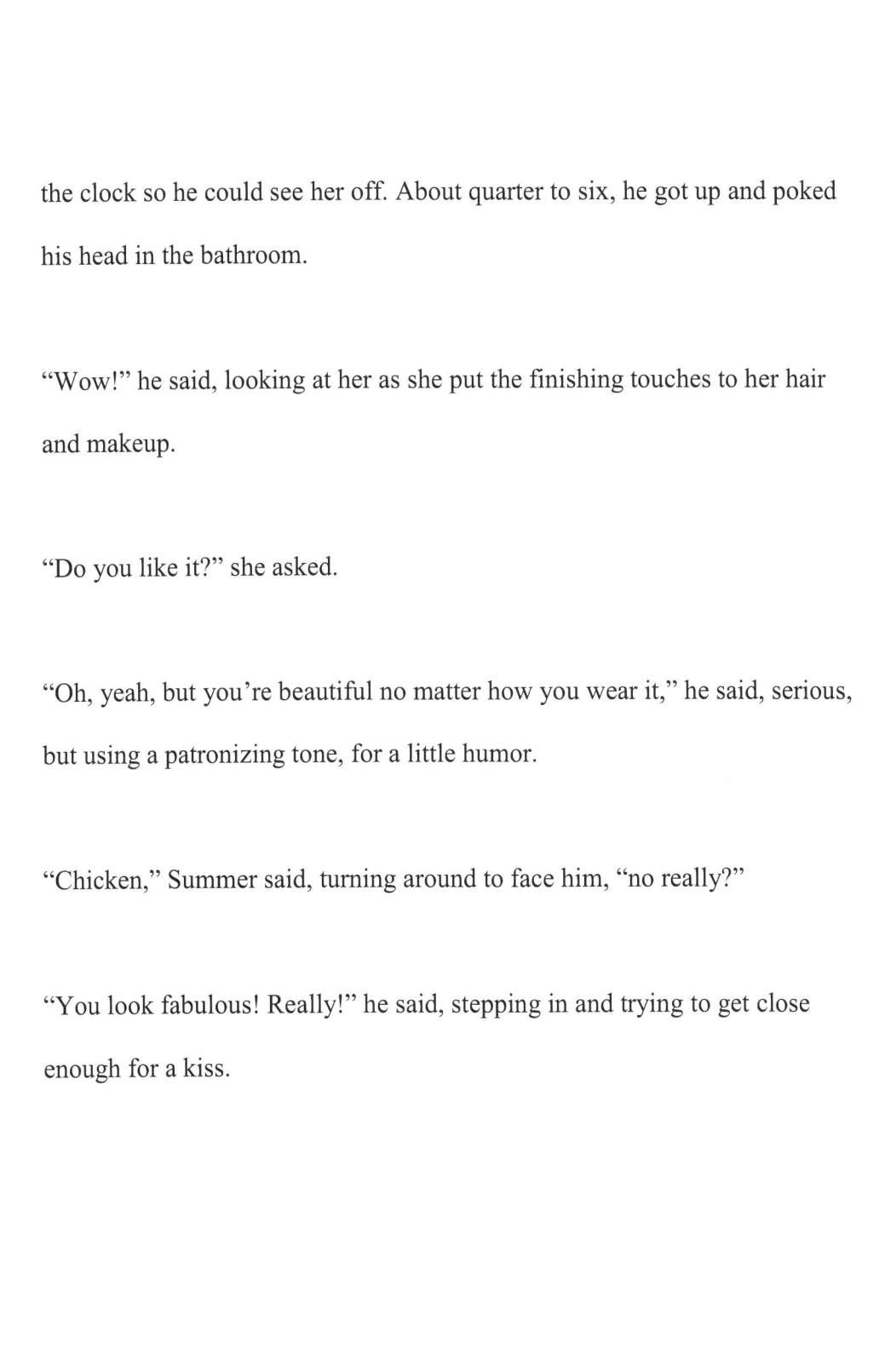

"Wow!" he said, looking at her as she put the finishing touches to her hair and makeup.

"Do you like it?" she asked.

"Oh, yeah, but you're beautiful no matter how you wear it," he said, serious, but using a patronizing tone, for a little humor.

"Chicken," Summer said, turning around to face him, "no really?"

"You look fabulous! Really!" he said, stepping in and trying to get close enough for a kiss.

"Careful! You'll smudge my lip stick," she said, and slipped past him, pretending to kiss his cheek on her way.

"Well, the transformation is complete. You are a New York kind of girl. I just had one of those 'insights' of what I have to look forward to in married life," Daniel teased, referring to her comment the other morning.

"I just wanna look nice, I want to make her proud," she said, and gave him a little peck on the cheek, and then put on her shoes.

"Don't worry, she's gonna parade you around, like you're her very own," he said.

"What are you and Billy going to do today?" she asked, getting a feel for the change in her center of gravity, as she stood up, in her high heels.

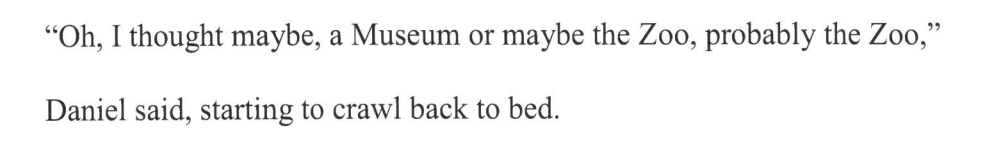

"Oh, I thought maybe, a Museum or maybe the Zoo, probably the Zoo," Daniel said, starting to crawl back to bed.

"What do you think you're, doing?" Summer asked, with a little smile on her face.

"I thought I'd go back to sleep until Billy got up," Daniel said.

"Oh, I'll bet he's up," Summer said.

Okay, I'll be out in a few minutes," he said, as he got up and put some sweat pants on.

"Morning!" Summer said, as she walked in the galley area and saw Evelyn sitting at the counter with a cup of coffee.

"Morning! Well, don't you look nice," Evelyn said, dressed to the nines herself, as she got up to get Summer a cup of coffee.

"I can get it," Summer said, stepping behind the counter and getting a cup out. "Ready for more?" she asked, holding up the pot.

"Please," Evelyn said.

"Morning," Daniel said, as he popped in.

"Morning," Evelyn said. "You're up early."

"Well, I thought I'd see if Billy needed anything, so you two could get a good start," Daniel said, making it sound like it was his idea.

"I told him to sleep in and stay in the room, until you came to get him, he was sound asleep when I left him," Evelyn said.

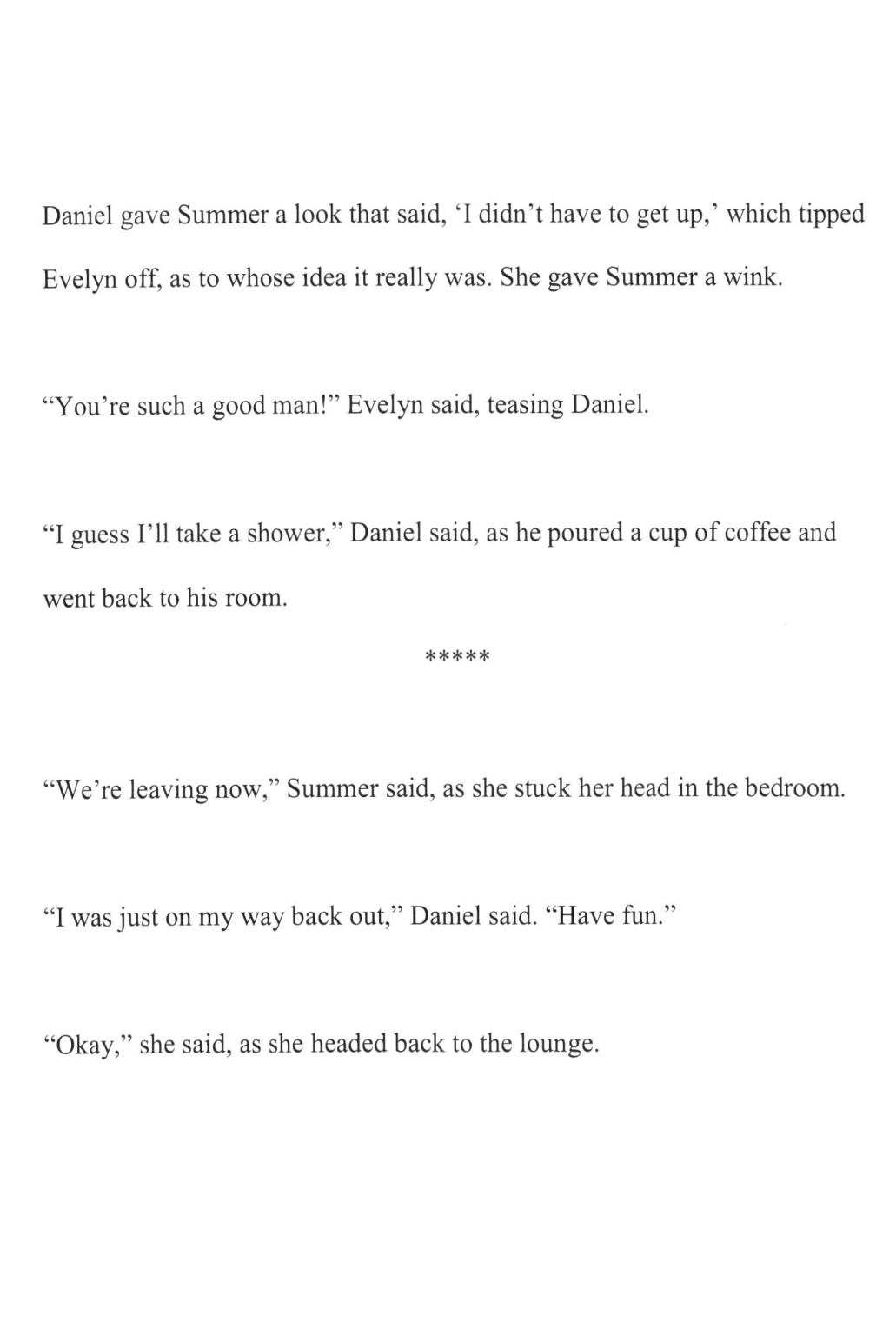

Daniel gave Summer a look that said, 'I didn't have to get up,' which tipped Evelyn off, as to whose idea it really was. She gave Summer a wink.

"You're such a good man!" Evelyn said, teasing Daniel.

"I guess I'll take a shower," Daniel said, as he poured a cup of coffee and went back to his room.

*****

"We're leaving now," Summer said, as she stuck her head in the bedroom.

"I was just on my way back out," Daniel said. "Have fun."

"Okay," she said, as she headed back to the lounge.

Daniel was only a minute or so behind her, but when he came out, he could hear them, already on the main deck. He poured a cup of coffee and went up to see them off. He watched, as they walked down the dock and toward the gate. He went back to the counter and finished his cup of coffee, then, he went to check on Billy.

"Morning!" Billy said, as Daniel opened the door a crack, to see if he was still asleep.

"You're awake," Daniel said, seeing Billy, still in bed, but watching TV.

"Yeah, Grandma said to wait in here until you came to get me," Billy said.

"What do you want to do today?" Daniel asked.

"Let's make pancakes!" Billy said, and jumped out of bed.

"Pancakes?" It's been a while since I've… okay, let's make pancakes," Daniel said, and they went to the kitchen.

Daniel had just put the second batch on the griddle, when his phone rang. Caller ID identified it as Steve.

"Good morning," Daniel said.

"Morning. I've got someone that would like to talk to us about manufacturing solar panels in Browning. Are you free today?"

"Yeah, I'm hanging out with Billy today. We could come by the Office. What time?" Daniel said, watching Billy wolf down the first batch of pancakes.

"How about twelve-thirty? I'll order lunch and we can see what he has to say," Steve said.

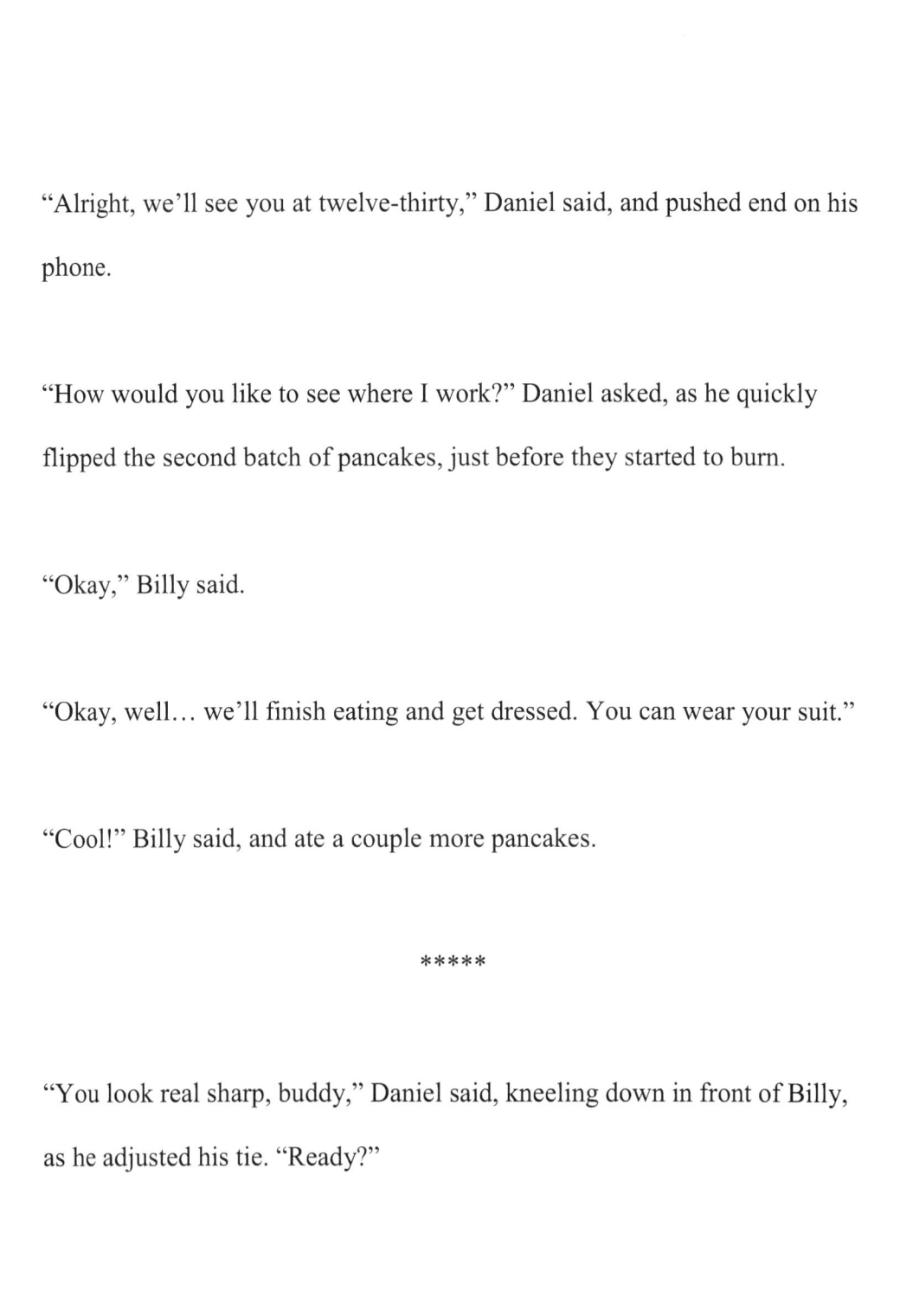

"Alright, we'll see you at twelve-thirty," Daniel said, and pushed end on his phone.

"How would you like to see where I work?" Daniel asked, as he quickly flipped the second batch of pancakes, just before they started to burn.

"Okay," Billy said.

"Okay, well… we'll finish eating and get dressed. You can wear your suit."

"Cool!" Billy said, and ate a couple more pancakes.

*****

"You look real sharp, buddy," Daniel said, kneeling down in front of Billy, as he adjusted his tie. "Ready?"

"Yep," Billy answered

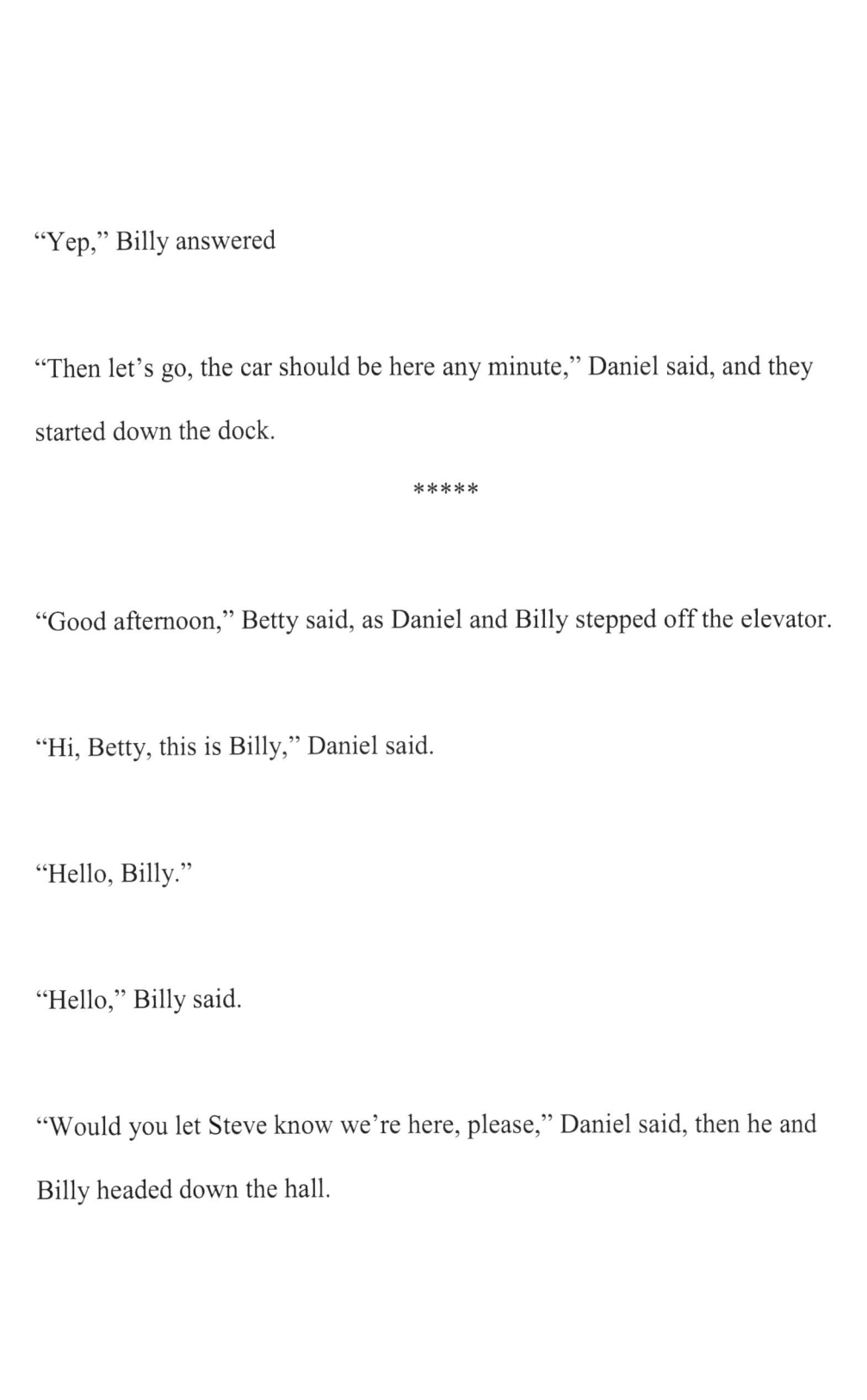

"Then let's go, the car should be here any minute," Daniel said, and they started down the dock.

*****

"Good afternoon," Betty said, as Daniel and Billy stepped off the elevator.

"Hi, Betty, this is Billy," Daniel said.

"Hello, Billy."

"Hello," Billy said.

"Would you let Steve know we're here, please," Daniel said, then he and Billy headed down the hall.

"This is it," Daniel said, as they walked in.

"Cool!" Billy said, walking to the wall of glass and looking out at the city.

"It is, isn't it," Daniel said, thinking back to when he was about Billy's age. "Okay, here's the deal, we are going to have lunch here in a little while, with a couple of guys and talk about Solar energy, then you and I can go check out the zoo, alright?" Daniel said, briefing Billy.

"Alright," Billy answered. "Are you the boss, here?" he asked, looking around the room.

"I'm a partner, Steve is a partner and the man that's coming to talk with us is a client of his. This client might be interested in starting a business back home, that would bring lots of jobs to Browning… that would be good, wouldn't it? So we have to make him feel welcome, like a guest in our home, okay?" Daniel said.

"Okay," Billy said.

Just then there was a knock at the door.

"Come in," Daniel said.

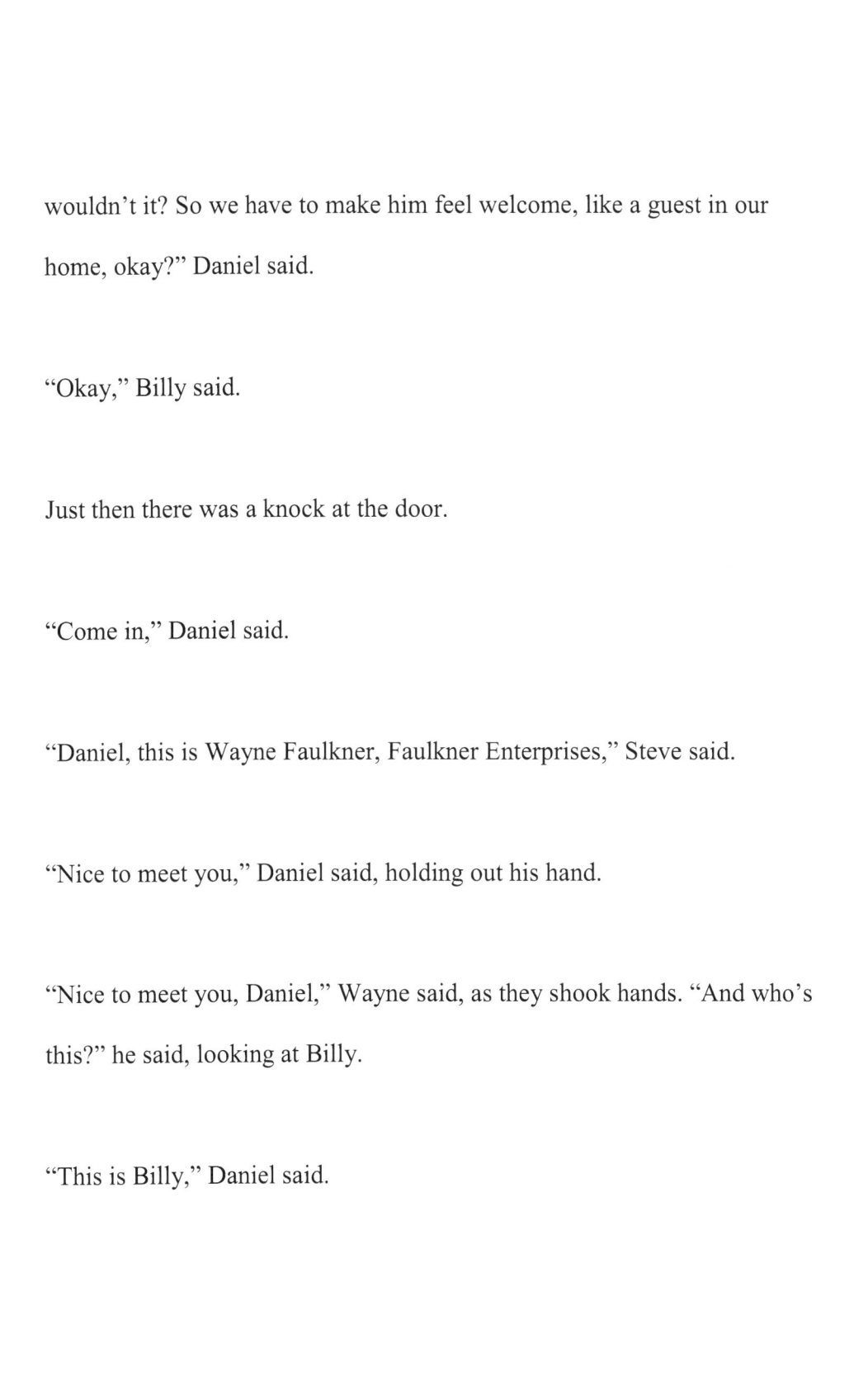

"Daniel, this is Wayne Faulkner, Faulkner Enterprises," Steve said.

"Nice to meet you," Daniel said, holding out his hand.

"Nice to meet you, Daniel," Wayne said, as they shook hands. "And who's this?" he said, looking at Billy.

"This is Billy," Daniel said.

"Nice to meet you," Billy said, holding out his hand.

"Nice to meet you, Billy," Wayne said.

"Shall we have a seat?" Daniel asked, and made a gesture with his hand toward the conference table.

"Steve has told me you're interested in starting up a Solar panel manufacturing facility in Montana," Wayne said, getting right to the point.

"I think matching up the city of Browning with a product that harvests renewable resources would fit right in with the Blackfeet belief that all things are sacred and gifts from the Creator. The railroad runs through town, land is reasonable and there are people available to work," Daniel said.

"Naapi' (Old Man)," Billy said, in a clear voice.

The three men looked at him.

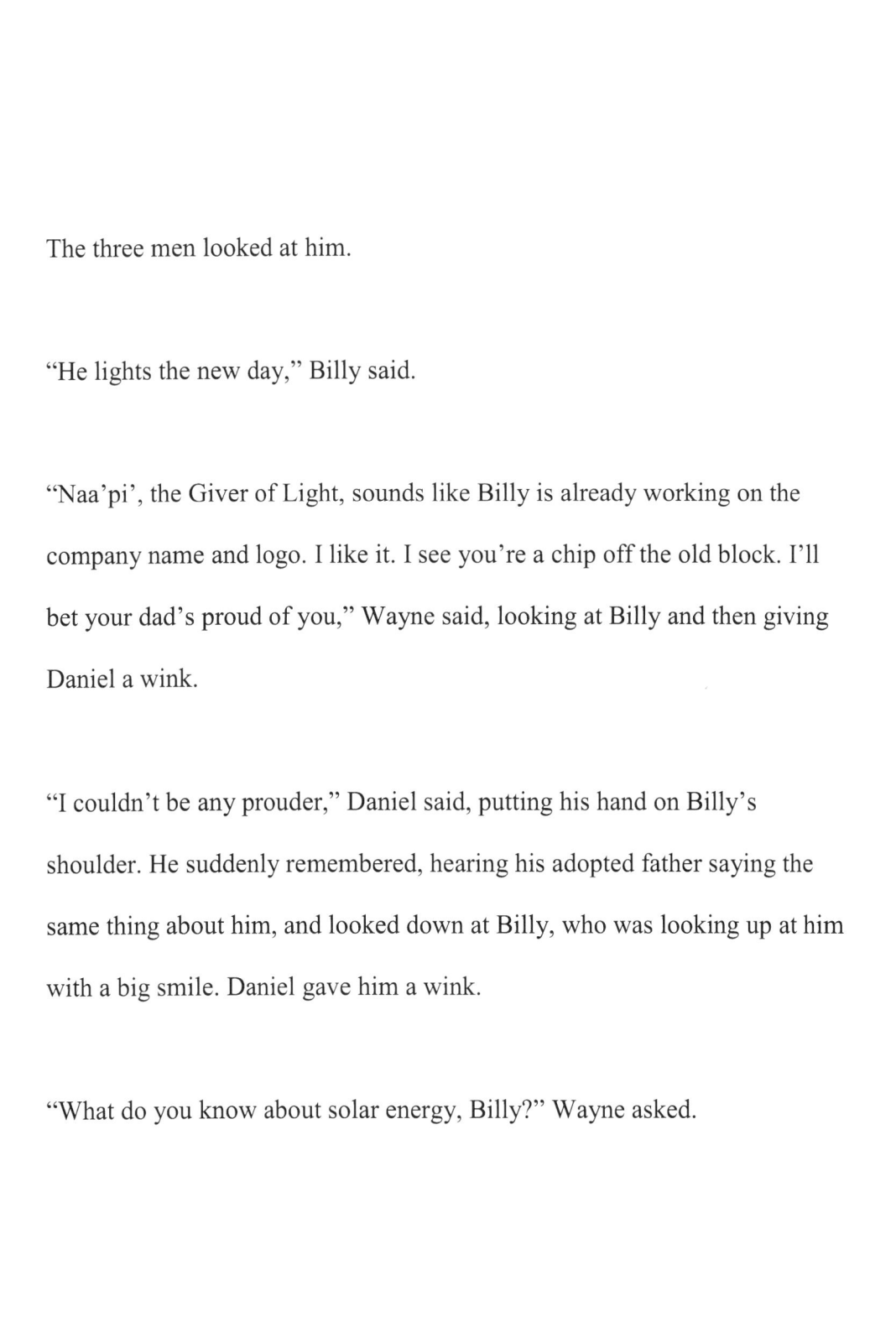

"He lights the new day," Billy said.

"Naa'pi', the Giver of Light, sounds like Billy is already working on the company name and logo. I like it. I see you're a chip off the old block. I'll bet your dad's proud of you," Wayne said, looking at Billy and then giving Daniel a wink.

"I couldn't be any prouder," Daniel said, putting his hand on Billy's shoulder. He suddenly remembered, hearing his adopted father saying the same thing about him, and looked down at Billy, who was looking up at him with a big smile. Daniel gave him a wink.

"What do you know about solar energy, Billy?" Wayne asked.

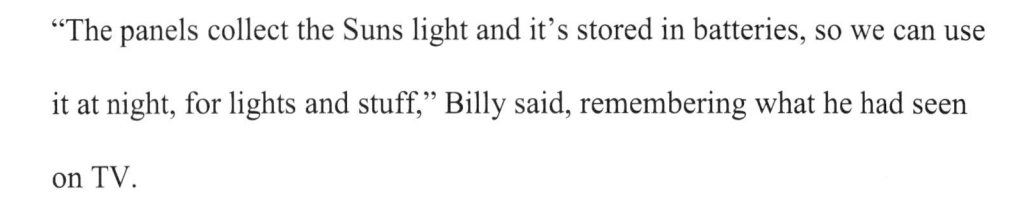

"The panels collect the Suns light and it's stored in batteries, so we can use it at night, for lights and stuff," Billy said, remembering what he had seen on TV.

"You are sharp as a tack," Wayne said.

Then there was a knock at the door.

"Come in," Daniel said.

Betty opened the door, holding several white plastic bags. Steve got up to help her,

"Thanks, Betty," Steve said, taking the bags and putting them on the table. "I ordered pastrami on rye, I hope that's alright," Steve said, handing a Styrofoam container to Wayne.

"My favorite!" Wayne said.

"Oh, good," Steve said, giving Daniel a little smile, as he handed him two containers.

Daniel smiled back at him; it was just like Steve to cover every little detail.

"Wow!" Billy said, as Daniel helped him open his lunch.

"Looks pretty good, huh," Wayne said to him, "You gonna eat all that?" he asked Billy.

"Yep," Billy said, and dug in.

"What kind of private backing are we looking at," Wayne said, after a few bites.

"Well, I'm really just starting to look into all of this, to see what might be possible. I don't have any outside commitments to the project, just yet," Daniel said.

"As you may or may not be aware, there are some pretty substantial government programs that can go a long way in helping this kind of thing get off the ground. One of my companies is helping the Navajo in Arizona with a wind turbine project. I have several people working for me that… let's say know the ins and outs of making these programs work for us, and are able to get things rolling, without a lot of trial and error. My standard offer is, a five-year contract, where I control fifty-nine percent of the company. I'll handle facility issues, raw materials, shipping and distribution. At the end of the contract, I will sell my shares back to the company for an agreed price or will absorb the other forty-one percent," Wayne said, and then turned his full attention to his sandwich.

"I'd like to look at one of your contracts," Daniel said, after a few bites.

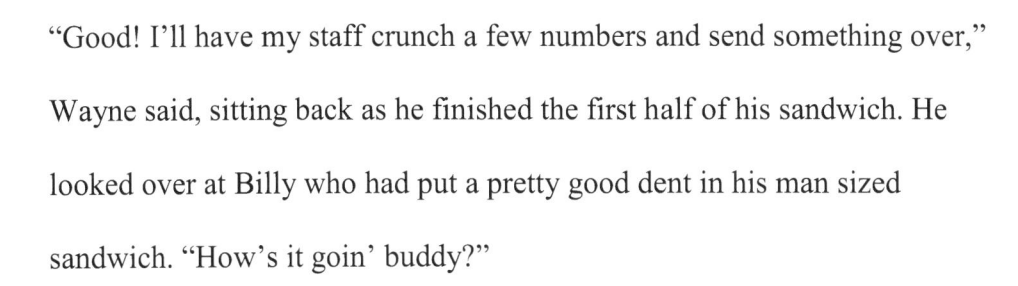

"Good! I'll have my staff crunch a few numbers and send something over," Wayne said, sitting back as he finished the first half of his sandwich. He looked over at Billy who had put a pretty good dent in his man sized sandwich. "How's it goin' buddy?"

"Good!" Billy said, determined to finish it all.

"Browning… that's near Glacier Park isn't it?" Wayne said.

"Yes, just East from there," Daniel said.

"My kids were always after me to take 'em. I guess I should have found the time. I was always traveling on business and when I finally got home it was nice to be there," Wayne said. "Now one of 'em is starting college, the youngest one is a junior in High School," he added, as he resumed eating.

"It's on my Bucket List," Daniel said.

Wayne gave a little sigh of contentment as he finished his sandwich and sat back for a few minutes, then he said, looking at his watch; "Gentleman, thank you for lunch, it was a pleasure talking with you, I look forward in working with you on this project, look things over and we'll be in touch. I've got to be back in Los Angeles tonight, and I'm scheduled to take off in ninety minutes."

Daniel looked at Steve, who pointed to the roof, where there was a Helicopter pad and a helicopter waiting to take him back to the airport and his private plane.

"Wayne, it was very nice to meet you and we'll be in touch," Daniel said.

"Wayne, a pleasure as always," Steve said, shaking Wayne's hand, and then walked out with him to the elevator.

*****

"Well? What did you think?" Steve asked, as he and Daniel walked back to the table, once Wayne was on his way.

"He certainly is a mover and a shaker, it will be interesting to see what he comes up with," Daniel said.

"He's worth over six hundred million dollars," Steve said. Then he looked at Billy and said, "you can be my wingman anytime… good job!"

"Good job," Billy said, as he swallowed the last bite of his lunch.

CHAPTER 25

"We're home!" Daniel said, looking at Billy, as the tires touched the runway.

The stewardess's voice came over the intercom, asking everyone to stay seated until the plane came to a complete stop. They watched as the ground crew brought the steps to the plane and opened the door. It was the only plane in sight, and as they made their way across the tarmac to the terminal, it was obvious they weren't in New York anymore.

"Hey!" Summer said and waved when she spotted April and Tommy among the group of people waiting beyond the roped off area.

"Did you have a good time?" April asked Summer, seeing the sparkle in Summers eyes.

"It was amazing!" Summer said.

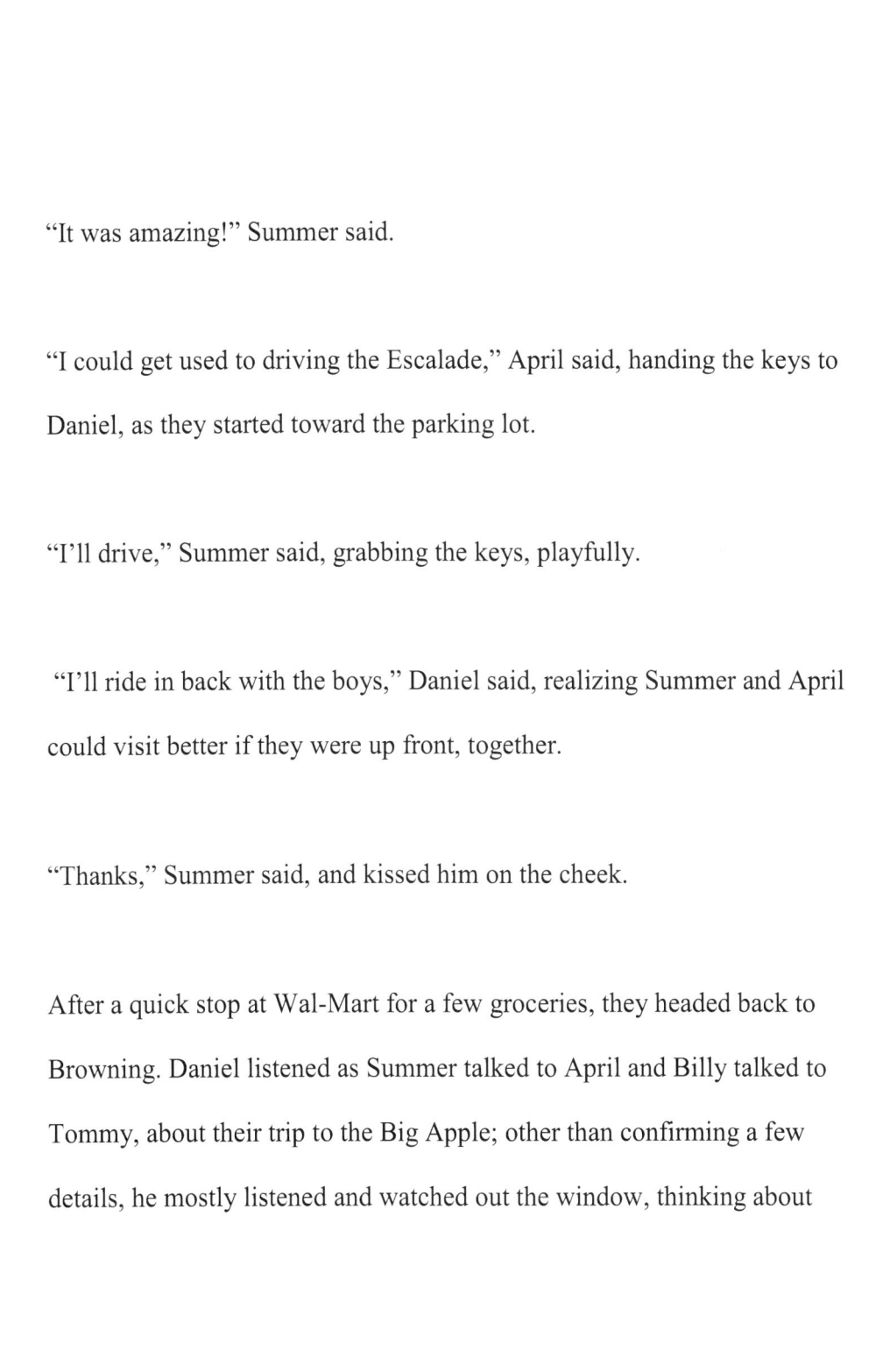

"I could get used to driving the Escalade," April said, handing the keys to Daniel, as they started toward the parking lot.

"I'll drive," Summer said, grabbing the keys, playfully.

"I'll ride in back with the boys," Daniel said, realizing Summer and April could visit better if they were up front, together.

"Thanks," Summer said, and kissed him on the cheek.

After a quick stop at Wal-Mart for a few groceries, they headed back to Browning. Daniel listened as Summer talked to April and Billy talked to Tommy, about their trip to the Big Apple; other than confirming a few details, he mostly listened and watched out the window, thinking about some of the possible opportunities that were on the table and the improvements they would bring to the community.

When Summer turned onto the dirt road that led to the house, Daniel felt a release, like when you walk through your door at home after being away for a while. The old house looked a little smaller to him, as they pulled up and before he even got out he was already thinking of those DIY projects.

They only had three carry-on bags. They had shipped everything else UPS. Billy thought they should wear their 'Montana clothes' and surprise Tommy and April with their 'new clothes'; so besides the groceries, it only took a few minutes to unpack and they didn't even have to change.

Daniel had thought Billy's idea was good, but had said, they couldn't go home empty handed, and suggested a couple small iconic gifts, so he helped Billy pick out an eight-inch Statue of Liberty and Summer found a silver apple with a bite taken out of it, on a chain, for April.

It wasn't long and Daniel found himself sitting in the living room, alone. Billy and Tommy had disappeared to somewhere outside and the girls were in the kitchen making a salad that Summer had tried at David Burke's Townhouse restaurant that reminded her of one Mary used to make, and wanted to see what April thought.

Daniel could see the chicken coop through the window and thought he'd go check on the chickens. He topped off the water and food, even though they were almost full. It felt good to be back. It was one of those cloudless, blue sky days, with no wind and he decided to walk back around the house, to the Spirit Garden.

He stood next to the two old folding chairs that faced the circle of metal figures for a few minutes and then sat down. He felt the warmth of the sun on his face, as a thousand things circled in his mind. So much to do and yet it seemed like it was going to be alright. He didn't hear Summer coming up behind him, until she was right next to him.

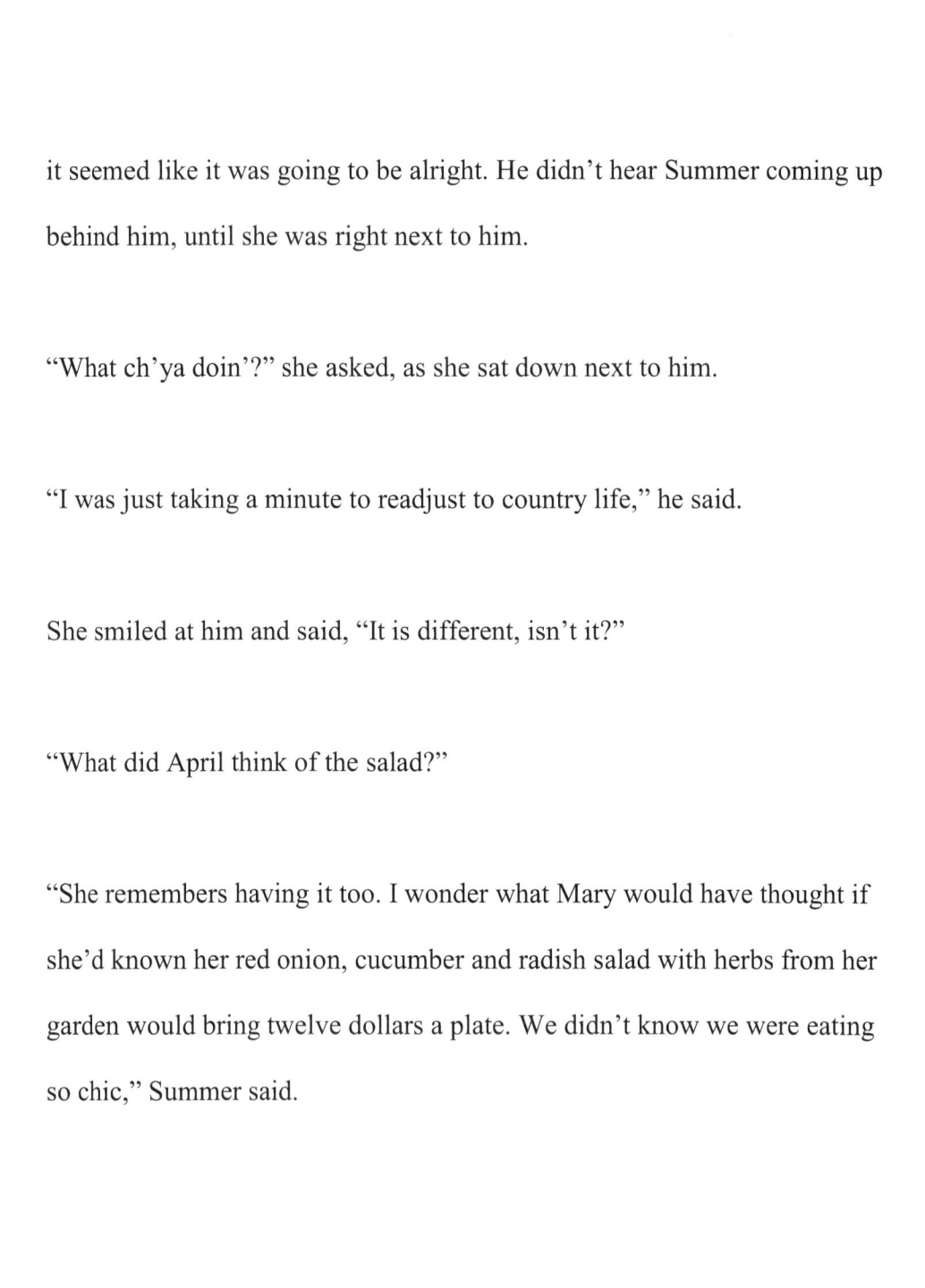

"What ch'ya doin'?" she asked, as she sat down next to him.

"I was just taking a minute to readjust to country life," he said.

She smiled at him and said, "It is different, isn't it?"

"What did April think of the salad?"

"She remembers having it too. I wonder what Mary would have thought if she'd known her red onion, cucumber and radish salad with herbs from her garden would bring twelve dollars a plate. We didn't know we were eating so chic," Summer said.

"So what advice has the Spirit Warrior given the leader of the Siksikawa? (Blackfeet") Summer asked teasingly.

"I was just listening to all the sounds," Daniel said.

"I found Grandpa Ray sitting here one time and asked him what he was thinking of, he said, he wasn't thinking of anything, he was listening," Summer said.

Daniel smiled at her.

"The reason I came looking for you, was to see if you'd like to do the grilling for Supper?" Summer said.

"I would," Daniel replied, seeming to appreciate the diversion, and so they started back to the house, holding hands as they walked.

CHAPTER 26

A few days had passed since their return to Browning. Daniel was sitting in the old shed looking through some boxes, when he heard a vehicle coming toward the house. He looked out as a brown UPS truck was parking next to the Escalade. The boxes from New York had arrived. He watched as Summer signed for them. Then the driver climbed back in his truck, turned around and drove away. A few minutes later, Billy came running toward the shed.

"Our stuff is here from Grandma's!" he said, to Daniel in a slightly excited tone.

"It is?" Daniel said, sounding surprised for Billy's benefit. "I'll be there in a few minutes."

"Okay," Billy said, and ran back to the house.

Daniel looked around the shed before he stood up. He had come to like spending time out here. It was a long way from his corner office, but sitting on a rusty metal chair with the old tools on the workbench, probably right where Ray had left them, was a great place to think. He thought about how time had stopped for these unfinished projects and how they were waiting for their creator to return and bring them to life.

In some ways Daniel could relate to them. He picked up the slab of wood with the bear on it and carried it over to the bench. He traced the outline of the bear with his finger, then turned to look at the deer antlers nailed to the exposed two by fours. In the rafters was several pair of massive elk antlers. Daniels eyes momentarily fixed on the short pieces of rope, hanging from the trusses. There were many marks from rope that had hung there before. He wondered how many animals had hung there over the years, and recalled the story Uncle Joe had told him. He wondered what it would be like to hunt for his own food.

When he made it to the house, Summer and April were folding some laundry in the living room. The boxes were piled up against the wall, unopened. Daniel came in and sat down in the chair in front of the window.

"You didn't open them?" Daniel said.

"We were waiting for you," Summer said, as they finished folding. She called to the boys and when they came out from their room, said, "Take your clothes and put them away and then we will open the boxes."

Several minutes later, they were back, sitting on the living room floor. Billy seemed more excited than Tommy. Now he could share more about his trip with him. It had been hard for him to keep everything a secret, but he had done it.

"We need a knife to open them," Summer said.

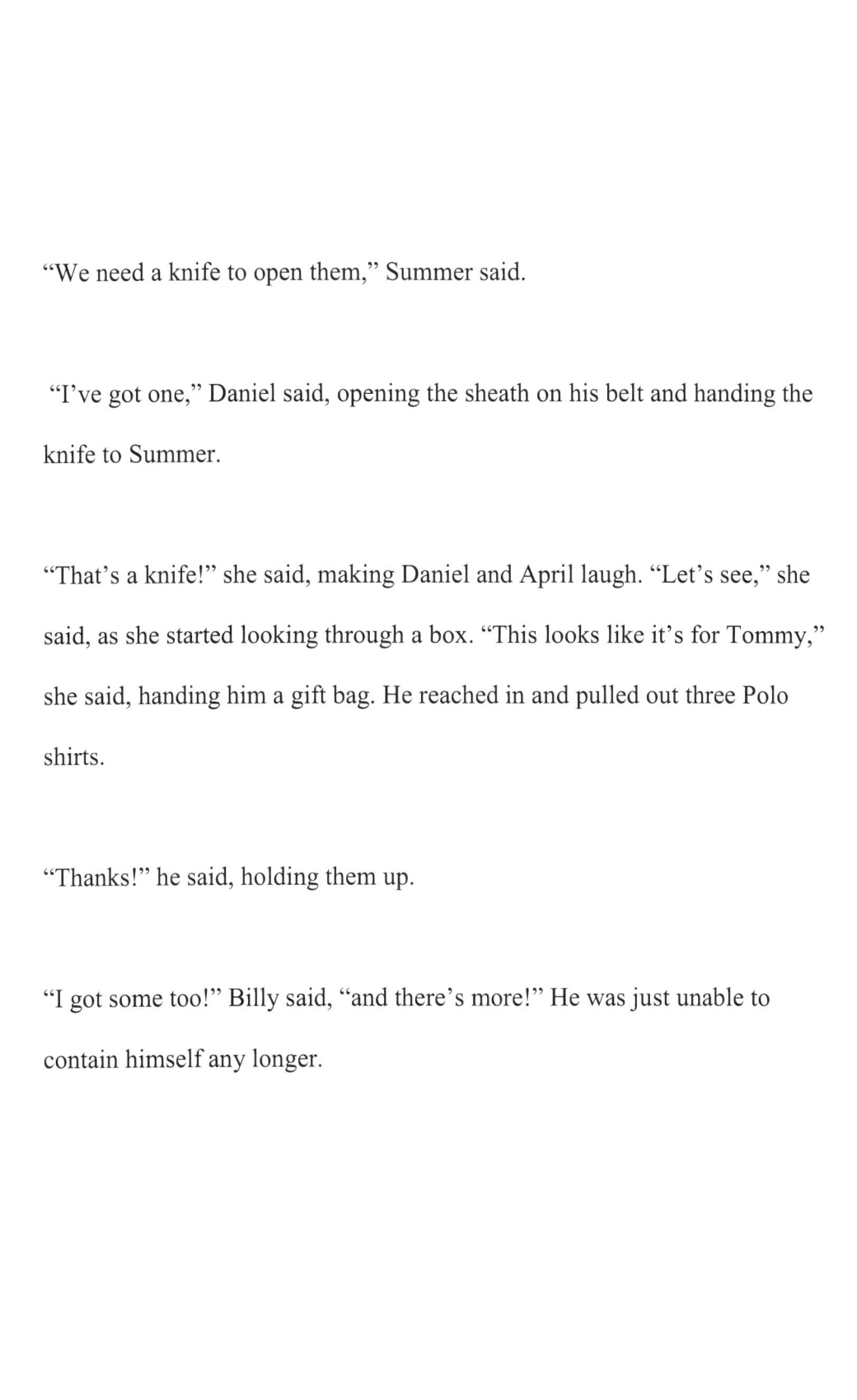

"I've got one," Daniel said, opening the sheath on his belt and handing the knife to Summer.

"That's a knife!" she said, making Daniel and April laugh. "Let's see," she said, as she started looking through a box. "This looks like it's for Tommy," she said, handing him a gift bag. He reached in and pulled out three Polo shirts.

"Thanks!" he said, holding them up.

"I got some too!" Billy said, "and there's more!" He was just unable to contain himself any longer.

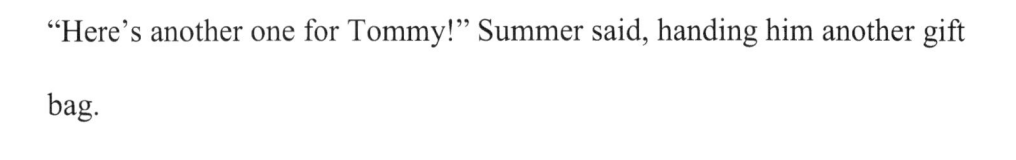

"Here's another one for Tommy!" Summer said, handing him another gift bag.

"Dress pants!" April said, as he held them up. "You're gonna look pretty sharp."

"This one's for you," Summer said, as she handed April a bag.

"It's beautiful!" April said, as she held up the dress that Summer and Evelyn had picked out for her.

"There's more!" Summer said, she too had found it hard to keep things a secret. She reached in the box for another bag and handed it to April.

April reached in the bag and pulled out a pair of shoes. She held them up and just looked at Summer. "Their fabulous!"

"There Versace!" Summer said.

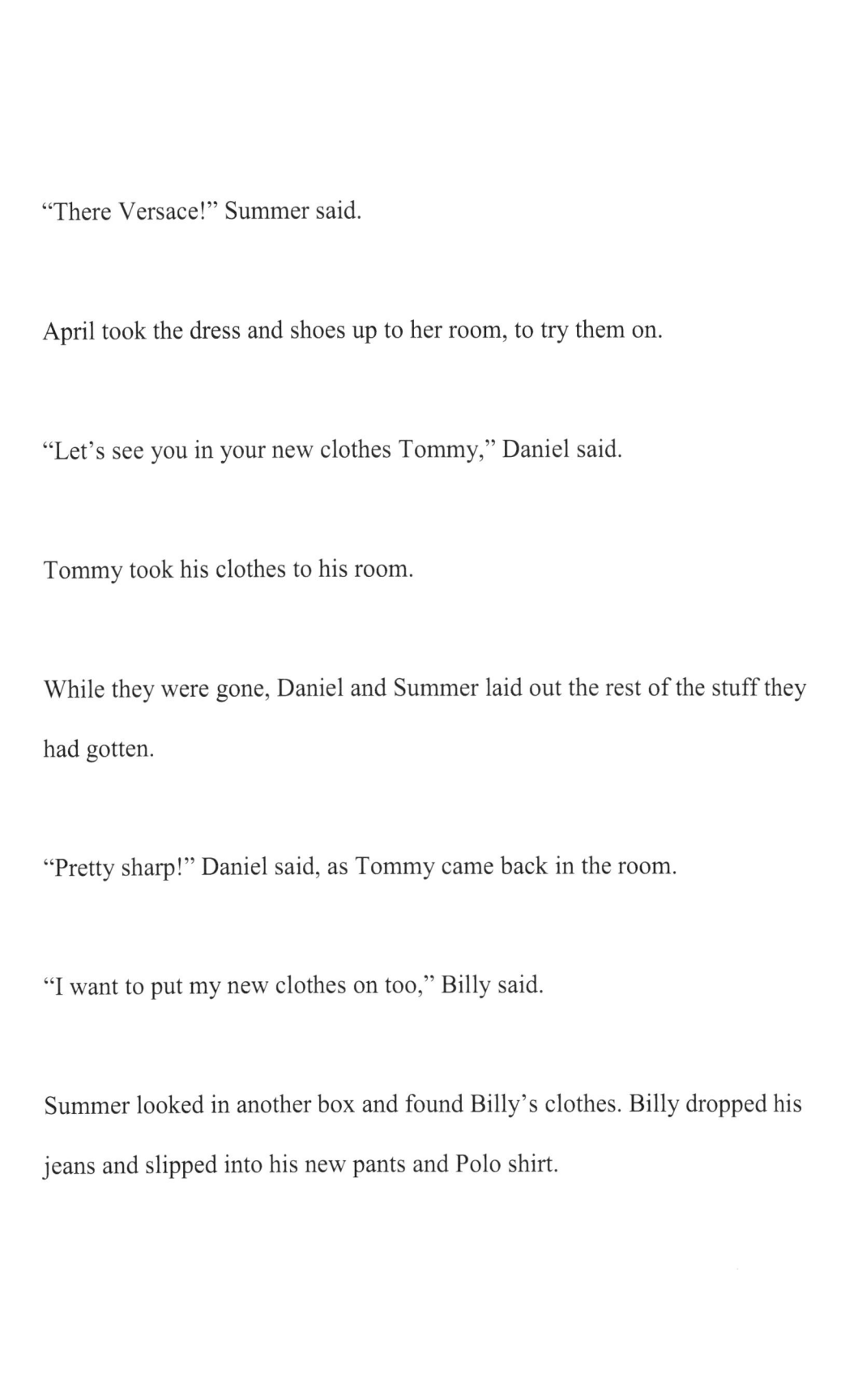

April took the dress and shoes up to her room, to try them on.

"Let's see you in your new clothes Tommy," Daniel said.

Tommy took his clothes to his room.

While they were gone, Daniel and Summer laid out the rest of the stuff they had gotten.

"Pretty sharp!" Daniel said, as Tommy came back in the room.

"I want to put my new clothes on too," Billy said.

Summer looked in another box and found Billy's clothes. Billy dropped his jeans and slipped into his new pants and Polo shirt.

"You're both looking pretty stylish," Daniel said.

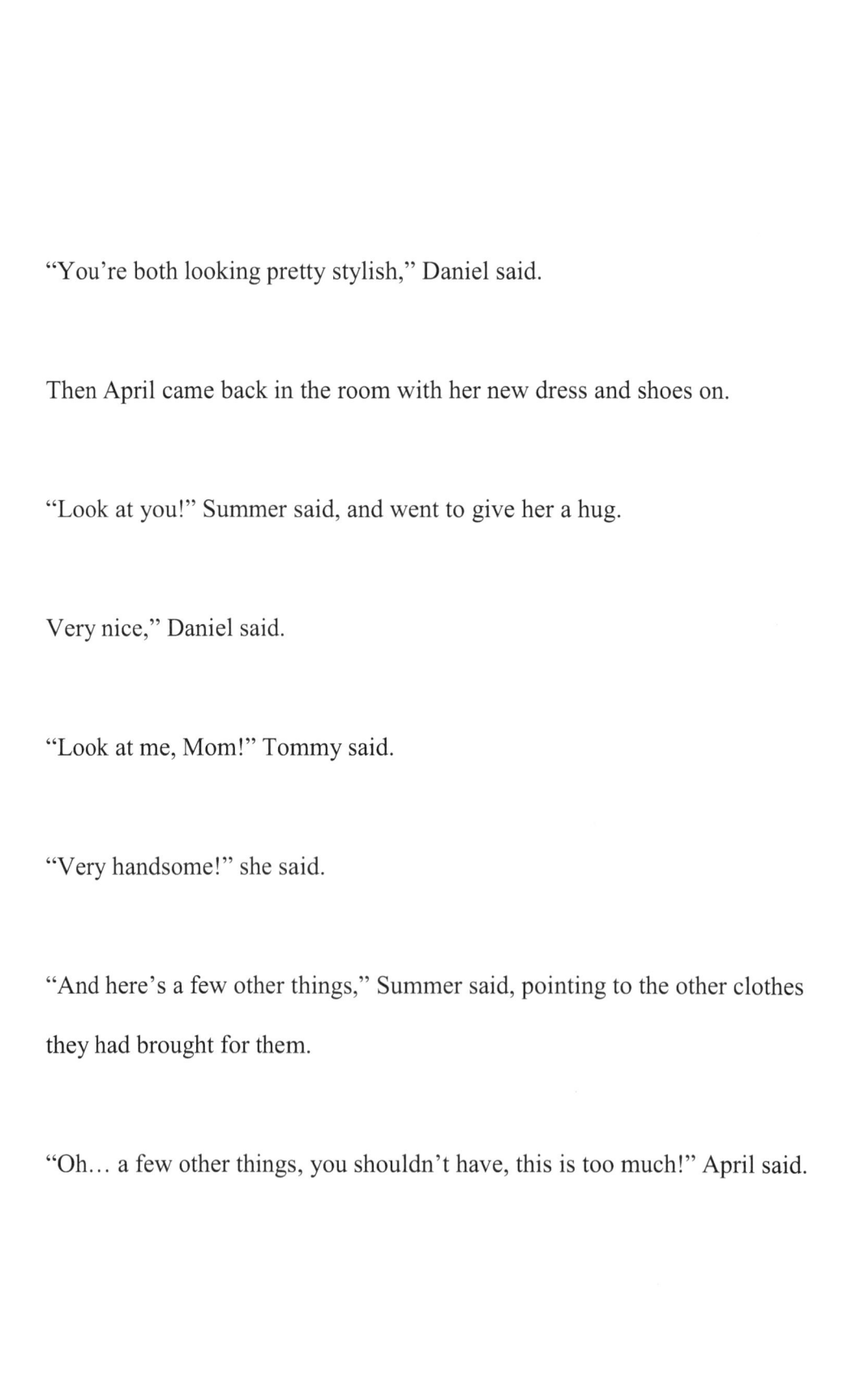

Then April came back in the room with her new dress and shoes on.

"Look at you!" Summer said, and went to give her a hug.

Very nice," Daniel said.

"Look at me, Mom!" Tommy said.

"Very handsome!" she said.

"And here's a few other things," Summer said, pointing to the other clothes they had brought for them.

"Oh… a few other things, you shouldn't have, this is too much!" April said.

"A Suit!" Tommy said.

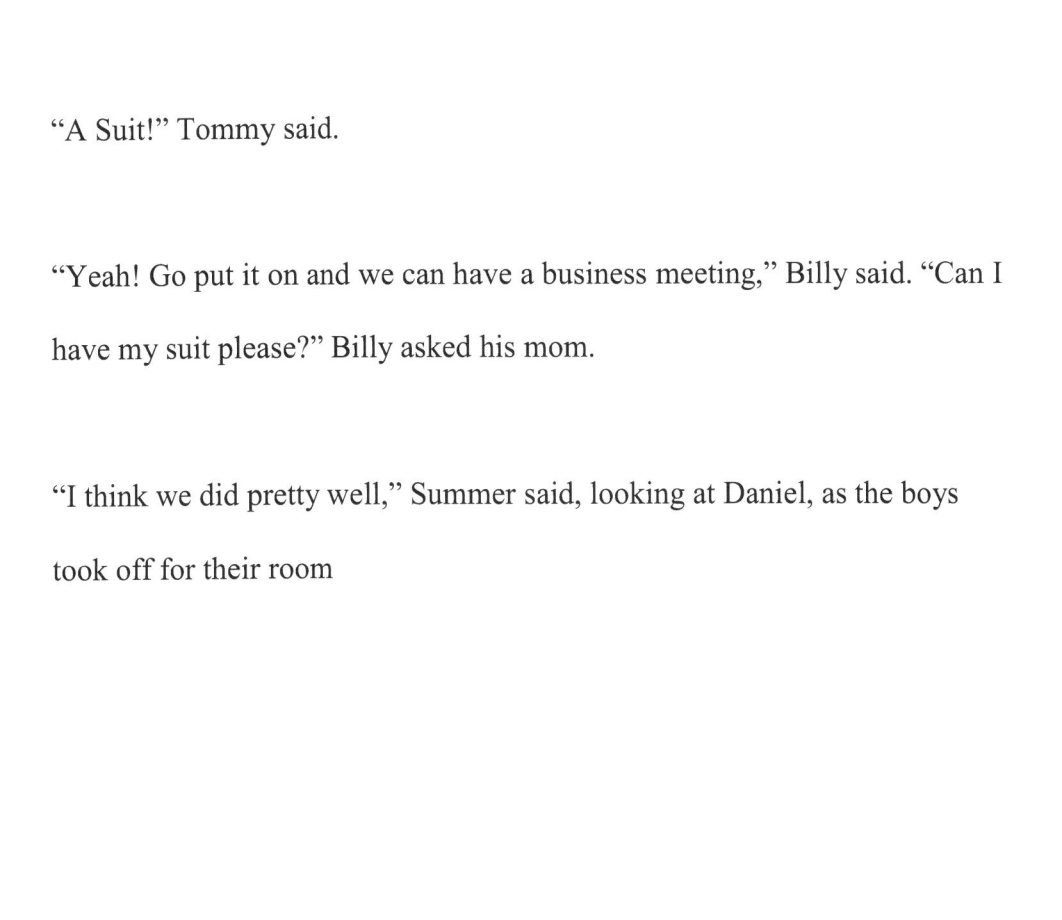

"Yeah! Go put it on and we can have a business meeting," Billy said. "Can I have my suit please?" Billy asked his mom.

"I think we did pretty well," Summer said, looking at Daniel, as the boys took off for their room

CHAPTER 27

It had been two weeks since they had returned from New York. Daniel was sitting in Mary's chair, talking with Steve, who had just finished looking over the contract, Faulkner's people had sent over.

"There are a couple of things we'll need to take a closer look at, but I think it looks pretty promising. I'll send you a copy," Steve said. "How does it feel to be back out there?"

"We're just starting to paint the outside of the house, it took a lot of prep work, but it's gonna look great," Daniel said.

"Well let me know what you think after you get the contract, I'll talk to you later," Steve said, and hung up.

Daniel was still sitting there thinking how good it would be for the community to have something like the solar panel plant, when Summer came out on the porch and sat on the arm of the chair.

"We could use a few things from town. Would you like to go in or should April and I go?"

"I think I'd like to talk with Chief. Why don't the two of us go?" Daniel said.

"I'll get ready," Summer said, hopping up and disappearing in the house. After a few minutes Daniel followed her and changed his shirt.

"Hey, the Jetsetters have returned. How's it going?" Chief said, from behind the counter.

"Good! How are things going with you?" Daniel asked.

"Good," Chief answered, in a tone that wasn't totally convincing.

Summer grabbed a cart and went to get the things on her list, leaving the men to talk.

"We got back from New York a couple of weeks ago. I've been getting the old house ready for painting," Daniel said.

"That old thing? It's not worth the paint or the labor, what do you get? Five hundred an hour?" Chief said, referring to Daniel's legal practice…. "So the trip was good?" he said, more seriously.

"Oh yeah! It was fun showing Summer and Billy around… I'd like to talk to you about a few things, I've been working on."

"Okay, let me get somebody up front," Chief said. "Jimmy can you come to checkout, please," he said, over the intercom.

Daniel saw a tall skinny kid with his hair pulled back in a ponytail coming from the back of the store.

"We can go back in the office," Chief said to Daniel, making a motion with his head. "Take over for a little bit, would ya?" Chief said, to Jimmy, as he led the way to the office.

"We are going in back for a few minutes," Daniel said, to Summer, seeing her at the dairy case, and pointed to the door Chief had just disappeared through.

Chief sat down behind an old wooden desk and made a gesture with his hand toward the chair across from him. Daniel sat down.

"When I went back to New York, I went back to find anybody that would back us in our fight to expand the range of the buffalo. I was mad as hell about what happened and determined to make whoever was behind killing those animals pay. My partner, Steve, helped me see things from a different perspective. He pointed a few things out, that made me see the bigger picture.... If we had good jobs here, then the people living here would have money and that would attract more business and we could build a stronger foundation for a better local economy. We'd have a bigger voice for the Buffalo.... I think we may have some people interested in helping start up a solar panel production site, right here. Something like that could really help get the revenue needed to make a real difference," Daniel said, taking a minute to compose his next sentence.

"The big picture is, the Rez. is the Rez." Chief said, folding his arms in front of him.

Daniel sensed something had changed since the last time they had talked.

"There will always be someone interested in "Helping Us!" Chief said, making quotation marks in the air. "Didn't you see our pencil factory on the edge of town? Someone figured out, there was grant money to 'Help the Native Americans,'" he said, pumping his fingers in the air, again. "We got a pencil factory, as the rest of the world entered the computer age and some big business man, that knows his way around Washington, walked away with millions of dollars of grant money that he channeled to other parts of his empire. At the end of our contract, his people convinced the council to buy him out, by showing them sales figures, made by using creative financing. It turns out, he used several of his other companies to buy all the pencils, at a contract rate, five hundred percent higher than average. The accountants of these other companies, used the inflated cost to help show a lower profit margin and avoided paying taxes. Then they turned around and donated them to charities around the world, for a tax break, of course. His companies even received an additional tax credit for buying from a company that was enrolled in the Grant program. Because, he owned the controlling stock of the pencil factory, ninety percent of the profits went to him. What do you think happened to all those pencil orders, once he sold his shares? How do I know all this? We had lawyers look into it. We were told it was all perfectly legal. That's how it is… really…. Katoyis (Blood Clot Boy) cannot slay all the monsters…. Tribal police found Nitsokan's (His Dream) hide. They found it when they went to Tony Coyote's house, to check on him, after someone said, they hadn't seen him for a couple days, they found it in the freezer. But no sign of him. They believe he left town."

Chief looked at Daniel for a minute, then fished around in his pants pockets and took out a couple of crumpled dollar bills. He straightened them out, put them together and then slide them across the desk.

"What's that for?" Daniel asked.

"Your retainer. I'm your newest client…. One night, a day or so after you flew back to New York, I got a call. Someone told me Tony had been downtown drinking all day. They said, he was talking about how he was getting things stirred up with the Cattleman and how he was gonna teach the 'fancy New York Lawyer' to mind his own fucking business. They also told me, that as he got drunker and drunker, he started talking about Summer and April and how maybe if something bad were too happened to the boys, they'd remember not to let outsiders in the Rez. As your client, I'm telling you, that later that evening, Tony and I had a face to face conversation. But when I left him, he was still alive," Chief paused for a moment and then continued, taking things in a different direction.

"I know you have a good heart. I believe the Elders, when they say you have come back to help 'The People.' But I don't want you to get hurt. I don't want Summer or Billy or April or Tommy to get hurt. There are others just like Tony, confused, filled with hate. First save those that can be saved. Then, try to do something for the rest em'. That is the only way to ensure our legacy," Chief said, and then smiled as he leaned forward putting his elbows on the desk.

Daniel sat quietly for a moment, thinking about what Chief had just said. He was probably right. He had wondered himself about their safety at the old farm, once things got stirred up. Maybe he was foolish to think he could protect them. Now he couldn't even be sure, from what direction danger might come.

"I should get back up front, before Jimmy gives away the store," Chief said, as he stood up.

"I guess, I'll go find Summer," Daniel said, following him back out into the store. He had a lot to think about. He found Summer pushing the cart down the canned goods isle.

"Hey…" she said, and then paused in mid-sentence holding a can of black beans; she was about to ask him if chili sounded good, but it was obvious Daniel wasn't thinking about dinner. "What's wrong?" she asked.

"Oh, nothing… I was thinking I'd like to go see Uncle Joe. Let's get some things to take to him." They finished shopping and went to check out.

"So how did you like the Big Apple?" Chief asked Summer, as he rang up their groceries.

"It was fantastic. I had a wonderful tour guide," she said, and looped her arm through Daniels and smiled.

Daniel paid and they made their way out.

"Take care," Chief said, as they went out the door.

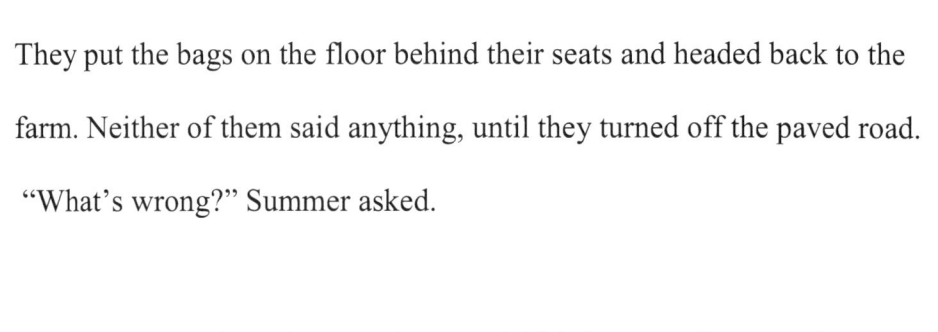

They put the bags on the floor behind their seats and headed back to the farm. Neither of them said anything, until they turned off the paved road. "What's wrong?" Summer asked.

"They found 'Nits-o-kan's (His Dream) hide in Tony Coyote's freezer. Nobody's seen Tony for several days," Daniel said.

Summer didn't say anything for a couple of minutes, then, she said, "This is the end of the county road."

"What?" Daniel asked.

"You asked me how far the county road went. Here, this is the end of it," Summer replied.

Daniel stopped the vehicle, "So, we could put a gate here if we wanted to?" he said.

"Yeah, I suppose," Summer answered, with a worried look on her face. "What's up?" she asked.

"When I asked you about the road, I was thinking about a security gate. I was initially thinking of the Cattleman's association or other outside groups opposed to reintroducing the Buffalo. Now I'm not sure who our enemies might be or for that matter who our allies are."

Then Daniel told her about his conversation with Chief. Summer didn't say anything, but, Tony's disappearance and finding the hide in his freezer, seemed to put her slightly on edge. She looked out the window as they made their way along the bumpy dirt road. Daniel parked and they went inside with their bags. April heard them pull up and came down from her room.

"Hey!" she said, as she came to help Summer.

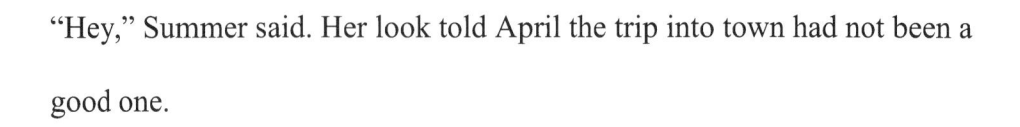

"Hey," Summer said. Her look told April the trip into town had not been a good one.

"What's wrong?"

"Oh, we'll talk about it in a little bit. Where's the boys?" she said, suddenly with a look of anguish, realizing they weren't right there.

"I'm pretty sure they are in their room, why?" April said.

Summer stopped what she was doing and left the kitchen to look in on them. April gave Daniel a funny look, as she finished putting away the groceries.

"I'm gonna go check on the chickens," he said, and turned to go out the door, in an attempt to avoid offering any possible explanation for Summer's concern.

"You have to see this!" Summer said, just then, popping around the corner with a big smile on her face. April and Daniel followed her back to the boy's bedroom. "Take a look," Summer whispered, and motioned sideways with her head.

"Hi, Mom," Tommy said, when he saw April. He and Billy were sitting at the little table in the corner of their room, dressed in their suits, playing checkers.

"Are you having fun?" she asked.

"Yeah, I'm winning!" he said.

"King Me!" Billy said.

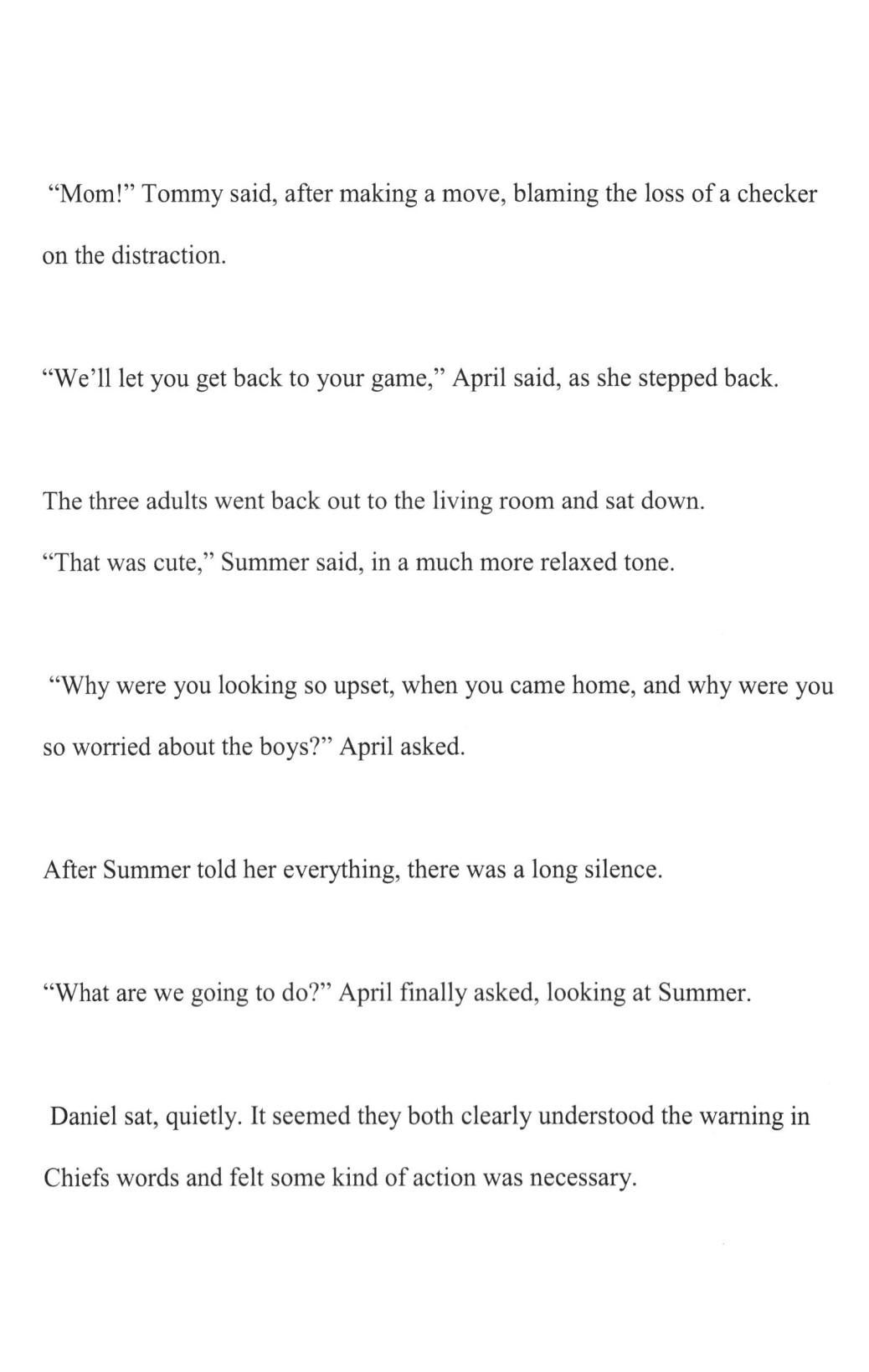

"Mom!" Tommy said, after making a move, blaming the loss of a checker on the distraction.

"We'll let you get back to your game," April said, as she stepped back.

The three adults went back out to the living room and sat down.

"That was cute," Summer said, in a much more relaxed tone.

"Why were you looking so upset, when you came home, and why were you so worried about the boys?" April asked.

After Summer told her everything, there was a long silence.

"What are we going to do?" April finally asked, looking at Summer.

Daniel sat, quietly. It seemed they both clearly understood the warning in Chiefs words and felt some kind of action was necessary.

"We could all move to New York," Summer said.

April gave a little laugh, then, she realized Summer wasn't kidding. She looked at Daniel and then back at Summer. Daniel just looked at the two of them, as they both let the idea hang out there. Summer told April about Evelyn and some of the things she had said to her. Daniel was a little surprised at how open they both were to the idea, as they discussed more of the pros and cons.

"Why don't we go on a road trip and spend a few days away from everything. We can stop and see Uncle Joe on the way," he said.

"I can ask Jenny Weasel Child to come out and take care of the chickens, she can always use extra eggs," April said.

"That sounds like a great idea," Summer said, looking at Daniel.

"Okay, when are we leaving?" he asked.

The sisters looked at each other. "We could leave tomorrow, sometime," Summer suggested.

"Okay, tomorrow it is," Daniel said.

They all sat there for a few minutes. There was an odd mix of excitement and worry, as each of them thought of what might lie ahead. Daniel got up and went outside. He sat down in Mary's old chair. It had become a place for reflection. He looked out at the chickens and to the horizon beyond, where the earth and sky became one. It all seemed so peaceful. But was it really? Daniel didn't know what to think. He got up and walked over to the chicken coop. He went in, checked their food and water, they were still full. He stepped out and latched the door and looked back toward the house. The new grill looked more at home, with the house freshly painted. He had thought of a metal roof… maybe adding on. But now? He made his way around to the back of the house, thinking how the girls reacted to Chiefs comments. As he neared the Spirit Garden, something caught his attention. A big mule deer buck, feeding just out of the circle, raised his head suddenly. Their eyes locked for a moment. Then the deer turned to its left and bolted. As it jumped into the air, a white wolf landed just feet from where it had been standing. The buck bounced off through the sage, the white wolf following close behind. Daniel sat down in one of the old metal chairs. "That was amazing!" he said, out loud, as he replayed what he had seen, in his mind. He took a deep breath and exhaled. "You don't see that in Central Park," he said. He sat there for a little while, looking at the Spirit Warrior. Then, something caught his attention, where he had first noticed the big buck feeding. Two figures seemed to come out of nowhere. Daniel recognized one of them as Mary; she raised her hand as they walked to the center of circle. The other figure was that of a man, he looked around the Garden and then directly at Daniel. Daniel could not take his eyes off him; it was as if the apparition controlled his will. Then he saw their lips start to move, but the sound of their voices was not in sync with them and it sounded like it was coming from far away.

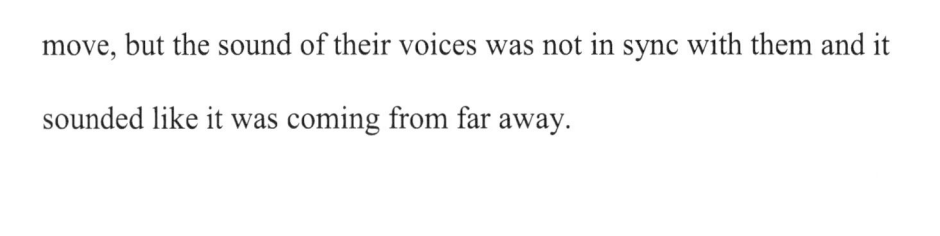

"Take the Women and Children. They are coming. Follow the Red Road," they both said.

Daniel could see Mary was looking at the house, tears rolled down her face. Then, they turned, walked out of the circle and disappeared. Daniel felt the trance loosening its hold on him, as he sat there starring at the spot they had vanished. He felt a hand on his shoulder and snapped his head around.

"Oh! It's you," he said, seeing Summer.

"You look like you've seen a ghost," she said.

"Two of them, you didn't see 'em?" Daniel said. He described what he had seen: The deer, the wolf, everything. "Take the women and children, they are coming," he said, repeating their words, as he looked in Summers eyes.

Summer sat down in the other chair and looked out into the Spirit Garden and then at Daniel.

"April is helping the boys pack. They are excited about going to the Park," she said.

"Good," he said, making a noise with his lips as he exhaled, and then stood up to walk back to the house.

CHAPTER 28

The next morning, after breakfast, the boys announced they were going to wear 'good clothes' and thought everyone should dress up. Summer and April didn't need much convincing. Daniel would have rather worn his jeans and boots, but could see it would make the trip even more special to all of them and that made him happy. After a stop at Jenny Weasel Childs house, they were on their way.

It was just after noon, as they passed Blacktail Lake. Daniel stopped when he got to the fork on top of the ridge and shifted the SUV out of 4-wheel Low and into 4- wheel high. He turned to look out over the mountains and caught Summer smiling at him. He looked in the rearview mirror and saw April watching him too.

"What?" he said, lifting his hands off the steering wheel.

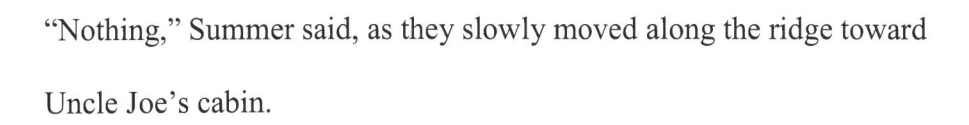

"Nothing," Summer said, as they slowly moved along the ridge toward Uncle Joe's cabin.

Uncle Joe was watching from the top of the steps, as everyone got out. Summer and April carried the bags of supplies from town and Daniel followed with a bag from the Ranch and Home Supply in Great Falls.

"Oki'nik'so'ko'ik'si'," (hello, all my relatives) Uncle Joe said, as Summer handed him, the flour, sugar and coffee. "Nitsiniiyi'taki," (I thank You), he said.

"Noshi," (Your welcome), she returned.

"Please… sit down," he said, before disappearing inside with the box and returning with two more folding chairs. Once they were all seated, Uncle

Joe looked them over. "You all look so nice. How was your trip to New York?" He said, turning toward Daniel.

"It was good," Daniel said ... "I got these for you, before we left... I hope they fit," he said, handing Uncle Joe the bag with the jeans and shirt.

"Thank you!" Uncle Joe said, looking inside the bag, but then setting it next to his chair. "What's wrong?" Uncle Joe asked.

"The trip to New York helped me see things in a different light. I thought I had things worked out. Then, when we got back, it all changed," Daniel said, as he went on to tell about his visit with Chief and the discovery of the hide in Tony Coyotes freezer and how they had decided to go to Glacier Park to get away from everything to think.

Uncle Joe looked at Summer and April with the boys sitting on their laps. After a moment of silence. He said "a road trip! It has been many years since I have been on the 'Going to the Sun Road.'"

"We were hoping you would come with us!" Daniel said, ready to argue the case.

"Yes, I think it would be a good thing," Uncle Joe said, getting up and taking his new clothes inside.

Daniel looked at Summer with a 'what just happened' look on his face. She seemed just as surprised, and just shrugged her shoulders. It wasn't more than fifteen minutes and Uncle Joe reappeared on the porch, dressed in his new jeans and shirt, holding an old travel bag in one hand and two gun cases in the other.

"I'm just about ready, will you take these, and I'll lock up," he said, and went back inside," pulling the door shut behind him.

Daniel stood there with an odd look on his face, as Uncle Joe seemed to be locking the door from the inside. Then there was a noise along the kitchen wall, over by the sink; several minutes later, Uncle Joe came walking from around the side of the house.

"Now I'm ready. It's been a long time since the house was locked down. But I guess with everything going on, it's best," Uncle Joe said, and smiled.

Daniel was still standing at the bottom of the porch, holding the gun cases, with a funny look on his face.

"Those used to belong to Eddie. I want you to have them," Uncle Joe said.

****

Back down the mountain they went.

As Daniel turned right on Highway 2, he glanced in the rear view mirror and smiled as he made eye contact with Summer. They were on their way!

They popped in and out of the timber as they headed west on Hwy.2, passing through the edge of Glacier Park, it was beautiful and for a couple of hours, they traveled along, everyone watching the landscape roll by and forgetting their cares. They made their way to Whitefish and drove around, checking out the lodging options: Holiday Inn, Inn Gate, Super 8. The girls decided on Holiday Inn because it was straight across from Perkins. Daniel went in the Office and came out after a few minutes with the keys to two rooms and moved the SUV over to them.

Daniel and Uncle Joe sat down at the little table in front of the window in their room for a few minutes, to give the girls a chance to settle in. Daniel started talking about the trip to New York and how much fun they'd had. He told Uncle Joe how his mother had taken to Summer and how Billy called her Grandma.

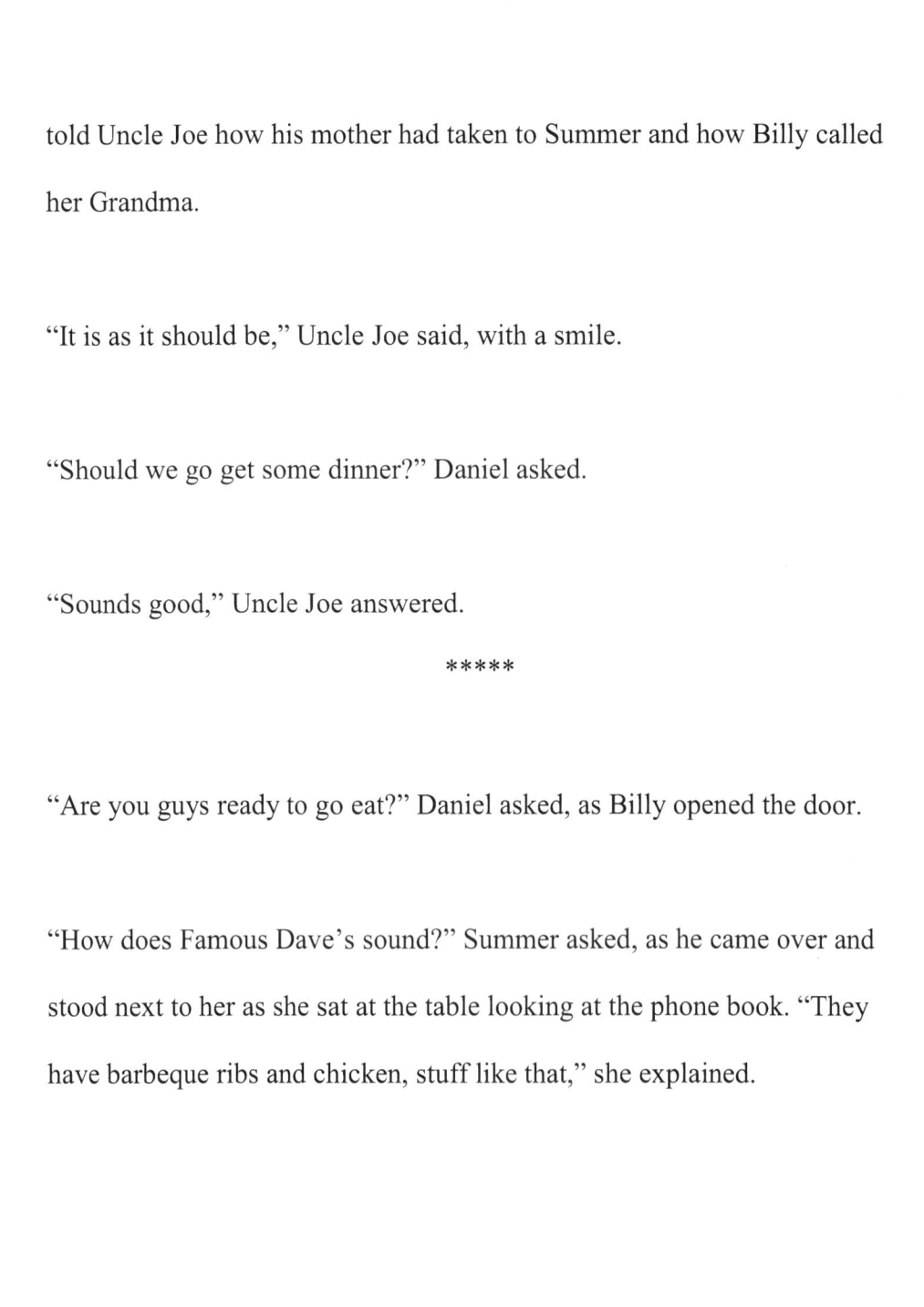

"It is as it should be," Uncle Joe said, with a smile.

"Should we go get some dinner?" Daniel asked.

"Sounds good," Uncle Joe answered.

*****

"Are you guys ready to go eat?" Daniel asked, as Billy opened the door.

"How does Famous Dave's sound?" Summer asked, as he came over and stood next to her as she sat at the table looking at the phone book. "They have barbeque ribs and chicken, stuff like that," she explained.

"If that's where you would like to go, it sounds good to me," he said, and off to dinner they went.

Later that Evening, back in their room, Daniel and Uncle Joe were once again sitting at the table.

"You are a good man," Uncle Joe said, looking at Daniel. "It takes a strong man, a good hunter, to take a woman with a child and her Sister and her son into his lodge."

"April is her only sister and the boys get along so well," Daniel said.

"You look after others, like it is your pleasure. That is what makes you a good leader," Uncle Joe said.

Daniel smiled, as his eyes shifted down to the table.

"Naapi (Old man) gave you a great gift, when he gave you, your adopted family. They taught you many things," Uncle Joe said.

Uncle Joe put his bag on the table. He pulled out the old felt hat and handed it to Daniel.

"I want you to have it," he said.

"Thank you," Daniel said, tipping it, to look in at the rabbits. In addition to the three rabbits was the old picture of his parents, taken before they were married. Daniel looked at Uncle Joe, "Thank you," he said again.

Uncle Joe then reached in the travel bag and pulled out his old pipe and tobacco bag. "This pipe and bag have been in our family for one hundred and fifty years. It has been handed down to the eldest son for six generations. One day, you will have them." He put the pipe and leather bag back in his travel bag and closed it. "Those guns were Eddy's. I gave him that shotgun when he turned twelve. The rifle he bought when he turned fifteen with money he earned by selling furs he got trapping."

Daniel didn't know what to say, except, "thank you, I'll take good care of them."

"I know you will," Uncle Joe said. Then he stretched, saying "I am getting tired, I think it is time for bed."

The next morning, Uncle Joe listened and watched, while they ate breakfast. What he saw made him smile. It was a good thing, and he silently thanked 'Naapi' (Old Man) for answering his prayers and returning Daniel to him. He was very proud to be part of this newly formed band.

"What do you say we do a little looking around town?" Daniel suggested as they were walking out to the Escalade.

"There's a Murdoch's in Kalispell," Summer said, doing her part by making it sound like a spontaneous thought. Daniel had mentioned to her that he wanted to get a few more things for Uncle Joe. She knew he meant well and understood where he got his generosity, but her part in the plan still made her feel a little guilty. She wondered how Uncle Joe would take it.

Two hours later, Uncle Joe was looking at himself in the mirror and smiling, as he adjusted the silver clasp of his Bolo tie, shaped like a grizzly bears head, and lightly ran his hands down his leather vest, and over the belt buckle made from the base of an elk antler. He had tried to tell Daniel, that it wasn't necessary to spend any money on him, but it hadn't done any good. He smiled as he looked at Daniel, he thought of Eddie and how proud he must be as he watched from the Sand Hills.

"It's best to just give in," Summer advised Uncle Joe, knowing how he was feeling. "He's just like his mother," she added.

Chapter 29

Daniel and Summer sat, snuggled together, on the oversized leather chair, thinking about the last four days. Everyone else had gone to bed, and the only sounds were the occasional pop and hiss of the logs, burning in the massive river stone fireplace. They watched as the logs melted into glowing embers and then white ash. In the morning they would be heading back to Browning.

"I loved hearing Uncle Joe tell the story of Sour Spirit and how he came down from the sky, to teach the Siksikawa(Blackfeet) about the Hunt," Summer said.

"And how he pointed him out to the boys on the side of the mountain, as we drove up the 'Going to the Sun Road… that's something the boys will remember for a long time," Daniel said.

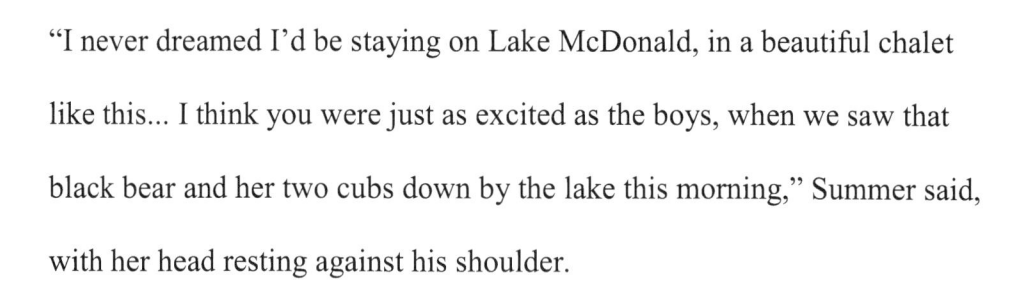

"I never dreamed I'd be staying on Lake McDonald, in a beautiful chalet like this... I think you were just as excited as the boys, when we saw that black bear and her two cubs down by the lake this morning," Summer said, with her head resting against his shoulder.

"What's the word for black bear?" Daniel asked.

"Sik'oh'kyai'yo'-wa'," Summer said.

"Sik'oh'kyai'yo'-wa'," Daniel repeated.

She looking up at him, the light from the fire danced in his eyes, she smiled and let out a sigh. She couldn't remember a time when she had been happier.

"It was the first time I'd ever seen a bear in the wild. It seemed to get Uncle Joe going too, and he's probably seen hundreds of bears," Daniel said, playfully defending his enthusiasm.

"Do you think we could ever convince him to come and see us in New York?" she asked.

"I wondered the same thing," Daniel said, with a little chuckle, as he imagined a walk in Times Square with him.

*****

The next morning Daniel woke up with his arm over Summer, as she slept, holding his hand in her hand up to her chest. He laid there for a minute and listened for any signs of others stirring, and heard nothing, all must be good, he thought and dosed off. A little later, it was Summer who awoke. She ran her right index finger up and down Daniels arm. Summer felt him stir.

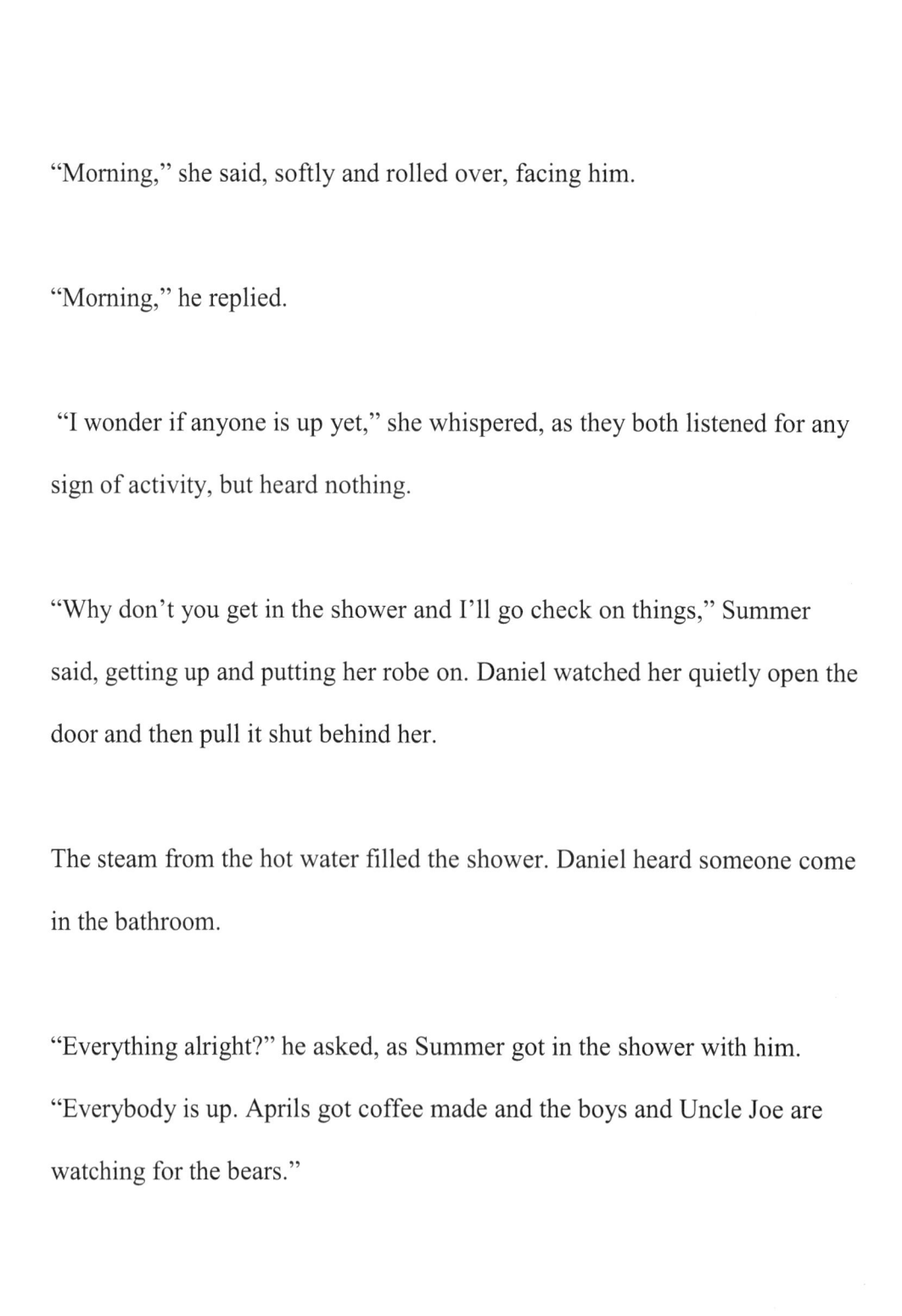

"Morning," she said, softly and rolled over, facing him.

"Morning," he replied.

"I wonder if anyone is up yet," she whispered, as they both listened for any sign of activity, but heard nothing.

"Why don't you get in the shower and I'll go check on things," Summer said, getting up and putting her robe on. Daniel watched her quietly open the door and then pull it shut behind her.

The steam from the hot water filled the shower. Daniel heard someone come in the bathroom.

"Everything alright?" he asked, as Summer got in the shower with him. "Everybody is up. Aprils got coffee made and the boys and Uncle Joe are watching for the bears."

They embraced and turned a half circle, putting Summer directly under the shower head. Daniel watched the water run down her body, as she ran her hands through her hair.

*****

"I see you've both gone green, now… saving water by showering with a friend," April said, as she saw them coming into the kitchen and heading for the coffee pot. "The boys have been keeping Uncle Joe busy, asking him every question they can think of," April said, "I think he likes it," she added.

"It has to get lonely sometimes, living way out there, by himself," Summer said, as she took a sip from her cup.

Daniel was looking out at the boys and Uncle Joe and noticed their posture suddenly changed, as they looked toward the lake. Daniel took his coffee and walked over to the sliding glass door. He carefully opened it and quietly came up behind the boys in a crouched position.

"The Bear and her cubs just came out, down by that stump," Tommy said. They watched as the two cubs crawl up on the stump, while their mother rubbed her side against it. Then the little ones started wrestling and tumbled off, letting out a bawling noise, as they continued rolling over each other.

The boys looked at each other for a second, with their mouths opened, and then back at the bears. Then the mother bear started back into the timber and the little ones followed, and they were gone.

"That was cool!" Billy said, turning around to look at Daniel. "Uncle Joe said they would come out. He said the words to make them come."

Daniel smiled at the boys and looked at Uncle Joe.

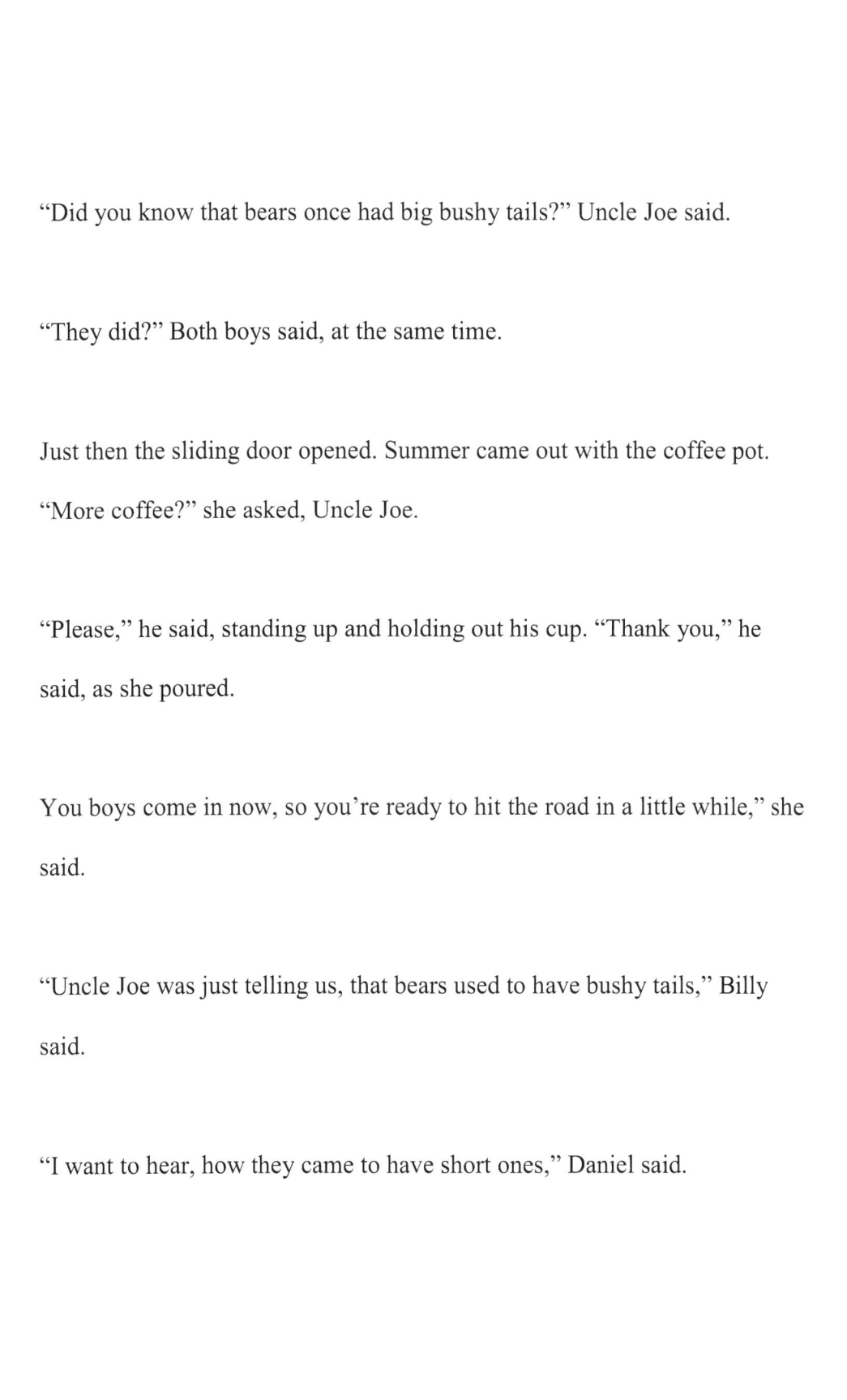

"Did you know that bears once had big bushy tails?" Uncle Joe said.

"They did?" Both boys said, at the same time.

Just then the sliding door opened. Summer came out with the coffee pot. "More coffee?" she asked, Uncle Joe.

"Please," he said, standing up and holding out his cup. "Thank you," he said, as she poured.

You boys come in now, so you're ready to hit the road in a little while," she said.

"Uncle Joe was just telling us, that bears used to have bushy tails," Billy said.

"I want to hear, how they came to have short ones," Daniel said.

"I think that's something we all want to hear," Summer said, going in to get April.

"This is what my father told me… he said, he had heard it from his father, who said, he heard it from his father, who told him, he heard it from an old man that suddenly appeared one day, when he was fishing and then just as suddenly disappeared. It is thought to have been 'Naapi' (Old Man.)
…. Once, bears had a long beautiful tail. All the creatures were envious, especially Fox. He devised a plan that would make his tail, the most beautiful tail among all the animals. He knew Bear was going down to the lake every day to fish, as winter approached, to fatten up for his big sleep. He also knew Bear didn't like to be out fished. He made a bet with Otter, that Otter could not catch the three biggest trout in the lake and then stole them from him. Next, he begged Beaver to cut a hole in the ice, because he was thirsty. Then he laid the fish by the hole and waited for Bear. When Fox

saw him coming, he put his tail in the hole. When Bear saw the big fish, he said, "what are you using for bait, my friend, Fox."

"Come out and I will show you. I have plenty for my family, already," Fox said, with a smile.

So Bear went out and Fox showed him how he caught all the fish.

"Put your tail down there and sit real still. When you feel one grab on, pull it out, quick," Fox said.

Bear did as Fox said, and Fox stayed to keep him company, and to make sure his plan worked. After some time had passed, Bear asked, why he hadn't caught a fish, yet.

"Oh, you will, you will, you must sit real still," Fox said.

Bear sat there, the sun had gone down. He was ready to quit.

"The big ones, come after it gets dark. Don't quit now! I'll come and check on you in the morning. I'll bring a big breakfast and you can tell me about your huge catch," Fox said, leaving Bear to his fishing.

The next morning, just as the sun was coming up, Fox came, as he promised, with a basket of berries and honey and fish.

"I'm so hungry! I didn't catch a single fish," Bear said, jumping up to eat. But the hole had frozen shut and with his own power, pulled his tail off. "You tricked me!" he roared, and rush toward Fox, who easily ran away, holding his tail high for all the animals to see. And, that's how come bears have short tails and why the fox should not be trusted," Uncle Joe said.

"Is that really how it happened?" Tommy said.

"That is what my Father told me, when I was a boy," Uncle Joe said.

"Come on in, now, so you are ready to go, when it's time," Summer said, as she and April stood up.

"How did you know the bears would come back?" Daniel asked, after the boys had gone inside.

"I asked them to come. I also put some peanut butter sandwiches out there, before I went to bed," Uncle Joe said, with a wink, as he settled back and enjoyed his coffee.

Chapter 30

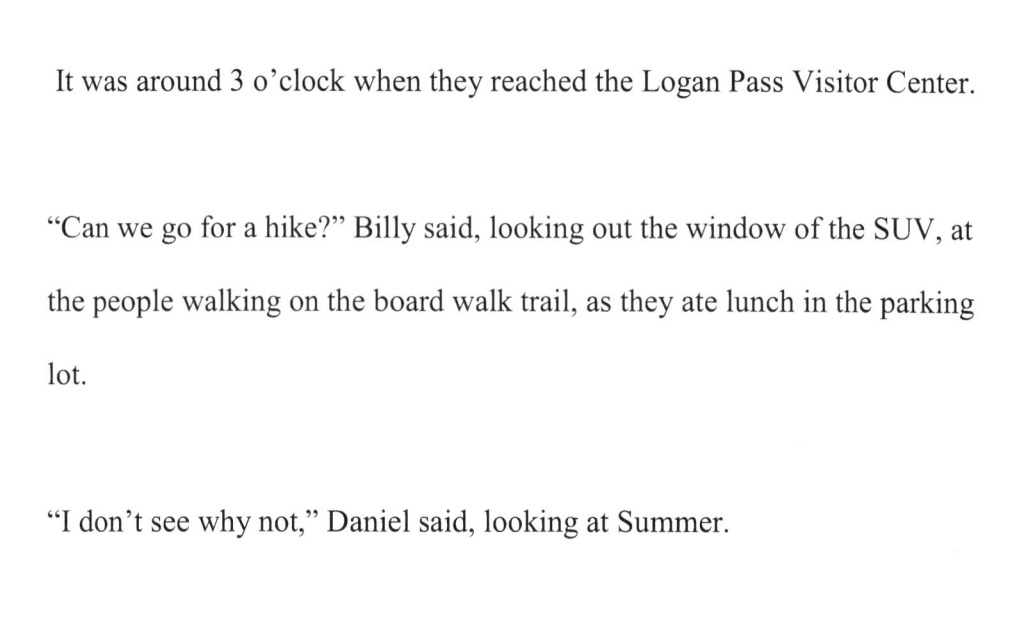

It was around 3 o'clock when they reached the Logan Pass Visitor Center.

"Can we go for a hike?" Billy said, looking out the window of the SUV, at the people walking on the board walk trail, as they ate lunch in the parking lot.

"I don't see why not," Daniel said, looking at Summer.

"A walk sounds like a good idea, not too far, though," Summer replied, trying to set some limits.

"I think, I'll just stretch my legs around the Visitor Center," Uncle Joe said.

"I think I'll keep him company," April said.

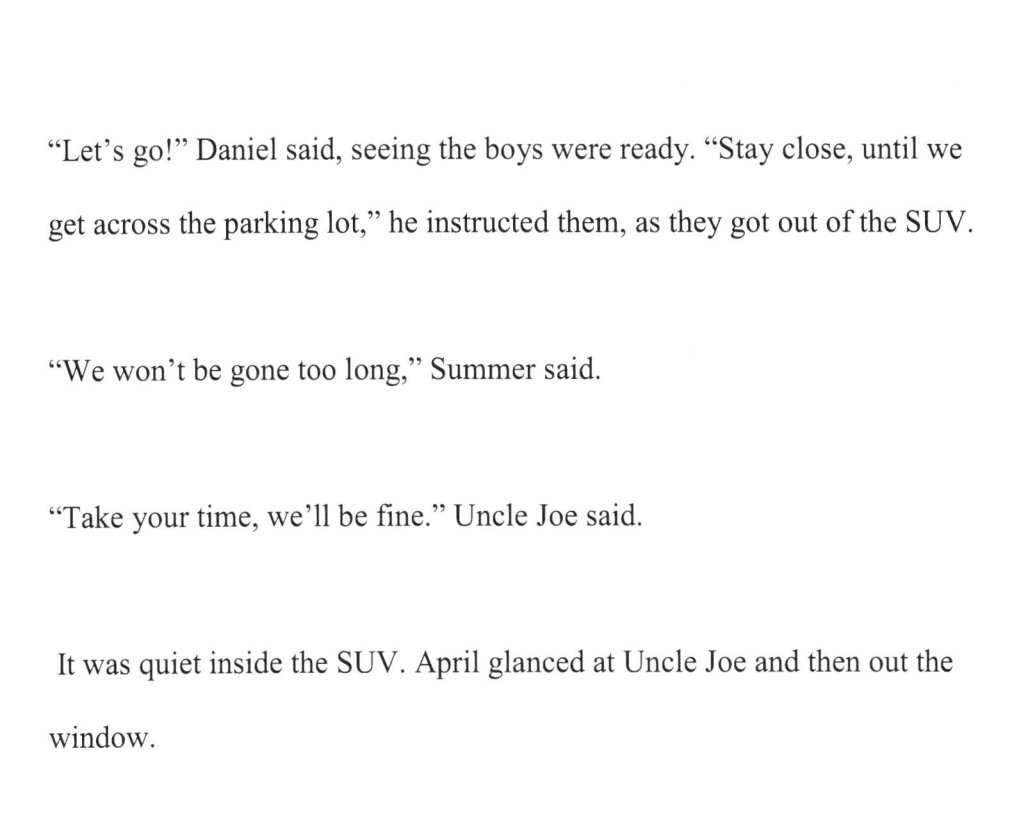

"Let's go!" Daniel said, seeing the boys were ready. "Stay close, until we get across the parking lot," he instructed them, as they got out of the SUV.

"We won't be gone too long," Summer said.

"Take your time, we'll be fine." Uncle Joe said.

It was quiet inside the SUV. April glanced at Uncle Joe and then out the window.

"What is it Ma'tsi'yi'ka'pi'si'ki'soom(April)?" Uncle Joe asked.

"I was thinking of this morning, when you were telling the story of how the bear lost his tail… I realized I hadn't heard one of those old stories in a long, long time. Now that Grandma is gone… there isn't anyone I know, besides you, that knows those stories. Who's going to make sure the boys know them?" April said sounding a little overwhelmed.

"It will be alright… Billy and Tommy, both have good mothers. You and Summer will teach them everything they need to know, about how to get along in today's world and I will do what I can to see they hear the old stories," Uncle Joe said, then gave her a smile.

It wasn't long after that, they saw Summer leading Billy and Tommy back to the SUV, with Daniel following behind. She didn't look very happy as she opened the door and got them inside.

"What's the matter?" April asked.

"Oh, the boys got off the trail and the Ranger caught'em," Daniel said.

Summer gave Daniel a look. The next hour and a half was very quiet, and when they pulled into the parking lot at the St. Mary's Lake Visitor center, Summer turned to the boys and said, "You two stay right next to me, got it?"

"Yes," they both said, at the same time, as they all got out to look at the lake.

The lake was like glass and reflected the snowcapped mountains in the back ground, like a mirror.

"I've been here several times and there has always been a chop on the water," April said, as they tried to take in all of its beauty.

"Let's go check out that trail!" Billy said pointing to a path leading down to the lake, as the group walked the path leading around the pavilion for a little break from sitting.

"No! We need to get a couple of things at the store, before it closes, so we can't mess around. Go use the bathroom and get back to the car," Summer said, still a little annoyed at Billy for horsing around at their last stop and being reprimanded by the park ranger.

"He's just having fun," Daniel said, after the boys had left for the bathroom.

"Oh, I know, I guess I'm just starting to think about what Chief said, and all that stuff about finding the hide in Tony's freezer," Summer said, trying to force a little smile.

"That's right. Turn that frown upside down! 'If you don't, a bird might land on your lip and take a poop," Daniel said.

"What, you think you're some sort of poet or something?" Summer laughed. "You better stick with being a lawyer," she added teasingly.

"I'm a good poet," he said.

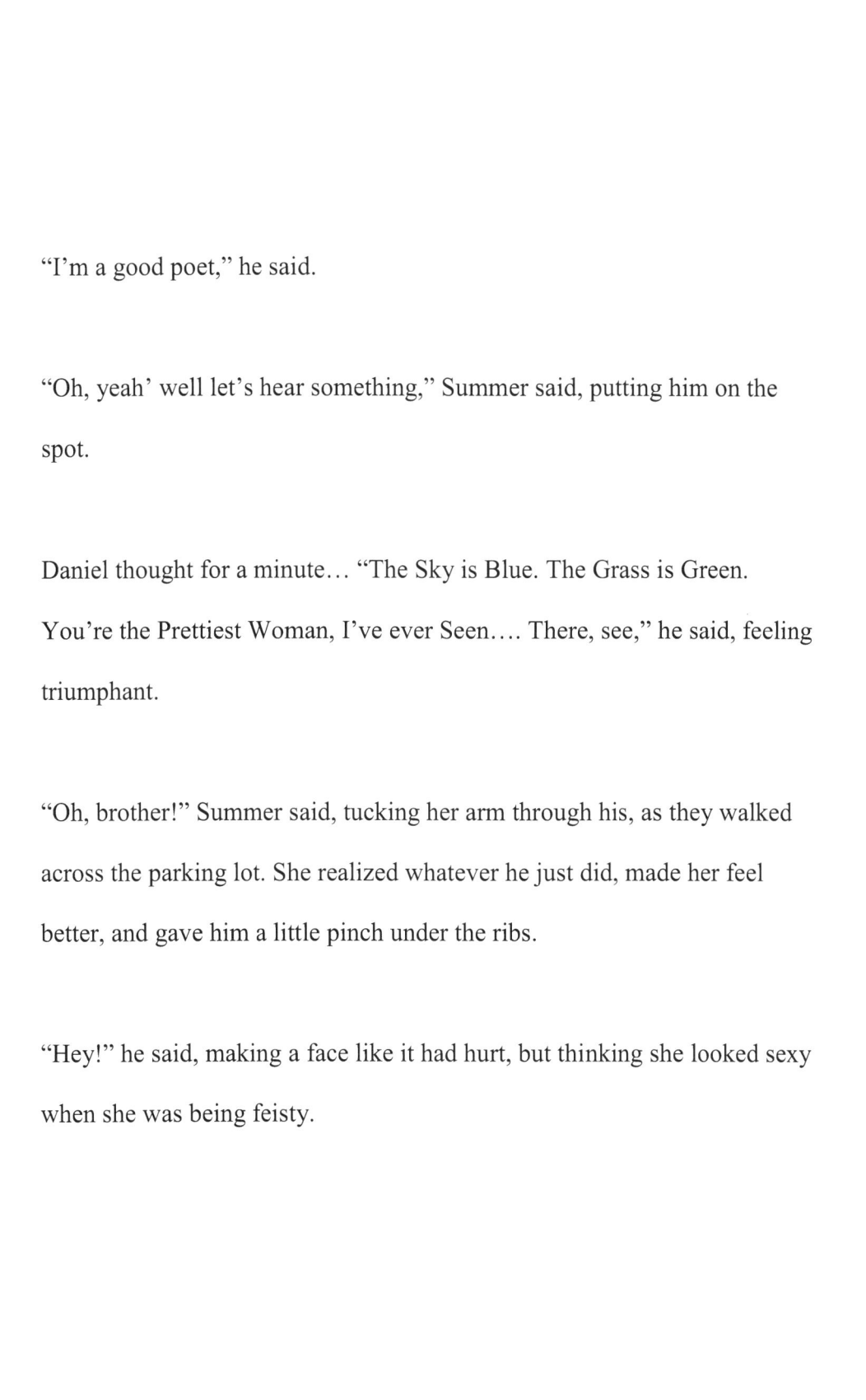

"Oh, yeah' well let's hear something," Summer said, putting him on the spot.

Daniel thought for a minute… "The Sky is Blue. The Grass is Green. You're the Prettiest Woman, I've ever Seen…. There, see," he said, feeling triumphant.

"Oh, brother!" Summer said, tucking her arm through his, as they walked across the parking lot. She realized whatever he just did, made her feel better, and gave him a little pinch under the ribs.

"Hey!" he said, making a face like it had hurt, but thinking she looked sexy when she was being feisty.

The boys were coming down the sidewalk from the restrooms and heading for the SUV.

"You better beat me back!" Summer called out to Billy, in a stern tone. She was just bluffing, but both boys quickened their pace to just under a run, remembering the words of the Ranger.

*****

"And that is why, all the animals think Owl is so smart," Uncle Joe said, finishing a story, just as Daniel parked next to 'The Buck Stops Here'.

The girls went inside, while the guys waited in the SUV. The plan was to go home and take Uncle Joe back to his place in the morning.

"Was it just me or did you feel weird in there, too?" Summer asked April, as they pulling away.

"I felt it too. I wonder what's going on," April said.

"What's the matter?" Daniel asked.

"The guy working in there, Peter Spotted Dog, he was acting kind of weird. Like he didn't want to look at us or say anything, he's always got some comment," Summer said.

"Wasn't Chief there?" Daniel asked.

"I didn't see him," Summer said, looking at April, who shook her head.

They pulled off the tar and down the gravel road that led to the old farm house. When they got to where they could normally see the house, they saw it was gone! Daniel stopped just past the shed and they all got out. They stood there stunned, as they looked at the chunks of charred rubble that was once their Grandmothers house. The gas grill, minus the propane tank lay on its side, the hose had been cut. Daniel realized this was no accident.

"It must have been the old wiring," he said, not wanting the boys to think someone would do this on purpose and hoping they didn't notice the missing tank. "Let's go check on the chickens," Daniel said, and led them over to the coop, which seemed fine. They topped off the water and food and found several eggs and brought them back to the SUV.

"What now?" Summer asked, "Do you want to stay at my house tonight?"

"I don't want to stay at my house, alone," April said.

"Well, I guess we're all going to your house," Daniel said, to Uncle Joe.

"I think that's a good idea, until we find out what's goin' on," Uncle Joe said.

Daniel put the boys back in the SUV, with Uncle Joe, then, went over and put his arms around both of the girls.

"It's so sad," Summer said, as she put her head on his shoulder. "First Grandpa Ray, then Grandma, now the house… It's all gone," she said, her shoulders dropping, as she exhaled.

"It'll be okay," Daniel said, not really knowing what to say, as he ushered them into the SUV. Then he went around to the driver's side, got in and slowly drove back down the dirt road. No one said a word until they got back on the tar.

"We should pick up a few more supplies, enough for several days," Daniel said. "You and I will go in," he said to Summer.

When Peter Spotted Dog saw them coming through the door, he turned and made himself busy. Summer started pulling the basics down, as they walked up and down the aisles. The cart was filled when they pushed it up to the checkout stand.

"Stocking up, huh?" Peter Spotted Dog said to Daniel, as he rang up the groceries.

"Guess it isn't good to shop when you're hungry," Daniel said, in his best New Yorker 'kiss my ass tone.'" Then he asked "Is Chief around?"

"He took a couple of days off. I think he said he was going camping," Peter Spotted Dog said, giving him a big 'Rez smile', which basically said, "go f*** yourself."

Daniel loaded the bags into the cart, as Spotted Dog packed them. "I'd help you out, but I'm the only one here," he said to Daniel, as he put the last items in a bag.

"We'll manage, thanks," Daniel said, as he started to push the cart toward the door.

After making one more stop, to top off the gas tank, they headed west on Hwy.2, back to Uncle Joe's. The sun had disappeared behind the mountains, when they reached Blacktail Creek road. The timber made the night seem even darker, as they slowly made their way up the mountain.

Once they got above Blacktail Lake, the night sky opened up, and Daniel saw more stars than he'd ever seen in his life. He stopped, for a moment, so they could watch the Moonlight dance off the water below. It helped lift everyone spirits, at least for the moment.

"Who's that?" Daniel said, twenty minutes later, as his lights reflected off a vehicle, about the same time they noticed a small fire burning near the house.

"That's Chiefs truck," Uncle Joe said.

"We'll go see what's going on. You wait here," Daniel said to Summer, as he parked, and nodded toward Uncle Joe, as they got out, leaving the motor running and the lights on.

When they walked up to the truck, Uncle Joe noticed something dark between the tailgate and the bumper. "Blood," he said, touching it with his index finger and rubbing his thumb.

As they got closer to the fire, they could see Chief sitting next to it, alone. He was holding a stick just above the flames, cooking something.

"oki ni-kso-ko-wa, (hello my relatives)" he said, as they stepped into the light of the fire. "I brought up some supplies… met that fork horn on the road, so I thought I'd give him a lift. I guess he hadn't heard, it's never safe to take a ride from a stranger," Chief said, and motioned with his arm toward the meat pole next to the house, where a dark shape was hanging. "Nice threads," he added, noticing Uncle Joe's new clothes.

Daniel went back to the SUV to help Summer and April get the boys and supplies to the house.

"What's going on?" Summer asked when Daniel opened the door.

"Chief came up to see Uncle Joe and bring him some supplies, he shot a deer on the way up, and I think he's been drinking."

Daniel led them up to the house with a flashlight. The box of groceries Chief had brought was on the porch. Daniel took the flashlight, found the door to the crawl space and unlocked it, then made his way up through the floor and opened up the house.

Summer lit the lamp that sat on the kitchen table, while Daniel held the flashlight on it, and the light gradually filled the room as it got brighter. Then they went to start bringing in the groceries, while April stayed inside with the boys, they were getting tired after all day on the road, and sat down at the table as she started putting things away.

"Are you hungry?" she asked.

"Can we have a peanut butter sandwich?" Tommy asked.

"Sure, you can," April said, recalling that she had just put some peanut butter in the cabinet. She made them each a sandwich and they sat and ate quietly, while Daniel and Summer came in with the rest of the bags.

"I'm going to talk with Chief," Daniel said.

"We'll be fine," Summer said.

"Fresh meat," Chief said biting into a smoking hunk of meat, as Daniel sat down on a chunk of wood across the fire from him, next to Uncle Joe. Daniel looked at Uncle Joe, who made a slight gesture with his head toward the meat pole. They got up and walked over to the deer. Uncle Joe reached inside the cavity and cut out the remaining tenderloin, while Daniel held the flash light. They went back to the fire and sat down after finding a stick to cook the meat on. It was hard but Daniel managed to sit quietly, as he held the stick over the fire. He had a thousand questions. But he wanted to see where Chief would take the conversation on his own.

"So, you went to The Park," Chief said, carefully enunciating his words so as not slur them.

"Yes. It was magnificent!" Daniel said. There was a long silence. "So, what brings you up here?" he asked Chief casually, as he looked into the fire, pretending to be occupied with keeping the meat from burning.

"I wanted to say goodbye to Uncle Joe before I left. I'm movin' to Mexico. I found a job online, workin' on a Sport fishing boat. I'm gonna be a fisherman," Chief said, as he finished eating the steaming meat and tossed his stick into the fire. He then reached into the bag next to him and produced a single can of beer hanging from a plastic six pack holder and held it out to Uncle Joe and then to Daniel, both of them shook their heads, declining the offer. Chief opened it and held it up as a farewell solute. Uncle Joe gave a nod toward Daniel, as a signal that the meat was probably ready to eat.

"Not bad," Daniel said, taking a bite.

"Good! eh? The Rez version of 'Beef and Burgundy,'" Chief said, snorting as he took another drink from the can.

"You gonna move with 'em?" he asked Uncle Joe. "Might not be a bad idea," he added, downing the remaining contents of the can, gave it a little shake and tossed it into the fire. "I'm gonna turn in," he said, and stood up. He headed for his pickup, making the occasional misstep. The dome light glowed like a lightening bug, when he opened the door and then it was black.

"Did he say anything before I came down?" Daniel asked.

"He knows something, but he said very little. Let's turn in, too, I'm tired," Uncle Joe said, and stood up.

They walked up to the house and found Summer and April, sleeping in the living room with the boys. Uncle Joe got a couple of blankets to cover them. Daniel thought about waking Summer, but she had Billy tucked in her arms and didn't want to disturb him, so he went to his room. He drifted off almost immediately into a deep sleep, and as he slept he started dreaming.

He dreamt he was a Golden Eagle flying high above the mountains. Riding the Thermals, higher and higher, as the morning sun warmed the air. Below he could see Blacktail Lake and everything that was going on around it: A moose stood at the water's edge drinking. Out near the middle, fish surfaced, as they fed on insects. He tucked his wings and dove toward the lake, cutting the air like a knife going through warm butter. It felt so smooth and natural as he adjusted his wings and extending his talons and grasped a rising trout. The tips of his wings barely clearing the surface, as he made three powerful beats to lift himself and the fish up from the water. He landed on a large branch and holding the fish with one foot, used his beak to tear into its head.... He felt himself slowly being pulled back to consciousness. Summer was perched on the edge of the bed. She stroked his arm again and he opened his eyes. She smiled at him.

"You were dreaming," she said.

"I was an Eagle," he said, closing his eyes and opening them again. "Morning," he said, looking up at her.

"Chief is gone. He left before it was light. The sound of the truck starting woke me up. I thought of waking you, but didn't think it really mattered. I wonder where he was off to so early. Coffee is ready, whenever you are," she said, kissing him on the cheek as she stood up. "Breakfast will be ready soon," she added, and returned to the kitchen.

Daniel got up and got dressed. He remembered there was no running water and made his way out to the kitchen after combing through his hair.

"Morning," the boy's and April said all at the same time, as Daniel stepped into the room.

"Morning," he said, to the group.

"Uncle Joe is out on the porch," Summer said, handing him a cup of coffee.

Daniel took a sip and then went out and sat down on one of the old wooden chairs.

"Do you think Chief is really going to Mexico?" Daniel asked.

"He is a good man. I have never known him to be part of anything that did not honor 'The People,'" Uncle Joe said.

Just then they could hear the sound of a vehicle coming, maybe more than one. Moments later, two black Yukon's with Government plates came into the opening, one parked behind Daniels suv, the other to the right, parking exactly where Chief had parked, destroying the tracks he had left behind. The four doors of one vehicle seemed to open at once and four men in black suits headed toward them. Daniel noticed that two men in the other vehicle got out but stayed next to it and someone in the back seat stayed inside.

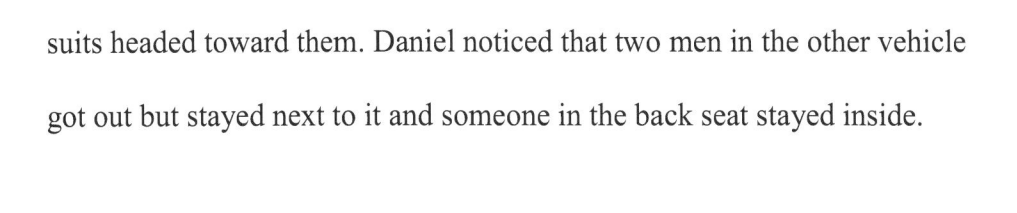

"Agent Lursen, FBI," the lead man said, stopping at the porch steps. "We are looking for Mr. Joseph Standing Bear."

"I am Standing Bear," Uncle Joe said.

"Have you seen this man?" The agent asked, holding out a picture of Chief.

Before Uncle Joe could answer, Daniel spoke up, "I'm Daniel Williams, and I represent Mr. Standing Bear. What's going on?"

The agent looked at Daniel and then at Uncle Joe. "Is that correct?" he asked.

"Yes," Uncle Joe answered.

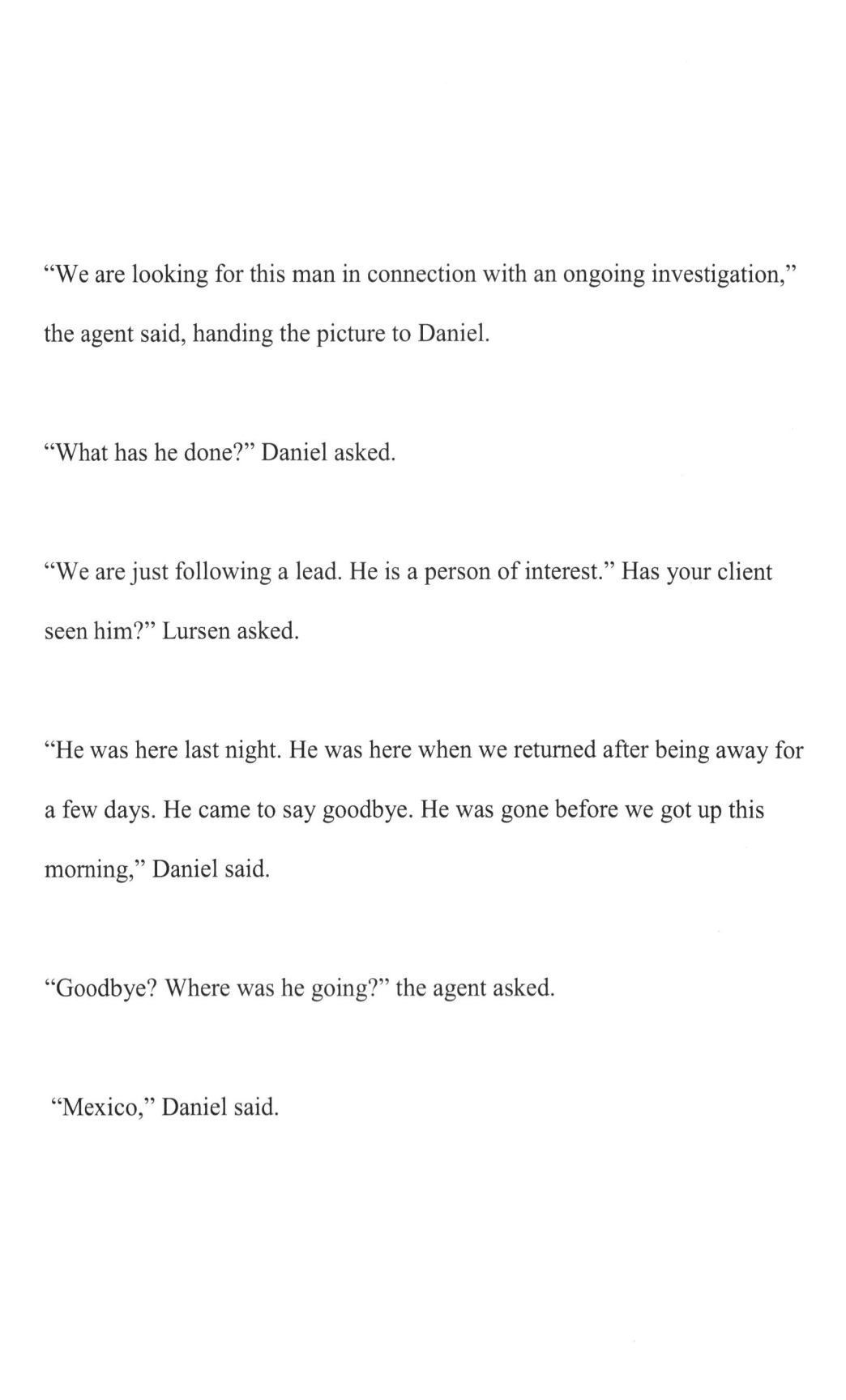

"We are looking for this man in connection with an ongoing investigation," the agent said, handing the picture to Daniel.

"What has he done?" Daniel asked.

"We are just following a lead. He is a person of interest." Has your client seen him?" Lursen asked.

"He was here last night. He was here when we returned after being away for a few days. He came to say goodbye. He was gone before we got up this morning," Daniel said.

"Goodbye? Where was he going?" the agent asked.

"Mexico," Daniel said.

"How long were you gone? Where did you go?" Lursen asked, as he started writing in a small note book.

"We went to Glacier Park. We stayed four nights. Mr. Standing Bear has been with us since Tuesday," Daniel said.

"We may need to speak with you again," Lursen said, holding out his card. Daniel came down the steps and took it. "Keep in touch," the agent said, as he turned and went back to the vehicles. Several minutes later both vehicles were turned around and heading back down the mountain.

"What was that all about?" Summer asked, stepping out on the porch.

"They're looking for Chief," Daniel said.

"I wonder who was in the back of the second vehicle. Somebody stayed inside and the other two stayed right next to it," Uncle Joe said.

"I noticed that too," Daniel said, nodding his head.

"Did you tell him about the fire at Grandma's?" Summer asked.

"No, the agent had a few questions and left. I didn't get a chance," Daniel said, with a little smile. "We should probably go talk to the Tribal Police or the fire department and see if it was reported. Who was the girl going out to check on the chickens?" he said.

"Jenny Weasel Child," Summer said.

"I think we should talk with her, too," Daniel said, pausing for a moment to sip from his cup.

Summer could see the wheels turning. Uncle Joe sat and drank his coffee. He listened and was pleased.

CHAPTER 31

When they reached the Highway, three State Police cars were blocking the forest service road. The officers were conducting searches on vehicles traveling from either direction on Hwy.2 and were caught off guard by a vehicle coming from behind and used an excessive show of force to cover up their embarrassment.

"Step out of the vehicle!" a bald officer, wearing sunglasses and protective vest, shouted as he pulled his gun and charged toward them, closely followed by another officer, who could have been the first one's twin.

They took them to a state police vehicle, while two others search the Escalade. About ten minutes later, one of the Black Yukon's pulled up,

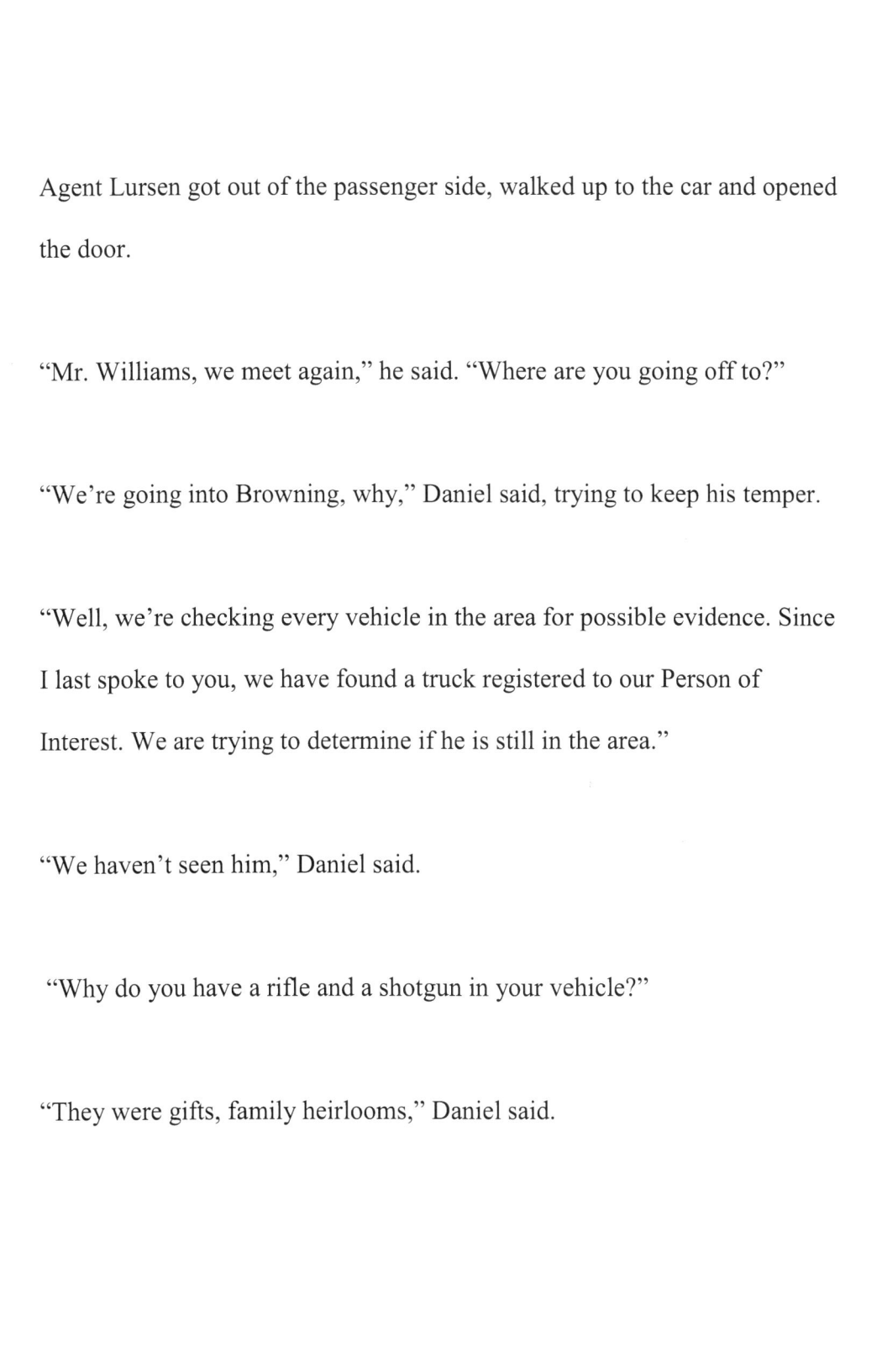

Agent Lursen got out of the passenger side, walked up to the car and opened the door.

"Mr. Williams, we meet again," he said. "Where are you going off to?"

"We're going into Browning, why," Daniel said, trying to keep his temper.

"Well, we're checking every vehicle in the area for possible evidence. Since I last spoke to you, we have found a truck registered to our Person of Interest. We are trying to determine if he is still in the area."

"We haven't seen him," Daniel said.

"Why do you have a rifle and a shotgun in your vehicle?"

"They were gifts, family heirlooms," Daniel said.

"Alright, you can go, but if a body shows up with a 7mm mag slug or a load of buckshot in it, I'll be looking for ya," Agent Lursen said, and walked them back to their vehicle.

*****

"Where does Jenny Weasel Child live?" Daniel asked, as they passed the art gallery.

Summer directed him to Jenny's house. He parked on the street and they walked up to the door.

"Hey, Summer," Jenny said, as she opened the door. She tried to smile but awkwardly bit her lip. She seemed nerves and her eyes quickly shifted downward.

"Hey, Jenny... we came home last night to find the house burnt to the ground. What happened?"

"I went out there to check on the chickens on Wednesday, everything was fine. I fed 'em and gave the cats some water. Later in the afternoon somebody saw a lot of smoke coming from out that way. Two fire trucks went to check it out and, I guess, found the whole thing on fire. I heard it was all they could do to save the out buildings. I haven't heard how it happened. I'm so sorry."

"We're heading out there now, to see what's what, is there anything else you can tell us? Any suspicious vehicles hanging around?" Daniel asked.

"Everything seemed just fine, sorry," Jenny said, looking down at the ground.

"I'd like to talk to the firemen that went out there," Daniel said, as they pulled away.

Summer directed him to the Fire Station. It was a small volunteer station. The posted hours on the door read: 'MWF.9:00-2:00. In case of an emergency call 911.' It was Thursday. They decided to just drive out to the farm and take another look around.

"Let's stop at the store and get some dry cat food," Summer said.

"Okay, I could use some water, too," Daniel said.

When they walked in, Peter Spotted dog was just finishing ringing up two young guys. They were getting a twelve pack of beer. Neither of them looked twenty-one.

Daniel and Summer went down the first aisle and looped around, Summer picked up a twenty-pound bag of cat food.

"I'll take it, Daniel offered."

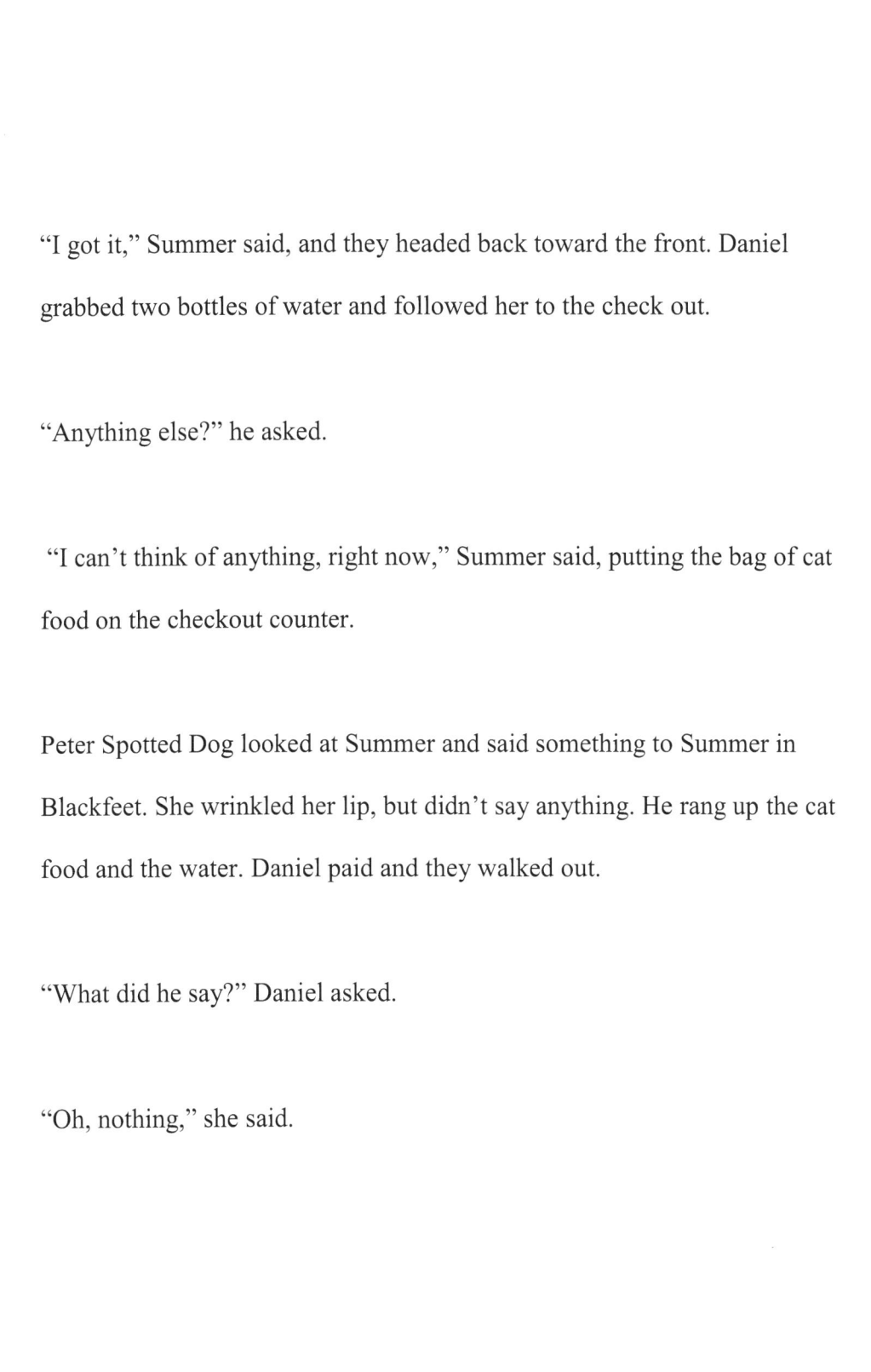

"I got it," Summer said, and they headed back toward the front. Daniel grabbed two bottles of water and followed her to the check out.

"Anything else?" he asked.

"I can't think of anything, right now," Summer said, putting the bag of cat food on the checkout counter.

Peter Spotted Dog looked at Summer and said something to Summer in Blackfeet. She wrinkled her lip, but didn't say anything. He rang up the cat food and the water. Daniel paid and they walked out.

"What did he say?" Daniel asked.

"Oh, nothing," she said.

"That was an awful funny look you gave him after he said it," Daniel persisted.

"He said, if my Kitty was hungry, he'd be glad to feed it, Spotted Doggy style," Summer said, trying to dismiss it. "That's how he is," she added.

"I see," Daniel said. "I'll be right back, I forgot something," he said, as she climbed into the passenger seat. He closed her door and went back in the store. Several minutes later, Peter Spotted Dog came around the corner of the building followed by Daniel. "Mr. Dog has something to say," Daniel said, through the opened window, and stepped aside. Peter Spotted Dog stepped up to the window. His lip was cut and his right eye looked very red.

"I'm sorry for my remarks, it won't happen again," he said, and turned to Daniel.

Daniel flicked his head at him, dismissing him, and then went around to the driver's side.

"Was that necessary?" Summer asked.

"Probably not, but it felt good," Daniel said, giving her a little smile, as he backed up.

"What about the cameras?" Summer asked, thinking it probably did feel good.

"The same cameras that caught him selling beer to minors? I don't think there will be any problem," Daniel said.

*****

It didn't seem real as they looked through the windshield at the rubble that had once been a house. Daniel noticed the shed door was opened, and walked over to it. It was empty. "That's too bad," Daniel said, looking at Summer with a disappointed look on his face. They walked over toward the chicken coop. The chickens were gone. The water can and feeder was gone too. "Well I guess we don't have to deal with finding them a home," Daniel said, letting out a sigh, as he walked away from the coop and started toward the house.

"Someone was busy," Summer said, noticing the grill was gone, too.

Daniel headed for the path to the back yard with a concerned look on his face. He suddenly stopped. The spirit warrior was standing there, surrounded by the four other figures. Daniel walked over to the old metal chairs and sat down. Summer sat next to him.

"I want to take them with us," Daniel said.

"I think, Grandpa Ray would like that," Summer said, putting a hand on his leg. "I wonder if the 'shoppers' found the old shovel behind the chicken coop?" she said, standing up. "I'll be right back."

Daniel sat there a minute and then went out to the center figure and knelt down. He brushed some small rocks away from the top of the coffee can and tried to wiggle the figure. It was firmly in the ground.

"Grandma used it to turn over the compost pile," Summer explained, as she held out the old shovel.

Daniel took it and carefully dug around the coffee can. He wiggled the figure again. It broke lose, and he pulled it free, and then went around the circle carefully unearthing the other figures.

They each carried two of the figures back to the SUV. Then walked back down the path, Daniel picked up the Warrior figure.

"Let's take the chairs and the old shovel, too," he said.

Summer folded the old metal chairs and carried them and the shovel, back to the vehicle. "I guess that's that," she said, looking around.

They drove back to town and back to Summer's house. She put a pot of water on the stove and got a couple of cups out. Daniel looked across the table as they waited for it to boil. He was thinking of their first date. He reached across the table and put his hand on top of hers. She smiled at him. She has been thinking about it too.

"So, what's next?" she asked.

"I was thinking about, a little nap. We haven't had much alone time," Daniel said, with a devilish grin.

"I meant what we are going to do about everything. But I might be persuaded to take a little nap. After my tea," Summer said, and smiled at Daniel as she went to take the whistling kettle off the burner.

Daniel tried to think of a topic of conversation, but really all he could think of was…so he just smiled at her from across the table and made an attempt to appear as if he was enjoying his tea. He finished his tea first. but waited a minute and then took his cup to the sink. He moved behind Summer and lightly put his hands on her shoulders and started to slowly rub and massage her neck. She let out a deep sigh.

"That feels good, she moaned, as she reached over her left shoulder and touched Daniels hand. She stood up and turned around to give him a hug. But she wasn't done torturing him yet.

"Are you sure sleepy is how you feel?" she asked, teasingly.

*****

"Have you given any thought as to where we all are going to live, when we get to New York?" Summer asked, starring up at the ceiling, lying next to Daniel, when he rolled over and faced her, as he woke up.

"Don't worry it will all work out just fine," Daniel said, reassuringly. "We'll take it one day at a time." I'm sure Billy and Tommy would like to live on the boat," he said, with a little chuckle, after a moment of thought.

"Terrific! Three little boys on a boat," Summer said, teasingly.

They lay there for a while longer, Summer had a million questions, but Daniel had already dosed off, again. She laid there thinking and listening to him breathe. She felt him stir and gently rubbed her hand up and down his arm. Maybe Daniel could take it one day at a time, but she had tasted the Big Apple and now was ready for another bite!

CHAPTER 32

Daniel nudged Summer, and nodded toward their welcoming committee, as they stepped from the loading gate into the airport terminal.

Evelyn handed the sign that read, 'WELCOME HOME! WILLIAMS FAMILY,' to the man standing next to her, when she saw them making their way toward her

"We're back!" Daniel said.

"I'm so glad," Evelyn said, hugging him. Then she put her arms around Summer's neck. "Welcome home," she said, as she hugged her.

"Grandma!" Billy said, as he put his arms around Evelyn's waist.

"Billy!" she said.

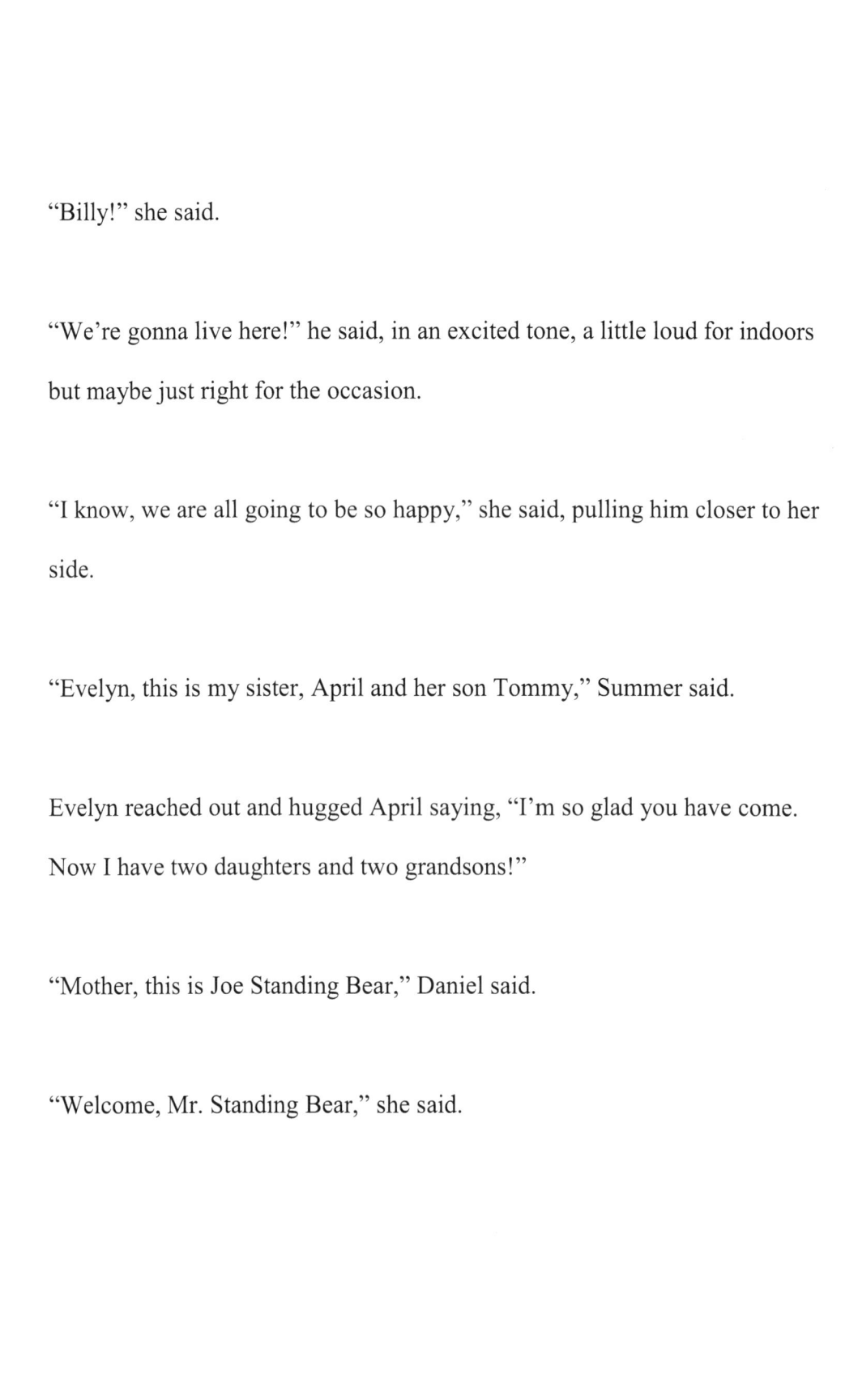

"We're gonna live here!" he said, in an excited tone, a little loud for indoors but maybe just right for the occasion.

"I know, we are all going to be so happy," she said, pulling him closer to her side.

"Evelyn, this is my sister, April and her son Tommy," Summer said.

Evelyn reached out and hugged April saying, "I'm so glad you have come. Now I have two daughters and two grandsons!"

"Mother, this is Joe Standing Bear," Daniel said.

"Welcome, Mr. Standing Bear," she said.

"Joe or Uncle Joe, please," Uncle Joe said, lightly taking Evelyn's hand.

"Yes, of course, I'm Evelyn or Grandma," she said, as she glanced at Billy and Tommy.

"Shall we get out of here?" she asked, then turned to Tony, her assistant and said, "Help them with their bags, please." Then, she proudly led her family away.

Tony called the driver to let him know, that they were on their way to the loading area and seemed to herd 'his people and their things' effortlessly to the car as it pulled into an opened spot. He put the small carry-on bags in the trunk, as the driver opened the doors and got everyone inside. It seemed like a well-rehearsed scene from a movie. April and Uncle Joe were impressed. Summer smiled at her sister as they drove off.

"I've got a little surprise," Evelyn said, giving Daniel a mischievous look. "After I talked to you a couple weeks ago, I started thinking. Your apartment wasn't going to be big enough for all of you. So I did a little looking and found a house out on Staten Island. We have it for six months with an option to buy."

"Sounds good," Daniel said, knowing it would have been useless arguing with her if he had any objections. It took three hours, but when they pulled into the driveway, both Summer and April gasped.

"It's beautiful!" they both said, at the same time. They all got out and walked up to the front door. Tony and Daniel each carried two bags and Uncle Joe carried his.

"Will there be anything else?" Tony asked Evelyn.

"No, that should do it, good night."

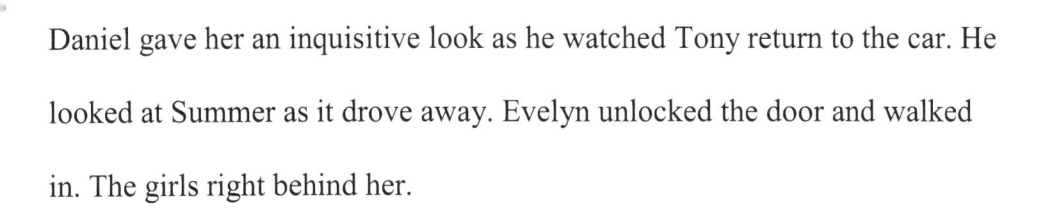

Daniel gave her an inquisitive look as he watched Tony return to the car. He looked at Summer as it drove away. Evelyn unlocked the door and walked in. The girls right behind her.

"It's beautiful," Summer said, looking around.

"There are five bedrooms, 6 and a half baths, family room, dining room and kitchen," Evelyn said, as if she was a realtor.

"Five bedrooms!" Daniel said, smiling at her.

"I took the liberty of getting some basics," Evelyn continued, turning her attention to Summer and April, pretending not to have heard him. "I thought we could always do some shopping," she said, giving them a wink. "Let's go take a look at the bedrooms," she said, starting up the stairs. "This is the boy's room," she said, opening a door. It was furnished with two single beds, two dressers and a small table with two chairs. The boys went in and flopped on the beds.

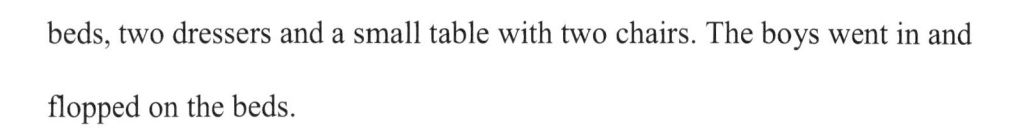

"They seem to approve," April said, and took the boy's bags in and set them by the table.

"Come and see your room," Evelyn said, to April, as she turned and led them down the hall. "I thought you'd like to pick out a bedroom set, so I just focused on the bed," Evelyn said, as she reached around to the inside of the doorway and turned on the light.

"Thank you!" April said, as she walked in.

"That door goes to a bathroom shared with the next bedroom. I thought I'd take that one, when I'm here," Evelyn said.

April opened the door and peeked in. She looked at Summer.

"Pretty fancy, Summer said, and made a face at her.

"Joe I thought you might like this room. It has its own bath room and a little deck," Evelyn said, heading for the door across the hall.

They went in. A bed same as Aprils was against the far wall. Uncle Joe walked over and put his bag on it.

"Very nice," he said, as he turned and smiled at Daniel.

"The Master bedroom is this way," Evelyn said. "It has an excellent view of the ocean," she added, as she opened the door.

Summer and April walked in. They walked over to the French doors that opened out to a small deck.

"Master bath and walk-in closet," Evelyn said, smiling at Summer. Evelyn could tell she was pleased and that made her happy. "Well, it's late. I'm sure everyone is tired. There are towels in all the bathrooms and I picked up a few things for breakfast. We can have some coffee and then go exploring or whatever," she said, directing the last part toward Summer and April, and turned to go back down the hall.

Good night," Summer said, and reached out, catching Evelyn by her arm "Thank you so much!" she said, and gave her a hug.

Evelyn put her arms around her and said "You're welcome, dear. It's my pleasure!"

"It's perfect, thank you." Daniel said, giving her a hug.

"Good night," they said, all at once.

Summer and April went to tuck the boys in and found them both asleep on their beds. They got them undressed and into bed and then went to their own rooms.

Daniel was brushing his teeth when Summer came back to their room.

"This was quite a surprise," she said.

"She seems to have thought of everything," Daniel said, hanging a towel on the rack after wiping his face. He turned toward Summer and put his arms around her and said, "Here we are."

"Yep, looks pretty good to me," she said, squeezing him around his waist. "I'll wash up and be right in."

Daniel went and got in bed. He stretched out, remembering how good a Tempur Pedic mattress felt. Summer was only several minutes but found him fast asleep. She thought about going under the covers and waking him up, but she felt a little sleepy too, and ooh, the bed felt so good. She snuggled into Daniel's back and was soon fast asleep.

The next morning Daniel woke up. He was alone. He got up and went into the bathroom. A wet towel hung on the rack next to the shower. He looked at the shower and thought it looked pretty good, so he grabbed a fresh towel and hopped in. As the hot water ran down his neck and back, he thought about the future and what it might bring. He thought how different his life was going to be, because of him listening to his inner voice and taking the journey. He got dressed and made his way down stairs. When he walked into the kitchen, he realized he was the last to get up.

"Good morning!" Uncle Joe said, sitting between Billy and Tommy at the counter, all three with a stack of pancakes in front of them.
"Morning," the boy's chirped together, between bites.

On the other side of the counter, Evelyn, Summer and April, seemed to have an effective production line going and were making pancakes faster than they could be eaten. Summer put the latest batch in the oven and then poured a cup of coffee and brought it to Daniel.

"Hey, sleepy," she said, handing it to him, and regretted not being impulsive last night, she winked at him and returned to her position next to April. They faced each other, as they quickly ate a couple of pancakes from the last batch.

"When you're finished, just put your plates in the sink," Summer said, as they did the same and headed upstairs.

"We can clean the kitchen up," Daniel said, as he watched them go. He looked at the boys and the kitchen, as he sipped his coffee.

"What have I gotten myself into," he said to Uncle Joe, with a smile on his face.

"It is Nits'o'kan (his dream)" Uncle Joe said, as he smiled and nodded his head.

The End.

Glossary

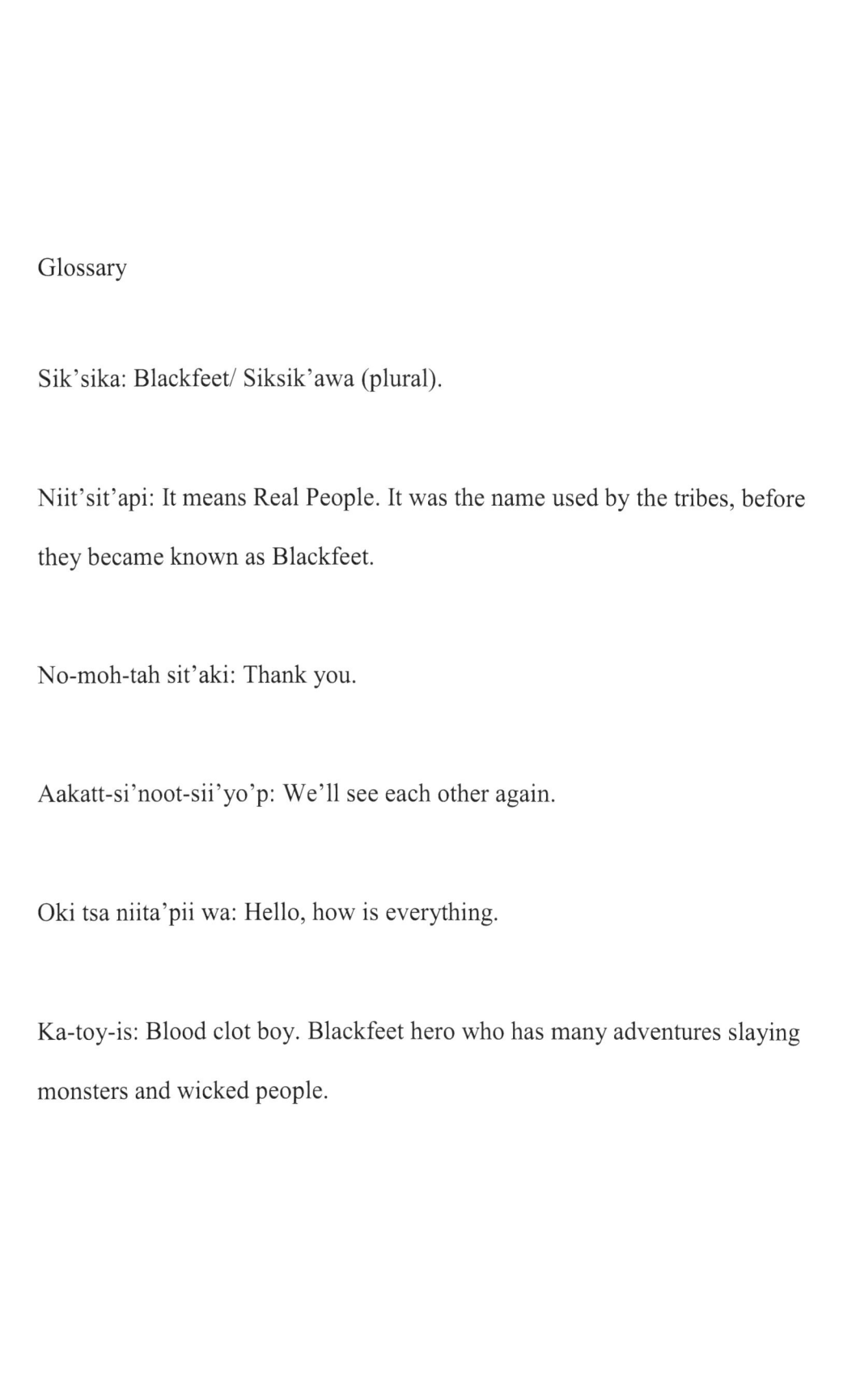

Sik'sika: Blackfeet/ Siksik'awa (plural).

Niit'sit'api: It means Real People. It was the name used by the tribes, before they became known as Blackfeet.

No-moh-tah sit'aki: Thank you.

Aakatt-si'noot-sii'yo'p: We'll see each other again.

Oki tsa niita'pii wa: Hello, how is everything.

Ka-toy-is: Blood clot boy. Blackfeet hero who has many adventures slaying monsters and wicked people.

Iini: Buffalo (singular) / Iinisskimm (plural)

Soka'pii Moss'kit'sip'ah'pi: Good Heart

Akai Aa'zist'awa: Many Rabbits.

I'taa'mik'skan'a'otonni: Good morning.

Oki'na'pi: Hello friend.

Ma-tsi-yi-ka-pi-si-ki-soom: April

Kayissta'pssiwa: "It is a Spirit."

Ni-po-wa: Summer

Aapi'si: coyote

Nah-ah: intimate name for mother or grand mother

Otah-ko'i'ssksisi yooh ki aayo: Grizzly bear.

Awakkaasii: Deer

Innoka: Elk

Aka'istaao: Many ghosts

Ma'oto'kiiksi: Buffalo woman society.

Naapi: (Nah-pee) 'Old man', trickster/ trouble maker, sometimes foolish. Responsible for shaping the world the Blackfeet live in. He does frequently help people.

His wife's name is Kipitaakii (kih-pih-tah-kee)

Apistotoke: (ah-piss-toh-toh-kee) Great Spirit, creator, no human form, is not personified.

Na'wak'o'sis: a plant said to have been given to the people by a Medicine Beaver. Used as Tobacco.

Ni namp'-skan: Medicine man

Nits-o'-kan: His dream

Ainihkwa: sing

Sipistoo: Owl

Pishkun: Buffalo jump. Translates to 'deep blood kettle.'

A'sita'aa'kiim: Young Sister

Made in the USA
Columbia, SC
24 July 2019

DISEASES/CONDITIONS AND ICD-9-CM CODES

Condition	Code
Abruptio placentae	641.2**
Acne vulgaris	706.1
Acromegaly	253.0
Actinic keratosis	702.0
Acute bronchitis	466.0
Acute and chronic viral hepatitis	070.9
Acute diarrhea (NOS)	787.91
Acute leukemia (plain leukemia)	208.0**
Acute myocardial infarction	410.9**
Acute otitis media	382.9
Acute pancreatitis	577.0
Acute peripheral facial paralysis (Bell's palsy)	351.0
Acute renal failure	584.9
Acute respiratory failure	518.81
Acute stress disorder	308.9
Adrenocortical insufficiency	255.4
Adverse reactions to blood transfusions	999
Alcoholism	303.9**
Allergic reactions to drugs	995.2
Allergic reactions to insect stings	989.5
Allergic rhinitis	477.8
Alopecia areata	704.01
Alzheimer's disease	331.0
Amebiasis	006.9
Amenorrhea	626.0
Anal fissure	565.0
Anaphylaxis, NOS	995.0
Angina pectoris	413.9
Angioedema	995.1
Ankle fracture	824.8
Ankylosing spondylitis	720.0
Anorectal abscess	566.
Anorexia nervosa	307.1
Aortic aneurysm and dissection	441.00
Aplastic anemia	284.9
Asthma	493.9**
Atelectasis	518.0
Atopic dermatitis	691.8
Atopic fibrillation	427.31
Attention deficit/hyperactivity disorder	314.01
Autoimmune hemolytic anemia	283.0
Bacterial meningitis	320
Bacterial pneumonia	482.9
Bacterial vaginitis	616.1
Benign prostatic hyperplasia	600
Blastomycosis	116.0
Bleeding esophageal varices	456.0
Brain abscess	324.
Brain tumors	239.6
Breast cancer	174
Brucellosis	023
Bulimia nervosa	307.51
Bullous diseases	694
Burns	940-949
Bursitis	726-727
Cancer of the endometrium	182.0
Cancer of the skin	172-173
Cancer of the uterine cervix	180
Cardiac arrest, sudden cardiac death	427.5
Care after myocardial infarction	414.8
Cellulitis	682.
Chancroid	099.3
Chlamydia trachomatis infection	079.88
Cholelithiasis and cholecystitis	574.1-574.9
Cholera	001
Chronic fatigue syndrome	780.71
Chronic leukemia	208.1**
Chronic obstructive pulmonary disease	491.2**
Chronic pancreatitis	577.1
Chronic renal failure	585
Chronic serous otitis media	381.1**
Coccidioidomycosis	114*
Colorectal cancer	153
Concussion	850
Congenital heart disease	745-747
Congenital rubella	771.0
Congestive heart failure	428.0
Conjunctivitis, acute	372.0**
Connective tissue disease	710*
Constipation	564.0
Contact dermatitis	692
Cough	786.2
Cushing's syndrome	255.0
Delirium	780.0
Dementia, multi-infarct, uncomplicated	294.8
Depression psychosis	298.0
Depression with anxiety	300.4
Diabetes insipidus	253.5
Diabetes mellitus, I	250.01
Diabetes mellitus, II	250.02
Diabetic ketoacidosis	276.2**
Diphtheria	032*
Diseases of the mouth	528*
Disseminated intravascular coagulation	286.6
Diverticulitis	562.11
Drug abuse (nondependent)	305.9**
Dysfunctional uterine bleeding	626.6
Dysmenorrhea	635.5
Dysphagia and esophageal obstruction	530.3
Ectopic pregnancy	633*
Elbow dislocation	832.0**
Encephalitis	323*
Endometriosis	617*
Enuresis	786.30
Epididymitis	604**
Episodic vertigo	386.11
Erythema multiforme	695.1
Fetal lung immaturity	770.4
Fever	780.6
Fibrocystic diseases of the breast	610.1
Fibromyositis	729.1
Fifth disease	057.0
Finger dislocation, closed	834.0**
Finger fracture	816.0**
Fistula (anal)	565.1
Fitting of diaphragm	V25.02
Folliculitis	704.8
Food allergy	693.1
Food poisoning	005*
Foot fracture	825.2**
Frostbite	991*
Gangrene	785.4
Gastritis	535.*
Gastroesophageal reflux disease (GERD)	530.81
Generalized anxiety disorder	300.02
Generalized epilepsy	345.1**
Genital warts (condylomata acuminata)	078.11
Giant cell arteritis	446.5
Giardiasis	7.1
Gilles de la Tourette syndrome	307.23
Glaucoma	365**
Gonorrhea	098.0
Gout	274.9
Granuloma inguinale (donovanosis)	099.2
Guillain-Barré syndrome	357.*
Headache	784.0
Heart block	426.1**
Heat exhaustion	992.3
Heat stroke	992.0
Hemochromatosis	285.0
Hemolytic disease of the fetus and newborn	773.2
Hemophilia and related conditions	286.0
Hemorrhoids	455.6
Herpes gestationis	646.8**
Herpes simplex	054*
Herpes zoster	053*
Hiccups	786.8
High-altitude sickness	993.2
Histoplasmosis	115**
HIV-associated infections	042.0
HIV infection, asymptomatic	V08
HIV infection, early symptomatic	042
HIV infection, late symptomatic	042
Hyperlipoproteinemias	272*
Hyperparathyroidism	252.0
Hyperprolactinemia	253.1
Hypersensitivity pneumonitis	495
Hypertension (essential)	401*
Hyperthyroidism	242**
Hypertrophic cardiomyopathy	425.4
Hypoparathyroidism	252.1
Hypothyroidism	244*
Immunization practices	V03, V04, V05, V06**
Impetigo	684
Impotence	302.72
Indigestion	536.8
Infectious diarrhea	009.2
Infectious mononucleosis	075
Infective endocarditis	424.9**
Influenza	487.2
Ingrowing nail	703.0
Insect and spider bite	989.5
Insertion of intrauterine device	V25.1
Insomnia (NOS)	780.52

DISEASES/CONDITIONS AND ICD-9-CM CODES (Continued)

Intracerebral hemorrhage 431
Iron deficiency anemia 280.0-280.9
Irritable bowel syndrome 564.1
Jellyfish sting 989.5
Juvenile rheumatoid arthritis 714.3**
Keloids 701.4
Laryngitis 464.00
Lead poisoning 984*
Legionnaires' disease 482.84
Leishmaniasis 085*
Leprosy 030*
Lichen planus 697.0
Low back pain 724.2
Lyme disease 088.81
Lymphogranuloma venereum 099.1
Malabsorption 579*
Malaria 084.6
Measles (rubeola) 055.9
Meconium aspiration 770.1
Melanoma, malignant 172*
Ménière's disease 386.0**
Meningitis 320-322
Menopausal 627.2
Migraine headache 346**
Mitral valve prolapse 424.0
Monilial vulvovaginitis 121.1
Multiple myeloma 203.0**
Multiple sclerosis 340
Mumps 072.9
Myasthenia gravis 358.0**
Mycoplasmal pneumonias 483.0
Mycosis fungoides 202.1**
Nausea and vomiting 787.01
Neoplasm of the vulva 239.5
Neutropenia 288.0
Nevi 216*
Newborn physiologic jaundice 774.6
Nongonococcal urethritis 099.4**
Non-Hodgkin's lymphomas 202.8**
Non-autoimmune hemolytic anemia 283.1**
Normal delivery 650
Obesity 278.0**
Obsessive-compulsive disorders 300.3
Onychomycosis 110.1
Optic neuritis 377.3**
Osteoarthritis 715**
Osteomyelitis 730**
Osteoporosis 733.00
Otitis externa 380.10
Paget's disease of bone 731.0
Panic disorder 300.01
Pap smear V72.3
Parkinsonism 332.0
Paronychia 681.0**
Partial epilepsy 345.4**
Patent ductus arteriosus 747.0
Pediculosis 132*
Pelvic inflammatory disease 614*
Peptic ulcer disease 533*
Pericarditis 432.9
Peripheral arterial disease 443.9
Peripheral neuropathies 356*
Pernicious anemia 281.0
Personality disorder 301**
Pheochromocytoma 227.0
Phobia 300.2**
Pigmentary disorders—vitiligo 709.01
Pinworms 127.4
Pityriasis rosea 696.3
Placenta previa 641**
Plague 020*
Platelet-mediated bleeding disorders 287.1
Pleural effusion 511.9
Polycythemia vera 238.4
Polymyalgia rheumatica 725
Porphyria 277.1
Postpartum hemorrhage 666.1**
Post-traumatic stress disorder 309.81
Pregnancy V22.2
Pregnancy-induced hypertension 642**
Premature beats 427.6**
Premenstrual tension syndrome (PMS) 625.4
Prescribed oral contraceptive V25.01
Pressure ulcers 707.0
Preterm labor 644.2**
Primary glomerular disease 581-583
Primary lung abscess 513.0
Primary lung cancer 162.9
Prostate cancer 185

Prostatitis 601*
Pruritus 698.9
Pruritus ani 698.0
Pruritus vulvae 698.1
Psittacosis (ornithosis) 073*
Psoriasis 696.1
Pulmonary embolism 415.1
Pyelonephritis 590**
Q fever 083.0
Rabies 071
Rat-bite fever 026*
Relapsing fever 087*
Renal calculi 592
Reye syndrome 331.81
Rheumatic fever 390
Rheumatoid arthritis 714.0
Rib fracture 807.0**
Rocky Mountain spotted fever 082.0
Rosacea 695.3
Roseola 057.8
Rubella 056*
Salmonellosis 003.0
Sarcoidosis 135
Scabies 133.0
Schizophrenia 295**
Seborrheic dermatitis 690.1**
Septicemia 038*
Sézary's syndrome 202.2**
Shoulder dislocation 831.0**
Sickle cell anemia 282.6**
Silicosis 502
Sinusitis, chronic 473*
Skull fracture 800, 801, 803
Sleep apnea 780.57
Sleep disorders 780.50
Snakebite 989.5
Stasis ulcers 454.0
Status epilepticus 345.3
Stomach cancer 151*
Streptococcal pharyngitis 034.0
Stroke 436
Strongyloides infection 127.2
Subdural or subarachnoid hemorrhage 852**
Sunburn 692.71
Syphilis 090-097
Tachycardias 785.0
Tapeworm infections 123*
Telogen effluvium 704.02
Temporomandibular joint syndrome 524.6**
Tendonitis 726.90
Tetanus 037
Thalassemia 282.4**
Therapeutic use of blood components V59.0**
Thrombotic thrombocytopenic purpura 446.6
Thyroid cancer 193
Thyroiditis 245*
Tinea capitis 110.0
Tinnitus 388.3**
Toe fracture 826.0
Toxic shock syndrome 040.82
Toxoplasmosis 130*
Transient cerebral ischemia 435*
Trauma to the genitourinary tract 958,959
Trichinellosis 124
Trichomonal vaginitis 131.01
Trigeminal neuralgia 350.1
Tuberculosis, pulmonary 011**
Tularemia 021*
Typhoid fever 002.0
Typhus fevers 080, 081
Ulcerative colitis 556*
Urethral stricture 598*
Urinary incontinence 788.30
Urticaria 708*
Uterine inertia 661.0**
Uterine leiomyoma 218*
Varicella 052*
Venous thrombosis 453.8
Viral pneumonia 480.9
Viral respiratory infections 465.9
Vitamin deficiency 264-269
Vitamin K deficiency 269.0
Warts (verrucae) 078.10
Wegener's granulomatosis 446.4
Whooping cough (pertussis) 033*
Wrist fracture 814.0**

*4th digit needed
**5th (or 4th and 5th) digit needed